Love. Local. Late-Breaking.
by
H. Laurence Lareau

D1124773

Prologue

Karli listened as the news director and general manager's leaden rejection made her stomach sink. The four years of extra hours, extra shifts, extra stories, and extra effort had all apparently come to nothing. She stared in shocked, frozen disbelief as she realized that the high quality and huge volume of her work as a television journalist meant nothing.

"How could you give the main anchor spot to her?"

"She has the *gravitas* we need, the overall look we need, the delivery we need to increase trust with the viewers and increase our ratings, Karli," the general manager said.

The news director was quick to add, "And Karli, you just don't have the kind of seniority to carry the weight of the station."

"You led me on the whole time I've been here, didn't you? Just so you could get more out of me." Karli was surprised at how calmly she expressed her fury at their betrayal.

"Led you on? What are you talking about? We never did that." The two heads glanced at one another, shaking their mutually reinforcing denials.

"No?" Karli responded. "*Do this series on your own time and you'll be destined for big things here, Karli*. Or how about *We need you to cover Thanksgiving, but don't worry, you're next in line for a big reward*. Haven't I done every crazy thing you've asked for the last four years?"

"Of course you have worked hard," the news director was taken aback. "The whole news team works hard. It's an expectation of this station—of this business—that reporters work hard. It takes years of hard work to develop the depth and maturity to carry a lead anchor's

2

role."

"So I've worked hard, I've developed sources and relationships, I've paraded the station's colors through the community, and now you tell me I'm shallow and immature?"

The news director heaved a belabored sigh, repeating a mannerism that Karli had always disliked. In this tense moment, dislike became loathing. She opened her mouth to protest, but the news director's raised finger triggered the restraint of four years' regarding this man as her boss. She paused while he spoke.

"Just because you don't have what it takes to be the main anchor *right now* does not mean that you aren't a solid newswoman. You have a unique ability to interview anyone from Joe six-pack to the governor with great effectiveness. You have a strong on-camera presence and a good voice. But you're not seasoned enough to be taken as seriously as a main anchor must be."

He shrugged, reacting to the rebellion on her face. "And we expect you to improve dramatically behind the camera, too. You usually catch most of the video necessary to file a solid story, but there's no question that you come up short on both the technical and artistic side of television news.

You don't think about audio until you're editing, if ever. You need more time in the trenches before you can expect to move up."

"Thank you for your feedback," Karli said, more by way of using her good manners to end the conversation than from actually wanting to express gratitude. She turned and left the business office and walked toward the building's other wing, which housed the newsroom.

She stormed down the hallway, vision blurred by tears of frustration. She half wanted and half feared meeting a fellow journalist who could see her tears and commiserate with her mistreatment. She was relieved, however, to get to an edit suite where she could slam the door and sob in sound-insulated silence.

Karli had a generous portion of the ego required for her chosen profession, and had believed—still believed—that success was only a matter of time. She had approached the interview and the morning's meeting full of confidence that she had earned her way to the anchor desk.

As she replayed the comments in her memory, they boiled down to thanking her for doing lots of extra work for free, expecting that she would do even more work for free, and somehow thinking that would 'season' her enough to make her anchor material.

And of course their ignorance extended to expecting her to become a better photog, too—which was nonsense, since she wouldn't have to shoot her own stories once she left podunk Palm Beach for a market big enough to be worth going to. Stations in moderate to major markets all employed professional news photographers, and journalists there looked down their noses on small markets where reporters worked as one-man-bands.

The anchor job wasn't really the object of her ambition, either, Karli reflected. She had applied for the job because it came open when the previous anchor had moved on to Nashville. Because she did not believe in half-measures, she had committed herself fully to landing the job.

Now that the opportunity had evaporated, that email from the news director in Des Moines, Iowa flitted across her mind. She pulled out her iPhone and re-read the email she had so lightly skimmed last night, when she had been sure of staying in Palm Beach as the main anchor.

"Karli," the email read, "Thanks for sending the link to your reel on YouTube. You're doing a lot of things we like to see here at Three NewsFirst. Please give me a call to talk about opportunities here. Regards, Jerry Schultz, New Director."

Des Moines has a reputation for really great news photographers, Karli reflected. Collaborating with them could help me to do really great reporting, the kind that can propel me on to even bigger markets where I can really have an impact. It's the center of a thousand-mile cornfield, but at least it's only a six-hour drive to Chicago. Good reporting should be able to reach a major market that's that close, even wading through corn.

The number was below his name. Karli tapped the link to dial it.

Chapter One

Just east of Cambridge, Iowa
Tuesday, July 16
Live shot for noon newscast

"It isn't safe here," Karli Lewis said. "We need to get the gear back in the truck and move." Iowa's humid west wind ruffled Karli's long, glossy black hair as she looked from the hazard sign on the train's side to her iPhone's screen. The midwestern haze caught light from the noon-vertical sun and scattered it in every direction, making shadows faint and blurred. Reflected heat radiated from the weeds and stubbled grass along the railroad tracks.

She waited tensely as news photographer Jake Gibson ignored her, carefully framing the cracked and leaking drums thrown from the railroad car in his camera's viewfinder. Karli checked her iPhone again and sniffed the increasingly acrid air, a growing sense of danger making her impatient. She took in a breath, preparing to telling Jake yet again that it wasn't safe to stay. Jake, still looking only into his viewfinder, pressed the *record* button and held up his index finger to quiet her while the video rolled. Years of news-gathering habit make Karli's silence automatic; the natural sound recorded through the photographer's microphone is often just as important as the video.

Everything he was doing got on her nerves. He was obviously competent, Karli observed as she watched Jake's strong, tanned forearms reach to carefully touch on the camera's controls. In spite of her impatience, she was impressed with the steady, masculine care he used with his equipment.

He was obviously in fantastic shape, too. He moved and carried dozens of pounds of video equipment effortlessly and very precisely. And when he was in the actual act of shooting, like now, his strength was coiled and motionless, almost as though he were cast in sculptural bronze. Karli resisted the temptation to ruin the shot and make that Greek sculpture of a man move. She watched a drop of sweat map its path down from his unmoving temple and along the stern line of his jaw.

Further irritating Karli, Jake concentrated only on his shot, oblivious to the sweat and her impatience. After an interminable five seconds, Jake stopped the recording, raised his eye from the viewfinder, and returned her impatient look with a questioning quirk of his eyebrow.

"Let's go," she said, dark blue eyes flashing from her tanned face. "*Now.*"

"This is the perfect spot to go live from," Jake responded firmly, locking his camera in place atop its tripod. "We're close enough that the railroad cars will be *right there* in the shot," he began, ticking the points off on his fingers. "The live truck has a signal locked into the station. We only have about ten minutes till the newscast starts. And we even have enough cable that you could do a walking live shot right up to the derailed train cars."

Karli could see by the dark eyebrows drawn together under Jake's light brown curls that he also was impatient—and he wasn't packing up his equipment.

She bent over, unplugged the cables leading to her earpiece and microphone, and strode, her tanned and athletically toned legs stretching swiftly right past Jake to his camera and tripod. She snatched them up decisively and headed for the live truck. "Pull the mast down right now, Erik!" she shouted. "We have to move to the west before the newscast starts."

Startled by her commanding tone, the engineer in the live truck started throwing switches and talking into his two-way radio. To the thrum of its electric motor, the long pole supporting the truck's microwave transmitter telescoped back into itself and the truck.

"Just who do you think you are?" Jake's furious question startled Karli. She hadn't heard his footsteps catching up. "We have an actual newscast to put on the air, and tens of thousands of loyal Three NewsFirst viewers are going to be watching a big fat nothing because *you don't feel safe*? I don't know what you did in the lazy tropics, but we're journalists here, and that means we don't just phone the news in—we actually cover it where it's happening."

"You can't talk to me like that," snapped Karli, who had turned away from Jake when he finally stopped talking. She turned back to face him just as she'd been about to dump the camera and tripod inside the van. "Good reporting is the same everywhere, and I spent four years doing good reporting in Palm Beach before I came here to the absolute center of flyover country."

"Uh, kids," Erik asked, sticking his head out of the van's large side door, "are we going to move or do you need to get a couples therapist? Because the mast is almost down and master control is asking when we plan on locking in a new signal."

Karli questioned, not for the first time, her decision to move to the center of Iowa for this job. She had chosen her career in broadcast news deliberately and against her father's wishes.

Her father had wanted—he still wanted—to put her on the fast track to prosperity and security. And he nearly always got what he wanted. He was a powerful and politically connected attorney in Charleston, SC. And he came from a long line of powerful Lewises. He was carrying on the tradition of marrying money, making more of it, and making sure that each succeeding generation fulfilled its role in Charleston's political and social elite.

Rebellion for Karli had taken the form of excelling in her chosen field. And journalism had definitely been a field *she* had chosen, not her father. Instead of plunking her in places she couldn't possibly have anticipated, where each person she met would have a new story for her to tell—including the lonely cornfields of Iowa—her father's plan would have put her near the center of a busy and deeply connected social network where she knew everyone and everyone knew her. And the plush public relations career he had planned for her dovetailed with his anticipated run for Attorney General.

But his plan was not hers. Karli loved meeting new people, learning their stories, and telling them in her reports—even considering the meager wages. But right now, in this heat, and with this photographer arguing with her, a little money and an air-conditioned office sounded pretty good. At least, she considered, she wouldn't have to schlep heavy video gear through tangled weeds in her Calvin Klein black heels.

She called her real ambition to mind, though: to do great reporting in a major market, where the issues had broad and deep effect, where good reporting was needed to unmask corruption and work to make power more honest and responsive to the people. Karli had fought hard to earn her reputation as a relentless and meticulously accurate reporter. She had also earned a reputation—one she was less conscious of—as a deeply compassionate interviewer, one who could quickly relate to people from all walks of life. Her curiosity about each person she met was intense and sincere. The attention she gave to the people she interviewed was complete and marked by the kindness and compassion that makes people feel like they're the only other person in the world. That disarming ability to reach people's hearts filled her interviews with revelations that flowed smoothly from the trusting intimacy people found with her immediately and almost universally.

What her stories in Palm Beach had lacked—and what she had come to Iowa for—was photography that could achieve that same kind of intimacy and complement the reporting she was learning to do so well. Working here in the cornfield brought her to a market where the news photographers excelled—especially Jake, if the gossip she'd gathered proved correct. And if she could report some stories that showed her working at her peak, supported by excellent news photography, that would catch hiring eyes in the big markets she was headed for.

"Hey! Easy on my camera!" a loud voice interrupted her thoughts. Looking back over her shoulder, Karli saw Jake's long, muscular arms reaching futilely for his equipment. Behind him, the whirling lights of fire trucks raced toward them.

She had already spent enough years in the news business to understand the stereotypical news photographer personality. "Look, Jake, lay off," she said. "Everyone knows that photogs only care so much for those long telephoto lenses because they're compensating for something. And we really need to get moving."

A dangerous light flickered behind Jake's limpid brown eyes. His 6' 3" frame froze, taut with tense emotion. He had been in the news business even longer than she, and he knew his stereotypes, too.

He replied, "If we're going to talk about what *everyone knows,* maybe we should touch on little reporter bunnies. Everyone knows that baby girl TV reporters come in two flavors: the most common are the attention whores who have enough intellectual capacity to know exhibitionism is healthier when it masquerades as reporting.

But they still put on a great show—on the air and in the bedroom."

His gaze bore into her as he continued. "You're probably the second type, though: the repressed prude who can't abide the thought of actual sex with a man, so you take your daddy issues with you in front of the camera. The attention of a news shooter and the viewers he stands in for are a poor substitute for the sex you're too frigid to actually have. And you think dry-humping your long-suffering, long-distance boyfriend is daring and maybe too racy for you. So you're frustrated and driven and angry and bitchy. And the only thing that you think will help is a bigger audience. But it doesn't matter how big the audience—or how long the lens—they can't relieve your frustration."

Karli actually heard herself shriek at this impertinence, and as she saw the handsome, devilish grin tugging at the corners of his mouth in response, she shrieked again.

Then she took a deep breath preparatory to shouting him off his high horse.

Erik the engineer had been listening as he readied the live truck's many delicate machines and instruments to move. He poked his head out again just in time for Karli's second shriek. "Hey guys, your stereotypical engineer can't promise anyone that he'll be able to get a signal out of the new location if we don't get there soon. I can't necessarily work a miracle every time, no matter how great my press has been."

"Save it, Karli," Jake said calmly, a grin now dimpling his cheek and chin. "The point is that maybe we are both actual people instead of the reductive stereotypes you have so handy." He reached across her to retrieve his camera, gently but irresistibly tugging it from her grasp, and continued talking as though to the camera. "And heck, if it were up to me, we'd use faster and shorter glass for just about everything and save the long lenses for helicopter rides."

Karli smelled Jake's skin as he pried the camera from her. His sun-warmed scent was a mixture of fading, spicy aftershave, clean sweat, and fresh laundry. She felt the fury begin to slowly drain from her system, sticking several times on the way out to demand *just how that prick could be so cavalier about calling her frigid and accusing her of having daddy issues.* She was here to do great reporting, that's all. She'd chosen television news because she had a front-row seat on life. Every day she found the extraordinary—whether she was meeting with Fortune 500 CEOs or Joe Six-Pack at the mini-mart.

And, Karli admitted to herself, she liked to be on camera. She liked to be looked at.

Because I like having the authority that goes with being on camera, she carefully thought to herself. *Definitely not because of anything to do with repressed sex stuff.* She searched within for a moment, and then came clean with herself: *Not mainly, anyway.*

"Not only are you rude, Jake Gibson, you're an idiot." Karli turned and began dragging cables back into the truck, making no contact with Jake's liquid brown eyes. She looked up at Erik, whose head had been swinging back and forth between Karli and Jake. "Yes, we are moving out. Keep everything turned on that you can for a very short drive, okay?"

Erik nodded and ducked back into the van. Jake stomped on the quickly tangling group of cables Karli was heaping helter-skelter into the live van. The cables stopped dead with the sudden weight and nearly tipped Karli off of her high heels. Just as she regained her balance and lifted her sparking eyes to Jake's, the fire engine rolled to a stop next to the live truck. Its PA system cut off her intended description of his shortcomings. "You must evacuate this area immediately," came the officially amplified voice. "The train was carrying dangerous chemicals. You must evacuate immediately."

Karli glared pointedly at Jake, tipping her head toward the engine and its message by way of silent but emphatic *told you so.* She resisted the urge to flip him the bird, only because they were standing right next to a van with Three NewsFirst painted on this side in three-foot letters. Jake took his foot off the cables and began to coil them himself, though neatly and quickly rather than in the tangled mess she had begun to create. She walked to the passenger side of the fire engine, looking for the ranking firefighter.

"Karli Lewis, Three NewsFirst. Where is your command post set up?"

***

With only five minutes left before the show started, they had moved the truck to the local Kum & Go franchise's parking lot near the center of Cambridge. Karli, Jake and Erik scrambled to set up and go live. Erik raised the mast and chattered into his two-way radio while moving joysticks to restore the microwave signal that carried sound and video back to the station's master control room. He also kept a wary eye out for more sparks between the reporter and photographer. The day was hot enough already, he thought, without another blow-up. Karli flipped back through her notes and paced the parking lot, mumbling as she rehearsed her report.

She couldn't help glancing, then outright peek-sneaking, as Jake, wearing a Three NewsFirst polo and 501s, strung audio and video cables from the truck and far enough across the parking lot that the noisily rattling generator powering the truck's array of broadcast equipment wouldn't be picked up as background sound. She noticed especially how he moved—somehow more lithe and powerful than the simple economy of movement that comes from repeating a practiced task. His strength was like a graceful cat's ever-ready yet relaxed power. Watching Jake's arms ripple as he spun out and dressed the cables, she remembered the irresistible strength of his hands as he'd taken the camera and tripod from her. And he handled the camera and tripod as smoothly as inanimate dance partners. His face and physique were the classic picture of handsome: waves of hair and a strong jawline framed expressive brown eyes and a razor-straight nose; a smooth neck arced to broad shoulders and a lean, muscled torso; the worn jeans rode over long legs and showed a distinctly impressive dimension around the button fly.

He's handsome, sure, Karli thought to herself. *Too bad he's an arrogant jerk. Regardless, I don't have time for news photographers who cop attitudes right before we go on the air. The decisions on location are* mine *to make, not his.*

Still, there was an unusual kind of sexy that made Jake different. He was good-looking, yeah, but it wasn't any particular thing about how he looked that kept drawing her eyes back to him. It was an unusual air of effortless competence, as though no problem were beyond his ability. Yet he wasn't cocky or arrogant; his was, rather, a calm presence that didn't seem likely to break a sweat over any difficulty. *This won't do at all,* she thought. She was attracted to this Jake. And she couldn't work with this photographer every day if she wanted to jump his bones. She needed a working partner to make her stories as visually brilliant as they could be, not a . . . well, not whatever Jake would be if she slept with him. And watching him move was compelling.

Karli took her spot and checked her earpiece. "Ready remote?" she heard Chuck Teros the director ask in her ear, followed by his call for the title sequence. She heard Erik's two-way radio echo through Chuck's headset, "We're ready to go live," and then heard the broadcast through her earpiece, with the opening music for the Three NewsFirst midday show and the announcer's voice trumpeting, "Live, from the News Center Plaza, it's Three NewsFirst at Noon."

Her sudden, reflexive cry of panic was silenced by the concern that her mic might be live, yet Karli felt a jolt of impending live-television doom shake her as Jake locked his camera into place on the tripod, straightened up, then ran away from the setup at a sprint. It was time to go on the air, but *Jake was leaving his camera*?

They hadn't been set up in time to do a live headline of their story before the newscast's open, but they were ready to go live as soon as the show started. Karli's earpiece brought the sound of the anchors on set in Des Moines reading her lead-in about the location of the train's derailment, between the Heart of Iowa Nature Trail to the south and Ballard Creek to the north. The director switched to video they had beamed back earlier of the evacuated town and the derailed cars. The video changed back to the newsroom's veteran anchor, Arthur Brinkman, who greeted Karli and introduced her as reporting live from Cambridge.

Just as the director cut to Karli on-camera, Jake sprang back into view, silently dropping a huge white box onto the ground near Karli's feet. Bright sunlight reflected off the angled white surface and into her eyes. Karli fought off the glare's distraction and began her report with the most recent development, the hazmat teams suiting up and starting to clean the spilled chemicals just across town, then she led into a recorded interview with a local resident who had heard the train squeal and thunder off the tracks.

While the sound and video of that taped interview rolled, Karli kept her eyes toward Jake and his camera. She couldn't help noticing Jake's hair curling behind the lens and his tall, masculine frame wrapped possessively around the camera and tripod. His muscular legs were locked into position to keep the camera rock-steady. The resident's sound bite ended, and Karli was back on, live.

"…Story County Sheriff's Captain Tina Mowbrey is with me here live." Jake smoothly zoomed out and panned to include the officer. "Captain, what progress are the hazmat teams making so folks can return to their homes here in Cambridge?

"We expect that work will be done within 24 hours. Any time you have chemicals leaking into the environment, that's a serious issue, and we are playing it safe. We're getting that under control, and the town is being evacuated now only as a precaution."

"Captain, isn't one of the chemicals leaking from the train sodium hydroxide, a chemical so corrosive it could injure or kill people who come in contact with or breathe it, right?"

"Yes, that is one of the chemicals we're dealing with. But we're getting it under control. We're glad to have the wind out of the west today, as that will blow any dangerous vapors away from town."

"Thank you, Captain.

"And Arthur," Jake zoomed tightly to Karli's face, her startling blue eyes turning underneath her long bangs to look into his lens as though directly into the eyes of the anchorman on set in downtown Des Moines, "as we said earlier, over 800 people have been evacuated from Cambridge today as a result of this toxic chemical spill on the east edge of town. We'll have more on the story this evening at six. Reporting live from Cambridge, this is Karli Lewis, Three NewsFirst."

"Thanks for that report," Arthur's deep bass rumbled in her earpiece. "Karli Lewis, the newest member of the Three NewsFirst team, live from Cambridge, where hazardous chemicals from a train derailment have caused the town's evacuation. We'll have more on that story throughout the day."

Arthur's co-anchor for the noon show, Bailey Barber, read the lead-in to the next story, about pesticide levels in Des Moines' tap water. Karli kept her eyes on the camera in front of her until she heard director Chuck's voice in her earpiece saying, "You're clear, remote."

Before she had the chance to feel the relief that always came as the adrenaline rush from a high-pressure live shot dissipated, Karli's iPhone buzzed in her pocket; the caller ID said Three NewsFirst. Expecting congratulations on a triumphant first day at the new station, she slid to answer: "Karli Lewis."

"Why weren't you ready to go in the break before the show? We sent you up there with our best photographer and engineer—so you could beat everyone else to the scene—and they tell me you made them move the entire shot *away from the scene?* You were supposed to tease the newscast!" Karli's new boss, News Director Jerry Schultz, was spitting mad. Her cheek and ear were practically wet.

"Uh, hi Jerry," Karli stammered. "We weren't safe that close to the leak. I googled the placard on the leaking containers, and I learned that sodium hydroxide is deadly. It is caustic enough to burn or kill people, and when it reacts with metals—like those train cars—it creates explosive gas. "

"You mean you couldn't have waited ten minutes until our lead story *actually led the newscast?*"

"The fire department came to evacuate us just as I told Erik to take the mast down. They weren't going to let us stay there, Jerry." Karli's voice shook with live-shot adrenaline and from the surprise and fear of the unexpected confrontation with her brand new boss on her first day at work.

"So the officials removed you from the scene?" Jerry sounded surprised, and Karli heard his chair groan as he shifted with his reaction.

"Yes, Jerry. They directed us to move at about the same time I said to take the mast down."

"Okay. Well, that can't be helped," Jerry conceded grudgingly. "At least you didn't fumble the shot once you did get on the air."

Is this what passes for praise here? Karli wondered. "Yeah, well, thanks. As far as I can tell, we were the only station to identify the chemical, and we covered the whole story from the resident witness to the evacuation and the danger from the chemicals and the cleanup. And I already have a line on some interviews with folks who've been evacuated." Karli didn't want to sound defensive, but she had done a solid job today. She had been working as a television news reporter for over four years after all, and she knew what she was doing.

Although her confidence could sometimes come across as a bit arrogant, Karli was deeply committed to excellence in her reporting, and it almost always came through in her reports.

The time she had spent in the tiny *Palm Beach* television market had taught her a lot about how to work toward her goal of reporting in one of the top markets. She had to cover stories that would gain national attention or at least report some stories that would win some of the big awards in the news business. It helped to be a member of the so-called Missou Mafia—alums of the University of Missouri (Columbia) broadcast journalism program—who have a powerful presence in newsrooms throughout the country.

As good as her reporting in Florida had been, it had been handicapped by the newsroom's lack of staff. She'd had to do her own photography and editing in addition to the reporting. And although she could run a camera competently, her training and interest focused on reporting and writing. Television is a visual medium, and Karli knew that winning big awards meant going to a market where she could work with hotshot photographers and editors. Operations like Three NewsFirst were among the best in the nation for that kind of talent. Or so she'd thought. Until her first day on the job. Today.

As she hung up from her call with Jerry, Karli's eyes brimmed with furious tears. *My first day. I save the whole crew from toxic chemicals, and the jerk photog bitches about it and tells me I'm a hack from the tropics. I nail the live shot, and my new boss thinks I'm a screw-up.*

I'm so glad I took this job.

Deep breaths, Karli, she thought to herself. *You're a short-timer. Stay cool.*

Get some good stories here for the resume reel and get the heck out of here and on to bigger news pastures, like a job reporting in a real *market like Chicago. And especially don't waste energy thinking about sexy photogs who won't do anything but hold you back. This too—all of it—shall pass.*

Chapter Two

Salon Cut it Out!
Ingersoll Avenue, Des Moines
Tuesday evening, July 16

Karli took a long sip from her diet Mountain Dew and, her back
to the mirror, regarded her new hairdresser's straight, fine features
and his deliberately tousled, product-laden hair. "Trevor, is it like
this for every new reporter here?"

"Like what?" Trevor asked as he ran Karli's wet hair through his
fingers, checking his work with a critical eye.

"Everyone is mean. Seriously mean. Like they want to see if they
can make me cry. Because they *like* to see the new reporter cry."

Focused on his work rather than Karli's complaints, Trevor tilted
his head to the side as he swung the chair from side to side,
examining Karli's new style. He snipped at some imperfection only
he could see, then finally met Karli's eyes. "Karli, you're *beautiful.*
We're going to move away from that girl-next-door look and show
everyone just how beautiful you are. Wait till I blow this dry. It's
going to open your face up for everyone to see."

Karli glanced down at the unusually large piles of hair on the
floor with concern and tried to imagine what the finished product
would be like. "Every move I make, everyone feels entitled to
second-guess me and tell me that I'm not doing it right or not doing
it the Des Moines way. Like that Jake—the photographer. He just
belittles me and looks at me like I'm an idiot. And he's even worse
than that.

Right when we went live, he tried to freak me out by flashing
this big white thing in my face. If I hadn't been live, I would've
screamed!"

Trevor nodded and started running product-covered hands
through Karli's hair. "Jake Gibson? He comes here, too. Well, pretty

much everyone from the newsroom does because there's a trade-out deal. He's gorgeous, isn't he?" Trevor's eyes twinkled salaciously at the mention of the lean, muscled photographer.

"Who cares if he's gorgeous? He's a dick! I found out that the stuff leaking out of that train was likely to kill us, and he couldn't do anything but tell me what an idiot I am for wanting not to wade in it," Karli fumed. "And then I nail the live shot and he just starts putting his gear away. No *nice job, new reporter who I'm going to be working with now.* No *glad you're on the team, new reporter who just saved my life and still got the story.* Nothing."

Then Karli remembered what he'd looked like while he'd bent over his camera, enveloping it with his broad shoulders and strong, carefully steady arms. *Okay,* she thought, *he's got a powerful, sexy presence.* Her pulse quickened slightly as she remembered his intense, liquid brown eyes framed by those light brown curls. *Okay,* she conceded, *he's gorgeous.* She felt her nipples draw tensely as she remembered how his muscles had rippled under the polo shirt while he moved equipment, and how the 501s had pulled taut across his hard ass, and how they had hinted at something special behind the button fly.

She shook herself back to the point. "So my next live shot is going to have to be good enough to win an Emmy to be good enough for middle-of-nowhere Des Moines. But Trevor, I don't care.

This job is really only a stepping-stone. I'm not going to worry about satisfying all these cornfield creeps. My reporting is going to get me a job in a top-ten market, where I can tackle national politics more than once every four years and cover official corruption and other issues people really care about."

"Des Moines isn't necessarily bad, you know," Trevor said. "It has been a good place for me. And do you really want to live where the corruption is?"

"Hold it, you're not from here?" Karli's voice rose in surprise. "When he sent me here, Jerry made it sound like you were the native son who was positively the only one who could fix my not-good-enough-for-Des Moines hair. So where did you come from?"

"You've never heard of it," Trevor said dismissively. "It's a little farm town I escaped from right after high school." Trevor fastened the diffuser to his blow dryer and began moving it carefully over Karli's hair as he shaped it with his left hand.

"I can't see ever fitting in here, Trevor."

"Really?" Trevor quirked an eyebrow at her, then gave her a long, appraising look, the blow dryer hanging noisily at his side. She watched his eyes run over her entire compact frame, starting with her new haircut and her startling, long-lashed blue eyes. Then he stared frankly at her smooth neck and at the small round breasts that rode high on her strong pectorals. He kept looking, seriously but somehow not leering, taking in her athletic figure's flat stomach and clean-lined, tanned legs.

"I need to update my radar," he concluded. Trevor indicated an exotic-looking hairdresser across the salon with a nod of his head.

She was tall—maybe 5' 10"—with lustrous, straight brunette hair cut asymmetrically and long. As she watched the stylist turn to escort her freshly coiffed client to the front of the salon, Karli saw the subtle contours of a long figure under red leather pants and a loose-fitting natural silk blouse.

"Leeza is back on the market," Trevor said. "She broke up with her last girlfriend about two months ago, and she's probably ready for dating again. You two would look great together." Trevor's eyes twinkled above the same naughty grin he'd had when talking about Jake.

It took Karli a few beats to figure out what Trevor was suggesting. Then her eyes popped wide open and a deep blush flowed over her face. "Oh my gosh, Trevor. I didn't mean different like that! I mean, I like boys!" She took a nervous swig from her diet Dew, then took another furtive look across the salon. There was no denying that Leeza was beautiful, but Karli wasn't... well, she wasn't like that.

"Sorry, Karli. It sounded like that's what you meant. And it sort of fits with you not noticing Jake," he said. Trevor's eyes drifted off his work and focused somewhere off in space. "If you like good-looking men, you pretty much have to notice Jake. And not as a jerk. He's *hot*—and genuinely caring, too."

"Oh." Karli finally realized what kind of man Trevor was. Her blush had barely begun to fade, yet here it came again, hot and embarrassing. "Trevor. It's flattering that you think I'm in her league—even though I don't play for that team. She's really exotic and beautiful."

"Really?" Trevor smirked and swiveled the chair so Karli was facing directly across the salon at Leeza.

Karli's cheeks flushed even more deeply. Her face was so hot she was practically sweating. While she appreciated feminine beauty, it was purely as a spectator, not as a ... a participant. Leeza's exotic beauty was what she pictured alongside a man like Jake, more than her own petite frame. *But he'd be so big and powerful,* Karli thought, feeling a distinct tingle between her legs as she envisioned Jake naked and moving toward her own naked body.

Her pulse was already pounding, but it spasmed even faster with panic as she remembered that Trevor cut practically everyone's hair at the station. She had to set the record absolutely straight before rumors started. She had just started this job, and here people would be hearing that she was a lesbian.

"Jake is much more what I'm interested in," she blurted in desperation. Then, realizing that she'd said the wrong thing again— *now everyone is going to hear that I can't stop thinking about being naked with him*—she hastily added, "But he's a distraction I can't afford. Like I said, I'm going to file a few award-winning stories, and then I'm out of here." She had learned during a college internship that dalliances with photographers could become very distracting indeed. The boy had been a nice guy and very attentive, but he had lacked ambition almost entirely.

"Hmm. You're interested in The Dick?" Trevor smirked and put the dryer away. He had pronounced the capital letters, and Karli knew her face showed that she'd heard them.

"Well, I could have been, if he hadn't accused me of having daddy issues. I guess." *Oh shit*, Karli thought. *I was trying to* prevent *rumors*.

Trevor indicated to Karli to stand up from the chair, turned her toward the mirror for the first time since she had entered the salon, and met Karli's reflected gaze with raised eyebrows. "What do you think?"

Karli looked at Trevor's proud smile, then gasped as her eyes moved to see the reflection of her new style for the first time. Seriously sharp bangs no longer covered her eyebrows, and the long, glossy hair that had fallen along her cheeks and down to her shoulder blades was gone. She saw her small ears without tucking her hair behind them for the first time in years. Shock turned to anger as Karli took it in and then stammered: "Trevor, you gave me a p-ppixie cut!"

Karli was furious. She had meticulously grown and cared for her beautifully long hair. With the high heels she took off only seldom, the long hair had always helped her look taller and more serious than the short stature—5' 1"—she believed hurt her credibility as a professional woman. Trevor had literally cut off her hope to appear taller than she was. *This—this insult to my dignity—was what they had sent me to Mr. Hair Genius for?*

Leeza drew near as Karli's irate stammers sputtered into speechlessness. "Trevor, who is this new person?" she asked. Even in her state of shock, it was obvious to Karli that Leeza was giving her a looking-over just as thorough as—and much more intimate than—Trevor's had been. Leeza's eyes languorously explored the smooth, tanned legs and roundly muscled backside that Karli spent so many hours in the gym to shape. Then Leeza calmly took in her round breasts and finally rested on the flashing blue eyes. "My, my, my," Leeza purred, "You have uncaged a tigress, Trevor."

"Those long bangs and straight sides were too college-girl cute," Trevor responded. "This opens her face up on every side and makes her more serious and complicated, don't you think?"

"Serious and *fierce*, Trevor," Leeza said. "By parting the curtains and showing the great bones that were hiding behind those bangs, you've made her honesty into something powerful. Hello, Sienna Miller-as-a-brunette; goodbye, college cutie."

Accustomed as she was to having people fuss over her appearance, Karli was still shocked. The radically different new haircut and Leeza's overt come-on were almost too much for her. They were very different from the professional squinting and primping she'd received at the hands of convention-driven makeup and hair professionals at her last job in Palm Beach. She reached unsteadily for her diet Dew, and breathlessly mumbled a thank-you that she hoped would work as an exit line. Trevor heard his cue, gently took her arm, and led her to the front of the salon. "If you really want me to, I'll tell Leeza you aren't interested," he mumbled into her ear.

Karli stumbled out of the salon and belted herself into her car. She put the keys into the ignition, then grabbed the wheel and yanked herself back and forth until the whole car shook. *Another jerk!* she thought. *He's supposed to make me look better than I've ever looked before, and instead he makes me look like a winged elf or something.* Here she gave the steering wheel a series of extra-hard tugs, still thrashing back and forth in the seat.

And to make matters worse, he's probably about to start a bunch of rumors that I'm either a lesbian or bi. No, it's worse than that. Jake pissed me off so much with that daddy-issue comment that I let it slip. Now Trevor's going to start rumors that I'm a bi nympho with the hots for that Leeza and for Jake, too!

Tired and fighting off tears of frustration, Karli stopped shaking herself and the entire car. After catching her breath, she carefully started the car, put it in reverse, and began backing out. Catching a glimpse of her new hairstyle again as she looked in the rearview mirror, she was startled anew and stepped on the brake to take a better look. She turned her head from side to side, slowly. *Who is this woman come out from behind the long bangs?*

She put the car back in park and opened the door to turn on the dome light. With her eyes nearly cleared now of the tears that had filled them but not spilled out, Karli looked more closely, with a television professional's trained eye, this time assessing the short hair's loose frame around her face and how it exposed her cheekbones and jawline from most any angle, sharpening her features with a look of keen intelligence.

Then she frowned into the mirror, drawing semicircles with her index fingers at the lower edges of the inky shadows cast by the overhead light. They all but hid her eyes. *I feel exposed,* she thought. What had Leeza called her—a tigress?

And then she thought about the rumors. And then she thought about Jake. "Jake is much more what I'm interested in." *Did I really say that about The Dick?* she grumbled to herself. *Of course,* she thought, checking the mirror again, *maybe Fierce Tigress Karli will be able to open his eyes about how good my reporting is.* Karli was surprised to feel a flutter just below her stomach as she thought how she might react if Jake were to show her some appreciation. *Okay, so he's gorgeous,* she thought. *But he's an arrogant asshole, and that trick about trying to blind me was a foul first-day prank on the new reporter. He's The Dick for that alone.*

Karli took a final look in the mirror as another car began to maneuver into a space on her side of the street. Its headlights flashed in her mirror, and she squinted just as she had when Jake had put that giant light in her face at noon. Still looking at her reflection, Karli noticed that the shadows from the overhead dome light—directly overhead, just like the noonday sun—had been obliterated with light from the other car's headlights.

He was lighting me to make me look better, so viewers could see my eyes, she realized. She shook her head as she closed the door and rolled down the window, realizing that it hadn't been a practical joke.

Chapter Three

Des Moines, Iowa State Fairgrounds
Thursday, August 8
Live shot for noon newscast

Karli swiped the alert off her iPhone's display. Even after three weeks, she was still getting texts from her father about how surprised he was with her new haircut and didn't she think that things were moving a little too fast at this new station if they thought they could just transform the Karli he'd known her whole life into some completely different person?

Glad to see anything that wasn't long-distance micro-management, Karli took in the crushing mass of sweaty Iowans and thought to herself that she had never seen a collection of people like these before. It had usually been hot in her last market, when she had been a reporter—and her own news photographer—in Palm Beach. But the folks at the Iowa State Fair, well, these people were definitely not used to year-round heat, nor did they look much like Floridians. And although Karli saw an occasional Hispanic or African American family, this crowd was overwhelmingly white. Either pasty white or sunburned white. But there weren't many glistening, even, beach-ready tans like those most folks had so carefully cultivated in Palm Beach.

Karli looked again at her iPhone for the notes her assignment editor, Vince Guzman, had given her about the fair. It was, he said, "a celebration of hogs, husband-calling and heavy metal hair bands" that had somehow made it onto someone's official list of *1,000 Places to Visit Before You Die.*

As she was reviewing her notes, a text message had popped up on the top of her iPhone's screen. She saw with a twinge that it was from her father—again—and all of his stern tones came through the text and into her head: "If you've had enough of Iowa yet, the senior partner of the public relations agency here says he'd hire you right away. Make \$\$\$! Love you!" The message finished with an emoji smiley face—something suspiciously out of her father's character. He had staff to handle details like that.

She sighed with exasperation and a measure of fear. She loved her daddy, but her heart sank at the prospect of having to concede that she couldn't make a career on her own. She would be crushed if she ever had to crawl back and do what she was told. Her whole adult life had been spent extricating herself from the luxurious and predictable web her father had woven especially to ensnare her into what he had envisioned as the perfect future for her. At his direction, she had been accepted to a number of prestigious southeastern universities. Without his knowledge, though, she had applied to the University of Missouri's broadcast journalism school—one of the finest programs in the country—where she had not only been accepted, she had been given an academic scholarship that very nearly paid all the tuition bills. And against his wishes and after many unpleasantly shouty or silent family dinners, she had packed herself into the Saab he'd passed on to her at graduation while he bought an American luxury car for its better political profile. So Karli had taken her high school diploma along in the Saab and driven herself to Columbia to begin classes. She excelled in school in spite of having to work nearly full time at a men's clothiers to pay her room and board.

And after the Saab company went into bankruptcy, the temperamental car's frequent cries for maintenance ate deeper into her tight budget all the time. Summers were spent working newsroom internships (by day, and retail at night to pay the bills) that resulted in a decent collection of resumé-stories up on YouTube. Those stories had been good enough to get her that first job in Palm Beach.

She had learned a few things about news and life along the way. News photographers in particular had been a minor field of study. She'd dated during her internships, and had thought she was serious about one of them. He was attentive and even charming, but he had turned out to have little or no ambition beyond each successive weekend. Karli, of course, was all about ambition. Having earned her own way through school, she was acutely aware of her education's value. Stagnation at a middle-market newsroom was not anywhere near the achievement she was looking for, but he had been perfectly willing to settle for that. Her internship had ended just as she'd realized the relationship had to end. Resolved to settle for nothing short of the best she could accomplish, she'd returned to Missou to take her senior year by storm. She had, too, impressing the most demanding professors and making an academic name for herself.

The job in Palm Beach had been lined up before graduation. Her parents had come to watch her walk across the stage in her cap and gown, yet they had been disconnected from what she'd accomplished, where she was headed, and the woman she had become. In their eyes, she remained the sweet little Karli they'd seen through high school, not the woman who had declined their offers of financial support and—always firmly—of relocation expenses to a school closer to home. They'd never understood why she felt compelled to sacrifice the comforts of an established social network and the comfortable lifestyle home offered.

After graduation, in an effort to reestablish some common ground with them, Karli had detoured her Saab to Charleston on the way to Palm Beach. The detour became a flurry of country club dinners, shopping at all the best stores—with her parents hanging bags full of clothes and shoes on her, in spite of her protests that she would manage for herself.

Her father was exactly the sort of man who bought clothes for her whether she wanted them or not and who would have found a plush job for her whether she wanted it or not. She stood firm on the job, though she gave in pretty quickly on the clothes. The job she was headed for fit her personality and ambitions. Any job her father found her would fit the money-centered world he ruled over Charleston. As he conceived it, he had pre-destined her for a role within that world, one where he could be sure she would have a jewelry-spangled life of country club receptions, glamorously philanthropic parties, and all the rest.

Charleston was a great city, and her father was near the center of the area's power structure. But he couldn't see clearly beyond that world. And he couldn't conceive that his daughter could make her own mark in a world that wasn't bound by strings he pulled. She loved his dark, handsome, consciously Rhett-Butler-esque style. He was proud to provide and plan for his family. She knew she couldn't fit into the sanitized and contrived life laid out for her, however well intentioned her father's designs might be.

Shaking her head and dismissing her father's text unanswered, Karli's attention turned again to the fairgrounds she had been unconsciously navigating with her face down in her phone. She had people's stories to discover and tell.

She looked up to noises of lemonade shake-up vendors hawking their goods and the shrill growls of chainsaws sculpting tree stumps into eagles and astronauts. She saw teenage boys slurping from oversized cups and gawking at teenage girls. The boys came in essentially two varieties: jeans, work shirts and boots, or gym shorts and t-shirts.

The teen girls were slightly more various, starting with jeans and workshirts and moving through all the way to daisy dukes and halters. Their footwear was completely mix-and-match, with flip-flops under hardworking jeans, cowboy boots under daringly short cut-offs, and vice versa. And Uggs under anything. In August.

In spite of their odd wardrobe selections, Karli saw that those girls were stunning. Toothpaste-commercial smiles beamed from faces that had an unusual openness and look of goodwill to all. Like girls everywhere, they giggled and squealed over whatever nonsense was on the smartphone screens they shared with one another, but theirs was a beauty more fully revealed and candid and less manipulative than the Florida girls Karli was used to covering or the South Carolina sorority girls she'd grown up with.

More homogenous were the retirees. The breathless, sweaty, lumpy uniformity of their bright white sneakers, khaki shorts, and fanny packs pressed along the main concourse and through each exhibit building.

They had once probably looked as sweetly attractive as the coltish teenagers and early-20s crowds, but that past was constrained by taut buttons and zippers. Fleshy creases described, strata-like, the years of accretion from countless hearty meals over their youthful glories. Still, youthful enthusiasm bubbled forth from them like a baby's saliva-laden laughter. Every sight or experience offered at the fair was another occasion for muttered exclamations of joy or restrained gestures of appreciation. Each booth's offerings were greeted as though they were completely novel—the latest material developed by NASA and put to practical application in, say, beehive framing.

Still, watching one of these jolly goliaths devouring a bacon-encrusted corn dog, Karli came up with a lead that she could never use in any story: *At today's Iowa State Fair, dieticians discovered the origin and destination of Middle America's ever-expanding middle section. With more on this flyover state's annual hickstravaganza of gluttony, Karli Lewis is live in the fryer zone...*

The youngest children, Karli thought to herself as she walked through the fair, were as beautiful and happy as any she'd ever seen. Their parents were loving but not overindulgent. Covered with silly hats and sunglasses, the preschoolers all were having a great time running through the seemingly endless animal exhibits, the kid zone, and all over the midway.

She and Jake had interviewed any number of these Iowans this morning, and they'd sent the video back to the station for editing. Now it was time for Karli to put her game face on and keep interviewing people about the fair. Today's stories were not likely to win any awards, but it was refreshing to relax through an easy day of reporting news as fluffy as the cotton candy being spun just a few feet away.

"Lookin' good so far, Karli," Jake said, his tenor voice enthusiastic. "What's the next group of fair-goers you want to charm into submission with your attentive ear and delicate questioning?" His eyes twinkled with mischief, and his left cheek dimpled over a troublemaker's grin.

He was so cute that he almost certainly knew he was cute, Karli thought. But he didn't seem at all aware that he put on a show just about every time he moved. And Karli was having a hard time not watching the show. He was built like a spokesman for Bowflex—but with his shirt on and no glycerin making his skin sparkle. His brown hair curled around the viewfinder when he was framing shots, and his eyes were as delicious as their milk chocolate color.

Karli was surprised she noticed, as no other guy had ever impressed her that way before. And boy oh boy did she ever notice it. She could deal with it when he was being Jake-the-Jerk; he was good at his job and made her better at her own. But Jake-the-decent-guy was something else entirely. He didn't show off his seriously great good looks. He was just comfortable in his own skin. Which made him even better looking and sexier. Most of all his smiles—at the curious, the elderly, and the awestruck kids—were all dangerously attractive. She found herself wondering when one would be directed at her. She also wondered when she would stop wanting to bring her lips to his.

Karli hadn't had huge experience with sex, but she had a feeling that Jake could make sex a major revelation.

Yet he was, after all was said and done, just another news photographer. In her experience they were mostly not-too-bright, ambitionless, but interestingly creative walking libidos with a camera attached.

Karli's musings were interrupted as a boy, maybe 12 years old, rushed close by her, yelling, "Sensei Jake!" Karli watched as the boy came to a breathless and beaming stop in front of her photographer, his face smudged with powdered sugar presumably from one of the fair's fried calorie-bombs.

"Hey, Brian!" Jake practically shouted, throwing his arm around the boy's shoulders and gently rubbing his knuckles on the blonde buzz-cut head. "When we're out in the world, you just call me 'Jake,' right? No need for studio etiquette here at the fair. But it's good to see you. Are you having fun yet?"

"Duh! This fair is the greatest thing ever!" Brian's smile practically cast its own light up at Jake's face. "You've got to check out the animals. I just saw, like, the biggest bull in the history of everything! He was huge—more than 3,000 pounds!"

"That big, really?" Jake asked with an impressed grin. "We'll probably be heading over there in a bit. Have you had time to do anything else?"

"Not much. But I want to go on the new rides, and they said there was going to be a magician show over behind the Ag building. And I'm hungry, and my mom gave me $15 to buy food. And I want a fried brownie."

"Brian Johnson, I want you to meet, uh..." here Karli saw Jake looking at her uncertainly, then back to Brian, "...my co-worker, Karli Lewis."

"Wow." Brian looked at Karli in gape-mouthed dismay.

"Um, I mean, I've seen you on TV."

Karli smiled, as to a new-found friend. "That's where most folks see me, Brian. And I'm glad you recognize me. I must be doing my job well to have made such an impression. Do you remember any of the stories I've covered?"

Brian hesitated, a look of confusion obvious on his face. "Not really, no. I mostly remember you because"—here his eyes flickered away from Karli's face and down to her white open-toe high heels—"because you're so pretty." Brian's head tilted slightly to one side, and he squinted back up at Karli's face, a shy smile creasing his face.

Karli was charmed. Brian was a very cute kid, and it was flattering that he thought her pretty enough that he actually got up the courage to say she was pretty to her face—or at least to her shoes. And he was only a boy, after all.

"Thank you, Brian," she managed to blurt after an uncomfortable pause. "You're a handsome young man yourself." *Where had that come from?* Karli wondered. *And since when could a little boy make her chest squeeze?*

Karli saw Jake nodding in approval though, and wondered if she was catching the Iowan knack of enthusiasm for all.

Jake put his hand on the boy's shoulder to signal the end of the introductions. "Karli is definitely good looking, Brian'" Jake said. "But don't forget that people are always more than how they look. It's much more important to know if a person is kind and cares about others—or if they are dangerously good at charming people off their guard so they'll answer all kinds of questions about things like fair food."

Jake's dimple came back alongside a teasing grin as he made that last comment.

Karli felt a different kind of warmth when she heard Jake's words of praise—both of her looks and her mind. Maybe because she had just been thinking about how handsome he was, but it wasn't the warmth of the blushes she'd felt at the hair salon. This was just as sudden, but it was down low and inside her. It felt kind of fluttery, too—like butterflies, but more intense and ready to drag more of her into its energy. *Now he's saying nice things about me?* she wondered.

Her attention came back to Jake and Brian's conversation, which had apparently moved on. "Well, there's nine more days of fair," Jake chuckled. "Make sure you save something."

"Duh! There's going to be new stuff every day, Sens... uh, Jake," Brian's smile stretched his cheeks into darling dimples. Karli grinned from sheer contagion, and she thought again that Iowa would soon have another heartthrob—one almost as handsome as Jake—as that sweet face grew up.

"Okay, kid." Jake thumped Brian on the back. "Just remember to get your mom a fried brownie, too. And get it to her while it's still hot. Now, scram. We're going live in a a couple minutes, and I need to get to work."

"See you soon!" Brian started off at a run, only to be brought up short by Jake's hand on the collar of his t-shirt.

"Brian, how do you greet and say goodbye to other men?" Jake asked, emphasizing the *other men* to include Brian in the group of adults.

"Oh, that's right!" Brian put out his hand and recited, as though by rote, "Hand out, thumb up, look 'em in the eye, and say goodbye!" Jake grasped Brian's hand, man-to-man, nodded curtly, and clapped the boy's shoulder with his other hand.

"Good job," Jake said. "See you 'round." Then he turned back to his work, tidying up the cables leading to his camera. Karli saw Jake sneak a glance back over his shoulder and smile—*another different kind of smile*—at Brian's rapidly retreating back. She saw the pride Jake felt in the boy's good manners, and she felt that warmth that had nothing to do with the weather or with blushing swell in her again. *Wait,* she thought, *Jake is turning me on by mentoring that boy? Really?* But she remembered the boy's delight at Jake including him in the world of men, and Jake's calm guidance toward good, manly manners. *Oh shit,* Karli thought, *it's hard not to be interested in The Dick.*

Karli was going live for the Three NewsFirst noon show, and she and Jake were supposed to be working on special State Fair-edition reporting the rest of the day. She had to deliberately clear her mind and get on the job. So she checked her iPhone for the time remaining and began her live-shot ritual: insert earpiece, clear throat, last sip of diet Mountain Dew, check notes, clear throat again, check microphone, stand tall, look at the camera like it was a person. Just as she felt ready to go on the air, Jake, who had left his camera standing alone, *again*, just as they were about to go live, came running up with a sneaky grin and his hand behind his back.

"Karli, this is for you—you need an authentic State Fair prop."

Looking both embarrassed and proud, Jake drew his hand from

behind his back and presented her with a genuine Iowa State Fair grilled-pork-chop-on-a-stick.

Before either one of them could say anything, Karli heard Arthur's bass rumbling in her ear, took the pork chop, and gave Jake's camera a significant raised-eyebrow look.

"... Live at the Iowa State Fairground's Grand Concourse is Three NewsFirst's Karli Lewis. Karli, can it be true that you've never been to the Iowa State Fair before?"

"Well, I'm not the only one enjoying a first today, Arthur. Five year-old Tiffany Buecher of Boone was here today with her parents. It was her first trip to the fair and her first attempt at eating one of these delicious pork chops-on-a-stick." Here Karli took a smiling bite from her inch-thick pork chop, clear juices dripping down its stick and onto her hand.

The director cut to a series of taped interviews Karli and Jake had done with various fairgoers, starting with little Tiffany's gleeful struggle to gnaw off a bite of pork chop, missing front baby teeth and all, as her chop clung precariously to its stick. Between wide-open efforts, Tiffany waved the chop-on-a-stick to emphasize her cries of mingled delight and frustration. Jake's camera brought viewers within what felt like hugging range of the little charmer.

The interviews went on to cover the highlights of fair food from tenderloins to corn dogs wrapped in bacon to funnel cakes drenched in powdered sugar, maple-flavored glop, and sprinkles of—what else—bacon.

Karli chewed frantically during the 90 seconds the tape rolled so her mouth would be clear when she came back on the air. As the taped segment ended, the director cut back to Karli live, her mouth and throat cleared just in time. "And Arthur and Bailey, you can be sure that those firsts—especially the food (here she brandished her chop-on-a-stick, Tiffany-style, toward the camera)—will be followed by seconds.

"Really, guys, this thing tastes great! And I can't wait for tomorrow, when I'll ride the Sky Glider for the first time. I've been watching people float by overhead all morning, and they look like they're loving it."

Arthur's deep basso laughter rumbled over the air as well as into Karli's earpiece. "Karli Lewis, it looks like you have that fair covered. We can't wait to see you gliding for us tomorrow."

***

Hearing the all-clear, Jake took his headphone off, hung it on his camera and began turning off and tearing down the blue-filtered lights he had set up to make Karli's sunlit face pop out of the busy background of fairgoers. As the crowds that had clustered around the live shot realized the show was over and began to move on, he saw Karli considering the pork chop.

"Hey, Jake, thanks for the pork chop. That really worked well in the shot. Um, do you maybe want the rest of it? This thing has to weigh almost a whole pound!"

After Jake shook his head, chuckling, Karli looked longingly at the chop, took a final bite and reluctantly dropped the rest into a garbage can.

"What are we doing now?" he asked her, folding the last light stand and stowing it in his kit.

Karli put down her diet Dew and took a look at the notes she'd put on her iPhone. "Why is a butter cow newsworthy?" she responded. "Wouldn't it melt in August in Iowa? And what in the world *is* a butter cow?"

"Hey, the butter cow is a tradition here, Karli," Jake said. "There's a lady—well, there was a lady—she passed away. Now there's a new crew. Anyway, they sculpt a life-size cow out of butter every year. It's on display in the Ag building." Jake stopped, saw no interest from Karli, and then went on. "It's a mandatory story, you know. We're going to have to do it sooner or later."

"We have nine more days to do our earth-shaking, award-winning story on the butter cow," Karli said. Her voice carried a sophisticate's contempt for all things precious. "The notes Vince gave me say today is the day for real animals. What did that boy say about a big bull? Let's go interview the thing and get our bull right from the source."

Amusement at her word-play flickered in Jake's eyes before he turned his back to her and began loading his gear into the golf cart they used to navigate the sprawling fairgrounds. She grabbed her diet Dew and sat in the passenger seat to check her iPhone for more notes on previous fairs and anticipated high points from this fair.

Looking up from his neatly stowed gear, Jake saw a small trickle of sweat tracing its way down Karli's temple—probably the first sign he'd caught that she was as hot as everyone else at the fair. Although he was sweating right through his company-issue Three NewsFirst polo shirt, she had shown no signs of perspiration or glowing or whatever up to this moment.

The sweat prompted him to look at her carefully—and to work at not enjoying it too obviously. Her tanned arms were smooth and strong, the Three NewsFirst logo perched jauntily atop her left breast, and her shapely legs led his eyes up to the generous contours she sat upon. Below her slender ankles, a pair of white high heels looked impractical and diva-esque in the walking-intensive fairgrounds.

Her glamorously photogenic face always captured his attention as great art would, but he felt a more personal attraction to her today and wondered what had caught his attention. He closed his eyes for just a moment to reflect on the urge and try to suppress it, smelled how the heat had amplified the vanilla and subtle spice of her perfume, and knew at once that it was her scent that had gotten its hooks into his libido. Knowing what had started the motor running did not, however, go any way toward shutting it down. Jake knew he would have to discipline himself to stay on task.

The big animal competitions started right away on the first day Karli observed aloud, so Jake steered toward the animal barns. "These kids can be really great stories, Karli," Jake said. "Have you covered many agricultural stories?"

"I certainly didn't grow up in farm country, if that's what you mean," Karli answered. "And how am I going to make this story not-boring? *I fed this pig a lot of food. That's why it got so big.* Right?" she asked. "These giant animals are just like all the human midway plumpers eating Fried Anything On A Stick, wrapped in Big Pig Bacon."

"Karli," Jake responded, shaking his head over a gentle chuckle, "these kids work hard to raise truly wonderful animals. Give them the credit they're due." By now they had rolled up to the animal buildings. Every species of farm animal seemed to have its own building, with some, like the horses, having more than one. Karli was surprised to see the Sheep Building's beautiful ornamentation, with sculpted sheep lounging, grazing, or caring for lambs all along the friezes set above the tall windows. And to think, Iowans erected this impressive building so they could use it only ten days a year.

The enclosures within were huge pens separated by broad aisles for gawking fairgoers to walk through. Loudly whirring livestock fans the size of big tractor wheels kept the many and mostly inoffensive smells of the different animals whirling in their noses.

After entering the Sheep Building, Jake watched Karli stop and look around. Coming in from the bright sunlight, the building was cast in semi-dark gloom, with countless Iowans milling around to look at one indistinguishable sheep after another. Jake touched her arm gently—so lightly that it was almost no touch at all—to guide her to a girl at the center of the crowd's thickest clump. "This girl won the biggest ram prize today." Jake said in her ear. "And this isn't her first fair, so she should be a good interview."

Nodding her thanks for the tip, Karli threaded her way through the crowd to the girl. Jake heard her introduce herself as Kennedy Shearer, a recent high school graduate headed for Iowa State's ag science program in the fall.

She stood in well-worn work boots, tight, faded jeans, broad, ornately buckled belt, and pearl-snapped workshirt. Kennedy had the lovely smile that shines from the tan faces of late-summer Iowa farm girls. Long, sun-bleached hair was pulled back from her face in a no-nonsense pony tail. Her teeth were brilliantly white in the light Jake set up for the interview, and they had the unnatural evenness of braces worn in younger days. Daily physical labor and good helpings of sturdy farm food had thickened her young body, yet her complexion glowed with youthful energy. A spray of freckles decorated her round cheeks and cute, snub nose.

Karli asked some basic questions while Jake fine-tuned his light and tripod. When he again touched Karli's arm and gave her a nod to say he was ready, Karli took the microphone he held out to her and gestured the girl to come closer. Kennedy stepped up to Karli, and Jake's head popped out from behind his camera.

"I put the light where she *was*, Karli, not here," Jake said. "Right there." He caught the girl's eye and pointed to where he wanted her to stand. She smiled and stepped back.

Jake could see that Karli was irritated by being bossed, and she darted a stern look at him and stepped towards the girl. Right into a pile of sheep droppings. Jake watched silently as they clumped up like so many semi-melted Milk Duds and smushed under and around her white open-toe heels. Karli suppressed most of her squeal as she felt the unwelcome texture of sheep turds under her shoe and touching her bare, newly pedicured toes. Jake watched as she looked down to see a marble-sized ball of sheep poop rolling off her big toenail. The rest of her squeal escaped and was quickly cut off.

The sheep girl laughed out loud. Jake made a little coughing sound.

Karli blushed with anger and shame as she looked back at the girl and her big ram. "Don't worry, Miss Lewis," Kennedy said, cutting her laughter as short as she could manage. "It won't hurt you any."

Jake saw Karli's struggle to paste the smile back on her face so she could finish the interview. Karli brought the microphone up to Kennedy. "What's your sheep's name, Kennedy?" she asked.

"My *ram's* name," said Kennedy, emphasizing her animal's sex, "is Barry White."

"Why did you name him Barry White?"

"Well, he had quite a way with the ladies before we pulled him out of the breeding herd," Kennedy smirked. "And I suppose he bleats kind of low."

Karli laughed in spite of herself. "So how big is Barry White?"

"He's 393 pounds, the biggest one we've ever brought to the fair. And this year there were more big ram contestants than ever before in State Fair history. So we're real proud of him."

"How did you get him so big?" Karli asked. "Did you feed him fair food?"

Now it was Kennedy's turn to laugh. "No, he didn't get any fried ice cream on the farm. We just kept him on feed and gave him a lot of personal attention. Genetics plays a big part in his size, of course."

"You say you took him out of the breeding herd—did he eat a lot to compensate for something?"

Kennedy's eyes twinkled in pleased surprise over her glowing smile, "Let's just say he didn't have to exert himself as much as he used to."

Jake also saw Karli's sudden look of astonishment as she learned that Barry White the Ram had huge testicles. Jake tilted his head to one side as he observed that the ram looked like someone had hung a pair of grapefruits between his hind legs.

Karli asked a few wrap-up questions about Kennedy's plans for the rest of the fair and whether she'd bring another ram next year, thanked the girl, and shook hands. While Jake took some close-up footage of Barry White's wooly face, he heard Karli extract from one of the judges that, as big as Barry was, he was more than fifty pounds lighter than the Fair's all-time record-holder.

They wrapped up and left the Sheep Building—*No, Shit Building*—Karli said, knocking her shoes on the edge of the golf cart to clear off the sheep shit—no, *ram* shit. "So what makes an Iowa farm girl like her tick?" Karli wondered aloud. "She's cute as can be, but she walks through shit every day and hangs out with animals. Why doesn't she spend her time working on something real instead of walking around on a farm with animal turds clumping up on her work boots?"

Jake saw Karli shudder with the comment, but he couldn't decide whether the spasm was prompted more by the manure or the manual-labor footwear.

"Were you just in there or not?" Jake asked. "That *cute girl* had a huge crowd around her. She raised that huge animal through a lot of hard work, and she's a big story today."

Jake watched as Karli whipped out her iPhone and spoke to it: "Siri, search for 'sheep equivalent of bovine'." She looked fixedly at the screen until it changed and she cried, "Ah ha! There it is: Ovine. I might need to know when it comes time to write Kennedy's story."

Jake continued to smile silently.

"Okay, Jake, so Kennedy is the champion of today's ovine world," Karli looked over, but Jake did not acknowledge her new vocabulary. "Unfortunately, that's a literally shitty place."

"Look, Karli, just because there's manure in the livestock world doesn't mean that it's crappy. The wool for your awesome newswoman outfits has to come from somewhere, doesn't it?"

Karli smoothed her skirt and looked over at Jake, who calmly started the golf cart back toward the station's on-site transmitter so they could beam the new footage back to the newsroom for editing.

Jake sensed Karli's attention and looked over at her. Abruptly he asked, "How's your shoe?" His face had the strained look of someone trying very hard to look compassionate while barely throttling back a convulsion of laughter.

Karli looked down at her white high heel in embarrassment. "I didn't think you saw that," she mumbled.

Jake's laughter popped out as though it had pushed a cork from his neck. "I didn't see it until you squealed. But, oh, the second time!" In the midst of his laughter, somehow Jake managed to squeeze in an inaccurate impression of Karli's squeal. He enjoyed the memory so much he laughed even harder.

Karli saw the humor. "I get it. It's funny when a stylish shoe squishes into the ram's turds." She tried to sound irritated, but she couldn't keep from giggling at the gooey memory. "Now, do you think we can cover a story that doesn't require me to dance on doo-doo? Or are there any of those here?"

"Oh, relax, Karli. There's a lot more than manure here." Jake was still grinning, and

he leaned toward Karli with raised eyebrows, inviting her to join in his fun as he sort-of sang, "It's dollars to doughnuts that our state fair is the best state fair in our state!" He finished and looked expectantly.

Jake saw Karli's blank look as he urged her to join in. "Did you just make that up?"

"C'mon! Don't tell me you've never seen *State Fair!*" Jake's eyes bugged out and his mouth fell open in shock.

"Um, we're at the state fair, aren't we?" Karli gestured to the fair all around them. "Like, here it is."

"No! The Rodgers and Hammerstein musical *State Fair*. It's set right here, at the Iowa State Fair. It's so good they made it into a musical—*twice*. Well, once and a half. The second one was terrible. And it was set in Texas, which is not at all right. But the original musical is fantastic. It's all about a girl who feels stuck in an insignificant place and is hoping for something new and exciting. And about a journalist who feels stuck in Des Moines and is bucking to get to Chicago. And the girl's brother and his fling. And a big pig named Blue Boy."

As he named each character, Jake's smile grew along with his enthusiasm for his subject. After a pause, a look of sudden realization flashed across his face and he threw his head back with

37

laughter. Then he met Karli's eyes with his own twinkle.

"Oh, and I almost forgot. The girl who feels stuck—she wears white heels all over the fair. But she never steps in any manure."

"You're pulling my leg, right? Like Broadway would ever do a musical about this fair. No way."

"Really, Karli, I'm giving it to you straight. It's a real musical, and there really are two movie versions. In fact, I have a copy of the good one. What say we have a pizza delivered and watch it in an edit suite? I can't do it tonight, but we could watch it right after work tomorrow."

As Karli met his eyes frankly, Jake realized that he hadn't had many chances to look directly into her eyes. He was usually looking all around her to check the background or at parts of her to check the lighting. They were a dark, speckled, complicated blue, and they were beautiful. *Those eyes could melt me if I'm not careful,* he thought.

Realizing that he'd been drifting away into her eyes, Jake blinked and brought himself back to the moment. "Well? What do you say? It'll be fun," he said.

"Um, sure. I mean, it'll be background for the rest of next week's stories, right?"

Jake looked around again at all the people, then nodded his head sharply as though he'd made a decision. He turned again to look Karli directly in the eye. "What do you say we beam this video back and then I take you around the fair for a bit without the Citizen Magnet?" he said, patting the bold *Three NewsFirst* sticker on his camera affectionately. "We're due for a break, and we've already got a bunch of video in the can from today. And I promise—no more manure."

***

After the gear was all locked up, Jake strung a camera around his neck and stuck a small wad of miscellaneous batteries and dongles into his pocket.

The camera wasn't much smaller than his usual television rig, but it was shaped very differently—like an old-school 35 mm still camera with a giant lens.

"It's my own Canon," Jake told Karli in response to her unspoken question. "It's an unbeatable still camera, and it captures video at least as well as the station's cameras. Kinda hard to hold steady for video though, without a shoulder mount. And it gets really hot if I shoot video for too long."

He swung the strap over his left arm, bracing the camera against his hip with practiced grace. "C'mon, Karli. Let's go see the fair like people instead of like outsiders."

"What makes you care so much about this fair, Jake? You're going to a lot of trouble to convince me it's more than death food and turds."

"There isn't that much to figure out, Karli," Jake said. "It's a big celebration—people and food. And the people all come together to share their interests and food with each other. That's a party, no matter where you hold it or what you call it."

Jake continued, still intent on looking directly into her eyes. "And this is your home now, too. You should get to know these people so you can cover their stories better." Jake saw Karli as she looked away to keep him from looking even more deeply into her eyes.

Jake took Karli's reticence as a challenge, and he welcomed it by leading her on a long march through the fairgrounds. She followed him through the exhibit halls where the competing entries in countless divisions were on display. The museums and historical societies had assembled elaborate recreations of Iowa frontier life. Huge areas were devoted to homemade beers and wines, doll houses and miniature rooms, wood crafts, arts and crafts, and a tremendous array of other creative efforts. Jake kept Karli moving along, pointing out that it would take nearly an entire week to pay close attention in just one of the many exhibit halls.

Every now and then, Jake stepped away when she dwelt on an exhibit longer than usual. He moved gracefully and quickly, raising his Canon and snapping frames of her while she took in the sights and eavesdropped on the conversations.

"Hey, I thought we had enough in the can," she asked. "What are you doing with that camera?"

"I don't like to miss opportunities."

Jake smirked as he framed the next shot. He knew what he was about; he had looked into her eyes and had seen more than a careerist reporter. Giving her the genuine fairgoer experience gave him the chance to capture her image when she was unselfconscious, not projecting for the viewing audience—when she was authentically herself.

And if she needed an explanation, it was simple enough to point out that she hadn't posed for any promotional photos yet. It made sense that he would take care of that business while they were goofing off so they would have a legitimate work excuse for simply enjoying the fair. He was sincerely interested in teaching her about this fair. And she had to admit after two solid hours of looking and listening that, when the fair was taken one person or group at a time, it was captivating.

"Jake, let's get back and watch your movie. My feet hurt. At least your homework assignment is something we can do while my heels are up." Karli stopped short, and Jake caught her cautious glance. He couldn't help grinning at her inadvertent double-entendre. Nor could he help thinking that the two of them doing things together with her heels up sounded like an exciting prospect.

"Like I said, I can't make it tonight, Karli," Jake said, and as he said it he realized that he genuinely regretted not having the opportunity to discuss double-entendres with her in a less-public setting. "I have to be somewhere. But can we watch it during the 6:00 show tomorrow?"

Chapter Four

*Des Moines, Three NewsFirst newsroom
during the 6:00 p.m. newscast
Friday, August 9*

At 6:15, the newsroom still crackled with energy even during the lull that came with each of the day's many newscasts. Tonight the raised central island that was the assignment desk emitted the usual sounds of several police scanners and of two editors trying to pry the last of tomorrow's planned stories from the far reaches of their telephones. As they spoke, their fingers flew over computer keyboards, taking information they'd need to send news crews out in the morning.

Crowding down from the ceiling and leaving a narrow space above the assignment desk's fortresslike wall, large monitors displayed the live broadcasts from competing Des Moines and Ames stations alongside the Three NewsFirst broadcast.

At floor level and several cluttered desks away from the noise and activity of the assignment desk, bright lights and a camera glared at a nervous young reporter about to go live from the newsroom—an unimpressive twenty or thirty feet from the studio—with a late-breaking and almost completely non-visual courthouse story. Jake walked briskly behind the shot and in front of the assignment desk, knowing that his motion through the out-of-focus background of the shot would add to the visual impression of a busy newsroom, even though he was just carrying a pizza back to watch a movie.

Jake nodded to production assistant Mary Rose Mayer where she stood behind a live-from-the-newsroom camera. She wore her short hair in contrasting shades of bright blue and platinum blonde, her eyeliner was heavy, her face was pierced in several places, and her jeans were artfully ripped. The sleeves were torn from her Three NewsFirst polo to reveal colorful tattoos on her deltoids, and the shirt was pulled tight over her flat stomach with a knot at her back. She smiled cheerfully and stuck her pierced tongue out at Jake before turning back to the camera.

Jake reached the edge of the newsroom and turned the gentle corner that led to a row of desks separated by small vertical fabric dividers. Contrasting with the newsroom's loud logo-colored blues, reds, and silvers, the warm browns and greys in the shooters' space were calm and quiet. And unlike the papery clutter on the newsroom desks, the photographers' spaces were filled with tangles of audio and video cables as well as variously disassembled cameras, microphones, battery packs and other field gear. The shooters, Jake among them, preferred to customize their gear and to handle maintenance and repairs on their own. That way their equipment could be kept out of the standardizing and sterilizing hands of the stations' and manufacturers' engineers as much as possible.

Snatching a Coke off his own worktop and reaching the end of the shooters' stations, Jake balanced easily on one foot to reach up and open the door handle of an edit suite with the other. "Don't tell anyone we're eating in the suite, please," he said. "There's about a jillion dollars worth of gear in here, and the engineers and front office folks would have a fit."

As he squeezed into the tiny room, Karli put down her diet Dew and offered to pay for half of the pizza. Jake smiled at Karli, surprised at the prickly reporter's show of decency.

Of course, her pizza had been an unusually special order: onions, but only if they were red; mushrooms, but only if they were portabella; pepperoni, but only if it was on top of the cheese. The sausage was the biggest challenge to get right. If it had fennel as a seasoning, Karli didn't want it anywhere near the pizza, not even if it was only on his half. Jake didn't trust the pizza joint's ordering system enough to make his own special half, so he contented himself with whatever turned out from Karli's exacting requirements.

"That's okay. I'll get it. I need to keep you fueled so you can learn that the Fair really has earned its state-symbol status." His voice sounded intimate in the claustrophobic space. Because it doubled as a sound booth for reporters voicing their recorded stories, the walls and ceiling were covered with dark grey Escher-patterned foam tiles.

Jake reached into his pants pocket and produced a slender,

rectangular present, wrapped tightly in heavy, tasteful paper topped with a ribbon and bow. "Open it up," he said as he handed it to Karli. She unwrapped the gift and found a brand-new, shrink-wrapped DVD of *State Fair* inside. "I thought you should have your own copy," Jake said. "So now we can watch your very own movie."

Karli murmured her puzzled thanks and began fighting with the shrink-wrap and then the adhesive factory stickers holding the sides closed while Jake moved a microphone boom back to the wall, asked Karli to pick up her diet Dew, and slid the pizza box to a delicate balance on the tiny work surface underneath the microphone where reporters put their notes. He gestured for Karli to take a seat, then turned to the complicated array of computer controls, audio mixer controls, and various drives and ports for video ranging from the outdated-but-still-used-for-file-footage broadcast-Beta tapes to digital card readers and DVDs. The suite was several times more complicated than the simple editing equipment Karli had used but never mastered in her last job and at college. As Jake reached back toward the door to dim the lights, he saw her eyes moving over the many control surfaces with more apprehension than understanding.

With the ease of much practice, Jake pressed, flipped, or spun a dozen or more controls to prepare the suite to play *State Fair,* powering speakers and drives and monitors, opening audio channels, and sliding open an optical drive tray. He put the movie in, waited for the menu, and selected play.

Reaching across Karli to snare a slice, Jake put his feet carefully up on an edge where they wouldn't bump any equipment, took a too-hot bite of pizza and breathed hard around it. As he struggled to chew and huff and swallow the cheesy heat, he twirled an audio control down to quiet the long title sequence. With his feet up, Jake's long legs pushed his chair all the way to the suite's back wall, taking up more than half of the room's free space.

"This movie is great, Karli," he said, breathing and mumbling around his cooling mouthful of pizza. "Not only is the story classic and the score fantastic, the technical work with the audio is awesome. Not just for the period but for musicals in general."

He looked over at her and saw that she wasn't paying attention to his cinematic insights. Instead, she was returning a steaming slice of pizza to the box and quickly blowing in and out around her own scalding mouthful, her brows furrowed in pain. She reached for her diet Dew, took a long pull, and waved Jake back to the screen, where an old man was driving along and silently singing.

Jake turned back to the controls with a sympathetic chuckle and rewound the movie back to the end of the opening credits. As it began to roll, he turned the volume up for the song. The sound poured from the studio speakers and filled the edit suite, making it their own, very cramped, private movie theater.

Having seen the movie before, Jake sang along with most of the score in a confident tenor. He knew the story would play just as it had every other time: the trapped-on-the-farm heroine falls in love with the world-weary and restlessly ambitious reporter from the Des Moines Register, her brother falls for the glamorous singer, the family's hog wins grand champion, and the mother's pickles and mincemeat beat the obnoxious incumbent's entries.

The edit suite was so small that every time Jake reached for a piece of pizza, his arm brushed across the warm, satiny-smooth skin of the legs Karli had propped up against the worktop. And she brushed her arm against his every time she reached for her Mountain Dew. Each touch surprised a hot electric tingle through his veins in spite of the extra-cold, equipment-preserving air conditioning. Jake hadn't consciously arranged the movie as a kind of a romantic encounter, but millennia ago some sequence resident on the Y chromosome had programmed him and all men to seek, repeat, and intensify the sensation of touching warm, silken skin in a small, cool room. And he could smell her perfume waft from her skin with each touch, too. Something vanilla and somehow asiatic teased his sense of smell and combined with the touching to make him ache on the level of instinct and hormone.

Watching her in profile as the switching light from the monitors played over the planes of her face, watching as her face shifted from unselfconscious laughter at the mother's boozy mincemeat and the hog's infatuation with a sow to compassion for the aching attraction pulling the brother to the glamorous singer, Jake saw a shiver that could possibly reflect the urges that rose from his own depths. But the booth was kept cold to protect the equipment, so that *frisson* could have been a genuine reaction to the temperature.

Karli's enjoyment of the movie thrilled him at the conscious level, where uninhibited laughter lit her face and she swayed with the tunes as Jake sang along. Unguarded like this, moving without thought of how *the viewing audience*—which presumably meant the news directors at big shops in Chicago—would perceive her, Karli was vibrant and exciting, far from the smooth, sculptural rigidity she usually projected.

Somewhere near the base of his spine, though, Jake's body thrilled in an unconscious way that urged him to feel her skin and smell her scent and taste her lips and elicit soft sounds from deep in her throat.

She ate hot pizza and swigged cold diet Dew through the movie, but she did not seem terribly affected by the movie romances, even when they fell apart. In the movie's final scenes, Jake saw Karli's biggest reaction: after the Des Moines Register reporter telephoned the heroine to tell her he'd landed a job as a columnist in Chicago and wanted to marry her, Jake saw Karli's fist pump and quiet victory cheer. After that, the movie quickly tied up all the remaining loose ends and concluded.

Jake raised the lights and lowered the sound as the closing credits rolled, then looked over at Karli with newfound interest in his eyes.

"So...?" he prompted.

"It was great. Really. Even the pigs were great." Karli's smile was interrupted by her loud impressions of the pigs' grunts and oinks. Jake's laugh was sudden and involuntary. Her pig impression was good, and it warmed him to her even more. He hadn't been sure she'd like the movie, but the fact that she did made his heart lighter. He had seen many qualities in her in the field and writing and editing—she had a very keen mind—but he hadn't seen much joy before this moment.

He ejected the disc and they both picked up the mess they'd made, laughing as they nearly conked heads bending over for a napkin and bumping into one another as they pushed chairs out of the way to get out. Each bump ratcheted up the sensitivity of the nerves in Jake's skin, and blood coursed ever faster toward and away from the warm spot in the small of his back.

Outside the edit suite, the mid-evening newsroom was quiet and empty. Anchors, producers, and editors were out having their late supper, and reporters and photographers were scrambling to gather and assemble their reports for the late newscast, leaving the newsroom populated by ghostly voices from monitors and scanners.

Karli smashed the pizza box into a trash can, laughing again at the pigs' romance. Before he became consciously aware of what he was doing, Jake reached out with a napkin to wipe a dribble of pizza grease that trickled from the corner of her lips. As suddenly as the hole you can't see until you've stepped in it, Jake felt an off-balancing shock run through his body; all of his blood suddenly surged to thrice its normal speed. Even as the dizzying sensation raced toward its peak, Jake saw a light flicker behind Karli's eyes, and the darkness at the centers of her eyes grew, compressing the encircling blue into a deeper and more intimate shade. Holding the napkin gently under her jawline and holding her gaze with his own smolder, Jake leaned his face slightly toward hers and heard himself speak in a husky voice. "You've got a little grease right here."

Jake found himself moving close to Karli as though to kiss her, and felt faintly surprised, like he was somewhere outside himself watching it happen. Although he had spent an illuminating day observing and working with both her façade and a bit of her revealed inner life, he hadn't consciously done anything to take them toward a physical encounter. But he felt all of his energies charging in that direction now; his veins thrilled as with high-tension electric current, his usually steady hands quivered, and his breathing was fast and shallow.

All day he had seen her beauty emerge from the places where she usually hid it, and it had somehow twisted around his own hidden places.

Karli's reaction was new. Jake had closed the distance to kissing range with many women before: their readiness had been easy to read—Karli's wasn't. Her eyes and the smell of her skin and the pulse beating in her neck all told Jake that she was ready to be his. Her raised eyebrows and her erect, squared-off posture told him to stay away. He saw all of this in an instant, then fumbled for something to do that wasn't kissing, in spite of the thudding pulse and the insistent twitch that urged him—*now*—to find the sweetness of her lips.

Jake wasn't thinking through the feelings, the urges, the choices. Evolution or God or something had equipped men—and Jake more especially than most—with a finely calibrated system to gauge a woman's readiness. Something—the pheromone density in the air or her posture or the pace of her breathing or some combination of those things or some other primal indicator—wasn't yet right. One more moment of intimacy, though, and they would both be ready. Instinct guided him to the movie's moment of consummation.

"When the heroine finds out that he really does love her and wants to marry her—that's pretty powerful, isn't it?"

Jake knew immediately that he'd said the wrong thing. Karli shook her head slightly and turned her blue eyes from his. She reached up and took Jake's hand and the napkin it held from her face.

"Shut up," she ordered him. "You think I was rooting for that insipid girl?" she asked. "No, Jake, I don't identify with girls who need men to define them. I was cheering for the reporter. He had finally found his way to a real news job in a real market. He had escaped Des Moines."

Chapter Five

Savery Hotel, downtown Des Moines
Friday evening, August 9

In spite of herself, Karli's face split into a broad smile as she walked toward the Coda Lounge and saw Assignment Editor Vince Guzman prowling the sidewalk outside the hotel, smoking a thoughtful cigarette. He caught a glimpse of Karli as she approached and gave her a grin.

"They're mostly in there," he rasped, tipping his head toward the hotel bar's entrance. He took a long drag on his cigarette, then continued, smoke puffing out with each word: "Be careful with 'em, sis. When the animals get off the leash, they can go pretty wild."

Karli saw the seriousness underneath Vince's playful tone. His concern for her sprang from an avuncular kindness that warmed her heart. He was one of the few who had truly welcomed her into the newsroom, as it was his responsibility to send stories her way. In Vince, she had found her first ally at Three NewsFirst.

Karli nodded her acknowledgement, patted Vince on the shoulder and said, "Thanks, Vince, but I think I'll stay in the safari wagon tonight. I don't want to get in the habitat and mix with the animals."

Vince snubbed out his cigarette with a smile and held the door. Karli braced her shoulders and marched into the bar. Many of the Three NewsFirst team's members were arrayed at several tables and the bar. Thelonious Monk's *Straight No Chaser* lilted smoothly in the background, beneath the journalists' always-intense conversations. Vince walked around her to sit with News Director Jerry Schultz, who chewed his pen and leaned into his subject as frantically as he ever did in the newsroom—only now he did it while holding a drink. He was making some earnest point to the seldom-seen-in-public six o'clock producer, Holly Cacciatore, who nodded as patiently thoughtful as ever while sitting back in her chair, one leg crossed over the other, a Birkenstock precariously hanging from her wiggling foot.

The loudest table was populated by a group of handsome twenty- and thirty-something men who had obviously gotten off to a fast start with their drinking. The table was rattling all of its empties and threatening to spill the full drinks from the pounding it took from the handsome blonde sports anchor Buzz Cziesla. Karli was able to overhear enough of the overlapping cries to understand that Buzz was protesting some heinous misconduct by director Chuck Teros in whatever drinking game they were playing. The darkly self-confident Scott Winstead, sports reporter and weekend anchor, spotted her as he looked up from the argument. He waved to her with a lascivious grin. "Gentlemen," he announced, loudly enough to halt the dispute for a moment, "our reason for living has arrived!" He rose to his feet and gestured Karli grandly to their table. "Get out your wallets and pull over a chair so we can buy this lady a drink."

"Thanks, no," Karli smiled. "This is kind of a girl's night for me." And as the boys protested loudly with promises of great laughter, free drinks, and only the most sincere sexual harassment, Karli headed to the bar where noon anchor Bailey Barber sat with production assistant Mary Rose Mayer, whose mostly platinum, partly blue hair and bare, tattooed arms contrasted sharply with Bailey's tailored suit.

Bailey always looked completely put together, Karli thought. Her straight red hair fell effortlessly around a porcelain-smooth pale face. Dark lashes curled around bright green eyes. And though she must have applied the horrible studio makeup at noon—makeup that even she would have to wear to look presentable under the bright lights— she now looked completely fresh and natural. A more serious, startlingly green-eyed, and slender-nosed Blake Lively type, Karli thought. And the tailored suit she'd worn all day still hung smoothly and without a wrinkle. In her early 30s, Bailey was not quite ten years older than Karli, yet the two had hit it off quickly. They shared the pretty woman's experience of not being taken seriously—simply because they were pretty.

"Hey, girls," Karli said, taking a stool next to Bailey.

Mary Rose reached for the full shot glass that sat on the bar in front of her and tossed back the drink with obvious relish. Karli saw that Bailey was just as appalled and impressed as she was at this display of drinking prowess. Mary Rose saw their reactions and cracked a naughty smile to herself before sticking her pierced tongue to the bottom of the empty shot glass, making it click. "It's okay to have fun, girls," she said, turning her sleepy-lidded eyes but not quite her subtle smile toward Karli and Bailey. She placed the shot glass back on the bar and tapped it with her index finger.

Bottle in hand, the bartender came to refill Mary Rose's glass and take Karli's order. "An amaretto stone sour, please," she said. "It's been an extreme day."

"Really?" Bailey asked. "It seemed to me like it was a pretty routine day, at least up until I left.

Did something break after the 6:00 started?" Bailey sounded puzzled and looked around the lounge, seeing the people who would be back in the newsroom if a big story had broken.

"No, it wasn't a work thing," Karli said. "Well, maybe it's kind of a work thing. It's complicated." She gratefully accepted her drink from the swift-handed bartender and looked into it thoughtfully.

"Complicated can only mean one thing," Bailey said, turning herself completely toward Karli and leaning eagerly toward her. "Man trouble."

"Well, I suppose you could call it that," Karli mumbled into her drink, taking a too-big first gulp. She did not have Mary Rose's composure at all, fairly gasping as she swallowed the cold, stinging sweetness. Mary Rose noticed, of course, and stood to make a large production of downing her own drink. "Ladies, I'm gone. My ride is leaving, and I have to go with it."

"Please, don't leave on my account," Karli said, feeling awkward and worried that she had broken up a friendly get-together.

"Honey, don't worry your pretty little head about it," Mary Rose said, patting Karli on the shoulder. "I really do have to catch my ride. And I'm sure we will have plenty to talk about other times." As she and Bailey bid each other goodbye, Karli couldn't help but notice that Mary Rose seemed as steady and sober as a judge in spite of her obviously earnest drinking.

"She's . . . impressive," Karli said, watching Mary Rose's retreating figure and then turning to the noon co-anchor.

"Sure, Mary Rose's impressive," Bailey said. "But she has nothing on you, Karli.

And she certainly doesn't have a complicated situation to tell me about. So dish already! What's going on? Who is he? What happened?"

"I'm not sure, Bailey." Karli began.

"You're not sure who he is?" Bailey teased. "C'mon girl, this is becoming *uncomplicated* much too quickly!"

Karli rolled her eyes and then turned to Bailey to match her posture of intense interest. Coleman Hawkins' *Body and Soul* came over the speakers and Karli took a deep drink before beginning. "Jake nearly kissed me tonight. At least I think so. It was confusing."

"Whaaaaat?" Bailey tucked her hair behind her ears to make sure she could hear everything. "What brought that on? I mean, I know you two work together a lot, but I thought that was because he wanted to work with a good reporter and you wanted a good photog."

"He *is* gorgeous, you know, and it's exciting to think about him, you know, that way." Karli reflected, remembering how confidently he had worked the machines in the edit suite and how his deft hands tweaked the tiny controls. Those same hands easily steadied the biggest equipment when they were in the field. And his spicy scent teasing her nose every time he'd leaned near her for a drink of his Coke or a piece of pizza. And that curly brown hair. She felt her nipples tighten and press against the fabric that restrained them.

Karli shook her head sharply, trying to get her thoughts instead of her hormones to focus on the situation. "But he's annoying, too. He thinks he's all that, just because he can take pretty pictures. Like I have time for any of his nonsense, anyway. I'm a short-timer, Bailey, and I definitely don't need a hometown boy who could tie me down here." Karli heaved a sigh over a deep swig. "So he's a great shooter who's gorgeous. Whatever."

"But why were you two in make-out mode in the first place?" Bailey asked, intent on what was, to her anyway, the interesting part. "We are agreed that he's gorgeous, but that doesn't mean kissing happens."

"When I was at Missou, they told us that we should go somewhere that has a lot of news, not a lot of competition, and—if we're lucky—people who can help us do the best work we're capable of. That's why I'm here, Bailey. To do great work and have top-flight photogs like Jake make it look as good as it can."

"Um. Your reporting isn't very good at the moment, Karli," Bailey persisted. "What got him to nearly kissing you? This is a breaking story, girl, and I want the scoop!"

"I don't see how he's going to support my best work if he's trying to kiss me, Bailey. It won't work at all. He is supposed to shoot great footage to make my stories look great. He isn't supposed to kiss me."

Bailey's eyes rolled across the lounge's ceiling and came to rest directly on Karli's blue eyes. "Yeah. I can tell you aren't into the kissing at all. That's why your drink is already empty. Tell me. Now." Bailey quickly caught the bartender's eye and nodded significantly to their empty glasses; he caught the hint and began mixing.

"It's hard not to be interested in kissing. I mean, he isn't just gorgeous; he understands what it takes to make a good story great. And he smells good, too—have you ever noticed that?"

"Hmmmm," Bailey recalled. "He always smells great, and I can't tell what it is. Spicy, just like I imagine he'd be in bed. Nobody knows much of anything about his love-life, though, which is hard to figure. He must have to turn girls away, but I've never met one of the rejects—or one of the lucky ones."

"But it's like he wants me to love Iowa like it's my home or something, and I don't want to," Karli said. "And tonight it was like he thought he'd converted me or something." Karli told Bailey about the pizza-and-State-Fair quasi-date they'd had in the edit suite. "And so he'd sung in that nice voice and we'd had a good time, and then he touched my face like he was entitled to—which was hot. Well, I thought it was, and then it turned out he was wiping pizza off my chin. Even then it felt like we were almost kissing—you know, the gaze into the eyes and then the stare at the lips." Just recalling the moment, Karli felt her pulse throbbing between and just above her hip bones, where her drink had made things warmer and more ready. She licked her lips and tried to return to her story.

"Oh, yeah—I know that moment," Bailey gushed. "That's hot." She paused momentarily, with a distant look on her face. "So what happened? That's a tipping point. So was there a fire alarm or something?"

"No, he just got all Iowan on me. He started talking about the romance in the movie and stuff, and it sounded like I was some helpless little girl, and it was terrible."

Bailey put her hand on Karli's arm and patted her gently. It was definitely time to tighten the bonds of sisterhood. The bartender placed fresh drinks on the bar, and the women raised them in silent toast to each other. "He's just a guy, Karli. It sounds like it all worked out for the best.

If you'd kissed him, then you'd have to deal with his attitude and all the rest. It would be messy, you know. It always is, isn't it?"

Karli nodded and wondered why her eyes were stinging so hard. "You're right, Bailey. He would just be a big problem." *A big, gorgeous problem,* she thought to herself. *A big, gorgeous, stuck-in-Des-Moines problem.*

Chapter Six

The emergency response vehicles had left and the rain-slick pavement had been cleared, but Jake was still crouched by the windswept roadside, his body curled around his camera and his grief. In his peripheral vision he saw Karli's high heels stumble over successive uneven joints in the sidewalk, but he didn't lift his eyes from the frame.

"I just talked with Jerry," she said. "He wants us to try to interview the parents."

***

He had composed the shot to show the viewer how a bicyclist felt riding along the busy street's painted parking-spot lines. Cars and trucks whizzed loudly through the frame, close enough to the camera that Jake could hold it loosely and let their wind-wakes buffet the image. Sporadic raindrops and spray from the cars spattered the lens and filled in for the tears Jake was too shell-shocked, angry, and in denial to shed.

Saturday morning had begun simply, with Karli and Jake filling in for vacationing colleagues. That had been okay with both of them: Saturdays were usually easy, feature-heavy and news-light. This story hadn't seemed like much when the assignment editor called on the radio and sent them to the address.

A car accident with injuries, so possibly newsworthy; more so if there were some traffic backups or if the injured had to be transported by helicopter or extracted from the wreckage with the jaws of life.

But when they got to the scene, they knew this day's story was going to be different. They'd seen the newspapers strewn along the roadside and the bent bicycle. The ambulance crew didn't show the intensity and urgency they usually had when they were busy saving someone's life.

Karli quickly confirmed that the story was out of the ordinary when she spoke with the police officer in charge of the scene. She spoke with him for a long fifteen minutes while Jake shot as much video as he could. He crowded the taped-off areas for close-ups of the mangled bicycle, crouched low and placed his camera on improvised supports to frame fluttering, rain-spattered newspapers in the foreground of his shots, and felt a deepening sense of foreboding with each new composition.

With the eye that wasn't glued to the viewfinder, Jake saw Karli talking to a reluctant-looking woman with a nondescript terrier on a leash and a plastic bag weighed down with fresh dog poop in her hand. Jake grabbed his gear and slowly walked over to their conversation. Rather than setting up his tripod right away, he bent to make friends with the dog while he eavesdropped.

"I don't want to say anything bad about anyone, but I saw that man just staring at the cell phone on his steering wheel the whole time," the gray-haired lady was saying, a distinct trembling in her voice. "It was horrible. I even yelled at him when I saw what was going to happen, but he didn't hear me."

Jake wiped the dog slobber off his hand and moved to set his tripod up and mount his camera. Karli had asked the woman, who was obviously badly shaken by having seen an accident, if she would repeat herself on camera. Jake heard the deep reluctance and turned his back so as separate himself and his equipment from the woman's attention. After a long five minutes during which Jake ran out of things to fiddle with, Karli finally coaxed the reluctant woman—who admitted that she'd walked away from the scene so she wouldn't have to talk to the police—to do an interview on camera.

After they'd finished with the reluctant witness's interview, the woman obviously considered Karli to be her new best friend. The woman's emotions were still fragile and unsettled, but Karli managed to extricate herself elegantly from the conversation with a hug and a promise to call the woman if she needed to talk any more.

As they walked back to the news car, Karli briefed Jake on what she'd learned from the police. Her face was stony as she spoke and didn't betray her usual eagerness for the story.

"This is big," Karli had told him, anxiety making her usually rock-solid voice shake a little. "A twelve year-old paperboy was killed here by that guy in a pick-up truck we just heard about. The cops say that the kid was riding on the right side of the road, wearing a helmet, doing everything right. But the guy just crashed into him—which is consistent with the texting—pinned him against a parked car, and killed him. I asked the cops if it was a case of the rain making the kid hard to see or something, but they say they don't think so. And they already have their accident reconstructionist out here taking pictures. He said he didn't see any evidence that the truck swerved—either to avoid the accident or to avoid something else and then into it."

Jake looked back over the scene and wondered if he could capture some video that told the different story better. "Were you able to get the name out of them?" he asked.

"Not for the record, no, because they're still trying to notify the family. But the kid's name was Darrin Anderson." As Karli spoke the name, Jake heard a roaring pressure in his ears and her face blurred and twisted as though he'd spun the focus element on his camera's lens. But he was looking right at her, with his own eyes.

"Darrin Anderson?" Jake sagged hard against his tripod, his eyes dropping from Karli's face to look at a place completely out of focus. The shock of hearing Darrin's name had thrown him completely into himself and out of the conversation with Karli.

***

Jake met the boy when he had done a presentation at Darrin's elementary school three years ago, explaining how karate's discipline could help people cope with different challenges and demonstrating some of the training exercises from his studio. Afterwards, a teacher had taken Jake aside and introduced Darrin as a student who might enjoy karate. Jake knew what the introduction meant: *Here's a kid who needs something durable in his life, something that's his.* Teachers were often good at identifying kids whose challenges made karate a good fit.

So Jake had invited Darrin to train at his studio. His parents drank all their money, so Darrin emptied garbage cans, swept the mat, and cleaned the gym mirrors in trade for the classes, uniforms, and equipment. After six months of unabated enthusiasm, Darrin's face lit up with joy as Jake handed him a key to the studio—along with a talk about the key being a sign of trust and something that he should not share with anyone else. Monday through Thursday after school, Darrin had ridden his bicycle from school to the studio, where he let himself in, did the chores, and then did his homework while he waited for the training to start.

And so it had gone for nearly a year. Then Darrin had gotten the idea that a paper route could earn him enough money both for karate and also for necessities that his parents couldn't provide. Jake had encouraged Darrin to pursue the job, believing that work and its rewards were important in forming a person's identity. And since Darrin had so little natural support in discovering who he would become, Jake believed the job was that much more important.

So Darrin had become a paying student—though Jake had given him deep discounts on gear and continued to pay tournament entry fees Darrin didn't even know about. Jake had even talked to a dentist about braces for Darrin and had arranged to pay for them, keeping just enough of a bill that Darrin rode his bike every two weeks to the orthodontist's office to pay $20 from his newspaper earnings and was none the wiser. Darrin still had his key, but the paper route kept him busy enough that he had to stop training on Tuesdays so he could stay on top of his school work. Jake required his students to bring in their report cards, and there were lost privileges for those who didn't earn straight As. To make up for the lost day, he usually let himself into the studio on Saturdays to train alone.

And Darrin had steadily improved as he grew and hardened into what would have been an awkward, floppy-footed adolescence. He was no natural athlete, but he was a sponge for karate. Jake recalled how he took the mat by storm every night, drilling every exercise as close to perfection as he could take it. Nor was there any grim determination to his training. It was all play for him—safe play in familiar surroundings with people he came to know and trust. Everyone in the dojo knew to expect Darrin to make them bust up laughing. He delighted in all the mistakes he and everyone else made while learning new skills or working on basics, and laughter was one of his best tools for creating openings in sparring sessions. Even senior students had trouble countering his techniques when he caught them mid-guffaw.

Darrin regularly competed in tournaments, and he did well though not spectacularly. He was much more interested in the camaraderie than he was in winning the competitions. He relished the time he spent with Sensei Jake and the other karate students, including the endless hours in his teacher's pick-up truck criss-crossing Iowa's corn and bean fields. And Jake had come to love the earnest boy less as a karate student than as the younger brother he'd never had.

Darrin had wanted to come in today and work on his new weapon routine—a choreographed exhibition of skill called *kata* in Japanese.

He was using one of the oldest weapons in the human arsenal for it, a stick. Most Asian martial arts taught the use of the bo staff, a weapon essentially the same as the quarterstaffs used in Robin Hood stories. Jake had done quite a bit of research to identify and plan the training for Darrin's new *bo kata*. He wanted it to be good enough to take to the late-January national karate tournament in Chicago. He and Darrin had both been excited to start the training and ultimately to go to a tournament with elite competitors from across the nation.

But Jake had been forced to cancel today's training session because he'd been called in to work at Three NewsFirst. And Darrin had begun his Saturday morning paper route later than usual because he didn't need to rush in to the studio.

And now Darrin was dead. And Jake knew it was his fault.

***

Karli's voice came back through Jake's fugue-state recollections: "I just talked with Jerry," she repeated. "The cops told the family, and he wants us to interview the parents."

"You'll need a different shooter then," Jake replied, still looking at his viewfinder. "I'm not doing it."

From the corner of his eye, Jake saw the surprise in Karli's raised eyebrows. And then he saw a conflict playing out across her face. They both knew they should go knock on the door and try to get an ambush interview. Jake had his own reasons for refusing, but he didn't understand what would make Karli hesitate.

"I'm not doing it either, Jake." Karli turned and began walking back to the news car. "Let's go."

Jake glanced over at the newly arrived crews from the competing stations. The most recent arrival was busily shooting a minimum of footage from the scene, and the other had just begun an interview with the police officer in charge. It would be standard for each of the crews to go to the bereaved parents' house to try to interview them, and he was sure the competition would do just that.

But what, he wondered, packing his gear into the car, would move Karli to skip the obligatory grieving-family ambush and not press him to back off his refusal? The feisty reporter he'd come to know would never back away without a reason, but he couldn't figure out what it was. Puzzled and relieved, he got into the driver's seat and saw Karli staring into the distance as she composed the next sentence to write in her reporter's tablet. "Where to?" he asked.

She gave him directions. Still numbed by his own staggering grief and loss, Jake drove carefully and quietly to Darrin's house. Karli told him to stay in the car, then walked to the house's front door, slid something through the mail slot, and walked straight back to the car.

Jake was emotionally spent. Just as he was about to say he couldn't focus one more frame, Karli saved him the trouble: "Let's go back and put this story together."

The Six O'Clock Newcast
Three NewsFirst Newsroom
Saturday, October 5

Karli sat at her newsroom desk, watching News Director Jerry Schultz, Assignment Editor Vince Guzman, and Producer Holly Cacciatore as they in turn watched three monitors—Three NewsFirst and its two major competitors—at the same time.

The three had come in to the newsroom on Saturday—even though it was their day off—as soon as the story had broken. They knew it was the kind of story that could change which station was number one in the ratings—it was that big.

Because it was that big, Karli was furious that Jake was nowhere to be found. He had just vanished after they'd returned to the station, and she was left without the photog who knew what shots he had taken and where they were. That slowed the editing considerably. Mary Rose had taken over for him in the edit suite, where she and Karli had found that they worked together quite well, if without the speed that went with knowing the footage.

Now Mary Rose's blue and platinum hair hung over the viewfinder while Karli sat at her desk in the newsroom, reviewing notes and waiting to hear her cue from the anchor on set in the next room. "...Karli Lewis has the story." Overlapping the cue was the director's voice in her earpiece: *And take Mary Rose's camera.*

Karli looked into the camera as though it were her best friend. Her deep, feminine alto opened the story gently: "An area family is grieving the loss of 12 year-old Darrin Anderson tonight." A close-up still photo of the boy's face and braces-tinseled smile dissolved to an exterior shot of his parents' house.

"The house where he grew up is darkened as family members try to cope with their sudden loss, caused when he was struck and killed this morning while delivering his papers." Flashing emergency response lights reflected off the front of a pick-up truck. A bent bicycle lay beside the road, damply fluttering newspapers scattered around it.

Her story went on to describe the results of the police investigation: Darrin had been riding appropriately on the correct side of the street and wearing a helmet. The pick-up had driven directly into him without braking or swerving. Karli's own investigation had yielded an exclusive interview with a witness who'd been walking her dog and had seen the driver texting right into the crash.

After tossing the story back to the anchors, she watched Jerry closely as he swiveled his decrepit office chair first toward one, then another of the monitors where each station's story was also wrapping up. The competition both finished with the reporter knocking on the Anderson house's front door and being asked to please go away. Three NewsFirst did not run a similar shot.

Karli's palms slicked with nervous sweat. She was acutely aware that she had not tried to ambush the family into an interview, even though it was an expected part of the coverage. But no family, she thought, needed to deal with the loss of a child while fending off persistent news vultures who came to pick at the fresh corpse. Not only did she not want to intrude on the family's grief, she didn't like the image of herself in a vulture suit, turning death into ratings.

Jerry plucked the pen from his shirt pocket and turned his chair around as the anchors filled the screen to lead into the next story. "If you didn't get anything, I don't suppose it's any great loss to leave out the family turning you away. There's emotional impact in that moment, though, that the others used to close the story." Jerry chewed thoughtfully on his pen, looking off into space and considering how the story would work best. "Maybe we should put it into the next show's version," he said, turning suddenly and intensely to meet Karli's eyes. "What do you think?"

Where the hell is Jake when I need him? Karli thought, wiping her hands on her crisp Ann Taylor shirtdress. *He didn't want to do that useless doorstep interview, either—heck, he flat-out refused— but he sure isn't here to help explain why. He is a monumental jerk for bailing on a big story like this.* Yet she wanted to deflect attention from the matter much more than she wanted to throttle Jake and then try to explain their choices. "Let me work on some bigger parts of the story, Jerry," Karli responded. "The eyewitness is exclusive and she's way more important than a non-reaction from the family. So I think we should do a reconstruction animation to show what she saw, from her point of view. I'll work with one of the studio crew to get that done in time for the show." Karli had made her decision back at the scene: it would be indecent to try an ambush interview on the grieving family's doorstep. Now she was simply trying to get Jerry to focus on the more important aspects of the story. "What else do you have going on this?"

Vince Guzman, Three NewsFirst's grizzled assignment editor, was in his late 60s but still had the urgent energy and chronically rattled air of a man who had spent his entire adult life listening to police scanners and working on two or more deadlines a day. He was of medium height, with salt-and-pepper hair and the rasping voice of a lifelong heavy smoker. He looked up from his computer screen and took his boss's unspoken cue to respond. "Sophia is on I-35 right now on the way to interview a professor from Iowa State who does a lot of work on traffic engineering," he said, an unlit and eagerly anticipated cigarette held between his lips and beating out the rhythm of his speech like a conductor's baton. Sophia Refai was the exotic weekend news anchor, and an experienced reporter. Her parents had moved to California from the Middle East, and she always carried her heritage with her in smoothly dark glamor and sophistication. She was perfectly capable of disarming a reluctant academic on a Saturday for an interview; that angle was in good hands.

Vince looked back at the monitor. "You might need this background for your part of the story, Karli. The metro's streets are *not* safe for bikes and pedestrians. The City has started spending some money on a few multipurpose routes, but the other cities are lagging. One of the City's traffic engineers is my next-door neighbor, and I buttonholed him today off the record. He told me that the street the boy was killed on is a perfect example of outdated, mid-20th century engineering principles. But that's off the record. Sophia should be able to get some sound bites out of that professor saying that the recent resurfacing and repainting of the street was completely wrong.

"Oh, and for your animation," he interrupted himself, "have Mary Rose press the buttons for you—she's fast and good at that kind of work."

Karli felt the kind of rush that came when she knew an important piece of a story was beginning to come into focus. She pulled out her iPhone and texted Mary Rose to tell her she was the designated animator, then began taking notes on Vince's research.

"The way it appears to have gone down," Vince began, "is like this: Some engineer with antiquated ideas and training took a four-lane street that nobody had parked on for 20 years and *improved* it by cutting it down to two lanes and adding parking spots along the sides.

"You saw the sidewalks along there, Karli. They're heaving with tree roots and cracks. Plus they're slap up against the street—no patch of grass to separate them from cars. They aren't safe even for walking, and it would be difficult to roll a bicycle or a wheelchair on them. So *of course* this rocket scientist of a city street engineer ignores the sidewalks while spending millions on the street. And of course the kid has to ride on that masterpiece.

"But there's nowhere else to walk or ride. That stretch is the only east-west route available for a mile or so north and south. Ravines cut off the parallel streets. So if you want to go either way, that's the street you're going to use, like it or not. And if you're a 12 year-old kid riding to where his paper route begins, you're going to have to ride in the traffic lane of what the engineer made into a narrow two-lane street."

"My traffic-engineer source tells me that any engineer worth his or her salt these days would have saved that kid's life by adding bike lanes instead of parking spaces.

"The best part," and here he waited for Karli to look up and make eye contact with him. "The very best part of this whole engineering thing, Karli, is that doing it right and saving that kid's life wouldn't have cost the taxpayers much of anything. Just the paint to make bike lanes and a center turn lane instead of parking spaces."

Holly Cacciatore, the evening newscast's greying-curls and Birkenstock-wearing producer, jumped in: "We have a freelancer in Iowa City who is interviewing one of the bicycle club's officers there. Iowa City won some kind of award this spring or summer," Holly checked her own notes quickly. "Yeah, here it is: Silver status from the League of American Bicyclists—in part because the city has striped a bunch of bicycle lanes on the streets. The freelancer shoots, too, so we'll have video of those lanes so we can show the viewers what contemporary street engineering looks like."

"Who is going to cover the texting-while-driving angle?" Jerry asked. "That's the direct cause of this, whatever the engineers may have done. And do we have enough crews to cover all of these angles? We need to call in some people so we can give this story the team coverage it needs. And I want live shots—on the scene and in the studio—for the 10:00."

Karli's iPhone chirped and drew her attention away from the rest of the conversation. When she looked up, her voice had taken on a new tone of excitement. "Is there a photog I can take on an interview right away?"

"They're all out," Vince said, shaking his head. "Max should be back in an hour or so, though. He's in on overtime, working on a Des Moines nightlife feature for next week."

Damn that Jake, Karli thought yet again. *I need him for this story, but he can't be bothered to come in and do his effing job.* After Karli found out that the weekend skeleton crew was stretched as far as it could go and that the reserves who had been called in wouldn't be arriving in time for what she needed, she found some available equipment and schlepped it all out to her own car.

She didn't want to take a marked news car to this interview. And it was probably best that she would be alone while doing and shooting the interview. She had done the shooting and interviewing all by herself for years in Palm Beach, so she knew how. She was surprised at how tentative she felt with the camera gear now, after having Jake shoot her stories for only three months or so. The camera had always just been a machine to her, but she had seen in the last few months how Jake transformed it into a storytelling tool, capturing images that she couldn't have conceived—and if she had been able to envision them, she was coming to understand that Jake had an artist's passion for creating visuals that she lacked the patience to develop.

As she drove to the interview, Karli reflected on how terribly sad the story was. The day had already been packed with emotional extremes and more were on the way. So she had a hard time sorting through her feelings. She was thrilled with the texting scoop, nervous and relieved about not doing the doorstep interview with the family, excited and apprehensive about the interview ahead, and there were still other subliminal feelings that were just beyond her ability to see or name them.

Both she and Jake had refused to go to the family's doorstep with camera rolling. Karli knew why she'd refused, but she was confused about Jake's reasons. *I suppose it makes sense that he would refuse the ambush interview if he knows the kid.*

And it had been obvious that he'd known the boy and that news of his death had devastated him. *He responded like it was his brother or son who'd died,* she thought. *Jake obviously loved this Anderson boy—like he loved that Brian kid at the fair. He was really very sweet at the fair, teaching that boy how to be a man with the handshake thing and all. He must've been teaching this boy, too.*

How does a news photog become so connected to these kids? she wondered. *He cares about them enough that he actually refused to cover the story by trying the ambush-interview at the family's door,* she thought. *And that's not like a guy who has been a news photog for as long as Jake has.*

Images of Jake flashed through Karli's mind: The rock-hard physique bent earnestly around his camera, all of his energy trained, laser-like, on the viewfinder; his lean form stretching up to adjust the light atop a fully extended stand; his furious face asking her how she covered news *in the tropics*; and his firm handshake with young Brian at the State Fair. He had *layers,* this guy. He wasn't just some shooter: he loved kids; he told her she was pretty; he gave her a pork chop like it was a diamond necklace; he shared his State Fair and the movie about it with her like they were treasures. Karli reflected that Jake was probably a good role model for the boys in his life. Then Karli remembered the building crescendo she'd felt right between her hip bones when he had complimented her, and she flushed with renewed excitement. *Who,* she wondered, *are you, Jake Gibson?*

Three NewsFirst Newsroom
The 10 O'Clock newscast
Saturday, October 5

Karli surprised all of the newsroom brass—and, later, especially the competition—when she asked the producer for a minute and a half to open the Saturday evening show. She had gone to her interview alone and had edited it with the help of a sworn-to-secrecy Mary Rose.

In the control room, Chuck the director had the technical director set up to run audio and video from the network feed and asked the engineer in master control to hand the station over during the last network commercial break. "Ready video 1 for the open," he called during the last commercial, his finger poised over a timer. As the last commercial faded to black, Chuck snapped his timer and called, "Roll video 1, speed, and take it." The technical director swung a fader lever to put the video on the air, and the sound engineer punched up the corresponding source. Energetic music mixed under the announcer's voice as logos and portrait-shots of the anchors swung dizzily through the frame: "With Sophia Refai and Stu Heintz, this is Three NewsFirst at Ten..." As the frantic music played through the monitor speakers, headsets, and earpieces that kept all the various crew members in sync, Chuck called out, "Ready camera 1 and open mic on Stu, in 5, 4..." On the studio floor, Stu Heintz, the new weekend male anchor, watched as the floor director counted out loud and flashed fingers to show, "...3, 2..." and then silently finished with a single digit that swung to point right at him as Chuck called out, "Take camera 1; ready 1 to pan for graphic."

Stu began the show with a thin, youthful baritone attempt at solemnity, "The NewsFirst focus tonight will be on the tragic death of newsboy Darrin Anderson."

"And pan camera one; fade in graphic," Chuck called. The bent bicycle appeared above Stu's shoulder, with police tape fluttering in the foreground.

"We will have team coverage from Ames and Iowa City," Stu continued, "on the street engineering that may have caused the boy's death."

"Roll video 4; and take it," Chuck called. "Bring that traffic audio under a little," he added to the sound man, as video of bicycles rolling alongside cars in separate lanes came up on the screen. The pre-edited video cut to a shot of thumbs flashing over a cell phone that rested against a steering wheel.

"That coverage will include analysis of Three NewsFirst's exclusive interview with the eyewitness to the accident and the problem of distracted driving."

"Camera 1, centered on Stu. Ready...take 1," Chuck called. Stu's deliberately earnest face again filled the screen.

"Plus, we will have local coverage of the community's reaction to the tragedy and what may come next for communities throughout central Iowa."

"Ready camera 2 with both of them," Chuck called. "Open

Karli's mic. And take 2." The control room monitor that showed the signal going out over the air changed to a two-shot of Karli on set with Stu.

"Three NewsFirst reporter Karli Lewis is here with the latest on the story. Karli, this is a story you've been covering since it broke."

"Camera 1, you've got to truck over faster than that. I need that shot!" Chuck called out over the headsets as a studio camera operator wrestled the huge studio camera into position to take a head-and-shoulders shot of Karli.

"What can you tell us about reactions people are having to 12 year-old Darrin Anderson's shocking death?"

"Stu, this is a parent's worst nightmare," Karli began, looking first at the anchor on set and then turning to the camera that swung toward her with her text scrolling over its teleprompter screen.

"Take 1," Chuck snapped to the technical director, as the shot of Karli came up on the camera's preview monitor at the last second. "Clip Stu's mic."

"I had an exclusive interview with Darrin's parents this afternoon. They are traumatized and grieving their loss, and they're terrified for other kids in their community. When I asked them what message they wanted people to take away from the terrible death of their son, they had this to say."

In her earpiece, Karli heard Chuck cue the video from the interview. Darrin's parents had the complexions and gin blossom noses of people who had long familiarity with alcohol, but they spoke clearly through their tears. The husband had his arm around his wife's shoulders. They were sitting on a brown and tan plaid sofa in a nondescript living room. "We love our son," the mother wept. "We still can't believe it."

The video cut to Darrin's father saying, "Everybody thinks texting don't matter if *they* are doing it. But it's them. It was this guy. And it kills," and at this word, Darrin's father stuttered with barely suppressed sobs. "It kills little kids like my boy." And Darrin's father put his face in his hands and sobbed.

"Close those mics!" Chuck called, as the gasps of surprised response from Stu and others in the studio had been slightly audible over the air. The sound engineer, looking shamed, snapped at his board. In the newsroom, everyone exchanged stunned looks.

Karli's story went on to tell what kind of boy Darrin had been.

Mary Rose had put still photos into Ken Burns-style motion to show pictures of Darrin's short life as Karli and people she'd interviewed told how he had taken the paper route to pay for karate and how the karate had given him confidence he'd never had before and had helped him become a straight-A student. The story ended on a photo of a bright-faced boy in a karate uniform with "Darrin Anderson, 2001-2013" superimposed over the bottom of the screen.

"Don't forget to open their mics," Chuck cautioned as the story came to a close. "Ready camera 2...get Sophia, too! Yes, all of them!...and take 2."

"What a terrible loss for that family and for the community," Stu said. "Did the family have anything else to say, Karli?"

"Take 1," Chuck called, cutting to a head-and-shoulders shot of Karli. "2, tighten up to just Stu and Sophia. Open Sophia's mic."

"Stu, the family is asking to be left alone for a while. They appreciate the many people who have reached out to them, but they told me tonight that what they really need is some privacy so they can try to begin to understand and cope with their loss."

"Take 2," Chuck called.

"Thank you for that part of the story, Karli," Sophia said, her face looking off-screen to where Karli sat. Then her eyes moved to the camera, and as she began speaking to the audience directly instead of to Karli, her head slowly turned directly toward the camera, an anchor's trick to create visual intimacy with the viewer. "Our coverage of Darrin's story continues tonight with this report on how Iowa is dealing with the texting-and-driving problem..."

The rest of the newscast demonstrated exactly why Three NewsFirst was a consistent number 1 in the ratings. The reporting delivered all the day's teamwork—the cell phone company representative acknowledged that her company's anti-texting campaign was a huge priority, the animation that Mary Rose and Karli had worked on together showed the truck's fatal path as the eyewitness had described it, a legislator said Iowa needed to toughen up laws about texting, the Iowa State University engineer roundly condemned the street design and sidewalk neglect, the Iowa City bicyclists spoke eloquently about how safely engineered streets worked for all kinds of vehicles.

"Finally this evening," Sophia Refai read in the broadcast's closing moments, "We at Three NewsFirst have been touched by

Darrin's story and heartened by a community that wants to share its support and grief in the wake of its loss. Funeral and visitation arrangements will be on the Three NewsFirst website as soon as they are finalized. Also, a special fund has been set up to accept memorial donations; details are also on our website. Three NewsFirst will be following this story to ensure that those responsible for Darrin's death are held accountable for making our area's streets safer."

It seemed like the entire Three NewsFirst team was in the newsroom late on this Saturday night, watching the broadcast. As Chuck called for all audio to be clipped and the closing shot to fade to black, the newsroom erupted in cheers. The team had pulled together and done some of the best work of their careers to cover Darrin's story.

Jerry high-fived Karli then leaned in to ask her under the self-congratulatory hubbub, "Hey, Ace—how'd you get that kid's parents to talk? The other stations are eating our dust tonight!"

Karli's palms again dampened with nervous sweat. She decided to come clean rather than change course to talk about the competition. "I wrote a note with my cell phone number and invited them to call if they wanted to talk. Then I slipped it in their mail slot instead of trying to catch them as they came to the door." Karli finished with a feeling of relief at coming clean about what she'd done, but she still feared what Jerry would say about her decision to deliberately avoid a necessary interview.

Vince had been listening in on the conversation, and he saw Jerry's deep intake of breath in preparation for a lecture about who had the authority to make that kind of decision. "Well done," Vince quickly rasped in order to head off Jerry's pointless lecture. "You got an interview with the parents, and nobody else got one." Here Karli saw Vince look pointedly at the news director, who took another deep breath, thought about it, and then nodded at Vince. Karli sighed with relief and gave Vince a quick look of gratitude.

"Vince is right," Jerry sighed. "Good job, Karli." His aging chair lurched as he swiveled it back to his desk.

Karli thanked them both and then looked around the people straying out of the newsroom and on toward a well deserved drink or to bed. Jake was nowhere to be seen. She went to his desk and saw that his computer was off and his coat was gone.

Where, she wondered, *are you? This was supposed to be the moment when we celebrated our glory together.* She reflected on the terribly downcast and quiet Jake who had come back to the station with her and left the editing to the always-competent Mary Rose. That had worked out fine because Mary Rose was doing the animation, but it was unusual for a shooter like Jake to leave important visual choices up to someone else. *And it's totally wrong for anyone to be a jerk and leave in the middle of a huge story like this. Is something wrong with him? He seemed quiet, yeah, but not like anything too terrible was up. It doesn't seem in character for him to just duck out when the story isn't done yet. And it doesn't seem like him to strand me so I have to face Jerry all alone about the decision not to ambush. Something is going on with him,* Karli thought. *Maybe he's sick or something. Or maybe The Dick really is a jerk.*

Chapter Seven

Karate Center
Southern Des Moines metro area
Monday, October 7

Brian Johnson came out of the dojo's locker room looking as proud as he felt in his clean white karate uniform and newly earned orange belt. Sensei Jake saw the boy's pride and energy and tried to figure out how to keep him enthused for this special training session. "Lookin' sharp, Brian," he said, reaching out to pin a black ribbon on the uniform. "Now remember," Jake said, grimacing with the effort of pushing the ribbon's pin through the uniform's heavy canvas, "today is silent training, and you haven't done that before. It's for special occasions only, and today we're training in silence so we can all remember Darrin. So once you're on the mat, make sure you let your breath and your uniform speak for you, okay? No words at all."

"Sure thing, Sensei Jake."

"Good. Make sure you look extra sharp tonight. This is an important session."

Ever since they'd covered Darrin's death, Jake felt as though he were always just a few seconds from shocked, useless immobility. He had worked on Darrin to get that paper route, and it had killed him. Jake realized now that he was not in any position to guide or advise people. He couldn't even help a little boy find his way without getting him killed. At least Karli had been more like a human being than he had expected about not doing the surprise interview with the parents. He still couldn't understand where that moment of...what was it? Kindness? Laziness? Fear?... had come from.

But he had been so relieved that she hadn't expected him to do an ambush-style interview.

Jake hadn't watched any news or read the paper since he'd

quietly left the newsroom late Saturday morning. He had had trouble keeping Karli off his mind—she had a highly unusual beauty when she was off-camera and off-guard. He recalled the deep kindness and compassion that he'd seen flicker across her beautiful face several times, most especially when she was deciding not to interview Darrin's parents. Contrary to all indications, she had a heart and even empathy for others. And he had felt a pull toward her that was more fundamental than any list of honorable qualities. Something about her hooked into his body's chemistry so that he felt incomplete whenever he remembered the smell and feel of her lightly perfumed skin. He looked at the yin-and-yang symbol on a student's equipment bag and realized that she was complementary to him on a very basic, even glandular, level.

But thinking about Karli was pointless. His terrible mentoring of Darrin was proof enough that he could never make the kinds of important decisions that go with a committed relationship and raising children. Jake wasn't so much trying to find a wife and make kids as he was disturbed at the cheerless prospect of a life alone and without the completion his emotions and urges told him he could find in Karli. But he was even more terrified of destroying someone he would choose to become responsible for—or even letting down the children they might conceive together. Which was thinking absurdly far down life's road—especially since Karli didn't seem particularly interested in him other than as a photographer.

So Karli thoughts were indeed pointless.

Jake had reflected long on Darrin. But Jake couldn't find any words for the loss that everyone was feeling. There *weren't* any words. So he had decided to emulate his first karate instructor and hold a silent class. Darrin had loved training and competing, and the best memorial Jake could conceive for him was a demonstration of how fully alive Darrin had been while training. And Darrin had looked so forward to this January's tournament in Chicago.

Jake had put up signs to warn spectators and students alike that there was to be no talking during the training session. He was surprised at how many people had turned out in tonight's silence. The visitor's gallery was overflowing, and two of the black belt students had gone into the back to wheel out a cart of folding chairs for the unexpected crowd.

There was almost no overlap between Jake's news life and his karate. Mary Rose, sitting straddle-legged on the mat and stretching out over her left knee, was the only person from the station present, her platinum-and-blue hair even more startling than usual above her crisp white uniform. And she was a newbie, as the white belt around her waist attested. She looked up from her stretch and gave Jake an approving once-over. Her nod, smirk, and wink told him that she thought he was looking sharp.

Jake looked over the rest of the students from the back of the studio. He had pinned nearly 40 black ribbons onto uniforms tonight, and the folks wearing them were all over 15. Jake would allow students as young as 12 to train in these sessions if they showed enough maturity, as Darrin had; but it was the session for serious, mature students, not kids. Noting the second hand sweeping to exactly 7:00 p.m., Sensei Jake stepped to the farthest corner of the mat, stood to attention, and bowed. When he strode onto the padded training surface, a 50-something man with a black belt around his waist jumped up from his stretching position on the floor and slapped his hands against his thighs as he stood to attention. All the other karate students heard the slap and rose as well. The black- and brown-belt senior students moved quietly among the color-belt students to arrange them by rank, facing the front wall of the dojo.

Jake moved to that front wall and turned to face the large class. He took much more time than usual to make eye contact with each person, to silently remind them that this session would be a solemn memorial to Darrin who had found a home with them. Many eyes he saw brimmed with tears that either fell or threatened to fall silently. Every face, though, was encouraging and proud. Sensei Jake's own eyes filled when even young Brian Johnson gave him a sharp nod to indicate that this was the right thing to do, that Darrin would have liked it, even if he couldn't laugh out loud.

After a series of formal bows to acknowledge the great martial artists in the karate tradition, Jake began the training by demonstrating and having the others repeat a series of lightning-fast blocks and punches, pivoting quickly to different stances for each set. After warming the class up with a sequence of hops and jumps and swinging movements, there followed a long series of basic techniques that Sensei Jake mixed together in different ways for the students to repeat after he demonstrated. Heavy breathing punctuated the techniques, as did the constant sliding and stepping of bare feet.

Everyone in the class moved together, with the different abilities associated with different-colored belts apparent to all. Movements from the senior students were faster and more precise. Their speed and power was evident in their uniforms' loud snapping sounds. After these drills, all of the students were sweating—most of them were nearly panting. Then Sensei Jake took the class through a series of rote attack-and-defend drills. The partnered-up students had practiced the drills many times together and knew what to do. As the time approached 7:45, Jake divided the class—still in silence—by rank groups to perform *kata*, prearranged solo sequences of karate movements.

Finally, Sensei Jake seated everyone on the back edge of the mat and then strode to one of the gear lockers. He took a two foot-long polished wooden case with a glass front from the locker and walked to the center of the mat. There he bowed formally to all the students and marched close to where they sat on the back edge of the mat. He placed the box down reverently and so the closest students could see the black belt inside with Darrin's name embroidered in gold thread. As Sensei Jake turned and went toward an equipment rack, students who could see the belt whispered and gestured to the others what was written upon it.

His back to the class, Sensei Jake took a breath deep into his body and visualized each movement of the bo staff kata he had planned to teach Darrin for the January tournament. Finished, he opened his eyes and took a staff from the rack. He then snapped into rigid martial formality and marched to the front of the mat. He bowed crisply to the class and began the kata. Each time Sensei Jake stepped into one of the kata's many stances, his legs, hips, and core took on a granite-like stability. Extending from that stillness, his arms propelled the bo staff into a furiously blurring aura of wood. The dojo was no longer silent as the staff's wood stroked the air into a series of humming vibrations, the canvas of Jake's uniform snapped, and the hissing of his intensifying breath all communicated the irresistible power he focused into each movement.

The performance transfixed everyone in the studio. Mary Rose sat cross-legged on the edge of the mat, a hand under each knee holding her own toes, her astonished mouth hanging slightly open. Senior students watched with rapt attention. The parents and other guests in the gallery sat forward, leaning in to better focus their attention on the barely contained explosion that was Jake's performance.

Jake finished the kata with a two-beat pause followed by a powerful final strike and a thunderous yell from deep in his abdomen, karate's spirit-yell or *kiai.* Coming after more than an hour's attention to the subtle sounds of a silent training session, the *kiai* startled everyone in the studio—on the mat and in the spectator's gallery alike. Sensei Jake then snapped back to attention, breathing heavily, as the small cries of surprise tapered off. He bowed to the room, took up the polished wooden box and placed it with the bo staff on a table a few feet off the training mat. An open book and a pen rested on the table for people to sign and jot memories of Darrin. He signed the book, paused to regard box and staff for a final silent moment, then walked quickly to his office, closing the door behind him.

The sweaty students left on the mat began to murmur questions about what was going on. They were cut off by the man who'd stood when Sensei Jake walked onto the mat, who held a stern finger to his lips and shushed them. He bowed as he left the training surface and went to the locker room without looking back to see that the others would follow. Some headed straight for the locker room, others went to the table to look at Darrin's posthumous black belt and to sign the book. Others paused in indecision, then headed for the showers so they could sign without dripping sweat all over the book.

As the mat silently cleared and it became obvious that training was over for the night, one of the parents, who needed to talk to Jake about past-due tuition, knocked on the office door.

Quiet sobs from behind the locked door were the only answer.

Chapter Eight

The Drake Diner
Des Moines, Iowa
Sunday, October 13

Karli tucked her iPhone back into her purse, shaking her head at the photo her father had just sent her from his latest formal lunch meeting with South Carolina's most powerful legislators. As she looked up, she saw the towering muscular uniform containing Officer Will McMillian shoulder its way through the Diner's entrance. She took him in as he scanned the booths and long, neon-lit counter, seeking her: a buzz cut topped his probably 6' 3" height, and judging by the impressive amount of rippling under the fabric he took weight lifting very seriously, yet his hands were as soft and uncalloused as Karli's own. He had the air of a former high-school lineman who had found in the gym and the police force socially acceptable ways to channel the aggression that had stayed with him since puberty. His dark eyes were a shade too small and close-set for him to be classically handsome.

She finally caught his eye and he smiled broadly, showing even rows of straight, whitened teeth. The breeze from the door swept away the delicious smells of the Diner's signature comfort food—especially the open-face hot turkey sandwich Karli had been sniffing—and brought a strong whiff of the officer's Brut cologne overdose. He strode past the hostess station over to her booth, shook her hand and introduced himself. "Will McMillian. Nice to meet you in person."

"Karli Lewis, as you know. So Officer McMillian, you're the one who made the call to my private cell phone number.

I still can't figure out how you got it, but it's creepy to have a perfect stranger call that number. What did you want to talk about?"

"Whoa, there," he said. "I was hoping we could talk about

whether we should talk before we get right down to talking." He grinned again and reached for the menu.

"Fine. You do the pre-talking, and we'll see where it goes. But I have to leave in 20 minutes to go to an interview, so don't spend too long on the warm-ups," she said, checking the Tag Heuer her father had given her for her graduation from Missou.

"That's what she said. . . in my dreams!" Will guffawed at his own joke. His laughter stopped abruptly as he saw that Karli didn't share his zeal for foreplay humor. He looked back at his menu to hide his momentary embarrassment. "Okay, here's the deal: We've been watching you for a while now, and we like your style."

"Who exactly are 'we,' Mr. McMillian?" Karli asked. Her pointed question kept McMillian on the defensive, and she could see he was going to need help to get the conversation on track. Especially since he was obviously attracted to the cute waitress who filled their coffee cups and asked for their orders. After he ordered— one of the Diner's signature and massive blue-plate specials—Karli watched him closely as he cleared his throat and returned to the conversation.

"Um, 'we' are the police, you know. We watch the news and pay attention to which reporters are doing a good job of being fair to everyone, even cops."

"So what do the cops want with me, Officer McMillian?"

"Well, we've been doing some really good things—busting some real bad guys—and we have some big stuff coming up.

So we wanted to get you to cover us when we do some of it."

"Are you offering me an exclusive on this really big stuff, or are you shopping this around to everyone?"

"This is just about as exclusive as it can get. Not even all the guys know you'll be getting this tip."

Karli looked skeptically at the big cop, who nearly filled his entire side of the booth. His cluelessness was just a bit adorable, she thought. He was the kind of guy she could lead around by the nose, and he wouldn't ever hesitate to do whatever she asked. It was written on his boy-next-door handsome face. She wrapped both hands around her coffee cup and leaned toward him, her eyes flashing with challenge. "So what is this super-secret amazing exclusive you have just for me?"

"Whoa, there," Will said, beaming around a mouthful of

meatloaf. He chewed quickly and swallowed before continuing. "There are still some things to talk about before we get to that."

"Such as...?"

"Well, we were hoping you could make sure not to show the faces of our undercover guys..." Will began.

Karli cut him off quickly. "You've never done this before, have you Officer McMillian? We are not out to compromise law enforcement or to place your officers needlessly in danger. Their identities, after all, are not the story. If this were a corruption story about, say, undercover guys selling drugs for their own gain, there would be another set of questions before we decided whether or not to reveal identities, but that's not this one, I'm guessing. So yes, of course we will pixellate any undercover faces we see. Just tell us which guys to keep safe."

"O-okay," the officer stammered. "So, um, we were also hoping you could make sure to tell the story so everyone knows who the good guys and bad guys are."

"This really is your first time," Karli said mostly to herself, barely disguising her scorn. "Officer McMillian, here are the rules. Please remember them for the next time you approach a reporter because they apply every time. I am not going to bargain about how I tell a story. I am the news reporter. You are the police. I won't use your guns or tasers; don't you start in with my pen or camera. If you want to look like the good guys, make sure you *are* the good guys. Then I won't have much choice about how to tell the story. Got it?"

Officer McMillian was rocked back by Karli's abrupt education on law enforcement-press relations. He reached under the table to adjust his pants as his reaction to her sassiness began to get the better of him. He was distracted. Karli watched him try to reach for and fall short of finding a face-saving witty retort, then move hastily to deflect his own attention and perhaps hers to the huge amount of food on his plate. After a massive mouthful and a hefty gulp from his huge glass of milk, it was apparent to Karli that she was a lot harder to talk to than he had expected the pretty reporter from TV to be. Accustomed to the arrogance of her fellow journalists—and one photog in particular—Karli found Will's defenselessness cute.

Lacking the ability to change course once he had set out, he pushed ahead. "There's going to be a multi-force raid on a big drug distribution operation on the near east side. The judge is signing the warrant tomorrow some time, and we only have 48 hours before it gets stale. So the bust will probably be Tuesday at 6:30 a.m.

There'll be feds as well as county and city cops, and it should be the biggest bust in Iowa history."

"Okaaay," Karli said, drawing out the word to suggest to him that she was waiting for more details, which the cop apparently didn't have.

"Look," he said, "everyone is going to see the drugs all piled up at the news conference, but you're going to be there to see the bust going down."

"Tell me about the *W*s, Officer McMillian: where and what kind of operation is this, who will be there when you do the bust, and how dangerous is this likely to be?"

"The operation is in the near east side, in a big old house. Vans and RVs and cars full of bulk drugs come from the west on I-80, then it's all broken down here and taken out in pretty much every direction. All the workers—probably 20 of them—should be there, and I don't know how many vehicles will be there to load outgoing shipments. It's possible that it will be dangerous. We know they have guns in there. But they aren't supposed to be the type to use them."

"How many law enforcement personnel will it take to bust a house full of people and drugs?"

McMillian stammered again. Karli could see that he didn't know as much about this bust as he'd thought. Disarmed, the officer looked less like the overly swaggering uniform who'd walked in and much more like a man she could talk to. And probably steer wherever she wished him to go. Big, manly, helpless and cute. "Well, l-l-like I said, there's going to be feds and county guys as well as city police. I don't know exactly how many."

"And the feds are going to be in charge?"

"No," McMillian's growing unease was showing. He was pale and little beads of sweat were showing where flat-top turned to forehead. "It's going to be a state warrant, I know that for sure."

Karli decided to relent a bit so as not to lose the story—or the man. "So how am I going to know where I'm supposed to be at 6:30 on Tuesday morning?"

Relief showed on the officer's face. He knew the answer to this question. "I'll text you when they send the vehicles out to serve the warrant, and you can get there in plenty of time to get what you need."

"This isn't a lot, Officer McMillian," Karli said. "But I'm going to trust you this time and see if you really have something here." She slid two dollars under her coffee cup and stood up from the booth. "I'll see you Tuesday morning."

She smiled as the surprised policeman tried to slide out of the booth and stand to see her out. He was so heavily muscled that the operation was too complex, what with napkin retrieval, milk glass placement, breathless sliding and so on, for him to get out and up on his feet before she had nearly reached the doorway.

"You'll see," he called. "You can trust Will McMillian!"

Karli nodded, gave a small wave, and headed out the door.

Three NewsFirst newsroom
Des Moines, Iowa
Monday, October 14

"Vince, I need to talk to you about crewing a tip," Karli said. She approached Vince during a momentary lull in the newsroom's frantic activity, so as to keep others from overhearing.

"What'cha got, kid?" Vince asked, never taking his eyes from the schedule on his monitor.

"A drug bust. Supposed to be the biggest in Iowa history, if the cop knows what he's talking about."

Vince looked up at Karli, examining her carefully. "Sophia has the police beat, Karli. Should she do this one?"

"No way, Vince," Karli whispered in indignation. "This tip came to me. I didn't go out and develop the source or anything. This was a cold call to me, because the cops like my reporting. They wanted to give the story—as an exclusive—to me, not Sophia."

"Okay, okay," Vince pressed his hands placatingly toward her. "What time?"

"I need Jake to be in the car, loaded and ready to roll, by 6:00 tomorrow morning. They're going to serve the warrant at 6:30, and I want to be set up to catch the door getting kicked in."

"Jake, huh?" Vince looked thoughtfully at his schedule again. "He has been taking personal time for a while now. I don't know if he's going to be in tomorrow."

"Vince, I need *him*, not some wet-behind-the-ears noob. This should be a big story, and I need some great video to make it work. Can't you get him for me?" Karli did her best wide-eyed pleading look and saw instantly that Vince was not going to bite.

"Besides," she quickly added, "this is the kind of exclusive that will set us up for ratings next month, plus we will be able to use it in promos for months. But only if we have great video. We get one shot at this bust—no do-overs. Give me the best, Vince."

She could see Vince considering her pitch—this time seriously. "Okay," he relented. "I'll call him. But I can't *make* him come in, okay? He has enough leave to take off till Christmas. I'll let you know later today." As he very deliberately dismissed her by turning back to his computer, Karli knew that she'd won and that Vince would persuade Jake to come back to her.

As she thought about seeing Jake again after his mysterious absence, she felt a warm anticipation of the brilliance he brought to her reporting. He had an understanding of what she was writing for each story that other photogs couldn't touch, and he framed that deep comprehension with images that complemented her efforts seamlessly, as though the finished story sprang from a single creative spirit rather than from two individuals working in different disciplines.

The iPhone buzzed against her hand, and Karli looked down to see the notification: a text from her father. Sighing, Karli swiped to unlock the phone and read, "Things are moving here. If you're tired of your corny life, I can put you in with some of the biggest names in town. Word is that Condé Nast tags Charleston as a Best City in the World. Not too shabby!"

Karli's chest heaved with another sigh. *Oh, Dad. You don't get it. There may be corn here, but at least it's real and not some crazy Lifestyles of the Rich and Famous nonsense. I'm going to beat everyone on a big story, and with Jake's help we're going to make it a landmark story for Des Moines.*

Thinking about working with Jake made Karli's pulse leap again, and the tension in her center coiled again as though ready to be sprung loose.

But why hasn't he been in to work? she wondered. *There wasn't enough rain to make him catch cold or anything, so it must be something else.* She thought of his steady hands guiding his camera to yet another great shot and felt a flutter in her stomach. *Fine,* she thought with an oddly reluctant feeling of resignation. *I admit it. I miss him. For more than just his pictures. But pictures are what I need right now.*

Chapter Nine

Des Moines, Iowa
Tuesday, October 15
5:45 a.m.

Jake rolled up to Karli's apartment building with all of his gear tucked neatly into the cab of his pickup truck. He watched with an artist's appreciation as Karli looked up from her iPhone, saw him at the curb and walked toward his truck. There was nothing of the hip-swaying model's strut in her walk; Karli moved more like a sprinter walking to the blocks—all her movements revealed a straight-ahead energy restrained by strict economy. The breeze her pace created fluttered the hair that was still cut short around her elegant features, and the bright parking lot lights behind her limned her physique and highlighted its compact strength. The time she spent in the gym showed in every line of her sleek workout shirt, which drew Jake's eyes to the small breasts riding high on her chest. The sight made Jake's hands twitch for his digital Canon SLR, but he had come for work. It was time to go shoot the drug bust, not Karli's bust.

Jake's breath caught at the suddenly imagined sensations his view of Karli unguarded sparked. She had a dramatic, sharp-angled beauty that glinted around the eyes. That glint underlined her beauty somehow, animating it with keen intelligence. She looked powerful, yet somehow deliciously accessible. Jake felt the insistent appeal, knowing that he wanted to be close to that Karli. Physically close, yes, absolutely; yet he was interested in knowing her, comprehending her, just as much. He shifted in his seat with the realization that the twitch he felt wasn't for a camera at all.

She opened the passenger door of his Ford Ranger and swung in her backpack ahead of herself. "Good morning, stranger," she said, her attention on jostling the pack into place so there was room for her feet. "We've missed you at work. Vince tells me you hit a rough patch. I hope everything is working out okay for you."

"Um, sure," Jake replied, surprised at Karli's oddly distant sympathy. "Everything's gonna be okay, I guess." He knew he was only making polite noise to humor her. Nothing would ever be okay; he had learned that much. But it was time to work, and he could at least take pictures without hurting anyone. And today he could help keep people safe by capturing a story about danger, while doing his best back-to-work work on a story that Karli obviously was into.

"Where are we going?" he asked.

Karli glanced at her iPhone's messages and gave Jake the address. "I just got the text as you were pulling up. Oh crap," she exclaimed, as her phone chirped an alert tone and a warning flashed up on the screen. "my battery. I forgot to plug it in last night."

She went over the scanty information she'd gotten from the police officer. Jake already knew all the details from his phone call with Vince, but he'd worked with Karli long enough to know that she liked to review her background information aloud more than once on the way to a story, so he waited for her string to play its full length into her back. "I was reading up on the web last night," she continued, adding something new. "And it looks like heroin rings are starting to work like rum-runners did during Prohibition: they work at high margins for upper- and middle-class clients and they don't go in for all the guns and violence."

"Well," Jake said, making the last turn before their destination, "let's hope they don't use their guns. Bullets can spoil good video."

After he parked the truck and snared out the royal blue PortaBrace bag that held all his camera gear, Jake looked around for the cops' vehicles. He saw the oddly lumpy tactical truck turning into the block behind him and began flicking switches to power up his gear and get it ready for recording. From his bent-over position, he swiveled his head to talk to Karli and found her breasts at an intriguing eye level. Changing quickly from natural appreciation, he looked carefully and sharply at them. He examined them openly, first one, then the other, until he heard Karli clear her throat with mild feminine indignation.

"Hey, Karli," he said, with a quiet urgency in his voice, "get your vest on. Even if the drug guys don't use guns, the cops might." The last comment was directed back over his shoulder as he strode off to shoot the cops filing out of their vehicle.

Jake found a spot with good perspective on the police truck, shouldered his camera, and leaned against a tree to steady the telephoto shot. He pressed the 'record' button as cops began jumping out of the truck like so many Rambo-clowns from a circus car. Once out, they were obsessive and nearly fetishy about adjusting their gear and checking their clattering shotguns, rifles, and pistols. The last ones out carried a four-foot metal cylinder with handles along its length. Jake recognized the door-breaking ram and readied himself to sprint after the cops and toward the entrance they were about to force. Just as he pressed the button to pause the recording, he felt a tap on his shoulder and turned to see Karli's eyes, wide open and terrified. Something had transformed the confident reporter he'd just driven with; something that rendered her nearly speechless.

Before he could ask what had her so scared, heavy-booted steps came to a halt on the other side of his tree, accompanied by heavy breathing that gasped, "Karli, you made it!"

Jake darted his eyes toward the cops with the ram; only a few seconds had passed, and they were not yet moving toward the house. Instead, he saw a grey-haired but sternly fit officer striding toward him instead of the house with a distinctly hostile look on his face. Then he snatched a look around the tree, saw Officer Will McMillian in cop camouflage that made him nearly as conspicuous in urban Des Moines as he would have been in a bikini, snorted in disgust, and looked back to Karli, a scathing remark about his bumbling acquaintance on the tip of his tongue. The snarkiness died before it could get out as he saw Karli's unusually pale, wide-eyed face. "What's wrong?"

Without turning her body, which still addressed Jake, Karli turned her head to glance distractedly at Officer McMillian and said to Jake, "What was that you said about a vest?"

"Didn't you grab a vest from the station?" Jake asked. Then, turning to Officer McMillian, "You're the one who gave her this tip aren't you, Wil? Didn't you tell her to wear a vest?" Jake's expression was one of disgust, and he shook his head in frustration.

The look of mute surprise on McMillian's face was a complete answer. "You moron," Jake said. "And I'm guessing that guy," and here he raised his lens to point toward an angry figure walking sternly toward the three of them, "is coming to ask what we're doing shooting his super-secret drug bust that nobody is supposed to know about, right?"

McMillian grew brightly red, and he began to mumble something about she-was-the-one-who-knew-it-all only to be cut abruptly off by the Clearly-In-Charge Man who had now arrived at the tree. "You can't be here with that camera, son," he began, "so stand down and clear on out of here." Then he glared at McMillian, obviously a member of the operation since he was wearing a vest with the word POLICE in six-inch highlighter-colored letters. "What are you doing with these news people?" he asked, as though 'news people' was a swear word. Then realization flashed across his face, along with sudden bulges in the veins of his neck and temples. "You tipped the press to this operation? You will be lucky to have a job waxing squad cars tomorrow, son."

"We aren't going anywhere, sir." Karli's clear voice cut through In-Charge Man's threats. His head turned sharply, snapping his menacing glare onto Karli's face. Seeing the shock in the man's eyes, Jake could tell he was accustomed to unquestioning obedience. And from the set of her shoulders, the man saw he wasn't going to get any obedience at all from Karli. Her face held none of the fear he'd seen when she was asking about vests.

Jake knew there was no time now, yet Karli wasn't wearing the Kevlar vest she should've gotten from the station or from McMillian. If the guns started popping, nothing protected her from stray rounds. Jake set his camera on the ground and began to pull his shirt off.

Karli was still talking to the In-Charge Man. "When the press is on public property like we are right now, we have every right to record what anyone can see. You have no legal authority to make us leave, and we aren't going to."

Looking around at the distant and keenly attentive group of suddenly idle police officers, Jake began tearing open Velcro fasteners. Karli kept talking, as calm as if she were live and on the air, though the In-Charge Man was balling up his fists and crowding closer into her personal space. "If you push the matter," she continued, "we will record every second of it so an army of lawyers can make sure *you* are the one waxing cars. And if you think you're cute enough to take our recording, we will subpoena every single one of those officers watching us right now. All it will take is one with the guts to tell the truth, and you will be joining all the people you've put behind bars over the years."

Jake picked his camera up and thumbed the 'record' switch. He slid right behind Karli, his front pressing neatly against her backside. Making a show of focusing on In-Charge Man's face, Jake fought to keep himself focused as he inhaled Karli's freshly showered scent and felt her firm curves pressing back against him. To let her know he was there and rolling and had her back, Jake dropped a reassuring left hand onto her shoulder.

Fury rolled off the In-Charge Man like waves of heat from a radiator. Jake was unmoved, though, as he had long practice controlling his breathing and posture to hold the camera nearly as steady as an actual tripod. And Karli held to her place as the Man's fury washed over her.

Looking from reporter to photographer with a final, mostly swallowed bark of rage, the Man suddenly turned and left without a word.

As soon as In-Charge Man's back was turned and Jake saw that he had displaced his anger into gesturing furiously at the police standing ready to begin their operation, Jake quickly put his camera down, picked up the vest, and slid Karli's arm through one of the openings. "That was great, Karli," he said, holding her wrist and pushing the vest onto her shoulder. "Let's strap this on you and go get the story." Her deep breath of relief made her chest move in a way that caught and held Jake's attention while he worked to secure the vest. He could tell from the sudden slackness in her posture that Karli was sagging with post-adrenaline relief now that she was done with the In-Charge Man. As soon as he had tightened the last strap, he found her eyes and heard her whisper, "Thanks, Jake. I feel a lot safer now."

Things kept moving fast, too fast for Jake to reply. He heard the thudding of McMillian's boots running away from their position and toward the other officers. Looking toward the cops, Jake saw that they were spreading out to cover all sides of the house. Glancing urgently from group to group, Jake saw with relief that the cops with the ram were headed to the front door. He snared his camera off the ground, quietly told Karli, "Come on!" and took off at a sprint to line up a shot of the door-busting.

From somewhere on the other side of the house, cops threw flash-bang stun grenades in through a window. That was the cue for the guys with the ram.

Screaming, "Police! We have a warrant!" the cops smashed the front door open, dumped the ram, drew their guns and charged into the house. As soon as the cops entered, Jake pushed in behind them. Drawing on skills developed through long and thoughtful experience, he made quick, extreme adjustments to his camera during the transition from the long, early-morning sunlight of the outdoors to the house's dim interior, all while rolling. He flicked through filters, increased gain, and re-balanced colors, all while recording the raid's tense visuals and sounds in vivid, intimate detail.

One of the suspects stared at a cop's pistol inches from his face, shaking in the broad-shouldered officer's two-handed grip. The cop was shouting so loudly—and all the other cops were shouting just as loudly, all at the same time—that his words were indistinct: "Get down, motherfucker! On the floor!" The man was transfixed by the gun in his face, paralyzed by fear, completely immobile.

Jake swung his camera to frame another suspect who was starting to leave his seat at a table about five feet away and put his knees onto the floor. Another cop charged up to him, shotgun jutting from his shoulder: "Don't move, asshole, or I'll shoot you!"

Movement was everywhere, and Jake turned to see cops kicking guns away from men they had just knocked to the floor while screaming, "Get your hands where I can see them!"

"Get up against that wall right now, fucker!" And Jake framed a shot of two cops shoving a man halfway across the room to where the wall was unobstructed. Then, his words punctuated by tugs of his booted foot dragging the man's ankle to one side, "Spread your legs now!"

And Jake swiveled again to another cop who was screaming at a man whose hands were placed on top of one another in a pile on his head: "Show me where the dope is, now, before I tear this place apart and you with it!"

Up close, the drug workers' quivering fear was nearly tactile. Jake backed out of the room into a doorway, rolling the whole time and reaching to feel blindly behind himself with his left hand so he could frame a wider shot of all the cops and suspects at one time. As he backed through the doorway and felt nothing behind him, he sneaked a peek out of the viewfinder to see where he was. His eyes nearly popped as he saw what looked like the main re-packaging room. He swung to pan across the room, but police officers entered right behind him and jostled him and shook his shot. Jake kept rolling. He recorded every moment as the cops discovered scales, packaging materials and tools, a table piled with guns and several fork-lift pallets of shrink-wrapped heroin. The shrink-wrap was peeled back from the top of one pallet where the workers had been taking large packages of heroin to the work tables for weighing and putting in street-sale size packages.

Once he'd caught two minutes of video in the workroom, Jake rushed back outside to the front of the house, where he re-set his camera's controls and snapped it onto the waiting tripod, and quickly adjusted the leveling claw to shoot the cops bringing suspects back out and into a newly arrived paddy wagon.

As the first scared suspects were escorted—a police euphemism for a fast-walk motivated by deftly applied grinding pressure where handcuffs met skin and bone—to the paddy wagon, Jake pulled back from his steaming-over viewfinder.

"You aren't on public property now, asshole," rasped the gravelly parade-ground voice of the In-Charge Man. "And I'm not in front of your camera. So put it down slowly." Jake heard an unmistakeable metal ratcheting sound and knew with a sudden jolt of fear that the In-Charge Man was about to handcuff him.

Chapter Ten

Des Moines, Iowa
Tuesday, October 15
6:45 a.m.

Jake's intestines shook with the realization that he was about to be arrested, handcuffed, and taken away to wherever the In-Charge Man's tender mercies desired. He had just escaped a guns-drawn, adrenaline-fueled violence festival without the bulletproof vest he had stopped by the station to put on this morning. Guns had been everywhere, drawn and ready, within easy reach, all loaded and ready to kill. He had seen—heck, he had captured in portrait-like detail—the transfixing fear overwhelming the drug-house workers as they anticipated a beatdown or a bullet's fiery penetration.

Now Jake realized that his own escape from the bust hadn't been complete. He hadn't been shot, but he had seen the In-Charge Man's fury, and he knew that he wasn't going to be led gently to a seat in a squad car once those cuffs were on. Jake's martial arts training had taught him how to take a blow, but the training hadn't exactly emphasized self-defense while handcuffed. *At least,* Jake thought, *nobody fired any shots. That means he won't shoot me. It would be impossible for him to explain me getting shot, outside the house, without anyone else doing any shooting.*

Luck seemed to be keeping more bullets from him than the vest ever could have. Jake's thoughts suddenly turned to Karli. He hadn't seen her since he had followed the cops into the house. She had the vest on, yes, but that wouldn't have saved her from In-Charge Man's handcuffs any more that it would've saved him.

And she looked so *good* today. It would be terrible for her to be cuffed and dragged off.

His wandering thoughts were cut off by the strong sound of her voice: "You may not be in front of his camera, but you're in front of *mine*," he heard her say. An actual human snarl and a further rattle of the cuffs prompted him to sneak a look back over his shoulder. He saw the back of In-Charge Man, who had turned to look down at Karli. She held her iPhone steadily toward his face and started speaking calmly before he could start yelling at her. "Here's how this is going to go. You are going to walk away from here and go about your business, while Jake and I are going to forget we ever saw you. If you turn up at the press conference, we will all greet one another as complete strangers, and we will have a nice, friendly interview. So how about you keep yourself from public embarrassment and get back to your bust?"

A long, unmoving silence followed Karli's speech. Jake kept as still as a rabbit under a hawk's shadow, while In-Charge Man and Karli stared resolutely at one another. Karli broke the impasse by glancing back at her iPhone's horizontal screen, then pinching across its surface to call up the zoom function. In-Charge Man snarled one last time, then turned and stumped off without giving Jake so much as a glance over his departing shoulder.

"Holy shit, Karli! You're brilliant," Jake said. "Thanks."

"We've overstayed our welcome, I think," she said, acknowledging his thanks with a quick shrug. "Let's get to the station before they come up with other ideas. We have a story to tell."

Jake turned to power down his gear, pack it up, and schlep the PortaBrace bag and his tripod back to the truck. He and Karli put the gear away and buckled in. Jake, sweaty from the strain of shooting but chilled by the fading of his adrenaline, turned the key and pulled the Ford away from the curb. A companionable silence rode with them for a few blocks, as Jake sighed in relief at the great save Karli had made to keep his wrists out of the In-Charge Man's cuffs.

She wasn't physically imposing. But she was a tight package physically, with the glutes and the posture and the strength and the focus. Her physicality was slim and tempered: knife-like, or maybe scalpel-like. Not physically imposing like a big man—like Will McMillian.

But man, was she ever imposing. She had utterly disarmed that In-Charge bastard *two* times, leaving him speechless and without options. And she had saved them both from being arrested—

however illegally the first time—and losing the story altogether. Come to think of it, he couldn't dream up a hotter combination than Karli's fearless, authoritative speech, her formidable, athletic physique, and her striking, photogenic countenance. She was intellectually stunning, physically arousing, and she had a face that blended those attributes with the kindness of someone who is deeply compassionate and interested. He felt the twitch beginning again and recalled the pulse-quickening combination of her smooth skin and vanilla-and-spice scent. They turned his systems on just as surely as the sight of a fox made beagles bark and give chase.

He had begun the day resolved to keep her safe. Yet she was the one who had saved them both.

Just as he took in a breath to say thanks again for the rescue, Karli, who had apparently been thinking thoughts of her own, turned to him and said, "Thanks again for the vest, Jake."

Startled, he turned to her and asked the question that had been bubbling in the back of his mind since he'd seen her scared face and heard her asking about vests. "Why weren't you wearing a vest, Karli? They're right there at the station, just for stories like this. And you may not realize it until you see the footage, but this was very nearly a trip to the shooting range."

"Didn't you bring it for me?" Karli asked, surprise in her eyes and her voice. "Isn't that what you put on me?"

"And if you didn't know about the station's vests, why didn't you ask the cops for one? They told you there were guns and that this was a big drug operation." Jake's voice grew more emphatic and stern: "Or did you think it was fine to get shot? Or did you think you would be safe on the sidelines wearing your photog's vest while he went into the building to get shot?"

"What?" Karli asked defensively, pulling at the vest's Velcro straps. "Are you saying you gave me *your* vest?"

"Which is better than that moron McMillian did," Jake said, his eyes flashing and his hands strangling the steering wheel. His fear for Karli's safety had come back to life, only now it was transformed into fury. "He crushes on you like he does every new face on the news, and he figures he'll make time by tipping the story to you. But does he ever consider that his gift of a tip might get you shot? Does he ever mention that a vest would be a good idea? No. Because he's a moron who thinks about everything only as it relates to his dick and whether he can get it serviced."

"This tip wasn't about McMillian having a crush on me, Jake," Karli said, shrugging out of the vest and dumping it on the seat between them. "He told me the police had been watching my stories and thought I could treat them fairly."

"That's completely bogus, Karli," Jake answered. "McMillian isn't connected with any police powers. Wasn't it obvious that he hadn't cleared the tip when the boss dude started chewing him out? He was just hoping to get in your good graces—and then into your pants."

Karli's mouth opened wider with each sentence, astonishment mixed with indignation on her face. "You pig!" she exclaimed. "Just because you're a photog who thinks with your dick, you think everyone else does, too. I'll have you know that Wil has been a gentleman to me, and there hasn't even been a hint of him trying to get into my pants."

"*I* think with *my* dick?" Jake turned his eyes from the road to glare hard at Karli, an odd and unaccustomed feeling of—what, jealousy?—focusing his eyes like lasers on Karli. "I've known your good friend Will since high school, and he has only ever talked to any woman because he wants her in the sack. But you know all about him from what, one in-person meeting, a phone call and an entire text message? Boy, you have read that guy's book cover-to-cover."

Jake swung his eyes in exasperation back to the road—just in time to see a cat run out into the street. He jerked the wheel and slammed on the brakes, squealing the tires, raising a cloud of stinky blue burnt-rubber smoke, and stalling the truck.

"Are you *crazy*?" Karli yelled, her eyes flashing with anger and fear. "It was just a cat, and you go screeching all over the road!"

The cat scrambled safely across the street. Jake laid his forehead on the arms he had crossed atop the steering wheel. He growled, "Shit!" through gritted teeth. He sucked in his next breath with a wet, shaking sound, then muttered down into his lap: "You're seriously telling me you want me to run over cats with my truck?"

"I don't want you to scare me like that!"

After another shaky inhalation, Jake raised his head from the wheel, started the engine again, shifted into gear, and began driving with hands at 10:00 and 2:00. He drove for a few minutes, listening to Karli's angry breathing gradually return to normal as her pen scratched in her notebook.

"I really wish I had the video of that cop trying to hassle you. My iPhone's battery was totally dead, though, so I didn't get a thing." Karli concluded in exasperation.

After a pause and more notebook-scratching she said, "It sucks that I couldn't do a stand-up while we were still there. Even five seconds of me in front of that house, explaining where it was or what they found there would've been a nice bridge between the amount seized and the actual raid, wouldn't it?"

Jake did not respond by word or gesture. He drove. Carefully.

"So I think we have to lead with the latest stuff. Vince or I will be able to call and get how many guys they arrested and how much heroin they found. You got video of the drugs and the guys coming out into the wagon, right?"

Jake nodded, but he said nothing. He continued cautiously driving.

"Maybe not, though. Didn't you say that there were a lot of guns in there? Maybe we should lead with video of the guns and drugs." Karli paused, chewing the end of her pen. "I wonder when the press conference will be. Either they'll have to get it in before noon today so we don't beat them and show that they're leaking, or they'll wait till tomorrow to see if we can get the rest of the story through the leak. Then they'll be able to fix the leak for next time." She turned to Jake. "Which do you think?"

Jake shrugged and drove, flicking his eyes from mirror to road and back.

Karli missed the shrug because she'd turned her attention to her backpack. She bent over to rummage through the bag, making frustrated sounds with each new grope into its dark depths. "I really need a diet Dew," she said, "and I thought I had one in here." She kept ineffectually pushing the same clutch purse and make-up kit around on the top of the bag's mounded contents. Then, finally, after picking the bag up into her lap, she stuck her arm deeply in. "Ooh, there it is," she cooed to herself, then dragged a diet Mountain Dew out from the bottom of the bag, gum wrappers and other backpack detritus stuck to its condensation-damp label. Jake watched out of the corner of his eye as she quickly wiped off the bits and flicked them mostly back into the bag. He saw that she disregarded the wet morsels of garbage that stuck to the Ranger's transmission hump as she twisted the top off the bottle and took a long, suction-y drink that pulled the bottle's sides in.

"That's better," she sighed. "Now, I'm thinking this should be a live-from-the-newsroom piece.

Do you think that would be better than on-set? That choice will be pretty important, because this could well be the piece that catches Chicago's eye. My reporting is going to be strong, and your pictures are going to make it sing if we can edit it well."

Jake shrugged again, unnoticed again, as Karli's eyes were back in her notebook. He kept driving to the station, at precisely the speed limit.

As they drew near to the station, Jake broke his silence: "I started this day with a single idea," he said, his eyes constantly roving in driver's ed textbook fashion. "I was going to make people safer today. I don't ever want to be responsible for someone being hurt again. Next time, buy a vest.

"And thanks for the saves. But I'm not sticking around to edit. Please tell Vince I'm not ready to come back yet. I'm sure you can talk Mary Rose into cutting the story together for you. She has great ideas and will do a super job."

Karli, who had been completely absorbed in developing her reporting ideas, looked up with delayed-response surprise. Seeing that Jake looked to be in earnest, she gazed searchingly into his eyes. Feeling the warm swell of tears begin, Jake looked away to pull into a spot, step on the parking brake, and turn the key off.

"Jake, what happened?" Karli asked, stuffing her notebook, pen, and iPhone into her pack quickly so she could keep talking as he got out to unload. "Why can't you come back to work? We're both fine, after all. And I need you."

At that last comment, Jake turned sharply to look back at Karli. "You can't need me..." he began, his throat feeling warm and husky.

"Yes," Karli interrupted, with a changed, businesslike tone to her voice. "I do. Without your video, I'm never going to get out of flyover country and into a real news market. I came here because there are supposed to be great shooters who can make my reporting come to life. But you're the only one here who has what it takes to really catch a major market's eye. So, yeah, I do need you."

Jake thought he had heard something else in her voice the first time. If Karli *really* needed him, he felt inadequate. He wasn't the kind of man who people could ever need. He couldn't be relied upon—well, he could: he reliably made dangerous choices. And that made a sore, scraping pain deep inside him. Karli was a dynamo, a real powerhouse, and she always seemed so close to having the kindness that he craved and couldn't deserve, but it was never directed at him. And then she would go all cold and career-bitchy on him, straight up announcing that she needed to *use* him instead of *needing* him.

As the thoughts raced through his head, she swung her pack onto a businesslike shoulder and reached out to take the equipment bag from Jake. He handed it over without a twitch. It looked like she really didn't need him, she really did just want to use him.

"Look," he said, heaving a deep, shaky breath, "it isn't like I need the job." He paused. "Tell Vince I'll talk to him tomorrow." With that, he climbed back into the truck, closed his door, and pulled away from the station. And from Karli.

He couldn't quite hear her over the truck's engine, but her lips were easy enough to read: "Asshole."

Chapter Eleven

Des Moines, Iowa
Tuesday, October 15
6:00 p.m.

Stu Heintz, the rookie weekend anchorman, took the news, and himself, very seriously. As the opening credits and music faded to a head-and-shoulders shot of him on the news set, he looked into the teleprompter mounted to the studio camera's lens and read the words scrolling up the display with a gleaming eye. "Tonight, an exclusive report on one of the largest heroin busts in Des Moines history. Three NewsFirst's Karli Lewis was on the scene with photographer Jake Gibson, where they followed the police into an eastern Des Moines residence where the drugs were being processed. Karli joins us now, live from the newsroom, with the story. Karli?"

Karli heard Chuck in her earpiece, telling her to stand by, telling the sound engineer to open her microphone, and calling for the technical director to cut to her camera in the newsroom. From beside the camera, Mary Rose pointed at her. Karli looked earnestly into the camera and began her report, catching Mary Rose's smiling thumbs-up: "The more than 1,000 pounds of heroin seized in eastern Des Moines today would have found their way across the midwest, police are saying. The search warrant served this morning yielded more than the heroin, too. Thirteen men were arrested at the scene, and police seized more than a dozen guns as well as about $24,000 in cash and relatively small amounts of marijuana and other drugs.

"Police say that they knew something big was going on in the quiet neighborhood house because there was so much traffic in and out. But they didn't expect to find as much as the roughly $30,000,000 worth of heroin that was wrapped onto forklift pallets."

As Karli finished her live introduction, she heard Chuck call for the package to roll, then for the cut to the recorded part of her story.

It opened with Jake's tense action video of the stun grenades shaking the house. In a continuous take, Jake's camera swung to the cops smashing the door down. As Karli's recorded narration went on to detail the scope of the bust, the video rolled mostly as Jake had shot it, with the audio of officers shouting with bleeped-out expletives coming up full volume between Karli's sentences.

Once the figures and likely drug cartel relationships had been spelled out by Karli's narration and sound bites from law enforcement, the video ended and Karli heard Chuck cue her back live. "Each of the thirteen suspects arrested at the scene will have their first appearances in Polk County District Court within 48 hours. Law enforcement personnel told me on condition of anonymity that all of those cases will likely be transferred to the United States District Court for the Southern District of Iowa—where the criminal penalties can be much more severe—within the next few weeks.

"Three NewsFirst is planning a series of reports over the coming weeks detailing the heroin trade in central Iowa and beyond." She had gotten Jerry, Holly, and Vince to all agree to the series this afternoon. "Up next week: a heroin dealer sold drugs to a customer who overdosed. Is it right to charge the dealer with murder? Join us for that story, for follow-up on the repercussions of today's bust, and much more."

Karli's voice dipped to indicate that the story was over as she signed off, "Live, from the Three NewsFirst newsdesk, I'm Karli Lewis. Stu?"

"Riveting video, Karli," Stu fairly crooned into the camera. "Great work by you and Three NewsFirst photographer Jake Gibson, with an exclusive on the largest Iowa drug bust in years."

Karli heard Stu go on to thank her for the report and heard Chuck call for her mic to be closed. She took her earpiece out and sighed with relief as Mary Rose switched off the portable lights that had been trained on her at her desk.

"Thank you, Mary Rose, for the editing and the lighting in here and everything. You did a great job with all of it."

"Hey, no worries, Karli," said Mary Rose, running her hands back through her blended blue and pink hair. "You wrote a great story, tailored right to that video and audio—it was easy-peasy. And Jake kicked ass, didn't he?"

Karli was grateful for Mary Rose's easy-going response. The day had been so fraught with different, intense emotions that she didn't think she could've handled one more temperamental coworker. Not only had Jake gone bonkers on her right after the bust, she'd had to coax her news director, producer, and assignment editor into letting her do the follow-up series of reports. Which was crazy, since she had enterprised the whole thing, doing preliminary research on drug-induced homicide, cartels in the midwest, addiction rates, and overdose deaths all in addition to the story and all in a single day.

Well, whatever. This was going to be the series that busted her out of Des Moines and into a real market. She had thought deeply about it, and the stories had all the ingredients: her writing and Jake's shooting would bring out all the sweeping effects and deep public interest in the state's—*no, the region's*—drug problem, as well as the effects that almost certainly were felt as far away as, say, Chicago. Karli knew where this was headed: straight to a major market.

Karli spent the rest of the newscast going over the printouts of her research and her handwritten notes, making to-do lists and outlines for the upcoming series. As she was wrapping up her work for the day and putting her papers in a folder to be organized later, the newscast ended.

"What the hell do you think you're up to?" Sophia Refai's deeply feminine voice rolled across the newsroom like autumn thunder. Karli saw the lean, dark figure striding across the room toward her with less of Sophia's usual runway-model's stride and more the march of a uniformed officer about to enforce the law.

Oh, no, thought Karli. *I'd forgotten about this angle.* She looked around, as though the question must have been directed to someone else. But there was nobody else in the newsroom.

"Yes, you, Karli Lewis. The police beat is MY beat, and I do not appreciate you elbowing your way onto my turf," Sophia said. Karli could tell that the anchor was only barely in control of her anger. "And I'm glad you've started the background on the series. Your research will come in handy as I report those stories."

Karli was taken aback to see Sophia's elegantly manicured hand outstretched, palm up, waiting to receive her notes and research. "You can't have this stuff," Karli gulped. "This is my work.

And Jerry already assigned the series to me." Karli slid the folder between the chair seat and her rear end, then leaned back and folded her arms.

"We will see who gets the series. But I warn you, stay off my beat, or life here will become very difficult for you." Sophia turned and marched back to the news set to record the evening's promos to air during prime-time commercial breaks for the 10 o'clock show. Mary Rose, returning to the newsroom after putting away the camera and light kit, turned to watch the pacing fury, then turned back to Karli with her eyebrows raised in unspoken question.

"Just a little jealous that I covered a police story without her permission," Karli said in answer to Mary Rose's eyebrows.

"Just a little?" Mary Rose asked. "That's enough that I'd change all my passwords and lock my desk if she was stomping around pissed at me like that."

Not wanting to show that she'd been intimidated by the anchor's fury, but grateful for the suggestion, Karli began clicking and typing to change her login password. She looked up at Mary Rose while she was making sure she could remember the new password and said, "I'd invite you out for a drink to celebrate the story, but I have to get my hair done. Maybe tomorrow?"

"That would be fun," Mary Rose said, grinning while holding her lip-ring between her teeth. After a pause, she let go and said, "I really enjoyed working with you on the edit today and that animation a while ago. I'd like to do more stuff like that, but they always have me stuck in the studio or the control room. Let's try for tomorrow."

"Great," said Karli, gathering her notes and purse and phone and stuffing them into her pack. "See you then." And she grabbed her diet Dew and headed for the door before Sophia could come back off the set.

Once in her car, Karli's day came rushing back at her. Jake had been such a hero this morning, coming back to work from leave to shoot amazing video for her. And he had put his vest on her before the action started. The video was exciting for her professionally: it was the kind of footage that could make major-market news directors sit up and pay attention, and it had obviously paved the way for her to get approval for the heroin series. The thought of the series revved her reporter's motor and just had to be the fast way to a major market reporting job. It was exactly the kind of hard-hitting news that great careers were built on. If she could get someone to shoot video and edit the pieces as well as she was going to research and write them, there was every chance that the series would propel her to a genuinely good job in a real market.

But Jake was the only reliably great shooter and editor on staff, and he had gone all weird on her. Karli remembered the first encounter with the boss cop in the morning, and how very hostile he had been. Jake's hands had been so strong and supportive when he'd strapped her into the vest right afterward that it felt almost as though he had caught her from a faint and lifted her into the vest. She had watched his soft brown curls wave around just under her chin as he'd checked the fastenings, and the wind had tossed them ever so slightly. That spicy smell, with maybe some vanilla mixed in, had wafted into her nose, too.

The memory of it caused her eyes to close and her head to tilt back to better re-live the sensation. With a quiet shudder, she realized that the day's fatigue had made her unusually susceptible to sensations that she was usually too busy and preoccupied to give any attention at all. Jake's scent hadn't made any impression on her during the frantic action of the drug bust, but the memory of it came on with a rush.

But he's such an asshole. He does all this great work and he looks like the regional representative for P90X and he smells like men's magazines want to smell...and then he ditches me.

AGAIN.

And leaves me hanging out to dry with another HUGE story.

AGAIN.

He. Is. An. Ass. Hole.

Chapter Twelve

As Karli walked from her car to Trevor's salon, she saw him recognize her through the window, give her a broad grin and wave, and practically skip to the employees-only door in back. After the stunning young receptionist had checked her name off the appointment book and walked her back to the chair, Trevor emerged from the back with clinking glasses in one hand and a foil-topped green bottle in the other. He set the flutes down at his station and began exposing the cork's basket. "I know you just got off work and haven't been to the gym yet, but Bailey was in at 5:00, and she said you scooped 'em all today, so it's time to celebrate." He eased the cork out with a small pop and a wisp of cold gas.

Startled at the champagne treatment, Karli stuttered, "Trevor, you know I'm not much for drinking—and I'm going to the gym right after we're done here."

"Correction, Karli: you *were* going to the gym. Your plans have changed." Trevor's eyes twinkled with a giddy, conspiratorial light. "Tonight you are going to savor your victory and tell me all about *every*thing." He handed her a full flute of champagne and raised his own to her before taking a sip and smacking his lips.

"There's nothing to tell about *any*thing, you goon." Karli chuckled with warmth at the realization that Trevor really appreciated her and was kind enough to want to celebrate her accomplishment.

She took a sip of the champagne, at first reflexively in response to Trevor's silent toast, then more deeply because the drily fruity wine was so much better than she'd expected. "I got a good tip," she said, "and we went out and covered the bust, then I did the follow-up work, then I did the live shot from ten feet away. Ta-da! No biggie."

"I know about the live shot—I actually watched the news tonight after Bailey told me to. You were great. And she says nobody else had video of the bust. That was exciting stuff. Did Mr. Hot do that for you?"

"He didn't do it *for me*, Trevor. It's his job to take pictures." Karli realized that she was implicitly agreeing that Jake Gibson was, in fact, Mr. Hot. *Oops.*

"But he hasn't been to work in ages, has he? Didn't he come back just to shoot that story for you?"

"Of course not, Trevor." Then Karli realized she wasn't being entirely truthful. "Well, I did ask Vince to get him in, but that was for the *story*, not for *me*." Even this, Karli knew as soon as the words were out of her mouth that she still wasn't telling the whole truth. "Well," she started again, determined this time to get it right, "I asked Vince to get Jake in to shoot this story so I could have it on my reel. The other shooters aren't as consistently awesome as he is."

"So he *did* come back just for you—I knew it!"

Oh. My. God. Karli thought to herself, hiding a surprised smile behind another sip of champagne. Champagne that was beginning to have, she noticed, a warmly dizzying effect. And the warmth increased as she finished her first thought: *He came back to shoot for me.*

Her iPhone buzzed: another text from her father. "Some of the BMOCs from your high school were at the golf outing yesterday— all out of law school or MBAs by now. All I had to do was mention your name and they were standing straighter and looking like the girls still in town could wait." She shook her head in disgust and clicked the phone back to sleep.

"Anyway," she said aloud, trying to get Trevor off the Mr. Hot subject (*How many nicknames is this guy going to have?*), "the story sets up a whole series on the heroin trade around here that I'm going to do during ratings sweeps next month. I've already started the background work, and it's going to be awesome." *Hold it, Karli!* she thought to herself, suddenly suspicious of the various warm feelings brought on by champagne and the thought that Jake had done the story especially for her. *Do I have some obligation to Jake because he* condescended *to shoot my story? Am I supposed to be all ready to sex it up with him, like Trevor seems to think, just because he* did his job *and took pictures?*

"Yeah, yeah," Trevor's voice cut off her grouchy line of thinking, and she brought her eyes back from the indefinite distance to see him deftly topping up her flute. "Tell me about today's story. It looked *scary* on TV. What was it really like?"

"It was scary, Trevor." Karli closed her eyes and thought back to the morning's excitement. It was hard to believe that the long day's deadline pressures had pushed the morning's adrenaline-laced events nearly out of her memory. "The stun grenades and guns and doors crashing down and the shouting and shoving and stuff— that was crazy, and it happened so fast and furious.

"But that was so scary it was surreal, like an action movie come to life, you know?" Karli paused, recalling all the adrenaline that had crashed through her system during the bust. "And the boss of the cops—even he was scary. He tried to kick us out of the neighborhood, he tried to arrest Jake, and he tried to bully me. But he wasn't all that. He folded when I called his bluff." Like a video replaying in her head, the scenes with the In-Charge Man played back through Karli's memory. *Jake even took his Kevlar vest off and put it on me when I was talking to that man. That was dumb. He was about to launch into that bust, and he stopped to put his Kevlar on me. Why would he be so stupid?*

After a longish pause while Karli went back over the morning's excitement, she looked into Trevor's kind eyes, paused, swallowed deeply, and said, "Jake took off his bulletproof vest and put it on me. That may have been the scariest thing that happened all morning, and I didn't even know about it until we were on our way back to the station. I thought he'd brought a vest for me."

Trevor's face gaped in surprise. "Wow. He really gave you his bulletproof vest? That's serious, Karli. That's really a serious thing, isn't it?" Then Trevor's eyes flashed with realization: "So all those pictures of guns and drugs and cops drawing down on the guys—he shot all of that without a vest on? Inside the house and everything? Or did he put it on you after that?"

Smirking to herself, Karli thumbed her iPhone back to life and quickly tapped out a message to her father: "The men here have walked in front of loaded guns for me, just lately."

"No, it was before he went in." Karli took another deep drink from her flute. She really wasn't going to go to the gym tonight after all this wine. "And I don't know whether to feel contempt because he was so stupid or to feel like he's some kind of modern-day knight in shining armor. I hate feeling stupid for not asking about vests beforehand and then showing up all clueless and damsel-in-distress."

"*Contempt?*" Trevor shrieked. "He was ready to lay his life down for you and you're turning your straight little nose up at him because he was being stupid? You really have no appreciation for what that means, do you?"

Surprised and feeling on the defensive because she hadn't expected that reaction from Trevor, Karli tried to backpedal. "Not contempt, Trevor, not really. But it wasn't the brightest move, after all, was it?"

Trevor's mouth opened and shut like an aquarium fish's. After a few seconds, he evidently decided that saying nothing was better than saying anything, so he put his glass up to his mouth by way of filling it with something other than the words that wouldn't come.

Karli watched and tried to get hold of her racing emotions. *He came back just for me, and he gave me his vest, and that probably makes him a real hero.*

Trevor had evidently given up on the conversation, as he had set down his glass and began wrapping a cape around Karli in preparation for her trim. While he busied himself with brushing out and oiling a clipper, she emptied her glass with a long, steady series of swallows. She took a hard look at herself in the mirror. *Why is contempt so much more convenient?*

Her phone alerted again: "Rational men play on the golf course, not in front of loaded guns."

Chapter Thirteen

Three NewsFirst Six O'Clock News broadcast
Coda Lounge, Savery Hotel
Saturday, November 16

The monitor over the bar showed Stu Heintz's eyebrows riding
high on his heavily made-up forehead. "That's all coming in the next
week, Sophia?" he asked, his thin baritone betraying genuine
surprise. "I'm sure everyone in the Three NewsFirst viewing
audience will be tuned in for your series. Heroin throughout Iowa—
that's a story that has been under-covered for some time, and I for
one had no idea how far-reaching the drug's effects have become.
Where will you be for your report on Three NewsFirst's six o'clock
news on Monday?"

The director cut from the two-shot of Stu and Sophia on set to a
head-and-shoulders shot of Sophia, who answered, "We're starting
at the end, where there's some hope about heroin. A federal judge
recently decided not to send Latrece Robinson to prison, even
though she had pled guilty to selling heroin. Between the time she
was first charged and the date of her sentencing two weeks ago, she
had turned her life around. She not only sought treatment to beat her
addiction, she got a full-time job doing honest work. She also
volunteered in a number of treatment centers, where she told other
addicts about the hope she has found. We'll meet Latrece and some
of the people she is trying to help up and out of addiction. And we
will hear what the federal judge had to say at her sentencing."

Karli turned her face from the television over the bar at the Coda
Lounge and furiously hissed to Bailey Barber, who sat on the bar
stool next to her, and Mary Rose Mayer, who sat on her other side.
"That's all *my* work. I found her before the judge ever made her an
easy story!" She lifted a full glass to her lips and drank deeply.

"Everyone who matters knows who did the work, Karli. Jerry,

Vince, Holly—they all know," Bailey replied.

"They don't matter!" Karli shrilled. "The news directors at the networks matter. The news directors in Chicago and New York and San Francisco matter. Jerry, Vince and Holly *do not matter.*"

"Karli, get some perspective, girl," Bailey said in tones of patience tried. "You haven't even been in Des Moines six months yet. Don't you think it's a little soon to anticipate your meteoric rise to a top market?"

Mary Rose raised a significant eyebrow to the vigilant bartender, then indicated toward Karli with a slight tip of her head. He reached for bottles and began dispensing more of the evening's remedy.

"Are you saying it's too soon to be ambitious? Or that I'm too wet behind the ears? Or that I'm not good enough? Or what?" Torn between anger and frustration and humiliation, Karli reached for her half-empty glass, drained it, and set it down with a little more emphasis than she'd planned. Prepared for all contingencies, the consummately competent bartender placed a fresh drink in front of Karli while effortlessly swiping a bar towel around the spilled ice cubes and taking the empty away.

"Chillax, girl," Mary Rose said with a chuckle. "It's some news, that's all. It'll be broadcast and then evaporate from the airwaves and our viewers' heads just like everything else we put on the air. There will always be more news—we fill a whole bunch of half-hour shows with it every day, you know." Mary Rose tossed back her shot of tequila, paused to sniff a moment as its heat spread down her throat, then reached for a cooling sip of beer.

Bailey had been watching Karli's dismissive shrug in response to Mary Rose's pep talk. "Look, I'm not saying you have to resign yourself to an entire career in this market," she began. "I'm not even saying that you should change your license plates—though it looks like your Florida plate is about to expire."

"Yeah, so you'd better move back to—where was it, Palm Beach?—soon," Mary Rose quipped, punching Karli's shoulder gently. "Or you're going to be stuck here like Bailey and me, with no future and nothing to live for."

"We're just saying that losing this heroin series isn't a career-shaping thing," Bailey continued, glaring at Mary Rose for her unhelpful interruption. "You'll find the right stories to propel you out of here. It is a good series, sure, but it is pretty meat-and-potatoes, don't you think? It doesn't require much in the way of investigative chops. It's just basic research and working cop sources. That recovered addict story is the only human part of the whole series. Not only did Sophia not do the work to develop that story, she didn't even want to keep it in when they gave it all to her. Jerry had to *make* her lead with it.

"If that series took you somewhere, you wouldn't want to be the reporter they hired once you get there. Sophia could be a solid police-beat reporter in any market, and this series sets *that* table perfectly.

"But you're the reporter who has a Midas touch with interviews. Who finds the only hopeful human angle on a heroin series? Karli. Grieving parents won't talk to anyone? Put Karli on it. Scared-to-get-involved lady saw the accident? No worries, Karli can have a nice quiet visit with her and she'll spill it all. Or how about this one—the biggest ram winner at the State Fair is a super-boring annual, but Karli gets the winner to crack wise about sheep sex."

Mary Rose smirked at this last example. "And you do know that sheep sex is the gold standard for Pulitzers and Emmys and stuff, right?"

At this, Bailey reached all the way around behind Karli to poke Mary Rose in the side as she picked up the thread of her thought. "You do not want to be the reporter who spends her career riding around in squad cars, hanging out in courthouses and trying to convince prosecutors to talk to you. Those stories aren't about people or about hope; there's nothing human about them except victims who can't or won't talk. You are not that reporter, and you shouldn't be moaning about missing the chance to saddle yourself with that career. The reporter you want to be at your next job is the one who breaks stories because she can convince people to talk about their lives."

Karli drained her glass with a thoughtful expression and considered Bailey's assessment. When she spoke, her words' edges were softened by the liquor. "There's a lot to what you say, Bailey. But it's still complete bullshit that Sophia has this series and I don't, and I want to be pissed about that right now."

"Yes!" Mary Rose cried, raising her beer glass. "Let's hate Sophia!" She brought the beer to her lips and drank deeply. "She's a snooty bitch anyway, regardless of this series thing," she whispered to Bailey and Karli.

"That's not terribly constructive, you know," Bailey chided. "So what's up with Jake and the kissing?" she said, shifting the subject abruptly. "Any news about that?"

"He hasn't even been to work in forever," Karli slurred. "How'm I supposed to kiss him if he's never around?"

Mary Rose, who had not heard about Jake and the kissing, goggled at her friends, her open-mouth and bugged eyes flicking from one to the other, looking for answers to obvious questions. "Jake and the Kissing? That sounds like a great band, but it also sounds like something I need desperately to hear about. When did you and Jake start in with the kissing? He has never even hinted that you guys were getting wild and nasty! And besides, Sophia wants him even more than she wants your series. I'm surprised she didn't slink that exotic figure into the kissing a long time ago!"

"Mary Rose, no. Just no. We never kissed at all," Karli said, defensiveness in every syllable. "And besides, he's a complete asshole."

"Then what's with the new band?" Mary Rose's face was covered with suspicion, as was the tone of her voice.

"It was just a thing," Karli sighed. "We watched a movie together, and then there was this moment when it seemed like we were going to kiss, but then it all went bust. So no kissing."

Bailey saw that Karli needed rescuing, so she chimed in with, "So what happened when he came back for the drug bust story? He didn't even stick around to edit that package, did he?"

Mary Rose cut in ahead of Karli's response: "No way Jose—or Josephine, I guess, since you're a chick—he split and then I cut it together, and I did an awesome job, too, I might add."

"And you're fun to work with, Mary Rose" Karli added. "But why again won't they assign you to field shooting—because of some departmental accounting thing?"

"Yeah, Mary Rose's great," Bailey seconded enthusiastically. "But what scared him away that day?" Bailey asked. "Everyone has been wondering, but Vince just says to shut up and tend to our own knitting."

"I don't know," Karli very nearly whined. "We had a scary morning, yet things seemed kind of normal when we headed out. Then he got all emo in the truck. He talked about not needing the job and not being able to keep people safe or make good decisions or something. He was all pissed about giving me his Kevlar vest, too, like it was some cop's fault, and I couldn't understand what the problem was there, either. I was trying to thank him for giving it to me, but it all blew up and went weird. It was like having a conversation with a mentally ill person."

"This is AWESOME!" Mary Rose boomed. She raised her beer and solemnly intoned,

"Here's to hating Sophia and to bullying Jake for being demented!" She chugged the beer, heedless of the scandalized looks on Karli and Bailey's faces.

Bailey looked thoughtfully at the new drinks the bartender brought upon seeing Mary Rose's glass lifted and then moved her eyes to Karli's face. "Hasn't anyone told you why he was on leave in the first place?" she asked so quietly that Karli turned her face and her full attention toward her. Meeting Bailey's strange look of sad compassion, Karli shook her head slowly. Bailey spoke with obvious effort. "Jake was very close to the boy who died on that bicycle. And Vince pumped some info out of the boy's school teacher. It turns out Jake was the kid's surrogate father: he paid for the kid's braces without the boy ever knowing; he took him to karate tournaments just about every weekend; and he really encouraged him to get that paper route. So it seems Jake is feeling guilty for the boy dying doing something he told him to do."

"Hold it, Jake not only knew that boy, he was like a big brother or a father to him?" Karli's astonishment transformed her sulkily drunk face into an alert picture of concern. Her heart sank.

"Yes," Bailey continued. "And he really doesn't need this job, so there's no big reason for him to come back. His father was a hot-shot exec at one of the big insurance companies in town, and he died a few years ago with enough life insurance in force to fund the economy of, say, Nicaragua. Jake and his mother were both beneficiaries, so they're both central-American-dictator rich now."

"But he isn't rich. He's a photog, for heaven's sake. And he drives a crappy pickup."

"Correction: He doesn't *live* rich. He lives like a photo-journalist. His mother and uncle and their parents were all part of a journalism dynasty at the Des Moines Register. Whether he acknowledges it or not, he is carrying on a long family journalism tradition. But that doesn't mean he isn't rich."

"Let me get this one more time: Jake Gibson is not only rich, he was also a surrogate father to that poor boy who was killed on his paper route? Really?" Karli was so astonished she slipped sideways half off her bar stool. Only the spike heel hooked over the foot-rail gave her enough leverage to keep from falling off entirely.

"And he's the one who you were almost doing the kissing with. Feeling any differently about that now?" Bailey couldn't resist needling Karli in her astonished state.

"Oh, Bailey, that's not it," Karli protested. "Or at least that isn't all of it." She looked thoughtful for a second, then went on. "I mean, he's all spicy-smelling and gorgeous and everything, yeah. But how am I going to get him to come back to work? I need him to come back."

"Whoa!" Mary Rose cried, her shot glass frozen in place, halfway to her mouth. "Spicy kissing? What's going on here? I ask about kissing and you say there's nothing, then you sound like there's really a lot of something. Do you need him to come back to work for the kissing or the shooting—and by that I mean video? Because even Max's video—well, let's just say that there isn't a turd that I can't polish up in post."

"Mary Rose, all the polishing in the world isn't going to make a story look as good as Jake's field footage will," Karli said. "And I mean no offense to you when I say that. You really are a whiz in the edit booth.

But I need Jake's work in the field if I'm going to have any chance at building a decent resume reel. And the fact that he moves like a panther and is a humanitarian and filthy rich and surrogate father to the needy and probably a fitness model have nothing to do with anything."

"So it really is all about you," Bailey's tone carried all the teasing exasperation that she tried to show with her granite-solid shoulders and stern gaze. "What a disappointment."

"No, that's not it, really!" Karli was alarmed at Bailey's apparent judgment. "I need to talk to him about that bulletproof vest—to say I'm sorry for being a pill about it and to thank him for caring so much. Trevor was pretty gentle about it, but he made it pretty clear that I was being a defensive bitch about the whole thing. It's a lot easier to be angry at someone than it is to be grateful, especially when being grateful means admitting that I was not as bright as I thought I was. If I'd thought about it for even a second, I would've thought to bring my own bulletproof vest. But I wasn't smart enough to do that, and that made me angry. So I was bitchy to Jake about all of it."

Bailey's eyebrows had climbed most of the way to her hairline from their former stern, straight line. "Is this the Karli who was just calling Jake *emo*?"

"Oh, heck yeah," Mary Rose was practically cheering. She raised her beer glass again, this time gesturing to the bartender that he should join in the toast at her expense. "Let's all bring the hate for Sophia, *and* push Jake around for being demented, *and* live a rich fantasy life about sexing with Jake, *and* under-appreciate Mary Rose the super-genius. Ladies and gentlemen, be upstanding for all of that shit!"

And with that, Mary Rose crashed her glass against the bartender's and chugged it all down.

As the Mary Rose show played out to appreciative grins from the bartender, Karli looked Bailey in the eye and protested, "I didn't know anything about him feeling guilty about that boy or about Jake not needing to work or anything like that."

Bailey regarded Karli for a moment. Then she smirked and asked, "So does this mean that you're interested in the kissing again?"

Mary Rose heard that, lifted her shot glass and practically shouted, "*And* to the kissing!" After she'd tossed the tequila back, she leaned in close to Karli and demanded, "You *are* still interested in the kissing, right?"

"Oh, jeez. I'm interested in the kissing. Of course I am. He's gorgeous. He's brilliant." Karli's gaze drifted off for a moment as she took a deep breath in through her nose. "But I thought he was complicated before all the stuff you just told me. I so don't need to get tangled up with anyone complicated. Especially his kind of complicated."

Chapter Fourteen

Three NewsFirst newsroom
Friday, November 22

John Bielfeldt's mildly bloodshot blue eyes scanned the assembled newsroom and production staff. Betraying no sense of urgency, he cleaned his glasses with the necktie that hung over his stiffly starched white shirt. "John is going to help us solidify our number one position in the ratings this month," said Station Manager Larry Norwich, "and he's going to help us prepare for the huge push we anticipate our competition will make for the February ratings sweeps."

John put his glasses back on and deliberately turned his—and presumably the staff's—attention to Larry Norwich, the startlingly short station manager. Norwich was standing on the first step up to the news set's riser so he could see faces past the first row while squeaking out his speech. On John's other side, news director Jerry Schultz's anxious smile twitched above the pinstripe suit he had bought thirty pounds ago. The slightly pilled collar on his broadcast-blue shirt further betrayed his effort to look fully management for the occasion.

Karli's sharp elbow in his ribs made Jake aware that he had rolled his eyes a little too obviously. She watched his hair swirl bounce as he twitched in response to her digging. "What was that for?" he hissed into her ear. His soft breath made Karli's spine tingle.

"This consultant is going to make us winners, you knucklehead," Karli whispered back, her hand on his muscled shoulder and her mouth close to his ear, where the spicy smell of him and his soft curls both tickled her nose. "Haven't you been listening?"

Karli felt Jake's hand reach around behind her to rest between her shoulder blades so he could lean in and whisper back: "This isn't his first time here, you know—and he isn't the first consultant to promise us big ratings. Besides, we have been first in every sweep for the last four years." Karli bridled at his unenthusiastic response but felt a quickening excitement at his touch.

"Well, I want to hear what he has to say," Karli whispered back, leaning in to enjoy the touch and smell and intimacy of him. "I think he'll be able to help me make an escape reel."

Bielfeldt was talking now, and they both turned to pay attention—though Karli's hand stayed on Jake's shoulder. "We're going to be working on the newscast's overall look and sound this year," he said. "That means we're going to look at the entire visual presentation of the station and the newsroom. The set, the graphics, the clothes, the hair, the makeup, the photography—they're all in play."

As he listed each visual element, the reactions betrayed individuals' anxieties. Stu Heintz lifted a hand unconsciously to his product-laden hair. Mary Rose glanced at the huge, stylized numeral 3 on the wall and squinted as if to see it in a different guise. Max looked nervously first to Mary Rose Devlin, the workhorse chief photographer, then to Jake, gauging their reactions to the consultant's comment about photography.

The consultant continued: "We've made appointments for each of the on-air talent. You'll be meeting with clothing and makeup experts. You'll get swatches and colors that we want you to use your clothing allowance for. Everyone's look is going to be freshened and compatible."

Arthur's voice rumbled its interruption: "Is anyone's job at stake this time, John?" The question prompted a host of murmurs from the assembled staff—he had asked the question that was on everyone's mind. *Ballsy* was the word most overheard; nobody else had Arthur's long tenure, nor his ability to walk off the job and into retirement at a moment's notice. And some of the employees recalled Bielfeldt's role seven or eight years ago in cutting nearly half of the newsroom personnel in a single month.

"Everyone in this business has to prove their worth every day, Arthur. You're each only as good as your last broadcast. You know that," Bielfeldt said, looking Arthur in the eye. "But I am not aware of any planned reduction in force, if that's what you're asking.

"Back on task, though. If this newsroom wants to consolidate and build upon its strength as a number one, the overall visual presentation—and each visual element within it—needs to be *inspirational.* So I'll be working with groups and individuals this week to develop some concrete skills on how to inspire viewers with your visuals. I look forward to working with all of you, especially people I've not met before."

Bielfeldt's mouth creased into a smile that reached nearly to the edges of his eyes. He held the insincere grin for a deliberate moment during which he looked pointedly at Karli, then turned to Norwich, who looked relieved to have an excuse to leave. Nodding and smiling his salesman's smile, Norwich led Bielfeldt out of the newsroom and toward the business side of the building. As the backs of their business suits retreated from the room, an energetic hubbub of conversations rose with increasing volume as the distance to the suits increased.

"Hey, everyone," Vince's smoky voice worked its way above the bubbling froth of conversation. "We have a newscast to put on the air in about three hours. Don't you have things that need doing?"

With varying degrees of resentment, folks returned to their tasks, though some isolated conversations persisted. Among them were Jake and Karli's. "I'm so glad you're back for this," Karli was saying, her hand again on his shoulder and her eyes glistening with interest. "Lots of my old friends have told me about consultants at their stations, and they mostly sound like they've learned a lot of cool stuff."

"I did not come back so I could waste hours of my life listening to Bielfeldt," Jake responded. "The guy shows up with yet another fashion trend every time he sets foot here, and none of it makes any real difference in how we cover the news."

"Whatever the reason, Jake, I'm really glad you decided to come back," Karli said, her flattened hand moving in circles over Jake's muscled back. "But you've never said why. Do you mind if I ask?"

Karli felt a surprising hand on her shoulder just as she finished her question, then a familiar gravelly smoker's voice spoke. "He came back because we need him. That's all we really need to know, kid. He's the best shooter in the shop." Karli turned to see Vince's warm eyes and gentle smile taking in both her and Jake. "And now that we're going to be working on the entire, *inspirational,* visual presentation of the station, we need the vision man more than ever."

Wondering if he was merely deflecting the question or if he was sincere, Karli raised questioning eyebrows and looked at Jake.

A light flickered somewhere behind Jake's eyes and vanished before Karli could find its meaning.

"I suppose I'm coming back partly just to prove to myself that I can," he said at length. "They say that a man isn't measured when he has fallen. It's when he gets back up that you learn his worth."

"But you were never fallen, were you?" Karli asked, looking earnestly into his face, then glancing at Vince for some kind of confirmation. "I mean, it was hard to cover that boy's story, but you shot the best video of the year that day. Even before you knew who it was, your pictures were the most emotional, memorable images I'd ever seen."

"Karli, I'm still trying to get back up," Jake said, his voice so calm and soft that she barely heard him.

"Of course that was the best video you've ever seen," Vince interjected, now gripping Jake's shoulder with nicotine-stained fingers. "Jake here is one of the best ever to shoulder a camera. The bigs are always telling us he needs to make a big move, like to a Sunday-morning network magazine show or something."

Jake looked gratefully up at Vince. "You're a good brand manager, Vince. But you of all people know that I couldn't ever fit in at those big shops. This is home, not New York or wherever. I like to be part of the entire, you know, *inspirational* story-telling process." He smirked at his use of the consultant's term and winked at Vince to make sure he was in on the snarky comment.

"Sure, kid. It's home, and you can't leave, right?" Vince teased. Then he made a show of shooing both of them out of the newsroom. "Go cover a story already, okay? I'm going out to smoke, and I can't be in here to make sure you don't trip over a suit on your way out."

Karli and Jake grabbed their gear, walked outside past Vince's smoking station, and piled into a news car where Karli picked up the conversation's thread.

"Apparently you're not into being part of the entire inspirational process when it's a story I'm reporting," Karli started, bitterness flowing from each syllable. "I get that you're good, Jake, but I don't get what I did to piss you off so badly. I get that covering that boy's story was hard on you—though I would've been grateful if you'd said something that day instead of just leaving without a word before the story was even ready to edit. I truly do understand that it must've been terrible to take all those pictures and then find out that it was your kid who'd been killed." Having run out of breath, Karli had to pause just long enough to inhale.

"But then you came back, and the same thing happened all over again," she continued. "You went out with me to the bust, shot some of the best spot news video of the year, and then ditched me before I'd even started writing." Karli's tone and furrowed brow showed her confusion and hurt. "So it must be me."

Jake had been stealing glances from the road to look into Karli's eyes during her entire speech. As she finished, he looked down the road briefly and then back to meet her with a steady, pained gaze. "The only thing about you that made me want to be away was fear of falling short in your eyes," he said, reaching out tentatively and touching her hand lightly before drawing it back. "But I can tell you that being back and working with you makes me hope that I'll make it back to upright."

Karli's eyes filled with mixed astonishment and confusion.

After a long silence during which her mouth opened and closed soundlessly several times, she blurted, "What?"

"Bielfeldt talks about inspiration like it's something new, Karli, but it isn't. Working with a reporter who is as interested in people and their stories as you are is an inspiration to me. In the field, when we're working on a story, you're over yourself the instant you start an interview, every time. You care about people's stories. And you tell their stories with a commitment to understanding. That's what I've always tried to do with my camera. Working with you challenges me to capture images with that same depth of understanding."

"So you aren't pissed at me for being bitchy about the vest?"

"Of course not!" It was Jake's turn to be astonished. "I was angry at Will for not giving you a vest and scared that you hadn't thought to get one for yourself. How could I be pissed at you? All I wanted to do was to keep you safe."

"Well I still feel terrible about not knowing what was going on with that boy..." Karli's voice trailed off into silence.

Jake's eyes filled with fresh pain. "I failed him," he said in tones of finality.

"That asshole who was texting is the one who failed," Karli

replied fiercely. "There was no way you could've known that some moron would do something that stupid. And you certainly didn't do like the municipal engineer and design that street to be deadly."

Jake's face was as unresponsive as granite. Karli could have addressed her comments to the faces in Mount Rushmore and gotten a bigger reaction. She could tell she'd gotten as far as this line would get her. It was time to change her tack.

"Vince needs me to advance the grand opening of the Winterset community theater's new space tomorrow," Karli said, checking her iPhone for notes and directions. "Why don't you drive out there with me and take some pretty pictures?"

Jake looked hard at Karli, his eyes giving nothing away. He slowly nodded and started the news car, pulling out of the parking spot in silence, the light snow that had fallen overnight dusting around the edges of the lot. Jake squinted at the grey sky's smooth ceiling and looked out to check for any kind of shadow at all. "I'm glad it'll be interiors. There isn't much to work with outside today."

Karli didn't press the conversation as they drove west through the truck-heavy traffic of Interstate 80 and then south along the much quieter US 169. After she read the latest text from her father and dismissed it unanswered, Karli passed the time looking for Iowa's strangest landmarks, dilapidated barns that slouched here and there, adding unusual texture to a countryside that farmers prided themselves on keeping meticulously groomed and regular. The old barns were often a collection of steadily increasing slants, the strongly vertical right angles of their early days gradually returning toward the earth of the farmsteads they had served.

After about 40 minutes of silence, they reached the downtown, and Karli mumbled, "405 E. Madison." Jake drove to the new theater space, they got out, collected gear, and went in to interview the performers and get video of the new facility.

They completed the easy shoot and piled everything back into the car, and Jake headed out of town, this time east on Route 92. "Are you going to take us back on I-35?" Karli asked.

"That's kind of a longer drive, isn't it?"

"Yes," Jake said slowly, stretching out the word. "But we're going to make a quick stop first. There's a place out here I want you to see." As he said this, he turned south off of 92 onto a country road.

Chapter Fifteen

Rural Madison County, Iowa
Friday, November 22

Karli looked out the car's windows at the stubbled fields with their light covering of snow, and couldn't imagine what out here in the middle of nowhere would stand out as *something worth seeing*.

"Reach in the back and grab my Canon, would you please?" Jake asked, pointing out the personal camera bag that always seemed to be near him. Karli did as he requested, then turned back to face forward in the car just as Jake began to slow down and pull off the edge of the road.

Though Karli could tell he was waiting for some kind of response, she wasn't sure what he'd been saying. She was still staring out the windshield at a gloriously red wooden covered bridge just ahead, arching over the road as though extending an invitation to its dark shelter. "It's from the movie, isn't it?" she whispered.

"Well, it's one of them," Jake replied. "There are six covered bridges here in Madison County. Remember in the book where his ashes were scattered and where he stuck the note up for her? That one's about 20 minutes in the other direction. But this one is also in the movie."

Finally hearing what Jake was on about, Karli's head snapped to meet his twinkling eyes. Without a word, she slipped out of the car, walking briskly in her excitement toward the bridge and glancing back at Jake over her shoulder. Just as her eyes reached him, she heard the shutter of his camera.

Jake dropped the viewfinder from his face and beamed at her. "That's it. Go ahead and check it out."

Karli had never seen a genuine covered bridge in person before, much less one of *the* covered bridges. And she felt a newfound joy at discovering she could be comfortable with Jake. She spread her arms wide and spun in place, looking from the sky to the bridge, the camera's exposures chattering just at the edge of her hearing. Karli's breath was taken away at the desolate beauty: On this windy grey day, in this cold season, in this part of the heart of the midwest, the bridge's dusty red glory stood over the nearly colorless surroundings, under the steel-grey sky, across the grey-brown flatness of the river.

The bridge's roof, dark walls, and wooden deck thrust a dark tunnel over the small cleft cut by the river. Dark shelter beckoned, a space apart from the landscape, secure from the wind that searched out the thinner parts of Karli's clothes and from the steep, slippery, snow-dusted and brushy river banks.

Jake came along in fits and starts, pausing to raise his camera's huge lens toward her, then jogging lightly to another spot on his zig-zag path. As Karli entered the bridge's chamber and began examining the huge arching timbers that spread along and inside the bridge's length, Jake caught up and began flipping open a thin black light stand with a small radio-controlled flash mounted to its top.

"I want to try to catch you inside, with the daylight behind and the opening framing you," he said, his hands busy with equipment and his head tipping awkwardly to indicate where he wanted her to stand. Karli saw his earnest attention to his craft and smiled to herself as he tested the flash transmitter and knelt, then laid down on the wooden deck to put his camera at the right angle. "Try some different angles," he called from the floor. "Look sideways, then 45 degrees toward me, and on around, okay?"

His studied focus on her and her alone was deeply flattering. Warmth greater than anything explained by the bridge's shelter from wind and cold swelled through Karli's body and cheeks and pulled her face into a broad, involuntary smile. Jake's shutter whizzed and snapped again and again as she basked in the obsessive attention he paid her with each movement and glance at her, at the camera's display, at the shapes the bridge formed around her. *This is amazing,* she thought to herself. *And he is so intense about these pictures, like it's a real magazine shoot or something. I didn't know he was so into still photography.*

She hadn't noticed before how sexual and attractive intensity of purpose could be. The way Jake wriggled on the bridge's deck, changing position constantly to capture different shots, was fascinating to her, as fascinating as he apparently found her right now. And he had chosen this romantic spot, a spot where just about every American woman alive in the last 20 years would feel deeply moved by a second-hand kind of nostalgia for a love she'd never actually had or lost. Her borrowed longing was reflected in a passion she saw all over this special place and all over Jake's powerful concentration on taking her image.

And as she wondered and watched Jake's decisive, strong movements, she had to take a steadying breath.

Karli's knees felt just a little wobbly as she realized that she was deciding to go with the passion Jake continually showed her and that this place stirred in her. And just as she came to the realization that Jake could indeed become more than just the photographer who propelled her into her next career move, he stood, gathered his gear and walked toward her with a smile that was all warmth and excitement.

"You really live in some of these pictures," he said, swinging his camera around so she could see the small color display on its back. He clicked swiftly through a bunch of exposures, and stopped on one where she stood framed by the bridge's opening. The light outside the bridge struck the snow-dusted road and tall grasses alongside it, right up to the edge of the bridge's opening. Inside, the interior bridge space near the opening slipped quickly into darkness. The angled flash popped Karli into the foreground, her smile much warmer than the usual on-set, fully made-up photo of herself she normally saw.

In another, Karli saw herself looking more joyful than she could remember being in a long time as she twisted back toward the camera with an excited smile, the bridge in the background being her obvious destination.

The images that Jake had captured showed Karli a side of herself that was never on camera. She was not telling stories of disaster or danger here. She wasn't telling any story at all. He was telling her story instead.

She looked up at Jake as he paused on yet another picture. A smile lit his face as he looked at the image of her. Then she saw him notice that she wasn't looking at the little display.

He glanced at her quickly, then turned his head from the camera to look her squarely in the eyes. And even though she had kind of braced herself for it, she felt a disconcerting quiver as she met his consuming gaze. He bent down to her, slowly, and she raised her face to his, her eyes flicking between his lips and his own eyes. He reached behind her with one arm while the other hand moved the camera away.

And just as they were about to kiss, he breathed a sudden, low laugh. Karli pulled her face back from his to see his smirk and sparkling eyes. "What?" she asked. Her voice came out more of a throaty whisper than she had expected or intended.

Jake didn't answer except to seize her gaze and chuckle low in his throat. His smile grew wider, and just as Karli was beginning to reply, she felt him bring her close with the hand pressed on her back. And he kissed her.

The kiss was gentle and careful at first. Karli felt Jake's lips asking whether he could seek more from her, whether she would match the heat that she could feel pouring from him. She answered the question with a small, slow bite on his lower lip and a rough sound deep in her throat.

Before the kiss could grow into more, Karli flinched at the sound of car doors opening and shutting just outside the bridge. Her eyes moved to the sound, and she saw a middle-aged couple walking into the bridge, reaching toward one another to hold hands. In spite of the crazily changing light, Karli saw them grinning together at the sight of her and Jake kissing inside.

The man—apparently the husband, since their cold-weather coats matched—raised his free hand and waved gently to them.

"It's good to know that young people know how romantic these bridges are," he called. "Heck, Oprah hasn't been here since that book club thing, has she?" This question was addressed to his wife, who shook her head and laughed quietly.

Flustered by the interruption and at being seen kissing Jake, Karli pulled away from Jake's strong arm and mumbled something about needing to pack up the gear. Jake put out a restraining hand as she began to fold up the light stand. "Folks, I'd be grateful if you'd let me take your picture here," he said. "And I'd like to hear what brings you here, too, if you don't mind."

Karli watched as Jake introduced himself to the couple and listened to the story of how they'd learned about the covered bridges from Oprah's show when she had actually moved the entire production to Madison County because she was such a big fan of the book. The couple was from Ames, north of Des Moines, and they'd never known about the bridges until that show. They'd gone on to read the book and watch the movie, and today they had both had the day off and decided to drive down for a visit because they hadn't been in 15 years or so.

Jake was looking hard at the couple and how they told their story by process of mutual, repeated interruption. Karli could see the moment when he decided he'd gotten enough of an understanding. He nodded one last time at some detail the wife had interjected, then quickly checked the settings on his camera as he raised it to his eye. "So you had kind of a long drive today, didn't you?" As the couple looked at one another to decide on an answer, Jake's shutter snapped and whizzed.

Karli shook her head as she watched him continue to engage the husband and wife, their relationship, and their relationship to the bridge. After he'd captured their images, he asked for their snail-mail and e-mail addresses, shook hands with them both, and nodded to Karli. She began folding the light stand for the second time as he walked over.

"They were beautiful, weren't they?" Jake asked her. "They've been married almost 30 years, and they still hold hands like teenagers."

"Thanks for the save, Jake," Karli said. "I was kind of surprised when they showed up, and you covered really well, taking all those pictures of them."

"Save?" Jake asked. "I was surprised, too. But they were awesome. Just wait till you see their pictures." Karli saw Jake's brow furrow as he contemplated her face. "You're going to freeze to death. Let's get back in the car and get going."

The ride back to the station was disconcerting for Karli, whose body was charged and ready for more action. She felt an odd melancholy from having the kiss interrupted and a nearly equal sense of relief. Her lips were still sensitive, and her thoughts kept drifting back to the series of moments: his eyes on hers, his lips moving toward hers, his hand pressing against her back, his small pause, her small nibble. Her groan.

She groaned at the wintry landscape outside the car's window. Still, she didn't mention the kiss. Neither did Jake. They watched

Iowa's snow-dusted farm fields flit past in their shifting geometric patterns, their furrows forming suddenly criss-crossing parallelograms that flowed through their eyes and into the distance.

She tried to understand the kiss. It was certainly memorable and emotional. But understandable? Definitely not. Jake was so hard to figure. He'd been as intense taking pictures of the couple as he had when he was shooting her. *But he kissed me afterwards.* And she realized that she'd kissed him, too—probably she had initiated the kiss. It wasn't just that he'd flattered her with the impromptu photo session—though it had certainly found its way to her softest parts. It showed in the photos that he had seen well past her surface—and he had for a long time now. His attention was scary because it came from his knowing her so intimately. *Intimate,* she thought. *That's a scary word. That's the kind of word that involves a lot more than kissing.*

Jake's attention had always been moving toward intimacy, she realized, toward understanding her, her motivations, her values, her self.

It was decision time, Karli realized. She was either going to have to choose to keep this inspirational, memorable, emotional, incomprehensible man at arm's length, or she was going to have to accept a kind of intimacy she hadn't experienced before. She was going to have to let him know her, deeply and honestly. Or she was going to have to keep it professional.

And she didn't know if she could push him away again. Not only because his passion was so overwhelmingly attractive, but because he was so obviously hurting and struggling to find his way. She couldn't bear the thought of rejecting him after that kiss and inflicting another hurt on him when he was already so battered.

She really couldn't afford to become entangled with this man, in this place, when she was moving on.

And Jake was capable of seeing her in ways deeper than she'd ever examined herself. The prospect of seeing herself through in his reflection made her feel too vulnerable, too exposed.

Just as Karli resolved to let Jake down easily and let herself off as well, his voice pulled her back from her musings. "So, would you like to come over for Thanksgiving dinner? I know you don't have any family in town, and we make it kind of a thing for as many friends as will come." Jake paused and then added, as if to close the sale, "You're guaranteed to get as stuffed as the turkeys. What do you say?"

Before she could come up with a different reply, Karli heard herself saying, "I don't have any plans for Thanksgiving, so that'd be great. Thanks. What would you like me to bring?"

"Just your smile and a big appetite. We have the chow more than covered—you know, turkey any way you want it, ham, dressing, potatoes mashed and sweet, cranberry, green bean casserole, homemade rolls, your nine favorite kinds of pie, and lots of places to collapse afterward," Jake's eyes twinkled with anticipation as he went through the menu. "Or if you want to have some fun before you come over, you could go to Ingersoll Wine and Spirits and ask them what kind of wine they recommend to go with turkey. I think those folks' heads are about to explode this time of year with answering that question." Jake glanced away from the road and back toward Karli. "You know the answer, right?"

This is not letting him down easily, Karli was thinking to herself. *This is getting together on a major holiday with his family.*
"Answer?" she asked, coming back to the conversation.

"Yeah, to the question of what kind of wine goes with turkey."

"Um, no. I'd have to ask, too," Karli admitted. "I'm not a big wine sophisticate or anything."

Jake chuckled at her response. "The best wine to drink with your turkey, at least as far as I've ever been able to learn from reading foodie magazines and so on, is whatever wine you like that's open or can easily be opened. All the snoots have an opinion, but they range from sweet whites to big, tannic reds and everything in between. So I figure that means anything is fair game. I like a dry white, like a Pouilly Fuissé, or a light-bodied red, like one of the million or so Beaujolais varieties."

"Wow," Karli said, a look of genuine astonishment on her face. "I didn't exactly figure you for a wine guy."

"Photogs just swill draft beer, right?" The corner of Jake's mouth Karli could see in her view of his profile twitched up slightly.

"Well, yeah. Mostly, anyway," Karli fidgeted the top off her diet Dew and took a swig. "I guess I've never seen a photog drink anything else."

"Tell you what," Jake said with clear, decisive tones, "I'll make sure your glass is never empty on Thanksgiving and that you taste some of my different favorites."

After agreeing, Karli again watched the Iowa landscape flicker by for a while. Then the kind of thing that often comes after a fancy meal seasoned with lots of fancy wine came vividly to mind. She caught her breath quickly and felt the blush start to heat her cheeks. She was looking forward to a taste.

Chapter Sixteen

Three NewsFirst Parking Lot
Tuesday, November 26

Karli zipped into a parking space at the station and noticed Jake's white pickup pull in just before her.

In spite of the chill in the air, she felt a little rush of warmth as she anticipated the upcoming holiday with Jake. They had kissed. And the kiss had been almost unbearably romantic, and she still nearly lost her balance every time she thought about it.

Now she was scheduled to attend a big fancy dinner with him and he was scheduled to get her all drunked up, and she was going to make sure she was as freshly showered as a girl could be after spending a long time eating and drinking.

And there he was, getting out of his truck. They could walk in together and not talk about romantic kissing or getting-drunk-and-kissing-more even though it would be in the air all around them.

So Karli grabbed her bag and her first diet Dew of the day and got out of her car just in time to see Sophia's long, elegant figure getting out of the passenger side of Jake's truck, a full gym bag over her shoulder and a smile on her face.

"Thanks for the lift, Jake," Karli could hear Sophia saying. "I really had a great time last night. I've never gotten pajamas sweaty like that before. Thanks for loaning them to me. I couldn't believe it after I got them off—you worked me really hard, you know?" And as Jake and Sophia came together around the back of the truck and on their way into the station, she slugged him on the shoulder with a broad grin.

Jake laughed in reply and said, "You totally had it coming. I wouldn't want you to think I was easy."

Sophia quirked a smile at Jake in response. Her smile turned into a wince as she tried to keep up with Jake's long, fast stride. "Hey, slow down there, big boy," she said. "My butt and legs are sore from last night."

"Whiner," he replied. "Being sore just means you were doing it right. Besides, you know you love it, so keep up already." With that, Jake tapped in the code that unlocked the newsroom's exterior door and swung it grandly open for Sophia to walk through. "After you, Miss Anchorwoman," he said, then stepped into the building behind her.

Karli sat, stunned and startled at what she'd just heard. *That BITCH!* she thought. *That ASSHOLE!* Karli's left foot remained on the ground outside her car, her right still on the car's floorboard. Her eyes stung with tears she immediately resolved never to shed.

After all this bullshit and not wanting to even like that dick, he sweeps me into this big romantic event and gives me a big romantic kiss. We kissed on one of the actual, physical Bridges of Madison County, for heaven's sake! And even then, even after he has completely melted me from the inside out—and here she caught her breath once again as the memory of that kiss sent a surge through her femininity—*I still don't want to get involved with him, so I figure we'll just pretend the kiss never happens. And THEN he brings on the charm offensive and the next thing I know he-with-whom-I-must-not-get-involved has talked me into a Thanksgiving Day wine-tasting and turkey party. Oh, that asshole. I can't believe I fell for his shit.*

The diet Dew she'd been crushing and shaking during her private, silent tantrum started to fizz green-yellow fluid out from the not-quite-tight-enough cap's bottom edge and then onto her hand. *Damnit!*

Karli took a deep breath as she reached for a napkin from the center console to wipe the bottle and her hand. *Okay,* she thought. *Sophia isn't to blame here. How could she know that Jake had taken me to that bridge and kissed me?*

Karli was not so naive that she didn't understand that there were situations that were so romantic they created a must-kiss buzz more or less on their own. Heck, formal dances in high school and college had led her into more than one forgettable kiss with more than one completely forgettable guy.

Jake isn't a forgettable guy, though, she thought. *And that was definitely not a forgettable kiss. At least it wasn't for me. Apparently it was forgettable for him, though, if he can go straight into sweaty-*

pajamas-land with Sophia.

What must that be like? she wondered. Feeling the tingles of arousal run through her body at the thought of 'sexing with Jake,' Karli firmly resolved not to let herself go there.

Now I'm stuck with going to his house next week for some dumb Thanksgiving dinner with wine. Ugh. Grabbing her bag and her Dew, Karli finally moved her right foot out of the car and headed for the newsroom.

Once there, she headed straight for the assignment desk, where Vince sat amidst the usual chaos of screeching scanners, mounds of papers, chirping phones, and coffee cups in varying degrees of emptiness, coldness, and moldiness.

"Vince, I'm sorry I pushed so hard to get Thanksgiving Day off. I've changed my mind. So I'll be in next week, okay?"

Vince moved his eyes slowly from his computer's monitor and toward Karli's face. "What in the hell is your problem?" he asked, no trace of sympathy in his raspy voice.

Karli was flustered at the usually avuncular Vince's uncharacteristic hostility. "Um, I ... uh ... I don't really have a problem. I just don't need the day off any more."

"The hell you don't," Vince rasped. "You haven't taken any time off at all since you got here, and you've worked a lot of extra shifts, too. Plus, you nagged at me until I talked about four other people into re-working their lives around the Thanksgiving schedule. So, no. You're taking the day off."

Visions of a wine-fueled afternoon of Thanksgiving misery flashed before Karli's eyes. She had to get out of this obligation, and work was the one excuse she could come up with. "Vince, I really ..."

"You really need to take the holiday off," Vince cut in, interrupting and shutting down Karli's last-ditch effort at getting back onto the schedule. "Besides," he added, "Jake was just here making sure that you had the day off. He said you were going to his place for Thanksgiving." Vince tilted his head down to look over his reading glasses at Karli. Then he took them off and sucked a bit at one of the temple pieces. "You wanting to work wouldn't have anything to do with Jake's Thanksgiving dinner party, would it?" Karli could tell from his steady gaze that he knew the answer and that there was no point in denying it.

"Vince, I just wanted to work. But since you won't let me, let's just say we never had this conversation, okay?"

Giving her a sage nod, Vince softened and held Karli's gaze a little longer. "Understand me, now, kid. That one is an actual human when you meet him in the wild, okay? He isn't like the other animals you meet in this racket. You don't need to take a chair and whip along with you—they won't keep you safe from this one, anyway. He's not Discovery Channel dangerous. Like I said, he's a human."

Karli stared back at Vince, stunned at this surprising and frustrating bit of candor. *Of course he is an animal,* she thought. *He does it just like all the other penis-brained jerks I've ever met: with anyone, any time. He must be an animal, too, to make her so sore. What must sex like that be like?*

Yet she heard something more than that in Vince's uncharacteristically long speech. And in his tone and on his face. Vince truly believed that Jake was somehow different. But Karli knew that he was wrong. Jake could certainly come across like something more than the usual, yet she had just seen who he was with her very own eyes. This wasn't the time to have that conversation with Vince, though. Karli nodded slowly, then turned away from him to head to her desk and begin the day's work. She turned back quickly as she heard Vince's usual tones addressing her.

"Karli, that's next week," he rasped. "Today you're going do a live shot of the Governor lighting the Capitol Christmas tree for the 5:30 and 6:00 shows. See if you can find something to give the story some meat for a change. Otherwise, it'll just be pretty video and no story."

"Oh, and there's one other thing, kid," Vince said in a lower voice, as though to invite a secret conversation. "Sophia made the case to Jerry that she should have Jake on every installment of the heroin series. He started it, you know, it needs a consistent look, it's a big series, all that. So he's assigned to that for the foreseeable."

Karli nodded again and turned away, her eyes filling with surprising tears. *Not only does that bitch take my series and all the credit for my work, she takes Jake, too. Can that be why they were getting all sweaty?* Shaking her head as though to chase these thoughts from it, Karli raised her chin with new resolve and went to power on her computer. The challenges of another day's reporting were a comfort. As she waited for the computer's reassuring start-up tone, she flashed back on her dilemma: she was going to have to go to Jake's for Thanksgiving, and she couldn't get out of it.

She worked on finding meat for the story—learning that the governor was going to tour an Iowa LED lighting company in Ankeny before the tree-lighting ceremony—she began working on an energy-efficiency angle. And it occurred to her that she could simply treat her Thanksgiving experience with Jake efficiently. She'd show up late, eat fast, and leave early. No pressure to hob-nob with Jake the Snake or his friends, just a quick meal like at Burger King.

Nodding smartly to herself, Karli began dialing an energy efficiency expert's phone number to find out how many power plants could go offline if people used LED Christmas lights instead of incandescent.

This was going to be easy. Efficiency was Karli's new watchword.

Chapter Seventeen

The Thanksgiving Party
Thursday, November 28

Karli drove in what felt like circles around the neighborhood to the south of I-235 near Theodore Roosevelt High School, looking first for Jake's address, and then once she'd found it, for a parking space. It seemed that on any other day a parking space would've been easy to find. This was a quiet, upscale neighborhood with long driveways and broad streets. But Jake's driveway and both sides of the street for a long block in either direction were lined with parked cars of every conceivable variety, from rusted-up-to-the-windows old sedans to glistening new German, Italian, and British imports and everything in between. Karli didn't usually notice cars, but seeing a battered, multi-colored trash heap next to a gloriously polished monster of a sedan was a surprising contrast. Especially when it turned out that the solemnly massive car was an actual Rolls Royce with the steering wheel on the wrong side.

Who comes to this Thanksgiving dinner? Karli wondered as she trudged along the neighborhood streets to get from her car to Jake's. The houses she walked past were modestly upscale Colonials, mostly in brick. Sneaking a peek through a dining room window in one of the houses, Karli saw a surprisingly Norman Rockwell family sitting down to a huge meal. The kind of Thanksgiving she'd grown up with had been a mostly dress-up affair, outside the house. Her father set the day's agenda of going to the country club for Thanksgiving.

That meant that the family dressed formally around noon and drove to the club for a dinner that, apart from the turkey, was not dramatically different from other dinners there. After the meal and some lingering over drinks, they returned to a dark home. Then it was pretty quiet until the shopping began the next day.

Here in Des Moines, Karli smelled the smoke from cozy fireplaces and saw houses glowing with crowds of extended families and driveways packed with cars, while others were silent and dark, their occupants gone elsewhere for the holiday. Finally she came to Jake's house, which had cars parked crammed into the full length of the driveway and all over the front yard. She marched up the driveway, carrying the random wine from Ingersoll Spirits and a bunch of flowers she'd bought at the grocery store on her way.

Because the lot was so big, the immense red-brick Georgian house looked deceptively small until Karli came closer. She saw the sweeping curve of a grand music room project eastward from the main house, the mullioned windows exposing a throng of people and the up-tilted glossy top of a grand piano rising in the room's middle. The entire roof of the huge room was outlined with white-painted railings that contained a spacious balcony apparently accessed from the master bedroom. Set back in a lot bordered by towering oaks, the house loomed ever higher over her as she approached the front door. Looking up, Karli saw that the six huge dormers projecting from the roofline were on the *third* story of brickwork. Candles—presumably electric ones—gleamed from each of the 20 or so front-facing windows. The aqua-tinted patina of the copper sheathing along the upper roof gave the house a college-campus look, one that was enhanced by the competing Drake University and Iowa State University flags that flapped slowly on poles leaning outward from either side of the front door.

The storm door in front was frosted with the condensation from the steamy breath of many conversations behind the open red wooden door. The hubbub of talking and laughter reached plainly through to the outside, but Karli's knocking apparently didn't reach in, as nobody came to open the door and clear the view. After her third try at knocking and sick of juggling flowers and wine, Karli decided she'd waited long enough and opened the door for herself. Warm humidity washed over her as she stepped through the spacious, coat-draped entryway and into a crowded room where a greasily pony-tailed and goateed young man was juggling oranges in small clear space in the middle. As he transitioned from a cascade to moving the oranges in a circular pattern, he dropped one. The audience caught its breath in unison as the orange bounced on the floor. The juggler's mouth opened in exaggerated astonishment and his eyes flicked toward Karli, who was trying to wriggle her way through the crowd to find someone—anyone—she knew. The juggler moved both of the oranges he still had to one hand, raised a quivering hand to point straight at Karli, and yelled, "Look at those beautiful flowers!"

The entire room of about 20 strangers swiveled their heads to look at Karli, who flushed with embarrassment at being suddenly the focal point of everyone's attention. She scanned the faces and found none that offered an escape from the sudden attention.

Several pairs of eyes seemed to be looking at her chest, which made her wonder if she was having some kind of wardrobe malfunction. Glancing down to check, she saw the bunch of flowers covering her, then raised them to the room with a shrugging gesture that she hoped would communicate that these were the flowers the juggler had pointed at and that she had to get out of the room to find a place to put them.

As she did this, she saw the juggler bent quickly over, pick up the errant orange, and begin juggling again. "Hey, folks," he called, "this act is *picking up*." And he went into a series of trick throws, tossing with alternating hands swinging behind his back so the oranges popped up over his shoulders and on into their pattern. "Don't think I'm trying to keep any secrets behind my back," he said with the insinuating kind of grin and waggling eyebrows that usually accompany dreadful puns.

Karli managed to cross through the small open space and on toward the next room. The juggler added a fourth orange from a nearby fruit bowl and told Karli in an exaggerated stage whisper that she would likely find a vase in next room, and if that didn't work, just ask Jane.

Wondering who Jane was and shaking her head at the strange beginning to the afternoon, Karli wound her way through a crowded doorway and into another crowded room, this time full of music and muted conversation. Against the other side of the wall in common with the juggler's room, a boy of about 10 years old was earnestly playing an upright piano, his tongue sticking out from the corner of his mouth and deep breaths filling the spaces where he paused to find the next sequence. Groups of kids of various ages clustered around tables laden with chips and candy. Parental-looking adults hovered in groups nearby holding drinks and talking in good-humored tones that tried but failed to be quiet enough for the piano to carry clearly. Karli saw no familiar faces and saw nothing that looked like a vase or a place for keeping vases. *This isn't an intimate family dinner. It's a three-ring circus. It looks like Jake invited half the neighborhood.*

As she looked around for vases, Karli noticed the unusual framed art displayed on the walls. Original single-panel editorial cartoons hung side-by-side. Photos, mostly black-and-white glossies that looked like they dated back to the late '50s and up to recent times, showed photographers training lenses on speakers with upraised fists rallying intent crowds or reporters taking pencilled notes next to busy police officers and bloodied prostrate citizens or walking on dusty tracks with farmers who grabbed the bills of seed caps in their permanent frustration with the weather. These were photos of journalists in action, right at the action, absorbing its smells and sounds and sights yet somehow not part of it. Karli saw herself in those photos, in the struggle pictured in each one, the struggle to pull the real and true significance out of the insignificant obviousness of every story's surface.

She headed for the plastered archway that led further back into the house. Karli felt a great relief at seeing Jake's familiar shiny brown curls bobbing over the crowd and heading toward her. She saw him handing a plate and glass to a woman who appeared to be in her late 60s. Rather than bending his tall figure, Jake knelt on one knee to make eye contact along with the delivery. He smiled broadly at whatever the woman said when he handed her the food and drink. Karli watched as he gave the woman his complete attention, as though she were the only other person in the world and not just one of the least mobile of his dozens of guests.

"Jake!" Karli called, too loudly for the too-loud piano room, as she felt more than one pair of shushing parental eyes glare at her. Jake's head snapped toward the sound of her voice, he leaned to the woman to say something that looked like an excuse-me, then he stood and moved quickly toward her, a smile broadening over his face. He looked radiantly happy in his usual jeans and an unusually formal and crisp blue-striped Oxford cloth button-down. The unexpected starchiness was compromised by cuffs that were folded casually halfway up his strong forearms. This was not the image of any photographer she'd ever seen before.

"Karli, I'm so glad you made it," he said, wrapping her in a sudden and unexpected hug. She barely managed to twitch the flowers out of the way to keep them from being crushed in the hug. As he pulled her close to his chest, she smelled his distinctive, spicy scent—overlaid with a distinct whiff of turkey—and felt him encircle her completely in his arms. Yet as soon as she turned her head to lay her cheek against his chest, she remembered that he was the filthy asshole who had slept with Sophia right after kissing her. She pushed away from him like she'd touched a hot stove. Jake looked down at her in mild surprise. "What's up?" he asked

Torn between savoring his delicious smell and kicking him in the crotch, Karli looked down and saw her flowers. They were going to save her for the second time in a few minutes.

"Um, I need to find a vase," she said, holding the flowers up to show Jake why she needed a vase. Jake looked back at her, a single eyebrow raised and a puzzled grin quirking his mouth. "Well, the juggler said I should get a vase. I brought these flowers for you," she stammered, then thought that didn't sound right at all. "Or, no, I mean, I brought them as a hostess gift. And they should probably be put in some water." Her voice trailed off indistinctly and she lowered her eyes in frustration at Jake's apparent good will and silence. *Why,* she wondered, *am I even talking to him?*

"Let's go meet Jane, and we'll find you a vase and get you a glass of wine, okay?" Jake said, his hand going to Karli's elbow to steer her through the archway and into what looked to usually be a dining room. The table was missing, though, and the buffets against each wall were heaped with mounds of cloth napkins, small plates, cutlery, and chafing dishes full of wonderful-smelling appetizers. Each dish was described with its own calligraphy card. Karli read and smelled shrimp and Andouille sausage in garlic butter with toast points for dipping, beef tenderloin sliders, mushrooms in red wine reduction, glazed baby back ribs, smoked salmon, bruschetta on homemade crostini, assorted cheeses with fruit, and several more that her eye wasn't quick enough to catch.

A sudden group of about half a dozen servers—each in black slacks, pleated tuxedo shirts, and black bow ties—emerged from what Karli assumed was the kitchen, bearing trays laden with stacked glasses and bottles. Jake stopped one just a couple of steps into the dining room. "What have you got there, Michelle?" he asked, eyeing the bottles in the center of the server's massive tray.

"This is the Beaujolais service," the server answered, reaching for one of her bottles and proceeding to pour a glass. "Would you like to try some?" she asked with a coquettish tilt of her head. "Or should I have one of the others come over?"

"Let's get one of these for Karli here first," he said, indicating with his head and neatly deflecting the server's flirtation. He steered Karli with a gentle touch on her elbow to a window seat along the least-trafficked side of the room. The server followed as Jake explained, "I promised her a variety of wines tonight, and I'd like her to start with one of my favorites."

He turned to Karli as the server nodded and began to pour and lowered his voice as though sharing a secret with her. "It isn't just inexpensive, it's downright cheap—even by diet Dew standards. But I can't taste the price of a wine very well. The flavors, on the other hand ... well, let me tell you what it tastes like to me: This wine tastes like it's made from baby grapes. It isn't some big, pompous, adult-tasting red wine, with all that tannic acid that makes your mouth as dry as a desert. It has an odd bit of powdery feeling on the tongue that I've always enjoyed and never understood very well. It tastes like how I imagine the frosty-looking yeast you see on grapes would, wrapped in a kind of yummy apple and pear and grape flavor, with maybe just a hint of tobacco. But you'll come to your own opinion."

Jake freed her hands of the bottle of wine she'd brought along and considered the label. He exchanged it for a full glass from the server and passed it to Karli with a look of happy expectation on his face. He then took another for himself and raised it to Karli, nodding to her in a silent toast and with a sexy half-smile.

As Karli lifted her glass to her lips, Jake handed the bottle she had brought to the server with a whispered direction.

Karli looked to the server for some escape from the obligation to taste, but she found only more encouragement there. Jake's long description of the wine's flavors had left her a bit befuddled. To her, wine had always been simply good, bad, or so-so. All of the flowery language about a beverage sounded a lot like overkill and affectation. With a quick roll of her eyes and a gusty sigh of exasperation, she raised her glass, caught her breath through her nose, and took more than a sip.

And her eyes closed suddenly as the many sensations Jake had primed her to experience played through her head. The tart fruit scents and flavors were obvious, and they rode through her nose and across her tongue on the frosty, powdery texture he'd described. The tobacco wasn't the horrible taste of cigarette Karli had experienced only once as an undergraduate. Instead, it was the delicious taste that the smell of fresh, unlit tobacco promised.

After the tastes had passed through her mouth, leaving a surprisingly clean feeling on her tongue, Karli opened her eyes wide with a look of startled appreciation. Jake was looking right at her, those brown eyes dancing in anticipation of her reaction. And he was rewarded with Karli's obvious appreciation. Karli had drunk wine before—many times. Yet this experience was heady like wine had never been before—not at all in a drunken way—this was the first time that she'd been cued to anticipate, then enjoy, the sensations.

"So you like it, then?" Jake asked softly. "Let's go find a vase while you finish that up, and you can meet—"

"Karli, it's so nice to meet you in person," Jake was interrupted by a short, energetic, bespectacled woman in her early 50s who was walking up to their semi-private nook, her hands outstretched in greeting.

"I'm afraid you have the advantage of me," Karli responded, reluctantly taking the woman's hand and permitting her own hand to be shaken.

"This is Jane," Jake said, with the tone of someone stating the obvious. Karli looked uncomprehendingly from Jake down to Jane, knowing she was missing something.

"I'm Jake's mother," the woman named Jane said, with an indecipherable look at Jake. "And it's very nice to meet you. Jake talks about you more than anyone else in the newsroom—and it's all good, too!" The woman's kindness was evident in her enthusiasm.

When Karli failed to fill the conversational gap with a response of any kind, Jane stepped right into the pause. "Jake's a critical thinker, you know. He doesn't compliment reporters unless he has reasoned his way to the conclusion that they've done something exceptionally well." Karli's inability to respond continued. The woman's warmth was an unexpected and pleasant surprise.

Karli looked in surprise from Jane's open face to Jake's. "I didn't know that about him," she faltered. Then she reached for the evening's fail-safe: "I, um, brought these flowers, and they probably need a vase and some water." She stuck the flowers out toward Jane, as much to erect a barrier to more conversation as to hand them over.

Jane exchanged another mysterious look with a shrugging Jake as she took the flowers.

"I'm sure there's something in one of these cupboards. Thanks very much for bringing them. Our table always groans with food, but there's never enough in the way of centerpieces or decoration. They're perfect." As she said these things, Jane moved away from Karli and toward a set of built-in cupboards that looked big enough to store just about anything.

"We'll see you when we sit down, okay?" Jake called to her back, then again he gently guided Karli, this time out a side door and back into the cold. "Would you mind keeping me company while I check on these turkeys?" he asked as he moved toward a pair of tall, sizzling metal cylinders connected to a pair of propane tanks. Karli had never seen turkey fryers before, but it was easy enough to figure out what they were. The smell was amazing, and set Karli's mouth watering.

"It looks like they're done now," Jake said, inspecting the frying birds. "Would you like to help me get them out of the fryers and on a cart for the caterers?" Jake picked up a pair of oven mitts, pulled them on and grabbed another pair to hold out to Karli.

"Um, I'm not really the cooking type, Jake," Karli said, leaving the mitts untouched. "How about I just watch or go get another glass of wine or something?" The gallons of vigorously boiling oil triggered her internal caution alarms, and the pause to recognize the danger gave her a moment to remember that she was angry with Jake and not eager to smooth that over. She looked at her glass and realized that she had emptied it. "I'll go find one of the servers."

"Well, then, I'll leave you in the best hands, okay?" Jake was gesturing through the glass of the storm door to someone inside.

Karli looked in the direction Jake waved and spotted the man as he started to move toward them. He was in his middle age, with grey hairs frosting his temples. His face had a faint look of bloodhound, with slightly drooping cheeks furrowed by the creases of laughter and age. Warmth fairly radiated from the brown eyes slanted down toward his cheekbones as they peered out from behind oversized glasses. A somewhat haphazardly formal shirt, tie, and sweater vest hung well on his lean frame. He walked toward them with the strength and twinge of an athlete whose lifetime of miscellaneous injuries had fixed their main emphasis onto long-suffering knees. As he approached, he extended a hand and asked in a voice as warm and comforting as his kind face, "Karli Lewis, right?" And then, as Karli nodded in uncomfortable acknowledgement, "I've used some of your reporting in my classes. I'm Gabe Evans; I teach journalism at Drake University."

"Very nice to meet you Professor Evans," Karli responded, shaking his hand a little more firmly. She was used to being approached pretty much anywhere by perfect strangers who expected her to greet them as old friends. Especially in WalMart. So often that she'd stopped going to WalMart. But meeting a journalism professor brought a broad smile to her face. She'd have common ground with him.

"So now you're in the best hands here—well, aside from mine." Jake smiled at Karli and gave Gabe a quick wink. "Ask for the white burgundy, if you can find the right server. You'll be impressed at how full and complex that flavor is, even for a white following a red." With that, Jake turned and began pulling on huge insulated gloves and reaching for tools. His attention was fully shifted onto the turkeys and away from Gabe and her.

Karli sneaked a peek at her iPhone to see if it was time to go home yet. She nearly dropped her wine glass when she saw that she'd only been at the party for twelve minutes so far. So many oddly uncomfortable things had already happened to her. It was definitely time for another glass of wine—whatever the variety.

Gabe gently guided her back into the dining room, where he caught a server's eye. As Karli secured and sipped a glass of the white burgundy Jake had suggested, she gave it all of her attention. The taste was so lovely—tart and chill, like an apple picked from a late-autumn orchard—that she closed her eyes to shut out distractions and savor it. After she had allowed it to roll through her mouth, she noticed that her stomach felt pleasantly and distinctly warm from the wine she'd already had. *I'll need some food if I'm going to have any chance at staying sober,* she thought to herself.

Opening her eyes, she met Gabe's smiling face. "I'm sorry, Professor Evans. Jake has gotten me so focused on tasting these wines that I got a little lost there."

"Just Gabe, please," he said. "Jane just told me that it's about time for us to head for our seats. And I'm pretty sure we both have assigned seats. We could head over there together if you like."

"Assigned seats?" Karli asked. "I thought this was an informal, family thing?"

"Oh, it's family all right," Gabe chuckled. "But you'll find that Jane and Jake have an expansive definition of family."

"So these people are not relatives, then?"

"Many of them are. Jane is the middle of seven, so her brothers and sisters are all here with their own kids and some grandkids.

And Jake's grandparents are here, too. They have brothers and sisters, and those all have offspring and so on," Gabe continued.

And as he explained that roughly 40 of the guests were related by blood or marriage, he guided her out the house's back door and into an enormous white tent, like the kind used for outdoor weddings. In summer. Here, it was a frigid Iowa fall day, but the grass had been covered with rolls of clean, fake turf, and Karli's quick eye caught a stalwart row of propane-fueled outdoor heaters spaced along the edges of the tent. And they worked well, as the temperature was comfortable—at least it began to be warm a foot or so above the ground.

Jake and his mother's *expansive* definition of family looked to be an understatement. Not only were all the people Karli had seen in the house pouring into the tent area from about three different doors, the tent already had several groups milling about some of the tables, apparently choosing seats.

There were at least a dozen round tables all set with white tablecloths, artfully folded napkins, heavy silverware, and at least three glasses at each place setting. At one end of the tent—which had to cover every inch of an entire, huge back yard—Karli saw a long line of tables supporting silver swivel-top serving dishes, two carving stations staffed by knife-wielding women in chef's whites and hats, and more kitchen staff in black cook's uniforms and hats carrying huge trays of food to the buffet line.

"Gabe," she said as they walked through the surprisingly well heated tent to their table, "this is no family get-together. This is nicer than most wedding receptions."

"It's no big secret, Karli, but it's easy to forget that Jane and Jake are comfortable, to say the least," Gabe replied. "Here in Des

Moines, being that wealthy is not very socially acceptable. So they only let it show once in while, and then only with the people who matter most to them. Like on Thanksgiving, when they host this little family get-together." As if by way of concluding, Gabe pulled out a chair for Karli and gestured her grandly into it.

She settled into her seat—a real chair, not one of the uncomfortable folding chairs she expected to find under a big outdoor tent—spotted the ornately hand-lettered place card bearing her name, and looked up to smile at Gabe while he pulled his own chair out and sat.

Before she could comment or even unfold her napkin, a server had snuck silently up on the side away from Gabe. "I see your glass is empty Miss Lewis," he said. "May I get you something you haven't tried yet? There are several interesting wines on offer tonight, all Gibson family favorites." The server darted a glance at a note in his hand and continued. "Perhaps one of the Marlborough varieties, from New Zealand? We have an excellent pinot noir and a very refreshing Sauvignon blanc."

After Karli took the server's advice and went with the Marlborough Sauvignon blanc—*by special suggestion of Mr. Gibson*—she leaned over to Gabe, who already felt like an old friend in this noisy throng. "There's too much going on here. Who are all of these people—they can't all be relatives, can they? And why am I at the table with the pretty name cards?"

Gabe's gentle smile was a reassuring comfort. "The people are Jane and Jake's extended family, plus the folks they consider to be like family. Friends that Jane worked with at the Register and at Meredith publishing are here. That's why I'm here—we worked together at both houses before she retired to her foundation and I went into my teaching career. And of course there are the people from her foundation and the organizations they fund, so that adds up.

"Some of the folks from Jake's studio are here, too." He paused and gave Karli a twinkling sideways glance. "And as for why you're at the table with the pretty place cards, that's an answer that you would know better than me. I do know that Jake's never had a woman at this table before. Females, yes, but never a woman his own age."

Karli's face flushed as she hid a grimace behind a sip of wine. After a slight pause, she met Gabe's calm, questioning gaze with a firm look of her own. "It seems to me that he runs through women pretty quickly."

Gabe's eyebrows raised with a question, but he did not have time to ask it. Jane was speaking into a microphone that amplified her voice enough to quell conversations. "Now that everyone looks to have found a seat, I wanted to formally welcome you all to Thanksgiving dinner. Jake and I are so pleased each of you could be here. We have so very much to be thankful for, and you all top our lists. Before we start in on the food, let's be thankful that Father Pellegrini can be with us again this year and ask for God's blessing."

Jane passed the microphone to a whip-thin bespectacled priest who was dressed all in black with a Roman collar, and had a head of thinning, graying red hair. His face lit up as he looked around the tent and from table to table.

He produced an iPad from the folds of his clothing, pronouncing it jokingly to be the *Holy iPad*, and referred to it as he proceeded through a long prayer giving thanks for all the works of most of the people present and requesting intercession for the people they helped and many others. Karli tuned out most of the prayer, which was mostly about a bunch of people she'd never heard of.

The wine's edge-softening warmth spread to her thoughts as she tried to process the intense quarter hour she'd been at the party. Jake had been utterly oblivious to the fact that he'd betrayed her immediately after luring her into thinking that he was passionate, caring, giving, and worth-tolerating-Des-Moines-for. And he'd been oblivious to the fact that he should acknowledge her fury. She was furious with him. And he hadn't even had the decency to feel her fury, the jerk.

Instead, he'd swept right up to her and cut off her chance to bust loose with the fury. Karli tried grinding her teeth to emphasize the fury she wanted to feel and realized that she'd just passed her teenage definition of intoxication: her teeth were starting to feel dentist-office numb.

She quickly reviewed the facts so far—a reporter's habit—while the priest droned on. *Jake had greeted me like I was the whole reason for the party. He'd left a guest to sweep me up in that huge and wonderfully scented and apparently sincere hug. He gave me a special wine selection and a mini-lesson in wine tasting. He instructed the servers especially about me. He made sure I had a*

144

special escort to the head table—and not just an escort, a fellow journalist who is familiar with my work. One who'd told me I was the first woman

Jake's age who'd ever sat at the head table.

Karli realized Gabe found that last fact to be more significant than she was comfortable acknowledging. But there it was. He was going out of his way to make her feel welcome. Nearly a hundred guests, and *she* was the one he was working hard to please.

As she was pondering the situation, she looked over to the carts bearing the fried turkeys and carving boards to the buffet line. Then just as she was about to start complaining to herself that he had ditched her *yet again*, she felt a gentle touch on her shoulder and heard Jake's voice whisper in her ear, "Sorry that took so long. I didn't realize how hard it would be to move those things around. They're *hot*. And heavy, too."

His smile was audible, and when she turned to see it, his face was still very close. His eyes were searching hers. *If his eyes weren't so intense, I wouldn't be thinking about the flowers coming in handy again*, she thought. Yet she found the insistent pressure of his penetrating gaze irresistible. The brown warmth of his eyes drew her attention away from the bustling tent, the priest's ongoing ramble, Gabe's avuncular presence. Her world shrank into the space spanning her eyes and his, while it expanded into the energy that charged the span with a tension that was intimate and sexual, yes, yet somehow more than simply lusty.

In spite of herself, she returned the grin that crinkled his eyes with pleasure. Apparently taking her smile as the permission he'd been waiting for, Jake pulled out the chair next to Karli's, whispered a *thank you* across her to Gabe, gestured to one of the wine servers for a glass of something, and composed himself to listen to the proceedings.

The air set aswirl by his movements smelled like a mix of his usual spicy, masculine scent mixed with the heady whiff of wine on his breath.

Karli watched his composed profile and tuned her attention in to listen to the priest, who seemed to be wrapping up.

"Of course we are here to give thanks for and to celebrate all of the many good works and the people who have given us so many great acts of goodness and kindness to celebrate," Father Pellegrini said with a gentle smile that encompassed the entire gathering. "Des Moines and Iowa and the United States and many places across the wide world are all better places for people to live because of them. Many more children have been provided with enough food and clean water, the ability to worship freely and safely, greater educational opportunity, and access to health care."

As Karli joined in the applause, she saw the sincere and deeply felt emotion in the priest's misty eyes. And seeing it, she felt a kindred warmth spread through her—not from the wine this time, though perhaps the wine had eased the way. The priest had described kindness and generosity that had the power to shape the future. And it was genuinely moving to think that children near and far were healthier and more safe—all because of the people gathered under this tent in the middle of flyover country. She felt glad to be among them.

Father Pellegrini continued as the applause began to fade: "Jesus told us in the Sermon on the Mount that the person giving alms should not let the left hand know what the right is doing. It's easy to think that sounds kind of silly—how can a person not know what both hands are doing?"

The priest flopped his hands around, making faces at each in turn and looking worried about his iPad.

He settled to a sudden and serious stillness. "Almsgiving has often been done for show, though. Like the company that makes the bits that drill holes for fracking oil loose from the ground. Although fracking involves known carcinogens and probably creates a multitude of health risks, the company made a donation to breast cancer research and then painted its drill bits pink." He looked up from his notes on the iPad, his eyes sweeping the room with sternly furrowed brows. "There the left hand is doing something bad, and the right hand is trying to make a show of almsgiving to distract from and maybe compensate for the bad.

"Even though Jane and Jake Gibson have both spent a lot of time writing and publishing the headlines, they're never in them," the priest continued, turning his smile to beam upon the two of them. "And they've even given me specific direction not to mention them tonight." Here, the priest gave a winking, we're-in-this-secret-together look to the gathering. "It's a good thing I only have to take orders from the bishop." Several chuckles bubbled up from various tables, and the priest continued, looking again at Jane and Jake. "Their left hands—their workaday lives, spent teaching at Drake and elsewhere, writing, making pictures for the news, teaching in the dojo—never hint that their foundation supports each of the efforts we celebrate here today."

Every table erupted in applause as Father Pellegrini gestured to the table where Karli sat alongside Jake and across from Jane. Jane smiled but raised her hands as though to shush the warm outpouring of gratitude.

Seeing that it had no effect, Jake took his glass in his hand and walked to the microphone the priest had left. "Everyone, I'd like you to please raise your glasses." The applause faded and the busy sounds of people turning to pick up glasses and shuffle chairs to more comfortable positions.

"I'd like to thank Father Pellegrini for coming tonight and asking for the blessing." Here he looked sternly at the priest and continued, "Of course, he won't be back next year, as he seems incapable of even saying grace without following some pretty simple directions." Laughter again bubbled through the room.

"Most of all, I'd like to raise my own glass to each of you. Each one of you is here for a particular and very special reason, and each of you deserves the gratitude of everyone here. You do amazing things, and my mother and I are proud and thrilled to know you. So let us please drink to each other." Jake raised his glass as the voices all called back, "To each other!"

Once the speech was over, one of the catering staff directed the four farthest tables to the buffet, while the wine servers again circulated through the room. Jake remained standing, shaking hands with people on their way to the buffet, smiling and patting backs.

Looking for something to occupy her hands while she waited her turn, Karli reached for her wine glass and found it full again. Gabe's droopingly sympathetic face again smiled her way. "You look like you might be feeling a bit lost tonight," he said, his face inviting Karli to unburden herself.

"I didn't want to be here at all," Karli began, feeling the bubble of fury that had been contained within her begin to break out.

She asked quickly to be excused, then stood and headed for the door back to the house.

"Why didn't you want to be here?" Jake's voice whispered in her ear as he intercepted her hand and slipped it into his arm. He guided her away from the entrances to the house and toward a gap Karli hadn't noticed before in the rearmost part of the tent. "Let's go somewhere we can talk." They passed out of the tent and walked quickly down a curving path to a two-story carriage house that had obviously been built to match the main house. There were at least four double-width carriage doors along the building's red-brick front. They entered a door that led into a heated garage where Karli saw the familiar Ford pickup parked near her and a sedan parked in its shadow.

Jake led her up an open staircase at the side of the garage area to a huge room that spanned the full front-to-back space of the carriage house. Karli took in the room at a glance: the ceiling towered above ten foot-tall freestanding museum-style display walls that were scattered across the floor. Discreet cables of small, directional halogen lights criss-crossed fifteen or so feet above the floor, casting small pools of light onto specific parts of the walls. Plainly framed color and black-and-white photographic prints—landscapes and portraits, some in close groups, some alone—perched in the circles of light. *So this is the studio Gabe was talking about when he said Jake's studio-people came to the dinner.*

Jake gestured her to a sternly modern sofa in the center of the room and asked her to wait for a moment. His voice carried back over the display wall he walked behind, explaining that this was where he lived, separate from his mother's house, yet still on the family property. "There's room enough here for a whole family, really," he said, returning from behind the wall with two full wine glasses. "It's pretty much wasted on me."

Karli accepted her glass in silence, trying to push aside the spectacular tastes of the wines, the tempting smells of the food, the special-seating attention and . . . oh, everything else. All of that was simply distracting her from Jake's betrayal. The bubble of Karli's fury expanded suddenly to the bursting point, and it flashed forth from her eyes as she turned quickly toward Jake.

"Why do I not want to be here?" she demanded. "How about you leading me on and making me think you were different from every other giant walking penis in the world and then turning out just like all the rest? That seems like enough to me." She stood abruptly, setting her glass down on the low table and moving toward the door.

"Karli, wait," Jake called to her. "I have no idea what you're talking about!"

"The hell you don't!" she spat back, turning to face him. "You slept with that bitch Sophia—right after that big romantic set-up to get me to kiss you."

"Karli," Jake said with a calmness that irritated her even more, "I have never slept with Sophia. I have never kissed Sophia."

"Right." Karli saw her own hands shaking with her rage. "That's why she was all come-hither and talking about how you'd worked her out of her pajamas when you gave her the ride of shame to work last week. Don't insult me with bullshit lies. I heard her myself."

"Pajamas?" Jake's brow creased as he searched his memory. Then, "Oh! Holy fire, Karli—she was talking about a *gi*!

I loaned her a gi, when she came to train at the karate studio. And I didn't work her out of it. She worked out *in* it. She wanted to do some weapons-disarming training for the ride-alongs we have to do with cops on the heroin series, so I invited her to train with us. That's all that was. She came to the studio for a workout."

"Gi? What the hell are you talking about?" Karli shrilled. "Sleeping with her in your studio doesn't make it not sleeping with her!"

"No, Karli, I didn't sleep with her anywhere," Jake said. "I have a karate studio. She wanted to learn karate, so she came to the karate studio. I loaned her a gi—a karate uniform—which looks kind of like white pajamas."

"What do you mean you have a karate studio?" Karli asked, confused by this bizarre and unexpected explanation. "This is a studio, right here, with all the pictures on the walls. Studio, see?" she asked, gesturing to indicate the room's many displayed photographs. "And why would she spend the night in a karate studio rather than here, anyway?"

"She didn't spend the night, Karli," Jake explained. "Her car was acting up on the way to the dojo, so she had to take it in for service the next morning. I offered to meet her at the garage and give her a lift in to work."

"Why do you even *have* a karate thing?" Karli's diminishing anger was now focused on the nonsense explanations he was offering. "Photogs have photography studios. *Nobody* has a karate studio."

Jake chuckled into his lap, shaking his head, then looked up at Karli with an inadequately suppressed grin. "I have a karate studio because I've learned enough karate to want to share it.

It's a way to make the world a more peaceful, safer, and healthier place. And it's a path many people choose to learn about how they can serve others." He rose from his seat and gestured Karli to come around one of the display walls.

"Darrin trained in my karate studio for a few years," he said gently, indicating a lone picture occupying the exact center of a display wall. A tinsel-smiling and sweaty Darrin beamed from the picture, holding a trophy topped by a little gold-colored karate man doing a kick. "He probably wasn't aware of it, but he served everyone else in the dojo each training session. When he was there, everyone shared his joy, everyone laughed more, everyone trained harder, and everyone learned more. He was a really special kid." Jake's hand reached toward the picture as though to touch it, but he held it back short of the glass, leaving only his shadow over the photo.

Stunned, Karli took in the photo. It was no snapshot. It captured the tournament atmosphere in the out-of-focus background; the sharp-edged focus on the boy pulled him out of the background along with his proud achievement. Fresh sweat beaded the boy's forehead and threatened to drip from an eyebrow and into his eye. Light poured from an out-of-frame source and onto the boy's shoulders and back, while a different light dropped shadows onto his cheek and jaw from the highlighted cheek bones and nose.

"So you were his karate teacher? *That's* how you knew Darrin?" It was obvious, but Karli needed to hear it out loud so she could jiggle this new information into place. Jake Gibson was a puzzle she hadn't been able to piece together yet, and here was a whole new part of the picture atop the box.

And he hadn't slept with Sophia after all.

Karli glanced silently at Jake's face, then moved on around the remaining walls, taking in the pictures—one wall held a group showing Jane one-on-one with children of different ages, laughing, reading, playing, working with pencil and paper. The photos were composed and shot to show the intensity she brought to each child in each situation. She was completely present for each of those kids, going with them into whatever adventure they were having.

Karli's breath caught suddenly as she turned a corner to find two facing display walls covered with photos of herself. There she was, listening to a middle-aged man in one of the State Fair pavilions, gazing at an unseen speaker with her hand on her chin, looking earnestly at her reporter's notebook amid the smoking remains of an office block that burned to the ground, smiling with a group of farmers alongside a harvested corn field. She saw in each picture a different part of her own personality, illuminated in ways nobody had ever shown her before, from the compassionate listener to the driven and focused career reporter. At first she looked at the pictures with the deliberate detachment she had learned to use when watching recordings of her reports. She was careful to evaluate how she held herself and whether or not she exhibited the earnestness and attention that she truly tried to bring to each of her stories.

And then she turned and saw the photo collage of her at the covered bridge, smiling back over her shoulder with the soft-focus bridge in the background, angled away from the daylit opening of the bridge and toward the great interior support timbers, close-up and just cold enough for the color to show in her cheeks, even in a subtly black-and-white image. Just seeing the images brought her suddenly back to the bridge, to the moment when she raised herself on tiptoe, toward Jake's solemn face, to their kiss. Her knees felt suddenly soft, her legs tingly, and she caught her breath again.

That moment had not, after all, been a lie. That passion, that intimacy, that breathtaking surge of passion had all been real. Karli closed her eyes to recapture the soft, firm wetness of the kiss, the tender bite on Jake's lip eliciting a soft inhalation from him, the pounding pulse that filled her head and chest and tender regions. She closed her eyes and the contemplative silence they'd both fallen into during the car ride back to Des Moines swept back over her, subsuming her awareness of her surroundings into a calm savoring of the sensations and exploration of the connection.

The warmth of Jake's gently open hand pressing between her shoulder blades began to swing her back to the present, through a muzzy blur of arousal and alcohol. She turned her face toward his and saw something in his warm brown eyes that sparked a connection, an intimacy. And she recognized it as the understanding that he brought to the video he shot for her stories, the pictures he had taken of her, and to their conversations. Jake tried always to understand her, and these pictures showed that he understood many aspects of her at least as well as she understood herself. *How does he see me so clearly?* she wondered.

As Jake opened his mouth to begin saying . . . something . . . Karli reached up and placed her index finger on his full lips, shushing him with a faint *sh*. Touching the warm firmness of his lips made her quiver with quick arousal, and the tingling shudder that ran down and back up her legs urged her on. She rose on tiptoe, her hand sliding along Jake's chiseled jawline and around the back of his neck so she could pull those full lips down to hers. She pressed the length of her body along his, feeling his hard stomach and legs and hips against her own. She felt his breath as he bent to her mouth, then their lips met with an insistent gentleness and parted together as their tongues met and moved together with rhythmic wetness. Her eyes fluttered shut as she was swept away on waves of intoxicating sensation.

The kiss intensified Karli's world, making the exploratory meeting of their mouths its center. Its outermost boundaries were the melding contours of their bodies, the blood pounding through her heavily breathing breast and everywhere she pressed herself against Jake's tall, masculine hardness. His mouth tasted of the amazing wine he'd given her, and his breath's sweet alcohol fumes mingled with his skin's spicy scent to flavor the air that swirled around their impassioned breathing. Gravity found dizzying new directions, pulling her legs and hips closer against Jake while tilting her head and neck back into almost a dance-couple's dip.

The sensitive nerves in Karli's neck lit up with electric chill as Jake's hand slid along her throat, his thumb and fingers covering the pulsing arteries on each side. The gentleness did no more than graze and then caress her skin. Electricity coursed between her tensing breasts, the growing wetness between her legs, her lips and tongue and neck and breath and pulse, criss-crossing and connecting each sensation.

As she and Jake gradually pulled apart from one another, Karli felt slightly off-balance, made dizzy not only by the surges of sensation and hormones and also by the substantial amount of wine she had consumed in the last hour. Jake's strong arms steadied her as each of them opened and connected startled eyes.

"Shit," Karli said. "I'm lost. That was amazing."

"You know," Jake said, "you're really good at that. *Really* good."

"I didn't expect anything like that . . . like that intensity," Karli said, reaching tentatively toward Jake, as though the moment, the passion, were fragile and could be broken by the wrong touch.

Jake took her hand and raised it back to his lips, delicately kissing her fingertips, then moving his eyes back to hers as his mouth formed a rascal's grin. She felt his breath on her fingers as, with a deep rasp to his whisper, he asked, "Do you still wish you hadn't come to my party?"

He moved her hand away from his mouth and moved gently toward her face again. This kiss was gentler, and felt for just a moment as though it could be nearly chaste. Their slight mutual hesitation ended all at once, and they were thrust back into the formless world of their passion.

After another breathless parting, Karli was swept away by the look of irresistible hunger in Jake's eyes. It ended when he shook his head and took a deep, quivering breath. "Karli, I hate to say this more than you can imagine, but I have to get back to the guests."

Karli saw him begin to fidget, picking up their wine glasses and looking toward the hidden part of his 'apartment' with a deep sigh, then tilting his head toward the stairs going back down to the ground floor.

"Do we have to go right now?" Karli asked, reluctantly accepting her wine glass back from Jake. "I mean, you live here, don't you? This is your place, right?"

Karli twitched in surprise as Jake leaned suddenly to her ear, where she felt his breath carry an almost inaudible whisper. "I want you," he said. "Now." And there was a pause as both he and Karli felt that statement's effect on their pulses. "But you are one of the big reasons I invited many of tonight's guests. I want to run you by the Board and get everyone on my side." Karli realized that he'd been ushering her toward the stairs as he said this, so he was unable to see the questioning eyebrow she lifted in response to his last statement.

She meant to follow up with questions about the Board, but as soon as they left the warmth of the carriage house and went out into the crisp winter coldness, a tuxedo-clad man walking toward them from the huge tent spotted them and called out. "Mr. Gibson, would you have a moment to provide some direction about the wine service? We're having more requests for the Pouilly-Fuissé than we'd anticipated, and we need to know if we should open more or if we should suggest alternatives."

"Do we have enough to serve everyone who's asking?" Jake asked.

"Your supply is ample, Mr. Gibson."

"Then please open as much as is necessary to keep it going as long as people are asking for it," Jake said easily. Then he turned to Karli. "Ms. Lewis, shall we return to the guests? I hear there's plenty of wine to keep the party going." Karli smiled back at his boyish grin and laced her arm through the one he extended for her.

They walked back into the big white tent and resumed their place-carded seats. As she sat down, Gabe leaned over to her with a grin. "It's good to have you back and looking a bit more cheerful. And it's probably the cold outside that put all that color in your cheeks, right?" Karli felt her cheeks flushing hot, but Gabe said no more. He just gave her a kind wink and suggested by gesture that they should take their plates to the buffet line. As she rose to walk with him, she noticed that Jake's distinctive smell lingered just below her nose.

As the evening progressed, Karli found herself sitting with a series of one or two people at a time, from Gabe and the priest to perfect strangers to three young siblings—the oldest might have been 7 years old—who earnestly shared their opinions about which kind of pie Karli should have more of. Being accustomed to meeting strangers and jumping right into conversations with them, Karli was perfectly comfortable making so many new friends in a single evening. And she often caught Jake's eye as he talked his way through a series of similar encounters. Each time, she felt a flutter as though they had just kissed a moment ago, even though they were separated by the crowd that heaved through the room, re-focusing from turkey to dessert and from one table to the next.

Finally, nearly everyone was gone from the party, though it looked like at least two families were staying the night. Jake broke free from exchanging good-byes with a departing couple and wound his way through the clean-up crew toward Karli, who was hugging Gabe good-bye as though they'd known each other for years.

"I'm afraid I have to go make up the guest beds in my place now,

Karli," Jake said. "Jane has a houseful, and I'm catching the overflow." Again, he extended his arm, and again she laced her arm through his. "May I walk you to your car?"

Karli nodded as they walked through the house to retrieve her coat, a bit disappointed that she and Jake wouldn't be taking up where they had left off. Jake grabbed an old barn coat for himself, and they went together out into the cold darkness of Thanksgiving night. The quiet blocks to Karli's Saab seemed to her much longer in the darkness than they had when she was coming to the party. *And I am not mad any more, either,* Karli thought to herself in mild surprise. *Jake didn't sleep with Sophia after kissing me. And he takes pictures of me that are more revealing than if I had my clothes off. And he makes me want to take my clothes off.* Despite the cold, Karli felt her cheeks flare hot again. *Kissing him is not like kissing other guys has ever been. I've never been kissed like that before. What is happening?*

She looked up at Jake's face, walking tall beside her, and wondered what he was thinking. "Is this your car?" he suddenly asked. "It's a Saab, right?" Karli swept her eyes away from his face and toward the car he indicated.

"Um, yeah, that's mine," she said, stammering as she came out of her thoughts and into the moment. She began patting her pockets to find where she'd put her keys, then felt herself turned and pressed back against the still-closed door of her car.

Jake's body pressed against her and his kiss came suddenly and without preamble. Her hands found his coat and pulled Jake against her more closely. She could feel the hardness pressing between her hip bones. The kissing lasted longer and longer and did not grow old. They finally paused, and, breathing hard, Karli whispered, "I want you."

"And I want you," Jake whispered through heavy breath as he bent to lightly run his teeth along her neck. "But not tonight. I have to go back and take care of people." Karli saw him pull away from her as though it took real effort. He said, "This is absolutely the best—certainly the most intense—Thanksgiving Day ever."

"So I should go now?" Karli asked reluctantly, her weight coming off the car and swaying toward Jake.

"Well, yeah, I think that's what has to happen," Jake said, bending to catch her by the shoulders and brush his lips ever so lightly across hers.

Karli opened her eyes yet again to find Jake's locked on hers. "I don't want you to go," he breathed.

"Making out in my car would be pretty juvenile, though, wouldn't it?" Karli asked in a moment of regretful lucidity.

Jake quirked a grin in response. "Yeah," he muttered.

"What kind of guy plies a woman with fancy wine and great food, brings the hot kissing, and then doesn't close the deal?" Karli was surprised that she'd come right out and said what was on her mind. She smiled, and she felt the glittering of the street lights in her eyes.

Jake dropped his head and chuckled into his coat. Karli watched closely as he raised his eyes back to hers, the erotic hunger flashing deeply within them. "The kind who's looking for an even better deal, I guess." He raised his eyebrows and gave her a naughty, twinkling look. "Or maybe just the kind who doesn't plan sleeping arrangements very well."

Chapter Eighteen

"Complacency is what kills top-rated newsrooms, Karli, and even though you're relatively new here, you're showing some of the signs." Karli furrowed her eyebrows and frowned her lips in her best impression of news consultant John Bielfeldt, then relaxed to an expression of appalled indignation. "Really, he totally had the balls to tell me that I'm complacent here." She drank from her third amaretto stone sour, made her own frown at the fact that it was empty except for ice, then looked around to catch the bartender's eye.

Wynton Marsalis blew his horn through the bar's speakers, laying down a calm, clear music bed for the gripe session.

"So what about your day showed complacency—the fact that you and Max hustled all the way out to BFE and back with stops along the way and managed to put together a huge story on how dangerous frozen ponds are? Not just with community reaction about those poor boys, but with ag experts AND an emergency room doctor?" Bailey was equally indignant. She had worked the phones for parts of the story and had seen the whole package come together on the air earlier that evening.

"He never mentioned *anything* about that story," Karli replied. "He picked on the little stand-up-and-sound-bite story I did on that car crash in Norwalk on the way back." Here Karli returned to her impression of the consultant: "This stand-up illustrates the problem. You're not doing anything to draw the viewer's eye to the visual story, you're not engaged with anything. It's just you saying that police aren't releasing names until families are notified."

"I didn't want to sound defensive," Karli said in her own voice. "But this was a car crash story. The mess had been cleaned up by the time we got there, we only had a few minutes to get anything at all on video and get back to the station so we could get it on the air. So I didn't say anything."

"Yes," Bailey said. "We all know that active stand-ups are better. They want us more involved in the story. But is the last-minute non-fatal crash story that you don't even think will air worth all that effort?"

"I don't know," Karli said. "The guy wants to be a college journalism professor or something. He doesn't seem to understand that we work in the real world and with real time pressures."

Mary Rose leaned in with a raised finger and an unfocused look in her eyes. After barely camouflaging a belch, she looked directly at Karli and spoke: "He isn't paid to tell us we're doing a fine job. Really, ladies, if he can't tell us to get all impossible, he goes broke. And you don't have to look at his cufflinks very long to understand that he does NOT want to go broke."

"I can totally see that about the frustrated professor," Bailey said. "We're all his little protégés, and he's going to teach us about reporting *inspirational* stories." Here she raised her wine glass and tried ineffectually to make her thin red eyebrows look gray and bushy like the consultant's.

"Think about the stories that had the biggest effect on you," she said in her best impression of a masculine baritone. "Each one of them was *inspirational*. There are three characteristics of every inspirational message. The message has to be Understandable, Memorable, and Emotional."

Karli and Mary Rose cheered Bailey's impression with delighted laughter. They could hear the capital letters in her pacing and emphasis. Encouraged by the warm reception, Bailey continued, á la Bielfeldt, "You're highly trained and already good at making your stories understandable, at taking language and ideas down to their simplest." And here Bailey took a deep drink from her wine, stood up from her barstool and began pacing back and forth to emphasize her pompous impression's points to Karli and Mary Rose, who swiveled in their chairs to take it all in.

"But journalism school's greatest weakness may be teaching people to disregard the emotional aspects of stories, and that's too bad. J-school talks about measuring a story's importance by assessing its impact or how many people are affected by it. That's all good, but most of the stories we care most deeply about are stories that affect us emotionally. To disregard emotional effect is to ignore a lot of the importance stories actually have."

Karli's expression changed from one of amusement to one of serious, if slightly inebriated, inquiry. Her fourth drink was now half-empty. "But doesn't that become pandering right away?" she asked. "If we use emotional impact as our yardstick, doesn't the news become an endless cycle of kitten-and-baby videos?"

"Kittens?" Mary Rose asked loudly. "If I want impact, I want to see stories about Jake and the Kissing. Update that story, Karli." Mary Rose took a languorous drink from her beer, then looked at Karli out of the corners of her eyes as she licked foam slowly from her upper lip, her tongue piercing flashing brightly. Karli looked down at the drink she held in her lap, but not before her cheeks showed red.

"I didn't say emotional effect was the only metric," Bailey-as-Bielfeldt intervened with a placating raised hand. "I'm just suggesting that good editorial judgment and reporting requires including emotional content. Say a plant is closing and a community will lose 600 jobs. The economic impact is vitally important, yes, and that's the story that we're all ready to report. But it isn't hard to find sources who say that self-esteem and marriages and child-rearing and all kinds of other things are wrapped up in having a solid job."

"Okay," Karli conceded, again engaged with the earnestness that comes with just about enough alcohol and as though Bailey really were the consultant. "Some of that, yes. But you know lots of news directors will say stories on emotional effects are puff pieces or hand-wringing or whatever. They aren't necessarily going to advance my career, in other words."

"My career, my career," Mary Rose mocked. "Haven't you got anything better to talk about?" She waggled her eyebrows first to Karli and then at Bailey. "The inspiration stuff is boring. And so is your career. Let's talk about sex."

Karli looked desperately at Bailey, hoping to avoid that conversation. "So, Understandable and Emotional we've got. What does he have to say about Memorable?"

Bailey shrugged. "He doesn't have much to add there. Just that memorable things come in threes. That's about it."

"Threesomes?" Mary Rose shrieked. "You two have been holding out on me!"

Karli was appalled that so many eyes in the bar had turned their way in response to Mary Rose's exclamation. "We did NOT have a threesome, Mary Rose," she said in her best shushing tone. "It was just the two of us."

Mary Rose ducked her head down secretively, and Bailey eagerly returned to her seat and leaned in toward Karli. "Two of you is plenty," Mary Rose blurted. "Girl, we need details. FULL details. Grooming and acts and dimensions and everything."

"And when did all this go down?" Bailey asked. "We haven't been out for drinks in forever."

"We didn't have sex, okay?" Karli's blush felt like it covered her whole body. "We just had another kiss." She caught herself and added, "Well, we had a few more kisses. But that's it."

Mary Rose's face looked suddenly downcast. "How come you run warm-up laps and never do the race? This is frustrating as hell, girl. I don't know about you, but I want more!"

There was a pause as Karli tried to figure out what to tell her friends. And as she thought about it, she recalled the heat and passion of the kiss in Jake's gallery. Just remembering the sensations made her pulse race and tightened the coiled energy inside her. The tingling between her legs confirmed that she wanted more, too. A lot more. Soon.

"Annnnd?" Bailey stretched the single syllable out impatiently.

Karli snapped out of her hormonal reverie and looked back to her friends. "It turns out that he is a karate instructor," she said. Then she drained her glass and gestured for more.

"What?" Bailey was incredulous.

"Of course he is," Mary Rose added. "But I didn't realize that was a necessary relationship qualification for you. Do you only shag karate guys?"

"No!" Karli answered. "I don't have sex with karate guys!"

"So why is karate a good thing, then?" Bailey asked, genuinely confused.

"Because that means he wasn't sleeping with Sophia."

"What?" said Bailey. Her confusion showed all over her face.

Mary Rose, who was also confused, didn't let her confusion slow her down. "That bitch," she said, "had better not be fucking Jake, or

160

I would have to hate him for being stupid enough to let her go there."

"Well, I thought she was, because of the pajamas," Karli said. "But the karate thing—really who even has one of those?—cleared that all up." She concluded with a glowing smile, her explanation complete.

"Um, Karli, I don't think you need any more to drink," Mary Rose said. "Or maybe you need a lot more. Come to think of it, that always makes for a better story. Let's have more." She clapped her hands together and rubbed them in anticipation, then raised a hand to catch the bartender's attention and gestured for a new round.

Bailey's frustrated glare conveyed to Karli that her explanation had somehow fallen short of expectations. "So I was pissed because he was sleeping with her after he kissed me on the bridge. . ."

"What bridge?" Bailey was interested but genuinely confused by now, and it showed in her tone and face.

"Ooh, I love stories with trolls," cried Mary Rose.

"You know, the covered bridge outside of Winterset," Karli said. "Where the book is set and where they did the movie."

"WHAT?" Bailey nearly shrieked. "He took you to a covered bridge in Madison County and kissed you there? That is probably the most romantic thing ever!"

"Well, he didn't kiss me," Karli said. "At least, not at first. I sort of started with the kissing. Then he kissed me back. Really well." Again, Karli's memory transported her to a moment of intense passion. Again, she felt the coiled tension inside of her—the aching wetness between her legs, the tightened flesh of her nipples—crying out for release. Again, she lost the thread of the conversation.

"On a covered bridge, no less." Bailey sighed wistfully.

"Right, so you kissed on a bridge. How far did you go?" Mary Rose asked.

Karli turned her eyes back to her friends and brought them back into focus. "We kissed there, and then I thought I heard him and Sophia talking about sleeping together, and that wasn't good."

"Yeah, but because he's a karate instructor he didn't sleep with her, right?" Mary Rose said. "I suppose that's like a self-defense thing, not sleeping with the super-bitch?"

"So anyway, he didn't, and then he took me up into his apartment-studio-thing and explained about the karate—which I still don't get because grown-ups don't do karate really, do they?—and then I saw the pictures he took of me and it was all sexy and then I kissed him again and he kissed me back again and then we should have done it but he had this huge party to be at and he couldn't even find a free bed in his own place so we couldn't do it." Karli finished breathlessly and looked for confirmation that she had spelled it all out in satisfactory detail for her curious friends. Somewhat puzzled yet smiling faces met her searching look. "So that's it. Kissing and that's all."

Scott Winstead, the darkly handsome weekend sports anchor, suddenly appeared in their midst. "Ladies, we need your company urgently," he said, gesturing to the table where Buzz Czielsa, the clean-cut and blondely athletic main sports anchor sat with director Chuck Teros. Noticing Scott's gesture, the boys waved cheerfully and even stood to pull out chairs where the women could sit.

"Crap, Scott, it was just getting good over here, and now you've spoiled it!" Mary Rose complained, rising from her chair and grabbing her drink. Bailey and Karli took her cue and began to move across the bar.

"We really ought to sit with the guys once in a while," Bailey acknowledged, taking Karli by the arm and steering her toward the table. "They're complete hounds, but they can be fun."

Sitting down at the table, Karli realized that she'd never spent any time with the sports team. Everybody said they were the funniest people in the station, and there was no denying that they were very handsome.

Scott had the café au lait complexion that made heritage an ethnic mystery. He had a kind of Latino air about him—*maybe Brazilian or something,* Karli thought, though his name was solidly none-of-the-above. *Boy oh boy, does he ever wear strong cologne! At least it's a relatively classy scent.*

Buzz was as wholesomely Iowan as could be: white-blonde close-cut hair, and he still rocked the physique of the Division I discus competitor he had been in college. Charlie Teros, the director, looked like a teenager next to the two specimens though he was probably ten years older. Charlie was sandy-haired, small, slight, and somewhat fidgety. He wore a very '80s mustache, perhaps to emphasize that he, too, was masculine, even in the hyper-manly company he kept.

As the seating was arranged, boy-girl, boy-girl, Buzz called the cocktail server over and ordered a round for everyone. Karli protested that she'd had enough and would be perfectly happy with a diet Mountain Dew, but Buzz insisted. And so Karli found herself with yet another fresh drink in front of her. She fished around in her purse, came up with her keychain, and demanded, "Who is going to take these from me so I don't drive tonight?"

Scott reached over to gently take her keys, wafting yet another cloud of his scent over her. "I'm still on my first drink, Karli, so I will stop now and be your designated driver," he said.

Buzz clapped him on the back and bellowed, "What we have here, my friends, is a genuine knight in shining armor. What do you think about that?"

"I think I'll have another drink," Mary Rose said, tilting back a nearly full beer and draining it in effortless chugs.

"Since Karli was my ride here, Scott, you now get to take TWO amazing women to their respective homes tonight."

If he was disappointed at Mary Rose's self-invitation, Scott showed no sign. He continued to beam his sparkling white smile impartially around the table as he slipped Karli's keys into his pocket.

Buzz, Chuck, and Scott were having an impassioned debate regarding the merits of the Iowa Hawkeyes and Iowa State Cyclones basketball teams. Of course, impassioned is the only kind of debate intrastate rivalries permit.

As they leaned into the table to pursue their good-natured and long-standing disagreements about Iowa's college basketball programs, Mary Rose leaned back in her chair and across to Karli. "Aren't you just ecstatic we left our great seats to come over here and listen to sports shit?"

Karli, her voice slurring noticeably and quite a bit louder than she had intended her effort at a stage whisper to be, responded, "I suppose they could be talking about muscle cars or something even worse. But you're right. How long do we have to stay?"

Bailey got up and walked over to sit behind Buzz in a chair from the next table. "So they invite us over to appeal to our love of sports debate? Really?"

Chuck had been sitting next to Bailey and watched her progress around the table with a hound-dog droop to his eyes. "C'mon guys," he called to Buzz and Scott, "the three most beautiful women in Polk County joined us and you've rubbed them wrong in under three minutes!"

Buzz and Scott snapped their heads back and forth around the table, observing exactly what Chuck had just described. They immediately fell all over themselves begging the women's pardon, apologizing for boring shop talk and so on.

"Hey," Mary Rose said, directing a challenging look at Chuck. "You owe Bailey and Karli here an apology. They're the two most beautiful women in Iowa, not just the Des Moines metro."

"I'll go farther than that," Chuck said with goopy sincerity. "Karli and Bailey are the two most beautiful women in the whole Midwest." And he made not-entirely-sober puppy-dog eyes at each of them, not bothering to hide the keen, if somewhat indiscriminate crush he had on both after spending large parts of every work day with their faces filling the control room monitors that constituted nearly his entire view of the world.

"There's no doubt," said Scott smoothly, "that you're all three the most beautiful women in this bar." He raised his glass ceremonially and said, "Gentlemen, let us toast the feminine magnificence that graces our table this evening. These women are, in the very finest sense of each term, Understandable, Memorable, and Emotionally irresistible. In short, *Inspirational*."

Buzz and Chuck erupted in laughter. "To the consultant-approved news faces!" Buzz cried, taking a huge drink. His laughter fading, Chuck reverted to the expression he usually wore with Karli and Bailey—sincere and smitten.

"I'd dump my beer on you jerks," said Mary Rose, gulping the last half of her drink, "if I wasn't putting it to a better use. Kiss my inspirational ass."

She stood up onto the seat of her chair—an unusual sight for the normally stolid and upscale Savery hotel—stuck her butt out and slid the waist of her jeans down just far enough to reveal the T-shaped top of her black thong. Buzz leapt from his chair as soon as he saw what Mary Rose was doing, grabbed her hips and planted a loud smooch hard on the right back pocket of her jeans. Chuck and Scott emptied their hands to applaud, and Mary Rose twisted, bent slightly at the knees, and raised a mock-startled hand to her mouth as she gave her backside an extra little waggle, Betty Boop-style.

Just as the noise died down and Mary Rose returned to her seat, Karli hiccuped. Loudly. And then her face fell into a half-lidded generalized grin, directed at nobody in particular. She reached for her drink, but Bailey snatched it away. "Oh no you don't," she chided gently. "You've had plenty enough, Karli. Time to go nighty-night."

"I wanna smooch Mary Rose's butt, too," Karli complained.

"You're darn right you do," Mary Rose said, moving her grin from Buzz to Karli. "Let's get in the car first though, okay?"

"I'd recommend it," Buzz chortled. "That's a world-class backside." He looked at Mary Rose with a lascivious sparkle in his eyes.

Scott rose grandly and gestured toward the exit. Mary Rose slid an arm around Karli to get her up and moving. Karli looked drowsily at her and leaned to whisper in her ear, "I want to smooch your butt because it's so cute. You have a really cute butt, you know? And that thong is really sexy." She finished with a loud hiccup.

Mary Rose laughed and urged the off-balance Karli along towards the exit with a minimum of stumbling.

Scott held the door for them and then walked ahead to his car, a low-slung Volkswagen CC sedan. He opened the front passenger door and Mary Rose helped Karli slide in, then Mary Rose got in the back seat. Scott patiently got both addresses and drove away.

"Mary Rose, you're closer, so I'll drop you off first, okay?"

"No!" Karli said. "I haven't kissed her sexy little bubble butt yet!"

"Karli, you don't need to kiss my butt tonight," Mary Rose said, reaching up to pat Karli's shoulder. "We can save that for next time, okay?"

Karli turned around in her seat, her voice slurred and her gestures big and sort of vague. "Okay, but you need to tell me how to be sexy. Because you're good at that, and all I do is get all worked up and then feel like I have to do it RIGHT NOW. Like, right now, that's how I'm feeling. Like I want to do it right now. You know that feeling?"

Mary Rose laughed again as she continued to pat Karli's shoulder. "You're doing just fine on the sexy thing, Karli. Dudes dig you like crazy."

"No, they don't," Karli began to transition to the tearful phase of intoxication. "They think I'm just a career bitch who has to be on TV because she has daddy issues. That's what Jake said. There's nothing sexy about me."

"Scott, back me up here," Mary Rose said. "Isn't Karli a hottie?"

"Heck, yeah!" Scott cried without hesitation. "I've thought so since her first day at the station. She's rockin!"

"There you go, Karli—dudes think you're hot. If there's ever been a dude's dude, it's Scott."

"That's me," Scott said beaming his bright smile back at Mary Rose and then Karli. "All man, all the time." As he spoke, he pulled over in front of Mary Rose's apartment building. "And here we are, Ms. Mayer. Do you need me to walk you to the door?"

"Don't get carried away, Prince Valiant," Mary Rose replied, leaving the car. "I can make it inside fine. Just promise me you won't go from knight in shining armor to retard in tin foil, okay?"

"Of course he'll take care of me, Mary Rose!" Karli called back through the open rear door. "He's a dude's dude and I'm sexy!"

Scott grinned at Mary Rose's face looking back in through her door, gave a one-shoulder shrug, and put the car back into gear. Mary Rose closed the door and stood on the curb, watching the car recede from view.

Chapter Nineteen

Three NewsFirst Christmas Party
Holiday Inn, West Des Moines
Friday, December 20

Karli watched the wind whisk the steam of her breath away from the hood of the heavy coat she'd worn to keep the wind out. The coat resembled a giant down pillow more than anything else. It was certainly not glamorous. She had reasoned that, although this party was supposed to be a formal occasion, the formal part didn't apply until she was inside and at the party. Her trek across the gigantic parking lot convinced her she had made the right choice. Although 24 degrees was practically balmy for a Des Moines winter day, the wind and the little black dress underneath her huge coat did not promise to play well together.

Vince was shivering around a cigarette outside the hotel's entrance, wearing no overcoat on top of his tuxedo. As Karli came close, he took his last drag, stubbed out his smoke and dropped the butt into the ashtray. He smiled broadly at Karli and offered her his arm to go into the lobby. "Glad to see you here finally, kid," he rasped. "So far it's just been sales and the traffic department that schedules everything to hit the air except news. The sales crew can't quit pressing the meaningless small talk and crappy jokes, and the traffic people only talk to one another around giant mouths-full of chow. You'd think they never ate at home."

"So why are we going in, then?" Karli asked with a chuckle at his descriptions of station personnel from other departments.

"We aren't, kid," he said. "We're going to the bar. The drinks aren't free there, but the company is a lot better." And saying this, he guided Karli to the Blue Bar in the steakhouse located within the hotel building. The host took her coat, revealing her Tadashi Shoji lace-inset black dress and walked them through a haze of delicious surf-and-turf smells and on into the bar. Vince helped Karli into her tall bar stool and then climbed onto his own next to her. He gave her an appreciative, raised-eyebrow look as he settled into his seat. "You certainly got the dress-up part of the memo, didn't you?"

Karli was pleased and surprised at Vince's uncharacteristic show of appreciation. Feeling a slight blush, she played along, making a show of crossing her legs and displaying her Jimmy Choo Alias lacy pumps. "Vince, I didn't think you ever noticed," she said, very nearly winking at her assignment editor.

The bartender came and took their orders for Karli's usual amaretto stone sour, Vince's dry gin martini, and the roasted ravioli appetizer. After he left, Vince turned back to Karli. "Kid, I'm an old guy, but I'm not blind," he said through a genuine smile. "I'm not dumb, either. You didn't wear that dress so old guys would leer at you. And you sure didn't wear it to impress the station management or the consultant."

He didn't ask a question, but Karli recognized the veteran journalist's interviewing technique of leaving a silent space to be filled. Most people feel obligated to fill the void with something, so they just start in talking without giving it much thought. She found the silence nearly irresistible herself. "You know us reporters, Vince. We love to look good any time there's somebody to pay attention."

"So what time is Jake supposed to get here?" Vince asked.

Karli took her iPhone from her clutch and checked the time. "It's about 6:40 now, so he should be here in about 20 minutes." Finishing, she looked up and found Vince nodding and grinning with a *gotcha* look of triumph.

"You'd better let him know you're in here, then, don't you think?" he asked. "We wouldn't want him heading to the big, boring room instead of feasting his eyes here, right?"

Karli blushed, pursed her lips to the side in Olympic *not impressed* fashion, and slid her phone back into her purse. "You of all people should know that he ignores his cell phone pretty much all the time, Vince. Heck, he usually doesn't even know where it is," she said. Then realizing that she'd shown that she knew some of Jake's intimate details, she tried to brush off the slip. "If he wants to find us, he will."

"Oh, he's motivated to look hard," Vince grinned, raising his martini glass to Karli in an unspoken toast. "I'd like to know what he's going to find." His raised eyebrows emphasized the implicit question.

"Hey, Vince!" called a resonant female voice. "Karli."

Karli looked up with a cringing feeling to find Sophia Refai looking deliberately away from her and raising her chin imperiously toward the bartender. "Hey, Sophia," she muttered, hearing Vince's more good-mannered greeting rising over her voice. Her attention was jarred suddenly away from Vince's voice as she noticed that the giant with the deep baritone and the product-laden hair was none other than Donald Harris, the distinctively gap-toothed features reporter from the perennial second-place newsroom. Karli was not surprised to see his arm reaching around Sophia's waist to a spot just shy of inappropriately low on Sophia's hip.

He was a notorious womanizer, one who took full advantage of his television-personality status to sweep essentially anything with two X chromosomes into his bed.

Sophia isn't interested in him, Karli thought to herself. *She's interested in shocking the entire station by bringing one of the competition to our party.*

And Karli saw Sophia discreetly checking in the mirror behind the bar. A knot of station employees hesitated at the bar's threshold, obviously noticing and commenting on Sophia's date.

Karli sighed with relief that she wouldn't be required to make Christmas-y small talk with Sophia, who obviously had other matters to consider. The relief even greater in light of Sophia's ongoing dislike for Karli. It had begun with the drug bust, but it was stronger and more obvious ever since she and Jake had, however quietly, become an actual couple.

Karli's attention was drawn away from the deliberate scandal as Margie Green's figure emerged from the cluster at the doorway and headed straight toward her. The community relations personality had already had a couple drinks, making her effusive personality crowd even closer than usual. As she drew close, Karli felt herself enveloped in a nearly visible cloud of Margie's liberally applied perfume and jingling costume jewelry. Margie's heavily made-up face shone with joy and affection for every person she met, and Karli found her eccentricity charming rather than off-putting. Margie extended both of her hands, palms down and many flashy rings up, to grasp Karli's and pull her into a two-cheek kiss of greeting.

Pushing herself away from Karli after the quick pecks, Margie gave her an appraising look.

"You are just the picture of a sleek and chic holiday party girl, Karli," she fairly gasped. "And those *shoes*! You could take the magazine covers by storm in those!" Margie's 60 or so year-old figure was tightly sheathed in a quirky, brightly colored dress that contrasted starkly with the red-and-green or little black dresses Karli thought appropriate to an evening Christmas party.

"Margie, you're too much," Karli said. "What's the party got for us tonight?"

"Of course Robert from sales made his infamous reindeer punch. Be careful of that stuff, honey!" Margie leaned in, a conspiratorial look on her face and a strong scent of the punch's main ingredient gusting along with her exclamation. "He has some voodoo secret to make that stuff taste like there's not a drop of the booze in it, but every year it makes a lot of people very drunk and very indiscreet. Sometimes I wonder if it isn't just an excuse for people to do what they really want to do but can't get away with." Margie's broad wink sent Karli into a quick spasm of poorly suppressed laughter.

"What would you like to have an excuse for?" Karli asked, trying to match Margie's obvious relish for the risqué.

"Oh, well, I think you already get to do what every girl wants to get away with, don't you?" The suggestive twinkle in Margie's eye and the gentle slap-and-caress on her thigh left Karli in no doubt that Margie was talking about sex—and specifically sex with Jake. The innuendo raised a quick heat in Karli's cheeks, which only made Margie's beaming smile broader.

Larry Robinson, one of the station's most eager sales personnel, leaned into the conversation abruptly.

His glassy grin and slightly swaying posture hinted that the highball in his hand was likely the fourth or fifth in a relatively short time. "You've got those sticky feet, don't you Karli?" he fairly yelled. When Karli looked at him in puzzlement, he elaborated: "You know, you're from Tar Heel country, right? Gotta watch out for those sticky-foot basketball players! They'll beat you every time, right?"

Karli tried not to roll her eyes and felt herself failing. "Larry, I'm from *South* Carolina," she answered. "The Tar Heels are *North* Carolina."

"Oh," Larry's *bonhomie* stalled abruptly at learning a fact known universally to the unintoxicated. "Well, don't put your sticky feet into that crazy Crimson Tide, right?" And with a firm nod indicating that he had managed to cover every base to his complete satisfaction, he slid across the room to his next encounter, leaving Margie and Karli to chuckle at his receding back.

"He needs an excuse for that," Karli muttered into Margie's ear, "but it probably isn't something he wanted to cross off his bucket list."

Karli caught a glimpse of Vince signing a check, tucking it back into the receipt book, and pulling the card from its little slot to return it to his wallet. He stood up from his bar stool, placed a light hand on Karli's shoulder, and rasped, "She's gone, but we'd better head to the party proper. This room is full of the folks we came here to avoid."

Margie's eyebrows rose abruptly as she mouthed a silent, "Sophia?" to Karli, who gave a small nod in return. The three of them picked up their unfinished drinks and moved through the crowd and on into the ballroom where the actual party was set up. A projector filled a screen big enough for a movie theater with a giant image of the station's call letters and the Three NewsFirst logo. Sterno-heated chafing dishes filled with miniature wieners, Swedish meatballs, bacon-wrapped water chestnuts, and tiny pizza puffs stood along one wall. Along the facing wall, a crush of station employees, raising and nearly sloshing cups filled with what looked like red Kool-Aid, dressed in t-shirts and jeans to business suits and everything in between, parted enough to permit only glimpses of three enormous punch bowls.

Margie and Vince steered a middle course toward the few figures that moved among the round, white-clothed tables that filled the room's cavernous center. Before they were able to pick an empty table, John Bielfeldt gestured to them with a somewhat vague wave of his brimful cup of Reindeer Punch. "Yuletide greetings!" he called, beckoning them to his table. Vince looked quickly around the room, Karli assumed for an excuse to sit anywhere else. She leaned forward to whisper in his ear, "It's okay, Vince. He can't possibly destroy our evening all by himself, can he?"

Vince shrugged and moved to the chair farthest from the consultant, pulling out the one next to it for Karli. Margie saw the gallant gesture, smiled broadly at Vince, and stepped nimbly in front of Karli to take the seat. Karli beamed over her seating figure at Vince, gave him a big wink, and drew out a chair for herself next to Margie's.

No sooner had she scooted in to the table than Margie turned to her with a salacious grin. "See that Hailey over there—that new production assistant?" She pointed with her forehead at a young, coltishly slender blonde standing at the middle punch bowl in a pair of jeans and a bright red Christmas sweater that emphasized curves that were, at least on her remarkably slender frame, distinctly prominent.

After Karli indicated that, yes, she saw her, Margie leaned in for a long-distance whisper. "If you had legs like that, wouldn't you be wearing a skirt to a party like this? Well, just watch how she walks, and I'll tell you something that will knock your socks off."

Luckily the girl was right over Bielfeldt's shoulder, as he was trying to get Karli's attention with a slurred inanity. "Do you have any big plans for Christmas this year, Karli?"

"No, John, I'm going to be working Christmas Day, so no big plans. I had Thanksgiving off, you know, and I'm the new kid in the newsroom, so I don't get two in a row off."

As Bielfeldt launched into a predictable when-I-was-a-young-reporter-working-holidays story, Karli let her attention drift over his shoulder to where the young Hailey walked to the table nearest her and winced visibly as she sat down, pausing mid-sit to put her drink on the table, then tug at the knees of her jeans before sitting all the way down.

Margie, caring nothing for Bielfeldt's tedious reminiscence, did another long-whisper: "She's got terrible rug burns on her knees. And so does that spicy sports kid, Scott. One of the engineers told me that he walked right by them on his way out at the end of the graveyard shift. They were so busy there on the newsroom floor that they didn't even notice him! And now everyone is calling her Rug-burn Hailey." Margie's rasping chortle rose above the room's general murmur of conversation and nicely covered Karli's astonished peal of laughter.

"I agree," said a mildly surprised Bielfeldt. "It *was* funny when that cop was grousing about working Christmas Day and accidentally broadcast his whole rant to the dispatcher. You see, my photog was in the front seat, twisted around to shoot the cop, and his knee had keyed the car radio..." Karli watched the consultant's eyes focus abstractedly into the distance as he recalled more boring details about his reporting youth. He paused momentarily to pour half of his remaining punch into his mouth, then he waved the cup in a semi toast, perhaps to his long-ago news photographer colleague, as he continued slurring out his memories.

Seeing that Bielfeldt was too far gone to take lasting offense, Vince rose from his seat and tilted his head toward the punch bowls. Margie nodded enthusiastically and grabbed Karli's hand, practically lifting her from her chair. Exchanging a mumbled excuse and a slurred *of course* with Bielfeldt, she rose and trailed in Margie's wake. The three filled their cups and took cautious sips as they surveyed the swiftly filling room. "Ladies, once we get the blooper reel behind us, I'm going to call it a night," Vince declared. "Everyone here is already bombed, and nobody is going to have anything sober to say for the rest of the night."

"That's what makes this so wonderful!" Margie practically cheered. She then flung her arms wide and began to sing from an old Broadway musical: "This is our once-a-year day! Everyone's entitled to be wild..."

"Margie, shush!" said a smiling Jake, who had snuck up on the little group and thrown his arms around Karli and Margie's shoulders, thrusting his head between the two and swinging it back and forth to take them in. "We shouldn't let ourselves get too wild, should we?"

"Bah!" Margie gusted boozily into Jake's smile. "We're here for the hijinx! I want to see the action, and soon!"

"You're in luck," Mary Rose Mayer called, walking briskly toward the laptop feeding the hotel's video projector. "I'm here, and I brought the hijinx with me!" As she said this, she turned her beaming smile to the laptop that fed video to the giant hotel projector. Clicking and tapping briefly, the huge screen's image changed to a splashy countdown. In the Channel Three colors, huge text screened back like a watermark read: "Time to bloopers." In the foreground, a giant "15:00" began counting down, second by second. Once it reached 14:45, the digital-clock format froze, then dissolved away. Pushed in from the left a verbal description of the time crawled onto the screen, proclaiming, "Fourteen minutes, thirty seconds." As that slid off the right side of the screen, text slid vertically along the side, this time saying, "Quatorze minutes, vingt-cinq seconds." That was replaced in its turn by something that looked like kanji characters, then five seconds later, something scrolled from right to left in what looked like arabic characters. Karli looked away from the screen toward Mary Rose and caught the quirking grin at the edge of her mouth. "That's really unusual. And awesome!"

Word of Mary Rose's innovative countdown apparently spread fast, as the ballroom began to fill quickly with folks who had been prowling the lobby and bar.

Karli watched Mary Rose and turned to look where she was looking: at the darkly handsome Scott Winstead, who was walking in with the usual bachelor crowd of sportscasters, photogs, and control room personnel. Mary Rose raised her hand for a high five in response to Scott's appreciative whistle at the elaborate countdown. No sooner had their hands touched, though, than Mary Rose reached down and slapped her hand across Scott's khaki-clad knee. Karli's abs tensed with suppressed laughter as Scott yelped in pain and danced quickly out of Mary Rose's reach. The group of assorted masculinity walking in with him burst into gales of laughter, mimicry, and fake-slapping toward Scott's knees.

"That is exactly," Jake whispered to both Karli and Margie through his own chuckles, "why I don't want to display any of my own hijinx—there's a price to pay for the Reindeer Punch excuse."

"Oh, but they were shagging yesterday!" Margie fairly yelled. "Long before they had any punch to blame it on. And besides, it's kind of sweet, isn't it? They got to share all that pleasure, and now they get to share a little memento."

Karli heard Jake's chuckling intensify, and she felt his breath stir her hair. The tingling down her neck and back made her want to squirm out from under his arm—or snuggle more closely into it. Either way, it set her tingling. *Maybe another Reindeer Punch would go down well after all,* she thought to herself. *Either it'll calm me down a little or*—and here she felt her breath catch—*give me the excuse I don't really need to do what I really want to do with Jake.*

Mary Rose's countdown kept the giant screen busy with different animations displaying different languages.

Suddenly the countdown shrank down to a small corner of the

screen as the screen filled with an extreme close-up of a male movie star's face. Those who were watching the screen started to laugh—the actor had played a newsman in a major movie. The star's eyes moved as though he were taking in the entire crowd, then he fairly shouted, "Everyone! I need your attention, please!" The abrupt and fully amplified sound startled most of the room to silence, and nearly every head turned toward the screen. "There are only ten minutes left! So it's time to make some NOISE!" The image shook as the volume increased to the level of actual discomfort.

Mary Rose screamed her best "woo-hoo!" as a heavy percussion soundtrack rose from under the actor's voice. The crowd in the ballroom erupted in applause and shouts. The screen changed to the station manager trying to shout, "I say THREE, you say NEWSFIRST!" Then the sales manager's face came on: "THREE!" And Karli heard Margie's shriek rise along with everyone else's voices: "NEWSFIRST!" Then the chief engineer came on the screen and struggled through, "Three!" The crowd responded with mingled laughter and cries of, "NewsFirst!" The chant was repeated with different managers from all the departments leading from the screen and the room shouting back.

Abruptly, the chant stopped. The percussion stopped. The countdown swelled back to fill the screen, this time with an odd progression of Roman numerals. *VII:V IX, VII:V VIII, VII:V VII.*

"Mary Rose, I think you've made yourself kind of a big deal with that bit of uproar," Jake said, his admiration clear in tone and expression.

"Thanks," Mary Rose replied. "I'm worried it de-escalated too quickly, though."

"You're leading into the blooper reel, Mary Rose," Karli said. "How can it possibly deliver on any kind of build-up at all?"

"It can't," Mary Rose shrugged. "But if everyone gets another drink in the next seven minutes, everyone will be too drunk to remember anything in particular about the bloopers."

Sophia Refai strode up to the group with her date trailing vaguely behind her. "That was a crass little stunt," she said as soon as she'd reached Mary Rose's side. "Are we actual journalists here, or is Three NewsFirst some kind of a sports team?" She looked pointedly around the room, and then back at Mary Rose. "I don't see any cheerleaders. Please tell me the rumors that you've arranged for them to perform are baseless."

Mary Rose looked right back into Sophia's sneering face with a casual smirk. "I heard you were going to be doing the splits and calling out names later," she said, glancing at the date-from-the-competition, who was aiming a gap-toothed leer at Sophia. "Your flexibility gets thumbs-up reviews, you know." Mary Rose's voice trailed off suggestively.

Apparently noticing Donald Harris's near-panting as he appeared to envision Sophia calling his name from a full-split position, Sophia snapped her head toward him. "Don't be an oaf, Donald. Let's find a seat before the video starts." And with that, she stormed off, leaving a strong scent of perfume in her trail.

"Are you really bringing in cheerleaders?" Margie asked in the hopeful tones of a child who has heard someone mention candy but can't actually see any.

"Margie, I don't think we could convince the dudes in sales to keep their clothes on if any genuine cheerleaders showed up," Jake said. "Reindeer Punch is the kryptonite that exposes all their weaknesses. Heck, it's a good thing there's only the overhead lights—if there were lampshades, we'd have naked guys walking around in them already!"

"What exactly do you think the cheerleaders have that isn't already here?" Karli asked, turning her face toward Jake's. "This dress isn't exactly floor-length, after all," she continued, running her hands along her chest and down to the not-very-low hemline.

Jake took his arms from around Karli's and Margie's shoulders and stepped through to get space for a full view of Karli's outfit. She immediately saw the appreciation shining in his wide-open eyes. He scanned her slowly up and down and then up again before bringing his eyes up to gaze steadily into hers. She felt his eyes moving over her almost as though they were his hands—and the feeling was electric. She tucked her chin slightly and, looking up through her lashes, asked in an intentionally throaty voice, "What's your kryptonite, Mr. Superman?"

Karli saw Jake swallow hard as he looked all up and down her again, and she felt a deep attentive silence fall within their little group. She wasn't accustomed to feeling, well, *sexy* was really the only word, but Jake's obvious and obviously sexual fascination with her appearance elicited a quivering, sexual response from her. She could feel her skin sliding underneath the smooth sheath of her dress and the slightly itchy edges of her lacy bra and thong needled her in a way that felt like anticipation of the slightly rough edges of Jake's hands and knuckles, of the slightly prickly rasp of his five o'clock shadow, of the slippery smoothness of his lips and tongue. The silence continued a beat too long, and the corners of Karli's eyes caught the others looking right at her.

Mary Rose broke the suddenly uncomfortable silence, stepping into the circle and saying, "Looks to me like that dress is made out of kryptonite." She turned to the entranced Jake and grabbed his elbow. As she tucked the elbow into her chest, bent his arm and then grabbed his hand with both of hers to bend his wrist and palm down toward the elbow, she continued, "Hey, he's so weak from that kryptonite dress, I can make Sensei Jake tap out!"

The pressure on his wrist suddenly became great enough that Jake snapped his attention to Mary Rose's devilish grin, then used his free hand to snake through her arms and pull his elbow free. Mary Rose was surprised to find that she was trying to bend a wrist that no longer resisted. She was even more surprised when she found that Jake had kept a grip on one of her wrists, slid his other forearm against her upper arm, and grabbed his own wrist to place a sudden twisting pressure on her shoulder—enough pressure that Mary Rose urgently patted her hand against the nearest bit of Jake she could find. "Hey! What the hell was *that*?" she cried.

Jake relaxed his grip instantly when Mary Rose tapped him. In response to her question, he chuckled and said, "I'm not sure. Something between a half-Nelson and standing Kimura.

You put that wrist-lock on me just enough to make the kryptonite vanish."

A little chuckle at this caught his attention. Margie leaned over to Vince and—in her extremely loud whisper, loud enough for the whole little group to hear—said, "I think he means that the dress covered Karli back up after he imagined it had vanished. Karli in her unmentionables is the *real* kryptonite!"

Karli appreciated Vince's effort not to laugh out loud—even though it failed—but she felt suddenly very self-conscious, as though she really had been partially undressed in front of everyone.

She felt the color rise in her cheeks and she looked from face to face, searching for some hint that she hadn't acted foolishly.

The clamor of several shouting voices broke her concentration. "ONE MINUTE TO THE BLOOPERS!" she heard an entire table of drunken station employees scream, followed by a "Woo-hoo!" that rang with the unique shrill that only an excess of drink can impart.

Karli and pretty much everyone else in the room looked up to see that Mary Rose's ingenious countdown had transformed into a series of animated Santas, reindeers, and elves, all indicating the decreasing time with numerals pulled from gift boxes, sleighs, hats, trees, and other Christmasy containers.

"We'd better find a seat, then," Jake said, lacing Karli's arm though his own. "If, that is, you want to stay and watch the drunks and the bloopers." He indicated with a nod of his head toward the Reindeer Punch table, where a studio camera operator was laughing uncontrollably at the puddle of red that spread over the table from his overturned cup. Karli felt Jake's breath on her neck as he leaned closer. "Mary Rose already showed me the bloopers," he whispered into her ear, his breath causing a tingle to spread along the side of her neck and on down between her shoulder blades.

Karli quirked a questioning eyebrow at Jake, posing an unspoken question. "No, there isn't much," he answered, and she couldn't tell if he was answering the wrong question on purpose. "The only two really good things are John's live shot where he said he was in Adel County, and then Brinkman had to tell him that he was in Dallas County, and then they cut back to John just in time to see him hit himself on the forehead with his mic. '*Aack--Adel is the county seat!*' That was really funny." As he finished this bit, Karli noticed that Jake had been leading them both toward the lobby. She looked over her shoulder toward the little cluster of Mary Rose, Vince, and Margie. Mary Rose saw her looking, cracked a huge grin, and gave her a double thumbs-up.

Karli smiled and then realized Jake was still talking. "So there's that, and then there's the time you fell all the way down when you were doing that walking interview with the farmer." Karli slapped Jake's arm as soon as she saw the grin tugging at his lips. "Hey!" he said, "At least that wasn't live, so it was never broadcast." Jake paused, the grin pulling hard now at his mouth. "Well, it wasn't broadcast until everyone sees it here tonight." The twinkle in Jake's eyes as he said this faded quickly to something much more intense. Karli felt her dress coming off in his imagination again and then caught her breath as it came off in her own imagination—with Jake handling the zipper. She felt her own eyes matching every bit of the intense smolder she saw in his.

She pulled Jake down and rose up the tiny bit her heels left to whisper in his ear. "Should we get a room?"

Chapter Twenty

Jake pulled back to look at her and he felt his pulse race and his eyes widen in surprise. "That escalated quickly," he muttered.

Just as he took a breath to give a more serious response, he noticed that at least some of the electric buzzing he felt came from Karli's phone. He felt her reluctantly pull it out. Her eyes still locked with his, she raised it to her ear and dragged her thumb across the screen. "Karli Lewis," she said. She held his eyes with her own, and he felt an ever-deepening arousal intensify. The room sounded like an urgently good idea.

As she listened, though, her eyes dropped from Jake's, then her arm came free from his, and her eyes took on the unfocused look of someone listening closely. "No, Jake's right here, so we've got it," she said. Then, after another pause, "Right. Text me the address."

No sooner had he seen her touch the screen to end the call than he felt her grab his hand and drag him toward the coat check. She was moving fast, and he fairly stumbled to keep up. "That was the newsroom," she said, her words coming all in a single breath and all connected. "There's a house fire in West Des Moines and it's bad and we have to go cover it and nobody else can do it because we're on a skeleton crew tonight for the party."

Karli had been waving to the coat check attendant as they walked up; she'd apparently made an impression when she and Vince had come in, as her coat was waiting for her without any need for the claim check.

"I have my Canon in the car, with enough other equipment that we won't have to go back to the station first," Jake said, taking her bulky coat and holding it for her to put her arms in. "Looks like this will come in handy." He watched with some regret as she shrugged its contour-disguising mass over the delicate dress. More clothing was not what he had been hoping for.

He followed as she now turned to the main entrance and the chill of the winter night air. "We'll take my car," he said, leading her to a low-slung black sedan. "My gear is already in the back." Jake held the passenger door, and watched appreciatively as she turned her back to the seat, lowered herself into the car, and swung her legs elegantly in. Jake hurried to his side as she buckled her belt. Dashboard lights gently rose, and Jake heard Karli's appreciative low whistle. "This is not at all like your truck."

Jake pulled the car out of its spot and out of the parking lot. Silently. "And I've never been in a car this quiet," she said. "I didn't even hear it start."

"I'm just trying to do my part for the environment with this one," Jake said, coming to a stop where the parking lot led onto the street. "Do you have the address yet?" Karli nodded and held her iPhone out for him to see. "Got it," he said, then pulled out onto the road. "I'm guessing the cops will mostly be at the fire to handle traffic control, so we should be okay to shorten the trip a bit." As he said this, he pressed firmly on the accelerator, and heard Karli's quick breath as the car jumped up to highway speeds and pressed them back into their seats. All without any appreciable sound other than the wind.

"What is this thing?" Karli asked breathlessly.

"Some kind of ninja car?"

Jake smiled over at her face, awash in the gentle light from the dash. She looked somehow off-guard and open, sweetly lovely and in the wide-eyed moment. Turning his attention back to the road, he pushed the car even faster and said, "Something like a ninja car, yeah." He had only had the Tesla a few months, and he still thrilled to the pressure of its intense acceleration. Added as it was now to the interrupted but lingering sexual tension, the thrill was even greater, and Jake hoped Karli felt every bit as much of it.

In a time so short it surprised even Jake—who had kept an eye on the speedometer's hugely unlawful readings—they rolled quickly and silently up to a block filled with countless flashing lights. Police cars stood at the ends of the block, and fire trucks clustered around the house, their spotlights pouring light onto the leaping flames as hoses poured water at their bases. Jake grabbed his camera and sound equipment as Karli pulled out her iPhone and opened the Notes app. She walked quickly toward the paramedics' ambulance, where people stood shivering in blankets at the open back door.

Jake snapped connectors together, the process so habitual that he had to give it only a small part of his attention. He was mentally framing the first series of shots: establishing, medium and then close on the fire itself, then the reactions of firefighters and the fire's victims. He'd have to shoot out of order, as the victims were likely to be whisked away by the paramedics any second. Plotting the series of images took just seconds. As the last connector snapped into place and the camera powered on, he raised it to his eye and rolled on the wide, establishing shot for a silent count of seven seconds.

Even as he pressed the button to stop recording, he took off running as quickly as his dress clothes and the cold weather permitted to cover the hundred yards to the ambulance. He stopped just far enough away to catch a quick shot that included the entire ambulance and the people clustered around the back. Karli was still there, talking to one of the people wrapped in a blanket. Jake walked up, uncoiling a microphone cable and handing the microphone with its big Three NewsFirst flag toward Karli without interrupting her. He stepped back and began recording her conversation in a loosely framed over-the-shoulder shot. He pressed his earpiece in a bit more tightly to monitor the audio quality; the microphone did a surprisingly good job of filtering out the many rumbling diesel engines powering firetrucks and the ambulance.

"...all our Christmas presents were right there under the tree where the flames were biggest," the woman sobbed to Karli. "And we were so excited to have a Christmas this year. Ned just went back to work after his injury at the Firestone plant, and we didn't expect to have much Christmas at all. And now...I guess we won't anyway."

"Did everyone in your family get out safely?" Karli asked, as though trying to help the woman find a silver lining.

The woman began to nod, then snapped her head up and looked toward the house searchingly. "I haven't seen Dexter..." she muttered. Then projecting her voice loudly, "Kids, have you seen Dexter?"

Jake had slid around as the woman spoke so he could capture part of the flaming house in the background. He pulled his eye quickly from the viewfinder to take in the full field of vision, and he saw a cluster of firefighters walking away from the house, hunched around something one of them was carrying.

He touched Karli's shoulder and leaned in to hiss, "With me!" into her ear, somehow managing to keep the shot steady. They walked quickly together to the group and found the firefighters holding an oxygen mask to the face of a little grey terrier. The men were silent as they set the dog on the ground and tried to massage it back to life.

Jake moved his camera in close to the group, putting the dog at the center, framed by the firefighters. While the shot rolled, he became aware of the persistent smell of drenched smoke. He knew the odor from covering many fires over the years, yet it never smelled familiar. It was a cloying, ruthless stench that signaled destruction and loss. And it came with particular strength from the group of men who had just come from the house.

As the seconds passed, the firefighters began to exchange looks that silently asked whether there were any point in continuing. First one, then another, shrugged in resignation. The one who held the oxygen mask to the dog's nose, however, hadn't looked up or noticed.

"Dexter!" the woman's voice shrilled from the ambulance, with audible tears. Jake slid back from the group to capture the woman throwing herself to the ground where the dog lay. He caught her stroking the dog's stiff fur and the terrible sound of her imploring the firefighters to do something, anything, couldn't they just do something? Her kids gathered awkwardly around her, crying quietly and trying to calm her. One of the firefighters picked up the blanket she had dropped and tucked it carefully around her, saying that they'd done everything they knew to do but sometimes that just wasn't enough.

Chapter Twenty-One

Des Moines
Friday, December 20

Jake and Karli left the edit suite somberly, having put together the story of Dexter's family and their destroyed Christmas. The story would lead the late broadcast, and a good Samaritan had already established a fund to help the family recover something from the fire.

"I hate this kind of story," Karli muttered as she slid her heels back on to leave. Jake had secretly enjoyed watching her pad around the station in her stocking feet, but it had only been a flicker of brightness in a dark night. The evening's earlier, sexy mood had evaporated with the smoky steam from the house fire, and he held no hope of re-kindling it. They both stank of smoke and they both were exhausted from the evening's huge emotional swings.

Jake lifted her bulky winter coat from her desk and held it for her. "I need a drink," he said, the flat tone of his voice mirroring his mood.

"Me, too," Karli said as she shrugged into the coat. Her voice was similarly bleak.

"C'mon," Jake said, his head tipping toward the exit. "I have to give you a ride, anyway, since your car is still at the party."

"No way. We are not going back to that stupid party."

"No." Jake said with a hint of a smirk. "That would be awful."

"Okay, then, Mr. Photographer. Get me a drink. A stiff one."

A stiff one, huh? Jake thought. *That opportunity went out with the fire.*

The two went out to the parking lot, where Karli paid attention to the black sedan's exterior markings. "A Tesla?" she asked. "This car is really just batteries? That's insane." She looked quizzically at Jake, as though asking him to deny that his car was electric.

"Actually, it's a Mr. Fusion churning up banana peels and beer," Jake said. He'd surprised himself trying to be funny, though it was a weak effort. So, "Yeah, batteries. Pretty strong ones."

As he pulled out of the station's lot, Karli again remarked on how silent the car was. Then she seemed to have exhausted her conversation. Not wanting to put any pressure on her when she seemed already so brittle, Jake steered silently through the snow-blown streets. He was silent. His profile showed only his focus on the road. Strong, stable, and confident after the emotional upheaval of the fire. As his carriage house swelled up in the headlights, the old-fashioned doors to the garage swung open. He pulled in with the swift assurance of a driver who knows exactly where his vehicle fits, then pressed the button to close the doors behind them.

He flicked on lights and quickly plugged a thick electric cable into the car as he walked to open Karli's door. Her legs swung out of the car and her eyes swung up to Jake's. "I thought we were going out for a drink?"

"Do you really want to go somewhere and have to listen to accountants talking about how people squander their bonuses or cell phone sales folks bitch about their sales numbers?" he asked. "I've got whatever you want to drink, and the lighting is way better than just about any bar, I promise."

Karli nodded, stood out of the car, and took her coat off in the heated garage. Jake held his hand out for it, and hung it on a hook at the foot of the stairs leading up to the living space. As they topped the stairs, Jake hit switches that turned on the lighting he'd designed. Although she'd seen it before, Karli was again taken by how elegantly the huge space was divided into smaller spaces simply by lighting effects. She sank gratefully into the couch and pulled the heels from her still-frozen feet. The stress had left her exhausted. Spent.

Jake moved to the bar area and lifted a bottle of white wine inquiringly toward Karli. In response to her nod, he grabbed two glasses and brought them to a couch by the fireplace. He set the bottle and glasses on a low table, grabbed a remote control and pressed a button to light the gas fireplace. After pouring, he handed Karli a glass and sat next to her on the sofa.

She raised her glass to him saying, "For tomorrow we may die." They clinked glasses somberly, thinking about the sudden catastrophes that afflict so many people who assume, like everyone else, that they're safe.

"Yep," Jake replied after they had both tasted the wine. "Let us drink and be merry."

"This tastes awful. I thought you were good at picking this stuff out," Karli said.

"It's the smoke. We stink something terrible, and the smell messes with the flavor of the wine."

"Half an evening, and I have to dry clean this dress already," Karli pouted.

Jake again looked appreciatively at the dress and the figure it limned so bewitchingly. "Black is a good color for remembering that little dog, at least."

"Stop it, Jake. I can't bear to think about that lady and her poor dead dog. This job makes me sickest when the story is just awful and sad and nothing else." Jake could see tears puddling up on Karli's lower lids, even though they didn't fall.

"All the profs in J-school talk about how it's okay because we're telling cautionary tales and encouraging people to modify their behavior. But that's bullshit. It's obvious rationalization. We cover these stories because they're horrible and voyeuristic and viewers can't look away any more than they can look away from an accident on the highway." She paused to drink deeply from her wine glass. She made a face at the taste of house-fire-scented wine.

"And it's so sad to see that poor woman's misery turned into a story like it really is news or something. It just isn't. It's not news that I want to report, anyway. It's just intrusive and heartbreaking, that's all."

The tears that had been brimming in Karli's eyes grew ever so slightly and spilled out onto her cheeks. She looked down at the glass she held in her lap, her shoulders shaking silently. After a pause, she looked back up at Jake. "Why do we have to do the shitty stories?" she whispered.

Jake reached his hands toward her face, cupping her cheeks. Silently, he wiped the tears away with his thumbs and looked into her questioning eyes. A sudden smile, wet with wine and humid emotion broke moistly open across her face. "Thanks," she quietly chuckled, "but your hands really stink like a fire scene."

Momentarily confused by the unexpected comment, Jake was

stunned by the fear that he was again being rejected on the brink of intimacy. He snatched his hands away with a look of embarrassment.

"Let me do something about that. Will you be okay here for about seven minutes?" As she nodded, he walked quickly around one of the dividing panels. He picked up speed, tugging his necktie loose and unbuttoning his shirt on the way through his bedroom to the bathroom. Once there, he turned on the shower and started stripping out of his clothes and piling them under the marble counter. That done, he stepped into the already steaming shower and quickly lathered himself up.

"Hey, Jake?" The call came to him faintly through the drumming of the shower's spray.

He took his head out from under the water and called loudly in response, "Yes?"

"Do you have any of those karate pajamas in my size?"

He pushed his face into the spray for a moment, feeling the warm water sluice over his skin and trying to remember what had come in his latest order from the martial arts supply wholesaler. "I think so," he near-shouted, "but you might be between sizes. How tall are you again?"

He thought he heard a tense laugh through the shower's splattering. "Five feet, one inch, Sensei Gibson," Karli said in a flat tone.

"Yeah, I'm pretty sure I just bought a couple of size 2 uniforms," he called out through the steam that billowed over the shower door. He paused to lather his specially scented shampoo into his hair. "Gimme a sec and I'll dig out a white one and a black one so you can choose."

It occurred to him that Karli had never said anything about being interested in karate. *Oh well,* he thought. *When the student is ready, the teacher appears, right?* And he stuck his head back under the spray.

A slight breeze swept the shower room, causing Jake to think again that the level-entry design could be improved by a door that went all the way to the floor. He was rinsing, face down toward the floor, with the water carrying dense suds down from his hair. Karli's small feet appeared on the floor next to him, in the edge of his squinting vision.

"Oh my gosh," he cried. "Don't ruin that dress in here!"

Karli's tense, quiet laughter resonated in the small space. Jake pulled his hair to one side and tilted his squint up Karli's legs to where the hemline of her dress was absent. He kept sliding his gaze upward until he reached the smoothly groomed space between the tops of her legs. He caught his breath with a sharp intake of surprise, which drew a spray of shower mist into his lungs and made him cough explosively. And the coughing made him panic that he had again said or done the wrong thing and that Karli would turn suddenly away from him.

Karli laughed again, and he heaved a sigh of relief that was immediately interrupted by the feeling of his stomach sinking. *What's next?* he wondered. He put a hand out to the shower wall, leaned back into the corner, and reached up to re-aim the shower head. "W-w-would you like to have the water?" he stammered, concentrating on looking directly into Karli's eyes and *not* at the gut-clenchingly amazing view of her naked figure.

She nodded, reaching for the body wash. "I heard the water and figured that I stink like a fire scene, too," she said, twitching a corner of her mouth up as her eyes returned to Jake's.

"And I want to be able to enjoy my wine."

He noted that she, too, was being careful about not letting her eyes wander. And he felt all the evening's intensity—the intense flirtation at the Christmas party, the thrill of racing to the fire scene, the vicarious horror of the woman's grief at losing her dog, the frustration and helplessness of having to report holiday misery stories, and the lingering stench of sodden ashes. The emotions washed over him in a fleeting moment, one that held their eyes locked in a mutual gaze.

And now, here he was in a steaming shower with a gloriously naked Karli turned away from him and making a bashful beginning at washing away the fire's smell. Turning away did nothing to make his view less arousing, he thought, taking in the gloriously rounded curves of her backside. He felt his blood begin to rush through his whole body, and he felt himself begin to indiscreetly stiffen. Embarrassed at his body's involuntary display, he reached for the shampoo bottle again and stammered quietly, "M-m-may I wash your hair for you?"

Karli turned to grin at him with a mixture of shyness and frankness that disarmed Jake utterly. He saw at once the confident strength that she always projected, along with a girlish caution that was wholly new. Her shoulders sagged with the stress and tearful fatigue of the dead dog's family. Jake saw her vulnerability and felt it call to his chivalry, his decency, his manhood.

He ran his fingers through her hair to wet it and then to lather up the shampoo. He bent to her dainty ear and whispered, "Are you ready?" As he whispered, he could feel his pulse thundering through his neck.

Karli turned toward Jake and the running water pushed fragrant suds from her hair.

Jake found her eyes and felt a surge run through him as she nodded her smiling agreement. She extended her arm around his neck and pulled his face down toward hers. Jake felt the kiss overcome his senses. The scent of the soap and shampoo, the spray of the water against his skin, the swelling humidity of the steam, and the sound of the water spraying then pouring off their skin and onto the shower floor all faded as he felt the sweet softness of their kiss. And the world of the kiss lasted for what felt like a thousand thudding heartbeats.

They parted ever so slightly and Jake's senses came rushing back altogether. He paused to savor the faintly soapy flavor of the kiss, opened his eyes, and saw Karli's eyelids parting. He took a breath preparatory to speaking, but Karli put a shushing finger to his lips. "Just shut up, okay?"

Another kiss, this time slightly less an experience of drowning in a shared sensation. Jake stayed enough within himself to reach his arms around Karli, to slide them down her water-slicked back to the round twin globes of her bottom. He had resolved to be gentle, to respect the fragility of her emotions. Yet she showed no interest in gentleness, pulling his neck into their kiss and coiling her arm around his waist to press his manhood ever more tightly to her. Still kissing her, now with urgent heat, he pulled her toward him, squeezing the strong firmness of his erection up between them, clenching her cheeks ever more strongly.

The kiss slowed and then paused. Breathing deeply, Jake opened his eyes to see Karli's water-drenched eyelashes, looking glamorously spiked and ready for a photo he couldn't take. He slid his hands up from her cheeks to the hard slenderness of her waist and then continuing up below her shoulder blades, where he spread them and prepared to pull her into the next kiss.

Her own arms had moved, though, and she leaned back into his hands to run her own lightly across the hard bulges of his pecs. He sought her eyes, but they were busy following her hands.

"This is what karate does for a physique, then?" she muttered, continuing to spread her hands along his flanks and then his backside. She leaned back and smiled up at him.

Jake twitched with need as he saw tightened, swollen nipples projecting from the smoothly rounded breasts.

"You smell pretty nice now," Jake replied. "But I think you may have missed a couple spots." Saying this, he ran soapy hands gently around her chest and then back and forth over her taut nipples.

In spite of their fiery kisses and the tight clinch that had impressed Jake's obvious enthusiasm into both of them, Jake sensed that Karli remained a little sweetly self-conscious.

Rinsed off and moving into the bathroom, Jake was as discreet as he could be in catching views of Karli's athletic body: Her back curving over to dry her legs or stretching to swing the towel around. The round strength of her butt. The smoothly hairless front. He was completely smitten with every feature, every curving contour and each perfectly placed mole. And he wanted to possess all of her, to stroke her to a thrumming, blissful fervor—to sweep the grief of the evening's story clean from her mind.

With their towels wrapped around them, they walked through the bathroom door to the bedroom.

Jake made a show of turning down a corner of the king-size bedspread and made a welcoming gesture to Karli. As she began moving toward the bed in response to his invitation, he bent and simply plucked her up into his arms and plopped her down onto the bed.

Wordlessly, he reached for Karli's damp head and pulled her to him for another timeless, pounding kiss. She rose to his touch with an intensity that stripped him of caution and summoned the masculine impulses instilled in his DNA from ancient times. His hands slid over the warmth of her soft, bare skin with urgent need, traveling across her back, down her side, and again grasping her bottom with a pressure he feared was close to bruising.

Karli's breathing became loud in response to his touch, and he chased the paths of his caresses with his mouth, this time stopping to swirl, then suck, then nibble on the nipples that had so captivated him in the shower. She rose to his mouth, arching her back and pressing the firm softness of her breasts against him.

Each movement, each touch came to him as an echo and reflection of Karli's rousing breath and grasp. He leaned away suddenly to fumble at the night stand for a condom, which he tore from its wrapper and put on as quickly as he could. After that clumsy eternity of preparation, he pulled her onto him, sheathed himself smoothly into her, and her gasp of pleasure tugged at his own inmost need.

He was intent on her pleasure, her release from the stresses that coiled around her. Yet the fresh sweet smell of her, the strength that underlay her softness, the sound of her breath in his ear all enveloped him in ecstasy.

They moved together and apart and together through long minutes of quiet, ecstatic exertion until Karli's breath came out as a shuddering, "Yessss!" Jake felt her grow tense around him, felt her arms clasp him tightly, and then felt her movements slacken and her forehead press to his collarbone. "Oh my God, Jake."

The animalistic spirit that had been guiding him preened itself, luxuriously stretching at her satisfaction. He withdrew himself and simply held Karli as her breathing slowed and her eyes came up to his.

"You're so beautiful," he whispered. "I could feel all your tension release." He moved close and leaned his forehead gently against hers, feeling anew the dampness of her hair, smelling the fresh glow of her skin.

"What about you?" she asked.

"Nice guys finish last, you know," he chuckled. The he held her for a long, lingering minute.

"I'll be right back," he whispered. On his way out of the room, he adjusted the dimmer panel so that two extremely dim pools of light shone onto the room's farthest wall, leaving the rest in near-absolute darkness. He came back into the bedroom with a jingle of glasses, set them on a nightstand, and returned to the bed. He poured and passed a glass to Karli.

"The wine tastes much better now," she mumbled. "But you haven't finished at all," she whispered, the tone of her smile permeating her voice.

Jake smacked his lips, surprised that he'd forgotten to taste the wine now that it wasn't polluted by the smell of soaked burnt house. "It has a really nice finish, too, don't you think?" he asked, looking at the glass and swirling the wine in it.

He looked up suddenly to Karli. "And, by the way, you're not finished finishing," he said, raising his glass to her in a careful salute. "That was just the stress-relief. We should both be a little more relaxed now," he said. "And *last* means after you're all done. So you'd better have a drink to fortify yourself for the rest of the evening."

Karli's eyebrows shot up. Jake laid a quieting finger to her lips and said, "Just have a sip. We don't have anywhere we have to go. And I want to show you just how deeply I feel about you."

She drank, and Jake noticed that his shyness had gone, for he took a long and languorous look at her body in the room's dimly scattered light, possessing it with his eyes as he just had with his body. *She is like her figure,* he thought to himself. *She seems petite and fragile, yet she has enough strength and depth and kindness to be my entire world.*

His eyes found Karli's peering at him over the tilted rim of her wine glass. She emptied her drink and turned to put it down. Her eyes angled back at him as a naughty grin tugged at her lips. "What was that you were saying about finishing?"

Jake felt the dizzying rush of arousal and quickly put his own glass on the table at his side of the bed.

Chapter Twenty-Two

Salon Cut it Out!
Ingersoll Avenue, Des Moines
Tuesday evening, January 7

"It's great and everything," Karli was saying to Trevor. "And it's not just, you know..."

"The scorching-hot sex?" Trevor asked with a conspiratorial chuckle, as he combed out a lock of her hair, stretched it between his fingers, and confidently snipped off an eighth of an inch.

"Um," Karli stalled, feeling her cheeks heat up with an intense blush. "Let's keep this on deep background, okay? No telling."

"Of course it's deep," Trevor said with a wink at Karli's reflection in the mirror. "If you want really good sex, he's got to really dig you. And he is totally into you. You should've heard him when he was in here last week. It's like he's a street person who suddenly inherited a huge house. He just can't think about anything else, and he can't shut up about how he *belongs* there and how it *feels so right.*

"He's so into you that I was kind of surprised you could walk straight when you came in. You must be in great shape. What kind of stuff do you do at the gym that lets you get all scorching hot with Jake and still walk around like it's just another Tuesday? Maybe I should try some of your routines..."

Karli was too scandalized at Trevor's frank comments to respond and sat tensely, torn between a shriek of indignation and flat-out silence.

She had spent enough time in Trevor's chair by now to know that he was probably about to start in on a story about how he had styled some porn star's hair and then tried the Official Porn Star workout and how it had left him a breathless puddle of sweat.

She steered toward less scandalous matters. "Tell me again why it is that people voluntarily live here in Iowa," she demanded. "Not that I'm thinking of staying. They had me out freezing my ass off yesterday, and the *whole story* was that it was *cold*. When the cold is the story, it's too cold."

"Oh, it wasn't that bad—"

"Oh it SO was that bad," Karli cut in. "The *high* temperature yesterday was *negative one*—the *high!*"

"But it doesn't last that long, really," Trevor began again.

"Trevor, the winds were gusting to almost 40 miles an hour. And it only got almost but not quite up to zero for an hour or so. It got all the way down to negative 12. That's *below zero*. Below zero *fahrenheit*. Without wind chill. That's crazy stupid cold."

"It's only a few weeks, Karli," Trevor started another time. "At most. Just enough to make spring and summer feel really special. And look at that fur hanging over there," he said, indicating a full-length mink coat draped as though on display, at the salon's office-door coat rack. "It's gorgeous, isn't it?"

Karli hadn't ever thought much about fur coats—weren't they for middle-aged women, for whom material things had taken the place of actual excitement?—yet the lustrous fur looked both beautiful and, most importantly at the moment, very *very* warm. *But in this weather*, Karli thought, *Jake is what I'd really prefer to be keeping me warm. That might be universal. Maybe that's why so many babies are born in September.*

"David came in this morning wearing that because he was showing off for his new boyfriend," Trevor was saying. "He was showing off way too much, though. Everyone in the shop is pissed at what a bitch he's been about *every*thing today."

Karli hadn't seen the normally cheerful Trevor actually upset before. She fixed an inquiring glance on him. "This place is a regular soap opera, isn't it?" she asked. He caught her look and immediately snapped his face back to its usual cheerfully naughty expression.

"Don't you talk to me about soap operas," he said with a smirk. "You're the one who is getting non-stop wild with the gorgeous Jake. That's way more exciting than David and his new little queen. And I want details."

"Trevor!" Karli nearly shrieked. "There aren't any details. He's just . . . really a wonderful guy." *Perfect,* she thought. *And that's what's really frightening.*

"No details? There can't *not* be any details!" Trevor paused to search Karli's blushing face. "Okay, so we're agreed that he's completely obsessed with you. So just tell me how—"

"Wait, Trevor," Karli interrupted. "You already got details from him, didn't you?" Her face began to darken at the thought of Jake reciting their bedroom activities to Trevor and anyone else.

Trevor's voice and face echoed his remorse at misleading Karli. "Of course not, Karli," he said quickly. "He wouldn't give up anything." And here he paused to lean in and whisper in Karli's ear, "Why do you think I'm asking you? If he'd already told me what a hot, tangled knot of passion you two are in bed, I wouldn't be curious. Besides," and here he delicately cleared his throat, "I'm not nearly as curious about what he has to say about you as I am about what you have to say about *him*."

Karli quirked an eyebrow at his face in the mirror. "Well," he responded with a naughty twinkle, "All he gave me was some nonsense about gentlemen not kissing and telling. Which is total BS. And even if it isn't," he added, his voice again dripping with tones of conspiracy, "you aren't a gentleman and neither am I. So start with the details already. Is he a good kisser?"

"Oh, man," Karli breathed quietly, her eyes half-lidded. Then she caught a glimpse of Trevor's leering face in the mirror and felt the shock of realizing he had nearly gotten her to tell details. "You jerk!" she said, and then noticed it had been loud enough that other people in the salon looked up to see what was going on.

Trevor slumped a bit, then snapped his eyes back up to the mirror to meet Karli's. "Okay, I'll quit," he pouted. "But there's nothing wrong with this question."

Here he paused to make sure Karli could see his serious, non-leering expression. "Is he The One?"

Feeling a bit guilty for calling him a jerk and calling attention to him, Karli considered how to give a fair answer. "He's unique, for real," she began. "He is creative in so many ways—the photography, the interior design, the still photography...he's got real stuff when it comes to visuals."

"And he's hot, of course," Trevor added with an over-the-top exaggerated wink.

"And he's *perceptive*," Karli replied in quelling tones. "Trevor, he sees things in me that I don't even realize are there until he points them out. Like, he's the one who told me that I prefer reporting stories that get inside the subjects' heads to stories that simply describe events. I always kind of knew that—interviewing people in depth has always been the best part of the job—but he was the first person ever to say it out loud. Spot news can be fun, too, but how many crashes and derailments and fires can you cover before they all start to run together?"

"Isn't that the exciting stuff, though?" Trevor asked. "Like when you did that drug bust? That was cool and scary," he concluded with a shiver.

"Oh, that wasn't really spot news, though," Karli responded. "We knew that was going to happen, so it was different from the kind of story where you just go to where all the firetrucks are going and then report on whatever's happening there." Karli paused, recalling with remembered anger how the drug series had been taken from her. Sophia had done a minimum of work developing Karli's research, too, and had mostly worked on making sure she had a maximum amount of time on camera.

"All those firetrucks are headed to Jake's because the sex is so hot, right?" The scandalous comment snapped Karli out of her reverie. She narrowed her eyes at Trevor and caught up the threads of the conversation.

"So he tells me stuff like that, which is just about annoying because he says it like it's obvious even though nobody else ever noticed. Then he tells me how it's part of what makes me so awesome in his eyes, and that makes me all warm and melty inside.

"It's not like every other guy who thinks he's saying something special by telling me I'm beautiful. I'm sick of hearing that. Everyone says it and it's never sincere and it is always manipulation. Jake tells me stuff that he understands. And to him it's not a compliment at all, it's just. . . *descriptive*, I guess. There's nothing manipulative about it."

"The other guys could just be telling it like it is, too, you know," Trevor said. "You *are* beautiful, you know."

"Oh, God, Trevor," Karli sighed. "Not you. You aren't even trying to get laid. And I'm not beautiful. I'm short. There's a difference." As Trevor tugged a little bit too hard on her hair and took a breath to continue the debate, Karli jumped in ahead of him.

"—and if you think you're going to get a tip yanking on my hair like that, you're crazy. Stop it."

"Fine," Trevor relented, "you're a pipsqueak. Whatever. That's who gorgeous Jake wants to shag until she can hardly walk into the salon. Right."

Karli glared at Trevor's reflection in the mirror for two silent seconds. "I'm not a pipsqueak, Trevor," she said. "Since you mention kids, though," she said, though Trevor had said nothing of the sort and furrowed his brow at her for making him responsible for the change of subject, "he is good with them. He's going to be an outstanding father—you should've seen him shaking hands with this kid at the fair. It was effortless how he helped the boy discover part of what becoming a man is, and the boy really thought Jake was cool. Not many kids think *any* grown-ups are cool."

She paused here and gazed into the distance. Then in a quieter voice she said, "And he practically was a father to that poor kid who got killed."

"And why, Karli, would that matter to you if he isn't The One?" Trevor asked, rather than joining her in a maudlin moment.

Getting no response apart from what had become a more or less fixed glare, Trevor tried to lighten the tone, muttering so she could only just hear it over the salon's energetic dance music, "So do you call him daddy when you're doing it? Because that sounds like it could get really kinky." He raised his eyebrows in two suggestively quick pulses. "He'd really be The One if you called him daddy and he gave you corsets and special padded handcuffs and stuff, wouldn't he?"

Shocked at Trevor's taste for the kinky, Karli flailed in the chair, trying to hit Trevor, but he had the chair up so she couldn't extend her foot all the way to the floor to swivel, and she was far enough away from the counter that she couldn't reach that with her hand. By the time she stuck her leg up to push against the counter, Trevor had a firm grip on the back of the chair, and they were both laughing.

"You're pretty easy to bind up, anyway," he said, continuing to laugh. As Karli tried again to turn so she could reach to hit him, he quickly reached for his blow dryer and wrapped the cord around her shoulders. She gave up, and they both glanced around the salon to see how much attention they'd attracted. As they both saw that it was too much, Trevor quickly replaced the blow dryer, cleared his throat, and fiddled with his fancy scissor-case while they both tried to quit giggling.

"So he's a great kisser—though you won't even come out and say so—he's great with kids, he says wonderful things to and about you, and he's got mad skills with the handcuffs and feathery whip." Karli again glared at Trevor in frustration at his never-ending dirty talk. "But," Trevor continued, "is he The One?"

"Maybe. Yes. I don't know," Karli stammered. "I so don't want him to be The One. I have a career. I'm leaving, and he's staying.

"But he gives these odd gifts. Girls always think they want jewelry and flowers and stuff—and that stuff is great in its way and I really like it all—but he gives stuff that comes from his passions, like wine from New Zealand, or a black-and-white portrait he shot, or a dumb pork chop on a stick."

Trevor continued listening and expertly snipping away at Karli's hair.

"He's always doing stuff for me, too, more than what a photog or just a guy normally would. He fixes stuff I didn't even know was broken, he carries my stuff, he even cleans up messes whether or not he made them."

Trevor ran his hands through her thick hair with a keen appraising look in the mirror, tugging it slightly here and there to confirm that both sides were precisely the same length.

"I don't know, Trevor. He might be The One, but he's totally not what I expected. And he's not going to fit with my life. I'm not staying here in this stupid deep freeze of a television market.

There are bigger things ahead for me."

His hands slicked with product, Trevor again ran his fingers through Karli's hair, shaping it to his own exacting standard.

"And besides, he's *weird*. What guy with a huge heap of money keeps working as a journalist because he has a sense of duty to the community? What guy who is a real adult actually has a karate studio? What guy has the time to do all that and still take long detours with me so we can see one of the actual bridges in Madison County or just talk through stuff?"

Trevor had been taking in all this extended monologue without comment or even much in the way of facial expression. As she finished, though, his exasperation was revealed in a massive eye-roll. "So he's The One," he sighed, "but you can't be bothered to deal with that because you have a job that you want to worry about. Am I getting this right?"

"You're so reductive," Karli said, anger ringing in her voice. "I'm not talking about just a job—this is a profession that I've worked my whole adult life to succeed in, and I'm just a great series or so away from landing a major-market job. So I'm not worried about a job, I'm staying focused on a goal I've had for years."

"Call it what you want," Trevor shrugged, continuing to tug and adjust a few hairs to make them just so. "I just know that honest-to-goodness true love doesn't come around very often. If you want it, you have to grab it before it slips away. And if you keep your hands full of career-goal nonsense, you won't have anything to grab it with."

"You're such a pig," Karli replied.

"You expect the woman to put her dreams aside so she can catch a man, but you'd never ask a man to do that."

"Um, I don't know if you've figured this out yet, but the relationships I usually think about don't involve subservient women—or any women at all." Trevor turned on the dryer and played it through a diffuser over her head. He paused and looked Karli's reflection right in the eye. "We *all* have to adjust a little when we have a chance at The One."

Karli blushed a little at Trevor's rebuke. Of course he hadn't been analyzing the relationship as a sexist. "It's not a very convenient time in my life to be worrying about true love. If I execute my plan well, I should be able to get to a major market in the next two years. Then I'll be in a different place."

"Yeah," he said, replacing his tools and tidying up the counter in front of his chair. "The place where your career eats every minute of your life, and you don't even know the names of the people who work with you, much less appreciate the pork chop-on-a-stick that they give you once in a while."

"Why do you keep harping on me?" Karli asked in tones of genuine frustration. "I've had a goal since my freshman year, okay? Is that such an awful thing?"

"All done!" Trevor announced as he unsnapped the cape and swirled it and the little snips of hair it bore cleanly off Karli. He returned the iPhone she'd set aside when she sat down, and she was immediately caught up by the text that showed up when she woke the screen: "There's a news anchor opening here in Charleston, kiddo. I met with the station manager yesterday, and he says they're very interested in you."

Chapter Twenty-Three

Three NewsFirst Viewing Area
Winter

Never had all aspects of his life felt so in synch. He and Karli had begun the background work on a first-ever Three NewsFirst documentary series on renewable energy in Iowa. The plan was for six half-hour episodes to run in mid-summer—all produced with only existing personnel and resources. The station's only additional costs would be minimal overtime (because Jake and Karli would have to donate most of their time to the project) and travel expenses for shoots outside the usual viewing area.

Jake's passion for renewable energy—*viz*, the Tesla—combined perfectly with Karli's relentless digging to look for political maneuvering that sought to block it. They had spent considerable off-the-clock time laying the groundwork for in-depth coverage of the issue and how it affected the people in his home state.

And the Karate Center had grown in recent months. Not only had the enrollment gone up, one of Jake's high school friends who had joined the military and been stationed on Okinawa where he had survived several years of intensive martial arts study had just returned home. He had very humbly asked Jake if he could continue his training at the Karate Center; Jake had immediately invited him to take on instructing duties and to work with him to revamp the curriculum.

The new energy and focus he'd found all began and ended with Karli. She was exhilarating; he was euphoric. He treasured home and family; she was both. She showed him passion like he had never known before; he mirrored it and more.

They were both too busy to spend all their time together, yet it seemed the days were complete only when they found time to touch base, to talk about their projects, to share notes or video clips or

201

helpful quotes, to touch one another, to share a glass of wine together, to eat together, to spend ecstatic nights together.

For her part, Karli felt a growing sense of confidence in her future. The documentary she and Jake were planning was the perfect kind of launch vehicle to propel her to the ranks of broadcast journalism's elite: an issue of national importance that she could explore through personal, local stories. She'd already found Amish farmers who were generating electricity with solar and wind installations, and she was very close to getting strong interviews with power company representatives and State-level politicians about the money pouring into anti-renewable campaigns from regional and national groups with interests in fossil fuel electricity generation. She had complete confidence that Jake's sound and images would combine with her reporting to make an Emmy-contending product.

Her father had tried to drag her home yet again, asking what it was about the major markets that attracted her more than a front-line anchor job in Charleston. He hadn't really listened to her answer, though Karli had tried to explain that major market reporters could cover bigger and more important stories and have a greater effect on the world. He just couldn't get it.

And she enjoyed her time with Jake. The conversations were engaging, the work was exciting, and the sex was electrifying.

She had even gone to watch a class at his dojo once, but that hadn't been anything she could get her head around.

Once had been enough, even though Jake had proudly given her her own set of karate pajamas. She suspected that gift had been as much to recall their first night together as to have anything to do with karate.

Neither one of them paid much attention to the weather news that snow had been falling all winter in record amounts to the north of Iowa.

Chapter Twenty-Four

Des Moines, Iowa
Sunday, April 20

"What in the hell do you mean *the water is off?*" News Director Jerry Schultz shrilled into Karli's iPhone through his earpiece's tin-can-sounding bluetooth. It was 5:30 a.m., Karli had been working since midnight to report the city's sudden water crisis.

"I mean it's already shut off, Jerry," Karli responded. "Apparently the early warm spell this spring melted a lot of the snow to the north. And of course it's been raining here and up north pretty much non-stop for a few weeks now. All that water came down here, so the Raccoon River flooded."

"The Raccoon always floods. So what?" Karli could hear the panicky raspiness of Jerry's voice. He was driving back, two days early and probably well in excess of the speed limit, from a meeting in Omaha.

"Jerry, it flooded a lot. So did the Des Moines River. A lot. And suddenly. It came down here overnight and it's not going away because there's a lot more behind it. The downtown bridges aren't safe to cross because the river is nearly at street level, pushing right up against them. But the worst part is that the water purification plant flooded and the motors that drive everything are under water. They're ruined and couldn't work even if they weren't under water. That means there is no municipal water service in Des Moines."

"What about the rest of Polk County?" Jerry asked. "Do other cities get their water from Des Moines?"

"Nope. The other municipalities have their own waterworks. But that's still 200,000 people."

"Nearly 210,000 in the city, Karli. Do you have what you need for interviews?"

"Jake and I just shot one with the water plant manager, who was not very happy," Karli said. "They won't let us into the plant because it's 'too dangerous.'" Karli made the air-quotes around that last bit plainly audible. "We have nightside video of the bridges and some early-morning exteriors of the water plant and other general flooding stuff. We're going to meet a live truck at Nollen Plaza in a couple minutes to send the video back and see if we can get Joe Sixpack to give us some reaction."

Karli heard an empty pause as Jerry collected his thoughts. "Have Holly and Vince checked in yet?" he finally asked.

"Of course, Jerry. The A team is in and on the job. Holly is lining up stuff with the governor's and mayor's offices, and Vince is on police and fire. Bailey is downtown with the truck's mast up and locked in, and just gave the anchor desk to Stu after about five solid hours. Drink some coffee and visit a restroom while you have access to water and get in to the shop."

"You're telling me the *bathrooms* don't work, either? Why not?"

"This isn't like a boil order, Jerry," Karli said, climbing into the news car next to Jake, who nodded that he was ready to roll. "The water isn't unsafe. There isn't any water at all. Turn on the faucet and nothing comes out. Flush the toilet and the tank doesn't refill. We stopped at some student apartments with a swimming pool and got some video of kids using buckets of water from the complex's swimming pool to flush their toilets."

Jake pulled away from the parking spot and pointed the car downtown.

"Holy shit." There was a long pause. "This really is big. Stay on the air, Karli. Make sure we stay on the air with this and that we have everyone in and on the job. I'm getting off at Jordan Creek for a pit stop, so I'll be in the newsroom within half an hour at the most. I'll bring in bottled water for the newsroom. And I'll be on the phone with them between now and then."

Karli recapped the conversation as Jake raced through the City's quiet streets to the where live truck's raised mast indicated they were headed. Several hundred feet from the truck, Bailey Barber stood, immaculately made up and coiffed as always, microphone in hand and facing a camera. As they got out of the car, Jake began handing an earpiece and microphone to Karli.

"What's this for?"

"Bailey doesn't have anything but what she can see. You need to get on there now and tell the story. I'll hook up the audio and let you know when you can use your own mic; till then, talk into Bailey's."

"What about the interviews? I need the interview with that stiff from the water plant to roll at some point," Karli said.

"Karli, you have the story that nobody else has. We were the only ones who went to the plant; the other stations don't have that. You need to tell the story. I'll get the video back for someone to cut. Just get on camera.

We have a lot of time to fill, and you have more story to fill it with than anyone else."

She nodded, pulled out her phone to check her notes while Jake guided her to Bailey's side. She saw Bailey's eyes flick over and recognize her, and Jake must have seen the glance, too, as he raised his palm toward her to prevent her from bringing Karli in too quickly. "Look at me," he whispered, so Bailey's mic wouldn't pick up the sound. Karli looked up to find Jake's fingers running quickly through her hair and brushing something quickly off her cheek. Her skin tingled at his warm touch, and his eyes grounded her. "You look like the complete authority on everything." He nodded his head toward Bailey, lowered his palm, and made a huge gesture that Bailey couldn't miss seeing.

Effortlessly, Bailey thanked the new weekend weathercaster—who appeared on the portable television propped up on the ground beneath the camera, a very young woman who had only joined the newsroom a couple of weeks earlier—and waited for the studio to switch from the set to the camera in front of her. "Joining me here in front of the silent fountain at Nollen Plaza is Karli Lewis, who has been working this story all night. Karli, what's the latest?" She extended her microphone toward Karli, who took care to keep her face angled as much as possible toward the camera even though she was addressing and standing right next to Bailey.

"We have learned why the water has stopped flowing, Bailey. I just left the Des Moines water treatment plant a few minutes ago, where I learned that the electric pumps that power the plant have been submerged under the Raccoon's flood waters.

Water treatment has stopped completely, so there is no water to pump through the city's pipes."

Karli began to explain the reasons for the flooding and what the next steps in restoring water service would be, and Jake sprinted for the live truck, where he jumped in, threw one of the dozens of switches, twisted one of many knobs, plugged a coiled cable into one of dozens of ports, and sprinted back toward Karli and Bailey with the cable paying out behind him all the way. As he drew close to them, Jake crept low and out of the camera's shot to plug the cable's other end into Karli's microphone. She immediately raised it to her face, giving Bailey and her arm a chance to rest.

As soon as the camera had zoomed in from the two-shot to a head-and-shoulders of Karli, Bailey stepped away and bent to listen carefully to the directions coming over her hidden earpiece. Jake hadn't stayed still for a moment, racing back to grab his camera and tripod. He carried them quickly to take up a position near the live camera, then he repeated the route to string a heavy cable from the truck to connect his camera as another video source. At the same time he played out the camera's cable with one arm, he strung an electrical cable next to it with the other.

Karli wrapped up her initial *ad lib* report and tossed back to Stu on the set. She glanced off camera for a moment and saw Jake running up with two bar stool-height director's chairs. He set the seats carefully just outside the camera's shot, angled toward each other and with the plaza's silent fountain exactly between them. Bailey climbed into one and arranged herself carefully.

As Karli and Stu talked about access to water, Jake smoothly set up and powered on a pair of lights mounted high on their stands to bring the talent in the chairs out from the background and flatter their features with properly angled shadows.

As he framed up a head-and-shoulders shot of Bailey, Jake heard his favorite director, Chuck, through his own earpiece: "Nod if that's you, Jake." He tilted his camera up and down quickly. "Awesome work, my friend." And then, to his technical director, "Stand by to take Jake's camera with Bailey on a one-shot...and take."

Bailey was effortlessly picking up on Karli's reporting, filling in with facts that could be helpful to viewers. "The Des Moines city officials have said that they will be placing kaibos throughout town, grouped so as to give the most people easy access. And I should point out here for non-native Iowans that 'kaibo' is a local term for a port-a-potty. It sounds like they're being trucked in from sources near and far to make sure people have access to sanitary facilities."

During this, Karli had climbed up onto the chair next to Bailey, and Jake had used the other camera to frame the two of them, with the waterless fountain that was in many ways the heart of downtown Des Moines in the background. Hearing her opening, Karli stepped in to follow up on Bailey. "Of course, you aren't required to use a kaibo. The sanitary sewer system is still working. In fact, photographer Jake Gibson and I stopped at a student apartment complex near the Drake campus today and found residents there taking buckets of water from the complex's swimming pool and using that water to flush the toilets in their apartments."

And so it went, with reports coming in from every live source the station could manage to rig, with video streaming back for editing and playback from the station's control room. All the newsroom personnel came in and pitched in, and the coverage went essentially around the clock (with taped replays from midnight to 5:00 a.m.).

Karli and Jake were together covering every new bit of the story they could find. They shot little kids saluting the Iowa National Guard troops arriving in town with a convoy of tankers to give out clean, drinkable water. They followed and interviewed volunteers identifying and helping the elderly and infirm. They ignored the barricades to interview and shoot the engineers and tradesmen working around the clock to restore the waterworks to operation. They shadowed the firefighters forcing everyone to leave the downtown areas because there was no water to fight fires in the high-rises. They sat and captured patrons at the restaurants trying to stay in business with bottled water, plastic cutlery, and paper plates.

They worked themselves into exhaustion every day, reporting live, shooting interviews and editing the stories, helping out with other crews, for up to 18 hours. Then they'd run to a hotel in West Des Moines, where there was water for drinking and showering. Clean, they would make tired love, collapse into urgent sleep, then rise to do it all over again. This cycle repeated every day for ten days.

The consultant, John Bielfeldt, had flown into town as soon as he heard the water was off, and he had worked just as many hours as the rest of the news team throughout the long days of covering the floods and the water shortage. He harped every day, to every crew, the importance of making each story *inspirational:* Understandable, Memorable, and Emotional. "Where's the footage showing me that person's emotion!" he'd cry. Or "What's memorable about that shot of the drinking fountain just sitting there? They *always* just sit there. Make it memorable—shoot someone starting toward it and then remembering it won't work!"

On the 11th day, they started the day at the Des Moines Register's temporary offices—even the newspaper had been evacuated from downtown Des Moines—downstairs in their hotel. The newspaper crew was a frustrated bunch. They, too, had been working themselves to death covering the floods, but their presses had been shut down by the evacuation. They were sending their very few pages to a busy press in a nearby town, but they were strictly limited in the number of pages they could print, so many good stories were being spiked. Still, when talking to one of the reporters off-camera and after Jake had turned off the camera, the rumor came up that the waterworks would be up and running again the next day.

Karli and Jake ran to the news car. While Jake headed onto I-235 to head downtown to the waterworks, Karli phoned the newsroom. "We're headed to the waterworks, Holly," Jake heard her say. "We hear they're getting close."

They pulled in to park as near the plant as they could and left the car at a brisk, adrenalized walk. As they crossed the mountain of sand bags that kept the river's waters away from the building, Jake shouldered his camera, his fingers playing without thought over switches to turn the camera on, set the white balance, snap in the filter for interior lighting, adjust the gain, and select audio sources.

Karli tried the door, found it locked, and knocked. Jake pressed the 'record' button and watched through the viewfinder as the door cracked open towards Karli and a timid man's face peered out. "Media isn't allowed..." he began, as Karli gave the door a sudden yank. The man, who had apparently been leaning on the door, stumbled forward enough for Karli to slip in behind him. Feeling the man's weight dropping against his hip, Jake gave a slight twist and bump to help the man to a face-first landing at the entrance. Then he followed Karli quickly into the dim building, readying the switch that turned on the brilliant light atop his camera.

As Karli wound her way to the room where the waterworks' pumps sat, they heard the escalating shrill of an electric motor powering up to speed. They also heard the urgent, breathy whisper of the man who had 'let them in' telling them to stop and turn around and understand that they just couldn't go there. Disregarding the man's earnest entreaties, Karli opened the door to the machine room. Jake snapped on the light and steadied his camera to take in the group of satisfied looking men and women who stood at a massive control panel that looked to have come straight out of a radioactive sea monster movie. Karli turned to take the microphone and neatly coiled cable that Jake held out to her, and they marched toward the group. Drawing near, she shouted above the increasing din of the machines, "How long until your testing is done and you start pumping water to the City again?"

A man gestured brusquely to an operator closer to the panel. Immediately after the operator reached to manipulate the controls, the thundering sound of the pumping machine began to die down in pitch and volume.

"Young lady, you have no right to be in here!" the man began.

"I'm Karli Lewis," she replied, "from Three NewsFirst." She nodded her head toward the camera that was hard to see under its bright light. "The citizens of Des Moines want to know how you're coming on restoring the water. And that machine sounded impressive just now. Is the waterworks ready?"

The man sighed and plucked the hard hat off his head to scratch at the thinning hair underneath. "Miss, we don't want to create any false hopes. Just because you heard a machine doesn't mean anything. We've told you we're installing replacement pumps now that we have the building pumped out, but I can't tell you any more than that we're testing them now."

"How long do you expect the testing to take?"

"You can't take a hint, can you?" the man asked, exasperation suffusing every syllable.

"Sir, the pump is connected to power. Is it also connected to the water purification system?"

The man turned to walk away from Karli and gestured to the group of hard hats clustered near the control panel. "Somebody get them out of here!"

Undeterred, Karli marched right after him, Jake tracking smoothly along with her. "How long until we can flush our toilets again?" she asked his retreating back. "How long till we can shower in our own bathrooms? Or do laundry? Or drink water that we haven't had to haul from Army trucks?"

The chief engineer kept walking, right through the pump room and through a door that he conspicuously locked behind him. Jake caught it all on camera.

Chapter Twenty-Five

Live on the news set, Bailey Barber was holding up the morning edition of the Des Moines *Register*. "There's a headline that captures what we all thought late yesterday afternoon when the water started flowing again."

Chuck was driving the show in the control room with the calm thoroughness that contrasted so sharply with his manner at any other time. *Camera two,* Bailey heard in her earpiece, *tighten up on that headline. Good, two. Standby to take two. And take it.* The image going out over the air changed to an extreme close-up of the newspaper's front page above the fold. In huge letters, the headline proclaimed: AND ON DAY TWELVE, WE FLUSHED.

Karli and Jake's Sunday story had caught more or less everyone's attention, and the complete approval of consultant Bielfeldt. In its wake, elected officials fell all over themselves to proclaim their earnest intentions to conduct government affairs in a transparent manner and with full respect for the public's right to know.

That, at least, was their public response. In less conspicuous ways, the news staff suspected, the elected officials redoubled the pressure they were putting on the waterworks engineers to get the water running again *immediately*. The officials managed to generate pressure in the water lines within 24 hours of the story's broadcast.

The city flushed, showered, drank and rejoiced in the glory of fresh, clean, flowing water.

On the set, Art's patrician face looked directly into the camera and his stentorian voice rumbled in response to Bailey's recitation of the headline: "The loss and restoration of water service to the City of

Des Moines reminds us that, now and ever since ancient times, civilization is buoyed by water—ready and universal access to clean, safe water."

The camera cut back to Bailey, who turned the full energy of her green eyes and perfectly made up face to the camera. "With the resumption of water service to the City's nearly quarter-million residents, Three NewsFirst will be returning to its regular broadcast schedule. We will continue to bring you the latest developments during our usual news schedule, and of course we will interrupt regular programming for breaking news. But we are now returning to that regular programming after more than eleven straight days of live news reporting on the water crisis in Des Moines. Thank you for watching. Art and I will be back at noon with all the latest news."

Having said that, Bailey looked down at the open MacBook sitting on the anchor desk, scrolled briefly to give Chuck's team time to cut the studio microphones, then looked up at Art to exchange a brief, inaudible comment that brought a telegenic and equally inaudible comment from him as the credits rolled over their image.

Jerry, Holly, and Vince, all sitting in the newsroom's raised nerve center spun in their chairs at more or less the same speed in a weary and joyous miniature victory lap. "Mary Rose!" Jerry yelled from his slowing chair. "How much of that do we have air-checks for? Please tell me *someone* thought to record every minute of the last 11 days."

"Do you mean *everything*?" Mary Rose asked, earnest sincerity ringing in her voice, "from when we first went live when the water went out until now?"

"Yes, yes, yes," he called back across the newsroom. "Didn't we record any of that stuff?"

"Well," Mary Rose said, staring earnestly at her computer screen, "it looks here like we got," and again she paused. Then she sighed and looked up at the elevated center desk. "Jerry, I don't know how to tell you this..."

"What?" Jerry asked, panic creeping into his voice. "Didn't we get *any* of it?"

"Only all of it, Jerry," Mary Rose said, her impish grin twinkling up at him. "I started a special deck rolling in Master Control right when we went on the air, and the engineers chipped in to keep at least one recording rolling all the way through till now." She paused, stood up from behind a desk, and took an exaggerated bow. "I kind of anticipated that you'd think this was important stuff to have, so I took a little initiative."

"Bless you, Mary Rose!" Jerry pumped two fists in the air.

Perched at a newsroom station near the assignment desk, Bielfeldt slid into the brief pause. "We should be in Emmy contention for this work, especially if we have all of that to edit down."

"So, um," Mary Rose said, disregarding the consultant completely, "can I maybe get out of the studio and into the newsroom now?"

Jerry was caught up short with this question, and he saw that the newsroom staff had all turned to look for his response. "Well, that's something I can talk to Larry about later today."

As the unusually populated newsroom heaved with a unison groan, he quickly added, "It's more that he'd have to fill your place in the studio, of course." He paused to let that settle in with the crowd of skeptics. Then, in a wheedling tone, he added, "Would you still do the animation work for us, even though that's technically studio work? Nobody can do that like you can."

"Of course I will," Mary Rose grinned. She turned a devilish grin around the room, then added, "Assuming the raise I'll be getting is enough motivation to do double-duty." The buzzing voices of reporters and photographers called, "Oh, snap!" among other appreciative sounds. Scott Winstead whispered loudly enough so that Buzz Cziesla could hear all the way across the room, "God, I wish I had her balls!"

"Wait," Karli interrupted. "John, were you serious about an Emmy?"

Buzz stage-whispered back at Scott, "You can have 'em. I want Karli's balls!"

Jerry grabbed Vince and Holly by the arms and steered them to listen to the exchange. Bielfeldt's pompous tones rolled through the newsroom like kettledrums. "The stories this newsroom has reported in the last week and a half have set a new standard for this market. You've inspired the people of this city to pull together and bear burdens that could easily have resulted in riots and looting.

"Your stories have been easy to understand, emotionally charged, and thoroughly memorable. All the work from the on-air talent has been seamless and excellent. And in spite of the daunting challenges of lighting and mic-ing impromptu locations as essentially full-blown news sets—in addition to covering their assignments—the field photogs have continued to capture powerful and beautiful images and sound."

Here Bielfeldt paused long enough to take in the entire room. His eyes stopped to hold Karli's gaze as he resumed, saying, "Unquestionably these efforts put you in contention for an Emmy." As he said this, an excited murmur rose among the assembled staffers.

Unfazed by the increased noise in the room, his gaze moved to Jake, who looked up after Karli dug an elbow into his ribs. "You're also certain to be in contention for National Press Photographers Association awards—national awards, not just regional." Two photogs whooped and high-fived one another over their cube wall as soon as he finished that assessment.

Jerry leaned even further forward, over the assignment desk's mounds of papers and clutter. "John, we need to talk about entry deadlines and what to submit and so on. Can we meet about that over dinner?" Here he turned to Vince and Holly, who both nodded to the implied request that they also attend.

"Of course," Bielfeldt replied, his self-satisfaction enhanced even more than usual by the news director's evident need for his expertise. "And I think it would be very helpful if Karli were to meet with us."

Jake raised a surprised single eyebrow at Karli, who had suddenly become very still and whose cheeks were coloring quickly. He whispered to her statue-still profile, "Did you pay him or something?"

"Well, uh, sure, John, if that's what you think," Jerry said. He turned to Vince, who gave his questioning look an easygoing shrug and to Holly, whose face broke into a rare tooth-exposing smile.

"Another woman at the table would be most welcome," she said, glancing across the room at Karli. "Don't you think so, Jerry?

"Well, yeah, of course," Jerry replied, his tone going from questioning to declaring. "Of course."

"That's settled then," Bielfeldt rumbled. "The restaurant at the Savery, then? 6:45?"

As the consultant faded from the newsroom, Sophia Refai

stormed up to the assignment desk, the papers in her hand carefully fluttered to make the most noise and draw the most attention possible. "Jerry," she said, loudly enough to ring through the entire newsroom, "Don't you think one of your female *anchors* should be in the meeting, rather than just a general assignment reporter?"

An obviously flustered Jerry looked to Vince for support, only to find him tucking a phone between his shoulder and ear as he leaned to dial. Holly was no better, a pencil clamped between her teeth as she pounded away at her keyboard.

"Well, Sophia—" Jerry began.

"If it's to be one of the female anchors," Bailey's voice carried from the hall to the studio, "I'd suggest it be the one with the most seniority."

Jerry's face fairly shone with hope. "I really think, Sophia," he started, "that Bailey has a point. But of course we should all stay looped in—"

"Fine," Sophia interrupted. "I think it's been too long since I talked to my agent."

She turned and stormed back out of the newsroom, tossing her fluttery papers into the recycling bin on the way out.

"Any time, Jerry," Bailey said with a twinkling grin.

"Yes, thanks much to *you*," Jerry replied, emphasizing the last word as he looked at the backs of Vince's and Holly's heads.

"Think of it," he went on, tilting his chair back and waving his hands toward the ceiling as though arranging a giant newspaper headline. "Three NewsFirst Wins an Emmy." And as his hands spread to display the imaginary words, his chair tipped too far back and dumped him on his back.

"You owe me Karli's balls plus five bucks," Buzz said to Scott, walking over with his hand held out. "I knew that chair would flip him before the year was out."

Chapter Twenty-Six

Coda Lounge, Savery Hotel
Des Moines, Iowa
Tuesday, April 22

Jake snared a chair, plunked his beer down, and sat at the table where Buzz Cziesla, Scott Winstead, and Charlie Teros all were fishing dollar bills from their wallets.

"That had better be a random dollar, Charlie," Scott said sternly.

"Of course it is!" Charlie cried in defensive tones. "I changed a twenty at the bar when I came in."

"Grab a buck, Jake," Buzz said. "We're going to beat Charlie at liar's poker tonight—now that he isn't filling his wallet with great serial numbers the day before."

Charlie glared at Buzz, not able to deny the accusation, but not pleased at the public shaming. "Two pair; nines over sevens," he said coldly.

Seeing that the game was already more serious than fun, Jake took a smiling sip from his beer. "I'm out, guys, unless you're okay with a spectator."

"That's fine," Scott replied. Then, turning to Charlie, he said, "Three eights."

Buzz countered with, "Full house. Three eights and two fives."

And so the game went on, with Jake peeking at all the serial numbers and keeping his face completely neutral so as not to spoil the game. After he had figured on a probable winner, he asked the table in general, "Have you guys heard anything about Bielfeldt's dinner with the gang?"

"Huh?" asked Charlie looking up from his dollar with a furrowed brow.

"Not a peep," said Buzz. "But what's to hear? They were just talking about deadlines and stuff, right?"

"I thought they might be looking at specific stories and live segments to submit," Jake said. "And I was wondering if they were going to use any of my stuff."

"You chowderhead!" Scott folded his dollar to hide everything but the serial number. "You consistently shoot the best stories in the house, and you're *wondering if they'll use your stuff?*" He sighed and turned to Chuck. "Five nines." Then back to Jake: "They're going to use your stuff. The real question is whether or not they'll even look at anyone's else's stuff."

Charlie threw his dollar on the table in disgust. Buzz and Scott cheered and high-fived one another.

"Okay, guys," Jake said, not wanting to leave Charlie to the sports team's tender mercies. "I'm in." He pulled out his wallet and shuffled out a one.

***

Across the room, Karli sat at the bar with Jerry, Holly, Vince, and Bailey. Jerry was handing a credit card to the bartender. "We've already blown a big hole in this at the restaurant tonight. Since I'm going to have to answer all of Norwich's questions about expenses, I may as well get some mileage out of the answers, right? So let's run a tab and see how much we can hold."

Karli watched the bartender give a sympathetic smile to the plight of a manager defending an expense account and then move immediately into taking orders. As he turned to begin making their drinks, Jerry's full face came into view as he leaned forward and practically onto the bar. "So what do we think of Bielfeldt's sunny optimism? Are we really going to win an Emmy, or is he blowing smoke up our asses so he can negotiate a better consulting arrangement?"

Not knowing anything at all about his consulting fees, Karli decided to sit back and listen rather than joining right in. The normally quiet Holly surprised her by being the first to speak up. "If he isn't sincere, he should be a trial lawyer or a politician. He sounded like a true believer tonight. Vince, you can sniff out a spin," she went on, turning toward the veteran assignment editor. "What did you think?"

"He was telling it straight," Vince rasped. "And I don't think I can disagree with him. I watched as much of all the stations' coverage as I could, and the others couldn't touch us."

"We didn't just beat them overall, we beat them in every category," Bailey chimed in. "Reporting, photography, location sets, community outreach—you name it, we had no effective competition from anyone."

"Don't leave out the anchor work," Karli said loyally. "And I agree. The other stations got really cheap about overtime and mostly kept to their regular shifts. We all worked like soldiers, and it really showed in how much content we delivered and in how good it was."

Jerry drank deeply from his glass and swiveled his chair to face the others. "I was so hoping I wasn't being delusional just because I've never been in sniffing range of an Emmy before."

He gestured to the bartender for another round. "Thanks to all of you for your clear eyes and great effort."

As he went on about his hopes for a big award, Karli tried to recall how many drinks she'd had that evening. At least two glasses of wine with dinner—probably three. And now an Amaretto stone sour under her belt and another on the way. No wonder she was feeling a little warm and fuzzy.

As her eyes focused again on her surroundings, she saw Jake, Buzz, Scott, and Charlie all coming up to the bar with empty glasses in their hands. Jake's smiling profile was as handsome as she'd ever seen it, with a couple days of unshaven bristle on his jaw and outlining his toothy smile. As she lowered her gaze to the fresh drink that appeared in front of her, her eyes traveled down his form to the noticeable bulge in the front of his Levi's. Surprised that she was so suddenly fixated on that bulge, Karli felt her cheeks flush hot. Turning toward the bar, she sipped from her drink and took a deep breath.

Breathing didn't help. It just gave her a tingly feeling between her legs as she recalled trying to control her breath the last time he had been down there. The usually cool Coda Lounge suddenly felt hot, and Karli wondered if she was visibly sweating.

She looked back over toward the *men*, and noticed how straight and strong Jake stood in his crisp, heavy cotton dress shirt—*would a photog wear Brooks Brothers, really?* she wondered. The cuffs were folded neatly back over his tan forearms, and the hand that held his glass was both strong and capable of great delicacy, both with his equipment and with...*well, MY equipment*, Karli smirked naughtily to herself.

As she watched him talk and laugh with the director and sportscasters, she realized that his eyes and creative genius had helped her to do the best work of her career—work that had found her at dinner with the news team's leadership, who accepted her in their group just like she'd always belonged there.

Not only is he smart and excellent at what he does, she thought, *he has become my best friend.* As disarming as his humility could be, there was no disguising the swagger he brought to his work and his off-duty life. *He's comfortable in his own skin,* she thought.

She looked unabashedly at him now, not caring who saw her deep interest. His lips were full and wet with beer, and she remembered the last time she had felt them on her breasts. Feeling the memory, she also felt herself stiffen with the memory and wondered briefly if her arousal were visible.

Peeking down at her chest, she decided that they weren't too obvious. But seeing herself roused to just the memory of his kisses, she found suddenly that she was thinking about how his hands had moved over her, and she noticed that she had become wet and even hotter and more tingly.

Karli watched the men all return to their table and start playing with their money. *I can't believe I didn't even like him at first. Not only is he incredibly hot—and yeah, I could see that right away—he is, like, the perfect guy. He has put up with my standards and even respects me for being a crazy perfectionist. He's totally patient with me and willing to stick with me while I grind out the last bit of a story. Even more, he is the best fit I've ever known. We seem to balance each other temperamentally—we challenge each other in the best ways.*

Loud cheers and cries of disgust drew Karli's attention to Jake's table, where the men were throwing dollar bills at one another. *What in the world are they doing?* Karli wondered. As the shouting died down, Karli saw Jake turn to look at her. His melting brown eyes caught hers tightly and let her know that he is in full agreement that it's time to leave the bar.

Bailey's voice cut through the pounding of Karli's heartbeat. "Are you about ready to head out, Karli?" she asked. When Karli turned toward her, she saw Bailey's significant eyebrow raised inquiringly. "It's been a pretty long day already."

Karli nodded. "I've been replaying the last nine months, Bailey, and I can't believe how much more handsome he's gotten. Every bit more I get to know him, the more I've seen it." She turned to look Bailey right in the eyes, and the buzz of the alcohol running through her head washed away the filter between her brain and her mouth. "He's so much like home. He holds me, he keeps me safe, he is patient with my weirdness, and he understands me. Plus, his cologne smells amazing."

"Sounds like he's Mr. Right?" Bailey's voice lifted to indicate the question.

"He really could be," Karli said slowly, considering the answer. "But he's going to have to just be a very precious Mr. Right Now. I cannot afford to get sucked into the Des Moines gravity well. The plan is to get to a really major market, and this flood coverage should be enough."

"You really like him, don't you?"

"Too much, Bailey. He's in my head all the time."

"Too much? What does that mean?" Bailey asked.

"He's the kind of guy I could give up my dreams for. And that's too much."

Bailey took a slow sip from her drink, giving Karli a considering look. Then her eyes shifted somewhere behind Karli, who turned to see what had drawn Bailey's attention. Just as she turned to look over her shoulder, the smell of Jake's cologne reached her nose. She inhaled it deeply, feeling her eyelashes flutter as the scent reached the instinctual parts of her brain. The ones that build even more of the tension and wetness Karli was feeling between her legs.

"Hey, Bailey," Jake said, and Karli felt his warm hand on her shoulder. Without waiting for Bailey's response, Jake turned and asked Karli if it wasn't time to leave. She looked into his eyes and realized they had seen right through her, over and over again. Even knowing everything about her, he still cared for her. As she replied,

"Okay," and grabbed her bag, she felt a nearly overwhelming feeling of love and loss. Jake was so wonderful, yet she couldn't keep him. She knew he wouldn't leave his work, his studio, his amazing carriage house, his charities, his mother. He was as entwined with Des Moines as her father was—though in a significantly different way—with Charleston.

She stood and bid goodbye to the news team, then walked out of the bar holding Jake's hand. *I can't worry about the rough parts tonight,* she thought. *I'm just going to enjoy how wonderful he is.* She glanced over at him and took a deep breath. *This may be the last time,* she began. She checked herself quickly. *I don't know how many more times I'll be able to be vulnerable with him and still be able to walk away.*

They reached the Tesla and climbed in. Buckling his seatbelt, he said, "Automatic door locks are just one more thing killing the last remnants of chivalrous manners. Back in the day, men used actual keys to unlock the passenger door, then they held it open. Now it's just a beep and then fend for yourself."

Everything that comes out of him smells like commitment, she thought. *I can't love him without getting lost. And besides, I have a plan. As wonderful as he is—pretty much everything I ever wanted professionally and personally—he is Des Moines, and I am SO not Des Moines.*

Arriving at Jake's grandiose carriage house, Karli felt immediately comfortable walking up the steps from the Tesla's place of honor to the living space upstairs. The photos, the completely controlled and directed lighting, the lingering smell of his cologne and the bleachy-clean smell of the karate uniforms he had washed and hung up to dry were all familiar and homey sensations for her, and they were reminders of other times they had been alone there together and of all the intimacy they had shared there.

Karli was first through the unlocked door. Jake came in right behind her, and she started just a bit as the door closed harder than usual. She turned to see if anything was the matter and found Jake just inches away and moving closer. His heady, spicy scent filled her nose, and her skin tingled where each little kiss's dampness evaporated cooly away. The smell of him—which was the smell of the carriage house, too—surrounded her comfortably.

He grabbed her by the waist and pressed his face to her neck, kissing lightly and mumbling, "I couldn't wait to get you away from all that newsroom crowd and alone." The absolute silence of the carriage house was filled with their breath and with the scratching of his unshaven cheeks along her neck. She could feel her nipples tightening inside her blouse. He was so all around her and so irresistible and so overwhelming.

Karli felt him move his hungry mouth along her neck, her heart pounding the march beat for his lips moving toward her own. He lifted her confidently and turned to press her against the door. She could feel the pressure of his bulge against her. Setting her down, he took her face in both hands and locked eyes with her. Even though she was still lost in his eyes, she felt her mouth reach for his and her teeth clamp lightly down on his lip.

His hands moved opposite to one another, his right sliding up to her chest, where she felt him discover the hard peak of her breast. His left hand slid down her side and raised her skirt. She felt his caress on the smooth globe of her ass, then felt his hand pause as he discovered the lacy edge of her thong where it slid down to hide between her cheeks.

His kisses grew ever more intense, and she felt the door's patterned wood press into her shoulders. She leaned back, pressed there by the weight of Jake's passion, pinned so that she had little need to bear weight on her stiletto heels. She felt his hand leave the roundness of her butt, then move around to slip underneath the suddenly itchy lace that barely covered her in front.

His breath carried a whisper to her ear, nearly unintelligible over her own heavy breath and the thudding of her heart's beat.

"My God, you are beautiful," his breath washed over and through her ear. "I've wanted to touch you like this for days." Saying this, Jake's fingers found the slick wetness under her thong and began moving in deliberate circles. Karli felt her body's responsive shudders almost as an involuntary reaction. And though Jake's fingers were gentle, his palm pressed hard against her smoothly waxed pubic mound, fixing her firmly to the door.

Karli tilted her head up and back against the door and felt the clenching inside her begin to feel more urgent. She'd been wound up so tightly that just a few thrusts of his fingers inside her—*just exactly like that,* she thought—and a little more circling would spring her. She lifted her leg slightly to better open herself to Jake's touch.

"I want to be inside you," he said. "Now." She felt him lift her leg even more, and she reached down to open the series of buttons that strained to keep his erection covered.

"Oh, yes," Karli whispered, feeling him spring out his jeans and into her hand. *This is the only place I've felt relaxed since I came here.* And Jake pushed himself inside her, the lace of her thong having already been moved to the side.

"You're so wet and tight," he said, through gritted teeth. He thrust himself slowly in to his full length, and Karli thrummed to the sensation. She felt him all around her, smelled the sweetness of his breath, felt the thrusting. *Oh my God,* she thought. *I'm getting pounded.*

He was pulling himself hard against her and pressing her hard against the wall, and his tongue was in and out of her mouth, mimicking his dick's strokes.

The entire world seemed to slip away from her, and all she knew was him and herself and how amazing every sensation in her entire body felt.

She heard Jake breathing with effort and moaning with pleasure. "Damn, you're hot," he groaned. She wanted to let go and feel the release of orgasm, yet she also wanted this to last forever.

Without warning, the wave broke over her and she clenched around him and the blood pounded through her and Karli found herself finishing with a suddenness and shivering intensity that surprised her. Her legs nearly failed her, and she almost collapsed to the floor.

"Don't worry," he said, holding her in his strong arms. "I've got you."

Karli felt her breath slowing along with a lull of mild, incipient disappointment that the orgasm had ended. The melting release swept over her, and she heard Jake whispering in her ear, "You're so beautiful when you come." Her eyes had started to open, but they fluttered closed with his words.

She felt Jake pull her from the wall, lift her, and carry her to the couch where they had shared so much unguarded conversation over the last few months. She slumped back onto the couch and felt him unbuttoning her and taking her clothes off.

She reached up to fumble with his shirt buttons, found that he'd already gotten them started, and ran her hands on the skin inside his shirt. His skin tightly covered hard muscles that rippled as he moved and as she moved her hands over him.

Her hands worked downward till they came to his huge erection. She ran her hands along the strong velvet length, realizing that she had finished first again. "You own every bit of me when we do that, you know," she muttered.

Feeling him like this, her lassitude vanished, replaced by a surprising new surge of sexual energy. Jake rumbled with a half-groan, half-growl in response to her gentle stroking. The sound found its echo within her, and she closed her eyes.

Then her shoes lifted and her legs went with them. She opened her eyes to see Jake holding a heel in each hand, and realized that he had removed all of her clothing except for the shoes, which he now used as handles to position her legs and steer himself toward her. "I can't wait to be inside you," he rasped. "You are so wet and tight and . . . just perfect."

As he entered her again Karli heard herself moan, "That's even better..." She felt Jake's full length sliding through her slippery wetness, and she lost herself again in the thrusting, the sounds of Jake's pleasure, and the warmly familiar smells that surrounded her.

The incessant buzz of her usual stream of thoughts slipped away, and Karli found herself concentrated only on Jake and herself and how amazing every sensation in her entire body felt.

She heard his breathing deepen and quicken to match her own. The finish was coming, and she ached for it, but she didn't want it to end the intensity of his obvious pleasure or her own.

She felt him relinquish the heels to wrap his hands at her waist and pull hard on her hips to bring them crashing together over and over. As he slowed, he rubbed a thumb steadily around her clitoris.

Karli crossed her high heeled feet behind Jake's ass to pull him into herself, and their eyes again met and locked. Jake moved his hand with more urgency and said, "Soon."

Karli felt the wave from afar this time, locking eyes with Jake and crying out a long, "Yesssss," just as he called out her name. She felt him come inside her, felt herself clenching tightly around him as she throbbed in climax.

She saw little beads of sweat on his forehead as he worked to get control of his breath. "You un-man me, Karli Lewis," he said. "I cannot imagine myself with any other woman."

Oh, wow, she thought. *That's a lot.* She goggled up at him, speechless.

She saw Jake's intent gaze turn suddenly sheepish, and his head turned with a suddenly shy smirk. "I guess I kinda took you there, didn't I?" He looked down and then back up to Karli's eyes. "With those heels, that skirt, and especially that thong, I don't suppose you're too surprised, are you?"

The two laughed quietly together, and Karli nodded. "Yeah," she said, "I was kinda hoping you'd notice me."

"*Notice* you?" Jake's eyebrows shot up together and his face took on a serious expression. "Karli, I can't stop noticing you or thinking about you or wanting you." Then, after a significant pause, he rose gently from the couch and said, "I'll be right back."

Karli watched the firm nakedness of his butt retreat, and then she felt a little chilly, what with being in the altogether and no longer moving in rhythm.

In just a moment, though, she saw Jake return with a pile of folded laundry in one arm, a basket hanging from the same arm, and a big grin on his face.

He plunked himself down on the couch and make a big swirly production out of silently handing Karli a warm washcloth.

Saying nothing at all about it, she watched him shake out a man-sized nightshirt and present it to her. "In case you get a chill," he said. She immediately pulled it over her head, rushing so as not to miss the sight of Jake sliding a matching nightshirt down over his head and over his otherwise naked body.

She laughed as he knelt fluidly on the floor in front of the couch and took her foot in his hand. "The shoe most definitely fits like it belongs," he said, gently easing first one, then the other of her high heels off her feet.

He then pulled a bottle of wine—*another New Zealand Marlborough*, Karli noted with approval—from the basket, followed by pears, a knife, a miniature cutting board, and two kinds of cheese.

As she watched the preparations, Karli touched the little bit of a rough patch on her neck left by his scruffy beard, smelled his smell on her, and savored the satisfied and swollen and sluggish after-sex feelings.

Jake's preparations were simple and homey. Karli took the glass of wine, grateful for the cooly crisp taste. She next bit into the salty-sweet of crumbling white cheddar atop a vanishing slice of pear. The tastes, the quiet, the comfort of the couch, and Jake's arm finally around her shoulders all felt unutterably safe and tender and permanent. She did not want to go anywhere, to think anything, to do anything.

Her phone chirruped from inside the bag she had dropped on the way in. Jake stepped quickly to grab and silence the call. Then he made a show of holding the power button down till the phone asked him to swipe to power off. Karli realized she had actually forgotten how to power her iPhone off, and she felt an odd twinge as the turning gear indicated an end to her electronic connection to the outside world.

"I don't plan on letting you leave," Jake muttered into her ear. "Should we order in pizza or something?"

"I had that big dinner with Jerry and John," Karli said. "But if you're keeping me for the whole night, I'll help you eat a pizza."

Jake reached for the landline to call for pizza. "I really want to keep you here for good, you know."

Ohmyfreakinggosh, Karli thought to herself. Then she thought, *I guess I'm not really surprised. And it feels really nice in a way. I knew I smelled commitment somewhere. But I* cannot *say I love him.* She took a deep breath and felt the muzzy warmth of the sex pull her thoughts out of focus.

Her sigh gusted across Jake's chest as he ordered a pizza for delivery—and she smiled to herself as she listened to him specifying sausage, but only if it had no fennel, and mushrooms, but only if they were portabella.

Chapter Twenty-Seven

Bravo! Cucina Italiana
West Des Moines
Friday evening, April 25

Karli leaned forward and hissed in an urgent whisper, "How in the world did you find out—they're not supposed to make announcements till the awards dinner, are they?"

Consultant Bielfeldt and News Director Schultz leaned comfortably back in their chairs, wide grins on each of their faces. Bielfeldt glanced over at Jerry, then lifted the bottle of pricey but unexceptional chianti to fill the beautiful stemware at the top of each place setting.

As he poured, he responded in tones of consummate self-satisfaction. "Karli," he said, "you understand that the news business is all about developing sources, don't you?" He beamed again at the news director and continued, "Well, my work in consultancy has put me in touch with quite a few of the industry's movers and shakers. And three of them sit on the awards panel."

"And my friends in the national association have confirmed John's sources, so this is firm. The reports that you and Jake did during the flood are going to win an Emmy."

Schultz raised his wine glass and tipped it toward Karli. "This is going to be huge for Three NewsFirst, and it's going to be huge for you, Karli. You're going to be the premiere field reporter for the entire state of Iowa."

Karli flushed with the surprise and gratification at winning one of television's most prestigious awards and with the unexpected praise from her news director. She took a deep breath to collect herself, then remembered dancing through the sheep dip at the Iowa State Fair and a hundred other indignities she had suffered covering both rural and urban stories in the past months. "The entire state of

Iowa, huh?" she asked, lifting her own glass to meet the others. "Well, then, here's to all three million Iowans," she declared, lifting her glass and then sipping.

"May each one of them know your name and face," the news director solemnly intoned, drinking from his own glass.

"And what sorts of things go with being *Iowa's premiere field reporter*?" Karli asked.

"Your duties won't be much different, really," Jerry said thoughtfully.

"You will, of course, have to make more public appearances," John interrupted. "Parades and charity events and beauty pageants and things. Your name recognition will be crucial for the station's success."

"That much time in the public eye might prevent you from tackling some lower-profile kinds of assignments, too," Jerry said, picking up where the consultant had left off. "Like your renewable energy series is a huge time commitment and might not fit into what's going to be a pretty much celebrity schedule."

"Wait," Karli interjected. "You're telling me that being a premiere reporter means I'll be doing *less* reporting and that the reporting I'll do won't be on in-depth pieces that can actually inform public opinion on big issues?" *And I'll be forced to go milk goats at the stupid State Fair, to judge the awful noise of the husband-calling contest, and to go shopping for prom dresses with the girls from the state basketball tournament. There's some hard-hitting journalism, all right.* She looked at each of the men, challenging them to back away from everything they'd just said.

"No, not at all, Karli..." Jerry began in wheedling and utterly unpersuasive tones.

Karli's phone buzzed in her bag, and she reached for it. Looking down at the alert, she smiled to herself. "Guys," she said, "I'm afraid I have to take this call. Please excuse me."

She rose from her chair and swiped to answer. "Karli Lewis." Then, as she retreated toward the women's restroom she said, "Yes, I'm so glad you called. ... No, this isn't a bad time at all, really. My plans just became very definite, and I'm excited we can talk about them."

Chapter Twenty-Eight

Cosi Cucina
Clive, Iowa
Saturday evening, April 26

Jake rose as he saw Karli directed to their table. He took in the entire picture of her, from the curved arches shaped by the dramatic heels to the amazing figure contained in her elegant dress to her shining face, and caught his breath. *She is absolutely the one,* he thought. He felt at his jacket pocket for the tenth time in as many minutes to make sure the little box was still there.

As the host made a fuss of pulling her chair out and seating her, Jake calculated the fractional second that had him sitting down just after her. The host filled her wine glass, topped up Jake's, and told them that Robert would be with them shortly. Jake quirked his most mysterious smile at her, raised his glass, and said, "Here's to you, Karli. You are an absolute vision tonight."

Jake saw Karli's smile reflecting the warmth he always felt in her presence, and she raised her own glass in reply. "Thanks, Mr. Devastatingly Handsome. You're something to look at, too, you know."

They both drank and then made small talk about menu choices. Once Robert had come and taken their orders, both Jake and Karli leaned forward across the table toward one another, taking breaths preparatory to speaking. When Jake saw that they were doing the same thing, he laughed and began to fish the little box out.

Karli laughed, too. Then, together, they both said, "I've got something—"

Jake laughed again, eased back into his chair, and said, "Okay, you go first."

Karli settled into her chair and took a drink of wine to fill the space. "You know I had dinner with Bielfeldt and Schultz last night, right?" Jake nodded, and Karli continued. "Well, they have inside sources, and they swore me to secrecy. But you're in this, so you deserve to know. And besides, I have to tell someone, and you're ... well, you're *you*, you know."

Jake was doing his best not to show the impatience he felt with all the unintelligible build-up. Then Karli leaned over the table and whispered, "Our stories are going to win an Emmy. It's locked up. We just have to keep it completely secret until the awards banquet in June."

The gratifying rush of warmth to his cheeks rode atop Jake's growing smile. "That really is news, Karli! Congratulations to us," he finished, raising his glass again.

"That isn't the news, really," she continued. "Jerry has offered me the job of 'Iowa's Premiere Field Reporter'." Her voice made the title's quotes and caps explicit.

"Well, that's something indeed!" Jake said. "I assume that means our renewable energy series and documentary is totally green-lighted now?" His excitement grew as he went on, "And you'll really be in control of other awesome new stories, too—stuff that can really change trends."

"Not really, Jake," she responded.

Then, to his surprise, she began to giggle. "They want me to judge husband-calling contests and milk goats and stuff. There is absolutely no way I am going to quit an actual career as a reporter and sign up instead to ride parade floats and be the celebrity starter for the charity 5K races."

"I'm sure they would be willing to let you do actual reporting if that's what you want," Jake replied. "Airhead TV 'personalities' are the ones who always *want* to be the celebrity rather than the actual journalist." Jake was gratified to hear that the station would be acknowledging that Karli had actual leverage to negotiate terms for a bigger role.

"Oh, but that part isn't the news, really, either," Karli said. "Some of the Emmy judges are higher-ups at the big network owned-and-operated station in Chicago. And they've offered me a job *covering a beat for me to develop on my own*, starting in two weeks."

All the blood in Jake's body slammed down to his stomach, and his ears filled with a loud rushing pounding. He slid the little box back into his pocket. His cheeks were suddenly cold and his lips numb. He fumbled his wine glass to his mouth and drained it with an enormous, untasted gulp.

"What did you say to them?"

"Well, I have to take the job, of course. This is what I've been working for ever since I started at Missou. Just think—the third-largest market in the nation, with more than twice as many people in the metro than there are in the entire state of Iowa! This is the dream job I've always talked about, Jake. And it's completely on my terms."

Jake slowly refilled his glass, then raised it to her and said, "Here's to your career." He dropped his eyes from hers to take a sip. It was not satisfying. Jake looked at and then carefully sniffed the wine to see if it had gone bad. It hadn't.

"Oh, it gets better, Jake—they said they'd like to interview you and see if you'd be a good fit there, too. They were really impressed with your work, too."

"Wow. That's really nice of them," Jake said, through as much of a smile as he could force onto his lips. "I'll have to see about that." *Never in a million years, Karli Lewis. I've looked down that road already, and there's nothing there but stress and backstabbing competition. And very little of the community participation that there is here. It's too bad you can't see it for what it is.*

"So, let's celebrate, Jake! I'm so glad I can share this with you, since you did so much to help my dream-job come true."

"Yeah, well, anything to help, you know."

Robert brought their dishes, and Karli dove in with real enjoyment. Jake picked at his food and did considerable work with his wine glass.

"So overall, the whole situation in Chicago is going to be fantastic," Karli gushed. "They've even got a downtown condo that the station owns where they'll put me up indefinitely. That means as long as I want, they're going to pay the rent for me. In downtown Chicago, that is a heap of money. And they're just giving it to me." Jake saw that Karli was genuinely puzzled at the station's "generosity."

"So, that condo is probably right there in the same building as the newsroom, isn't it?" he asked.

"Yes, it is!" she cried in tones of wonder. "How did you know that?"

"Oh, let me see if I can make this into a streak," Jake continued. "I'll bet there's a health club right there for you, too." Karli nodded, her eyebrows starting to come together and make vertical wrinkles above her nose. "And this one came as a real surprise: They will even cater in your meals if you're working late, won't they?"

"Yes," Karli responded slowly. Jake saw the tense questioning on her face, and quietly concluded. "They want to own your whole life, Karli. They want you to live and eat and work out on site so you won't have any pesky actual life intruding into your work life. They've recruited you into an occupational lifestyle, not into a job."

"But Jake, that's what I've been working for ever since Missou," she replied. "I am so fired up for this. Living the work and doing the work I want to do is what I've always been shooting for."

Jake looked at her, holding her eyes with his own till she looked aside and then down to her plate. *You don't realize that you're putting what you used to think you wanted ahead of what you have learned you actually want. And I don't know how long it will take you to figure that out.* He sighed, handed the passing server a credit card, and said, "Well, congratulations again. I hope it all works out the way you want."

"Jake, don't be like this," Karli said. "I want this to be a happy thing, and you're making it all dramatic and about something else." He watched her face scrunch up the way it does when someone isn't sure if they're going to cry or not.

"We've never said we're more than an in-the-moment thing, and I don't want to be made to feel all guilty because I'm making the big mean choice to leave you. Because I have my chance at what I've always wanted."

She paused and looked at her hands, folded over the napkin in her lap, then she looked back up at him. "You're really special, Jake, and you mean a lot to me, okay?" He could see her swallow and take a big breath.

"But I can't put my life on hold for a man, any man. My dad wants me to live the life he has cooked up for me, and now you're making me feel like I should be living some other life you decided on for me. Well, I'm not going to read my lines off someone else's script. I have to make my own choices about what my life is going to be like."

Jake took the little wallet with the receipt and his credit card sticking out of it from Robert, wrote in a tip, signed, and set it on the table. "Karli, I haven't said a thing about how you should live your life. I have congratulated you and wished you the best," he said. "You're right that I have other ideas, but I have never said anything about how I think you should live your life. If you're feeling guilty, it's not because I've laid that on you."

"Oh, so this is all my doing, then, is it?" Karli responded angrily. "If I'm feeling guilty, it's my own fault, right, and I should feel guilty about that, too, right?"

"That's not what I said, either."

"No, of course not," Karli's fury rolled on. "You're just the latest man who wants to control me."

Jake rose from the table and turned to leave. He went about two steps, paused, turned, and found Karli's eyes. "No, Karli. I'm not trying to control you. I'm trying to tell you that I love you. And that I love you enough to let you find your own way."

He began turning to leave, stopped, then reached into his pocket and turned back to Karli. "Here. I guess it's my turn, now that you're all finished," he said, opening the box and handing it to her. He watched her pull out the elaborate platinum charm bracelet with an appreciative gasp.

As she minutely examined each custom-made charm—a covered bridge, a tiny ram with prominent testicles, a miniature microphone, a camera, a little bulletproof vest, a bicycle, a tiny Three NewsFirst logo, and the initials J.G.—he turned and moved silently to leave the restaurant, and Karli.

Chapter Twenty-Nine

Karli's Apartment
West Des Moines, Iowa
Thursday evening, May 1

"That's the last of it," darkly handsome Scott Winstead said, slapping his hands clean of cardboard-box dust and examining the stuffed trunk of Karli's Saab outside her apartment complex. "These few boxes don't seem like they're worth the pizza and beer,"

"I didn't have room for much stuff in college, and then all I could afford at my last job was a really small efficiency, so I didn't get more stuff. This place is furnished, and I've been so busy here that I haven't had much need for, you know, things."

"You know how to travel light," Scott said, shaking his head. "I never thought I'd be here very long, but it's been five years now, and I'll bet I've accumulated enough stuff to fill one of those giant rental trucks." He shook his head slowly, as though considering the wearying burdens of moving to another city. "So how big is your new place going to be? Big enough to hang at least a picture or two?"

Saying this, he reached into the trunk and pulled out a picture. The frame was still bound at the corners with protective layers of cardboard linked with strapping tape. Scott turned the picture over and found a black-and-white close-up photo of Karli's beaming face, lit and shaded by a setting, golden-hour sun. Karli saw Scott react to the picture in stages: first, surprise that it was a portrait, then a quick glance at her face for comparison, then a lingering professional assessment.

"He really caught a look inside you, you know?" he said, looking carefully from the picture to Karli herself. "This picture has all the stuff that Bielfeldt was talking about when he was going on about being inspirational. Jake's composition—you off to the edge and against that soft background—is unforgettable. It's inspirational, too. Every man wants to make a woman smile just exactly like that. That smile is a discovery, the place where men find the promised land." Scott paused, looking hard at the picture, a corner of his mouth tugged in apparent regret or chagrin or something. "It had to be Jake, right?"

Kari nodded, stiffly, just as he looked up from the photo. Then he met Karli's eyes. "I had kind of hoped I'd find out if I could make you smile like that. But you were so bombed on the single night I thought I might have a chance..." His voice trailed off to a momentary silence. "I was getting kind of pumped when you went on and on all about being fully ready and extra-willing, but then I realized that you were slurring every single word. You were just too wasted. I couldn't even try for a kiss in good conscience."

"Please, Scott, let's not talk about that night. It took me two days of aspirins, water, and chocolate milkshakes to escape that hangover. And I'm not sure I recall—or even *want* to recall—all the details of my behavior leading up to the headaches."

"It's long gone, I know," he said, shaking his head. "And besides, you're headed off to the big show now, so it's not like there's going to be a less-wasted opportunity any time soon." He paused, then added, "Of course, I did send a new link to my reel a few days ago—maybe I'll be joining you someday." He shrugged, put the picture back, and swung the trunk closed.

He looked at the Florida license plate that still sat in the Missou frame. "You made it out of Des Moines before your Florida plate expired. That's fast work, Karli."

"I'm not leaving until after work tomorrow, but I have to be out of my place tonight so the new tenant can move in. And thanks to your help, it's all cleaned out now, so it's time for that pizza and beer. Mary Rose is letting me crash on her couch tonight, so she gets some, too."

They drove off separately to the Court Avenue area, where the nightlife emphasis means the beer usually sells better than the pizza.

Scott, who was parked behind Karli, could see enough to know that she didn't look back except to check for traffic.

Chapter Thirty

Fong's Pizza
Downtown Des Moines, Iowa
Thursday evening, May 1

"I hope it isn't too sappy, but I got you this card as a going-away thing," Mary Rose said, handing Karli a small USB drive. "Well, it has a kind of a card *inside*, anyway. I put a couple little things I made for you on it. You can check it out when you get to the new shop and have access to a computer again."

"Thank you, Mary Rose," Karli said, taking the thumb drive and then taking the other woman's hand. "That sounds like a lot of work."

"No big," Mary Rose shrugged. "You've been a good friend, and you helped me finally bust out of the studio and into the field." She ran her fingers through her bright blue hair and glanced over at Scott. "And it looks like I'm going to be shooting a lot of sports this summer, too. The Drake Relays may be over, but there's a lot coming up fast—the State high school track meet is just a couple of weeks away, and there's all the spring collegiate wrap-ups, and it seems like the summer balloons from there."

Scott looked at her in surprise, "Since when do shooters know about event schedules? I thought you just drove there and then bitched about having to carry the tripod."

Mary Rose treated Scott to a broad, triumphant smile that was interrupted by her tongue sticking out to make her piercing click audibly against her front teeth.

"You ain't seen nothin' yet, sweetie. I learned a few things about doing my homework before covering a story from our friend Karli. You're going to have to step up your game if you want to keep up with me." She gave him a mischievously challenging look, then bumped her beer into his where it sat on the table in front of him in a semi-voluntary toast. "Let the games begin." Karli watched as Scott's mouth silently opened and shut in speechless surprise.

"Careful there, Scott," Karli said. "She's full of surprises."

Karli's attention was drawn to voices shrieking greetings across the restaurant. One was a familiar voice, unfortunately. "Oh, geez. It's Sophia."

"Oh look, it's little Karli," she shrilled while tugging on the sleeve of the competition's Donald Harris. They walked noisily over to the table, making sure every eye in the restaurant was on them.

"Hello, Sophia. Still dating the competition, I see?"

"Oh, Donald isn't the competition any more. I thought you'd heard?" Sophia's eyes swept the room, making sure she still had the crowd's attention.

"Heard what? That Jerry lowered his standards enough to bring him on board at Three NewsFirst?" Karli looked straight at Sophia though Harris obviously took offense, to judge by his sudden snap of the head toward Karli and his fists balling up at his side. "You can try telling me that, but I'm not buying."

Sophia turned to her companion and placed a calming hand on his arm. "But Donald isn't *my* competition any more, Karli. This is all about *raising* standards. The up-and-coming station in Indianapolis was looking for a 6:00 and 10:00 anchor to lead them to the number one spot in the ratings. They happened to see my anchor work during the flooding, and they decided that they just *had* to have me."

"So you're moving to a second-place shop?" Karli asked, her voice brimming with false enthusiasm. "Congratulations. I'm sure you'll fit in perfectly."

"I'm going to be the *main anchor,* Karli," Sophia fairly spat. "Which is something you'll *never* be. You have to sit on a booster just to get your head over the top of the anchor desk."

"How much notice are you giving Jerry?" Karli asked, her eyes wide with feigned concern. "Filling your position is going to be *extremely* difficult."

Actually, it may be really hard to fill, Karli thought. *She's all bitch, but Sophia* is *very good on camera—good enough to balance out Stu. It's going to be hard for Jerry to find someone as good as she is to come out here to corn country for the weekend job.*

"They're designing and building a whole new set for me in Indy, so Three NewsFirst gets to keep me till the middle of June."

"The awards banquet is that first week of June, isn't it? Do you think you'll be invited even though you're on the way out?"

Karli's iPhone chirruped an alert.

She pulled it out and looked at the text from her father. "Mom and I are planning a visit to you in Chicago for the week of June 2. Booked at Intercontinental on Michigan. When you get tired of the big city, there will be a great job for you here. Can't wait to celebrate!" Karli replied with a smile emoji.

Smiling to herself, Karli looked up at Sophia. "I'm sorry, were you saying something?"

Sophia, obviously frustrated at being upstaged by a text message, glowered down at Karli. "Oh, nothing that bears repeating. Good luck in your new beat-reporter job." She said *beat-reporter* in tones implying it was several steps below *septic tank*. "Come on, Donald. Let's find a seat on the other side of this place." She snared his arm into her own and dragged him off, away from Karli's table.

"What about that awards banquet, Karli?" Scott asked. "You and Jake did some excellent work this spring—and Bielfeldt was talking Emmy, wasn't he?"

"I'd love to go, but I'll be plugging away at my new dream job. I'll have to leave it to you all to celebrate for me if there's any hardware being passed out."

"That's a shame, Karli," said Mary Rose. "It sounded like you have a really good shot at an award, and it doesn't get bigger than an Emmy."

"If I'm in the running," and Karli emphasized the *if*, "it would be great to be here for it. But I'm going to be working in the kind of newsroom where they practically *expect* Emmy awards. So there will be more opportunities."

"Do they have anyone like Jake there?" Mary Rose asked. "Or, for that matter, like *moi*? You're going to need an outrageously awesome collaborator if you're going to be all heroic there, you know. Or have you forgotten your one-man-band days so quickly?"

"There's nobody like Jake, of course," Karli said thoughtfully. And then, more briskly, "Nor like you, either.

How many crazy characters do you think they can fit in that newsroom?" Karli darted a glance at Scott inviting him to join in the teasing. "But they do have some really seasoned photographers, guys who've been shooting news since they used 16 mm film cameras."

"So you're saying those dinosaurs are going to be doing work that's up to the standard you've seen here? Really?"

"I'll turn on all of my motivational charms, Mary Rose," Karli said with an exaggerated wink. "You'll be impressed, I promise."

"Yeah, sure. I'll believe it when I see it. You're never going to find anything like me or Jake again. You'll be begging us to come take a gig in Chicago."

"And I'll be begging you to land me a gig there," Scott chimed in. "The sports work in a city like that is world's different from sports work in Des Moines." He paused and shook his head slowly. "An entire damned state, and not one single big league team in any sport. If it weren't for the Hawks and 'Clones, there wouldn't be much of anything."

Mary Rose stepped in immediately to offer a whole host of sports events unique to Iowa, starting with the Relays and continuing with the thousands of people who ride their bicycles all the way across the state every summer. As Scott warmed to his subject, he countered with tales of old-fashioned six-on-six grandmother league women's basketball. Mary Rose began to recite a list of Iowa's Olympians.

Karli tuned them both completely out.

She's right, I suppose. Jake really is an amazing photographer. And collaborator. And. . .what—Boyfriend? *That's an icky word. Friend with Benefits? Um, NO.*

Certainly there have been awesome benefits, but he's been a lot more than a friend. Lover?

As she was pondering what she should call Jake, Scott and Mary Rose both pushed their chairs away from the table. Mary Rose took Karli's plate and replaced it with the slim wallet that held the bill. "This is yours, Karli," she said. "You offered, we accepted. No take-sie back-sies."

Karli blinked, then looked at the wallet and, after a moment, reoriented herself. "Right, is it time to go already?"

Scott pointed out that they all had to go to work the next day, and things wrapped up with Karli paying the bill and all three of them walking out into the windy cool of the evening.

Chapter Thirty-One

Tuesday, June 17
Polk County Courthouse
Downtown Des Moines, Iowa

"Okay, Jake, let's head back," Sophia Rephai said, scrolling through the notes on her iPad as they walked briskly toward the courthouse exit.

"Um, Sophia?" Jake bid for the darkly glamorous reporter's attention. He kept walking and waited as she continued to review her notes and ponder the screen in front of her face.

Jake shifted the heavy tripod from one hand to the other and sighed. "Hey, um, Sophia?" Her heels clacked sternly against the courthouse's shining terrazzo floor, and she continued staring at the iPad.

"Yeah, we've totally got enough," she said. "This is a decent follow-up to that drug series. And we should have plenty of time to write and edit before the 6:00 newscast."

"Isn't this story about heroin killing people?" Jake asked, aware that the impatience was audible in his voice.

"That's what we just got, isn't it?" Sophia snapped. "The County Attorney just told us that three people have died from overdoses in the last month. Police officers are being equipped with that antidote stuff—what is it called? Naloxone?" Jake nodded his head in exasperation. "So we have a problem and some of the steps that are being taken to deal with it."

"You have the official story from officials, Sophia," Jake stepped in front of her and stopped so as to get her undivided attention.

"That isn't necessarily the story about what the opiate epidemic and overdoses mean in human terms, is it?"

Sophia shouldered past Jake and kept on toward the exit. "Look, you take pretty pictures, Jake, I get that. But we just got the story that we were sent out to cover. Now we need to go back to the station and put it together to broadcast for our viewers. That's the job."

"Sophia, this isn't a story about cops and prosecutors. Don't you get that? This is a story about human tragedy, about lives cut short, about the enslavement of addiction."

"Not the story I'm doing, Jake," Sophia retorted. "If you want to do a different story, you'll need to get a different reporter. But don't forget that I am the reporter and you're just the photographer. I make the decisions about what the story is and how we report it."

Jake sighed again, shouldered his tripod and shrugged through the door and out into the afternoon sunlight. Karli would not have put forth the least possible effort to produce the least interesting possible story, he thought to himself. And she would have looked for a human angle—like an interview with any actual person who had actually known anyone who had died from an overdose. He slammed his gear into the news car with unnecessary force as he reflected that the 'official' story that Sophia was reporting did nothing other than reinforce the public's view of opiate addiction as a problem of the underclass—one more deserving of resentment than of compassion.

He got into the driver's seat, keyed the ignition, and took a moment to direct a glare at Sophia. She was oblivious, however, her eyes locked onto emails on the iPad. Jake sighed again, put the car into gear, and headed across downtown toward the newsroom.

As he drove, he reviewed his day so far. He had awoken to blankets tangled around a huge bolster that he used to fill his arms while he tried to go to sleep. He checked out of habit, but there was no half-full water glass to rescue from its precarious perch just on the edge of the farther side's nightstand.

He showered and shaved without interruption. He made a single cup of coffee and didn't bother to steam any milk for it. Instead of firing up the stove and having breakfast with napkins and silverware at the table, he hastily beat and microwaved a pair of eggs in a bowl before dumping them onto whole wheat toast, then munching it all down at the counter.

On the way down the steps, he snared the previous night's karate uniform out of the washer, shook it out, and carried it down to the garage to hang on the line next to the steps so it could dry during the day.

He picked up the morning's Register where it had been delivered to his doorstep, chucked it into the recycling bin, and got into his truck for the quiet drive to work.

The drive was quiet—the steady murmur of NPR news washed over him without leaving any trace of meaning. Without the usual punctuation of her announcement of local angles to the national stories, nothing brought the stories out from the radio and into his mind.

Jake felt the absence of a colleague to commiserate with over the daily frustrations of the work—the deadline pressure that was forever increased by the unavailability of sources, the distance to be driven, the need for one more interview, the effort to shake all of the elements down and organize them into a compelling story.

He harrumphed to himself that he used to be irritated that the talk about work never stopped. Yet the work never stopped being interesting, and Karli never stopped being interesting, either. Whatever the subject, she was the most curious, most insightful, most analytical, and most compassionate person he'd ever known.

Again he turned to look at Sophia. She had flipped down the visor and was touching up her make-up in the little mirror. Noticing him from the corner of her eye, she said, "I think I have a decent stand-up written to link to the parts of the story. How about we shoot that with the station's big sign in the background?"

"Seriously?" Jake cried. "You want the Three NewsFirst logo to be the symbol of an addiction crisis?"

Sophia huffed in indignation. "No, I want the Three NewsFirst logo to be right behind me so our viewers know who they're watching deliver the day's news. And that's what we're going to do. So turn on the special pretty switch in your camera and make me look amazing."

She turned the full power of her smile on him, but he had been inoculated long ago. Jake took a sharp breath preparatory to continuing the argument, then thought better of it. Sophia's friendships lasted only so long as someone was useful to her. Then they stopped until the next time she could benefit. He bit his tongue, and kept driving to the station.

Working with Sophia to edit the story for broadcast was a protracted exercise in her self-promotion. The story wound up being every bit as soulless and mediocre as Jake had feared. He considered re-writing and -editing the story for the late newscast, realized that he would have to endure an endless series of diva harangues from Sophia, squared his shoulders, and got on with finishing the job.

When he got home from the dojo later that evening, the carriage house was again silent. He didn't have to explain what had taken him so long when her workout was long done and she had showered and what were they going to eat and would he like to go out to see the baseball game, the dance recital, the play, the movie, the jazz combo, or whatever it was that she'd gotten wind of tonight.

The television masked the chewing and slurping of Chinese take-out, yet it provided no real diversion. When Jake realized that he was beginning a third trip flipping through the hundreds of channels, he stopped, turned the TV off, and cleaned up the little folding boxes and chopsticks.

On his way to the bedroom, he grabbed the sweaty gi from his gym bag, stuffed it into the washer, and turned it on. Taking a lonely scotch and soda with him, Jake crawled into the still-tangled blankets. It was early, yet he was almost painfully fatigued. Leaving his drink untouched, Jake pulled the bolster to his chest and closed his eyes.

Karli would not be laying next to him, her head propped up on her hand, gesturing and whispering as she reviewed all the most interesting and exciting parts of the evening's amateur theater or jazz show or stand-up comic. He would not see her sigh with contentment at having fully discussed the event, nor feel her now-calmed arms around his neck. Her scent wouldn't reach through his nostrils to his hind-brain's triggers. He wouldn't feel her nip teasingly at his lips.

She wouldn't reveal her astonishing beauty to him yet again as they joined in another night's passion.

He remembered the intimacy and he squeezed his eyes tightly in an effort to turn his thoughts away from that lack.

Tuesday, June 17
Westin River North
Chicago, Illinois

"Holy fire!" Karli nearly shrieked into her iPhone. "Nothing has even happened yet to be news—it's the welcoming reception for a *Vitamin D conference!*"

"Karli, the event is sponsored by the National Institutes of Health. There are more than 250 scientists there—some of them the nation's top researchers. You can find a story."

"Yeah, breaking vitamin D news," she sighed. "What odds we start with a shot of the Vitamin D-enriched sun over Lake Michigan?"

"Go dig for a story, Karli. You'll find gold—that's why you're here."

"Right." Karli pressed the red hang-up button and heaved a sigh. She quickly checked her email and her text messages but found nothing that wasn't purely work-related or spam. "Okay, Ja— Um, Jim, let's get some B-roll of the reception room, okay?"

Jim, the grizzled veteran news photographer, hefted his camera to his shoulder and, without moving from where he stood, started rolling.

"Uh, that's a shot of a room, Jim. Don't you think it might look steadier if you put the camera on a tripod?"

"Nah, I'm steady enough," came the reply. "It's just an establishing shot."

Karli clenched her teeth and took a deep breath that had no effect on calming her. "Jim, the story really shouldn't start out shaky. Can you please put it on the tripod?"

"I've got that shot," he replied, shouldering his way into the reception and beginning to frame up another handheld shot of the milling scientists.

Karli fumed to herself and headed into the room behind him to look for someone to interview. About Vitamin D.

***

After torturing herself writing and trying to work around the dreadful video she had to work with, Karli turned in her wretchedly unsatisfying story about research demonstrating that people living at

Chicago's latitudes suffer from seasonal Vitamin D deficiency.

Then Karli walked straight to the news director's office. Turning the knob and walking in without waiting for permission, she saw the boss at his desk, writing notes with the telephone cradled between his jowly cheek and shoulder. She stood, arms akimbo and lips tight, and ignored the angry glare he directed at her in response to the interruption. The boss finished his call with a series of *uh-huhs*, and *rights* followed by a *thanks* and a *perfect*. Then, finally, a *good-bye*.

"What happened to this being a job where I get to cover the stories that I enterprise? I distinctly recall *not* signing up to cover Vitamin D conventions."

"Karli, we needed to cover that convention. One of our biggest shareholders has a husband who's a big-wig doctor at the National Institutes of Health. He's a Vitamin D guy."

"Yeah, I get that *you* needed to cover it," Karli retorted. "I did not need to cover it. In fact, I recall explicitly discussing that I wouldn't be covering bullshit stories."

"It isn't bullshit when one of the actual owners wants a story covered," the boss replied. "In fact, it's something you'll cover and be glad for the opportunity. There's nothing else to be said about it." Having concluded, he turned his attention back to his notes and reached for the phone.

Karli stood, quaking with indignation. *This is not what I signed up for.* After the boss had dialed his call and begun talking and again scribbling notes, Karli realized that he wasn't going to acknowledge her no matter how long she stood there. She turned and left, stopping just short of slamming the door behind her.

Back at her desk, Karli decided to blow off the several dozen emails that had accumulated in her inbox over the afternoon and shut her computer down. She walked away from her desk, wondering what had happened to the issues-driven reporting work she'd been promised.

And the photography had been so very bad. Most shots shook like an old sci-fi set when the starship was under attack. Many were underexposed—except for the interviews, where the subjects' faces were blindingly lit with a camera-top light that left the entire background as murky as a closing-time alley.

Stepping onto the elevator up to her apartment, Karli checked her iPhone's messages. Nothing.

When she was in Des Moines, she and Mary Rose and Jake and the rest of the news crew had kept up a more or less constant stream of texts, ranging from pet illnesses to good-natured teasing to gossipy nonsense to substantive work.

The last non-work text message she'd received was from her father. And that had been the day before. And it had been, of course, about how her Chicago experience would very soon permit her to take Charleston by storm.

She began a new text to Jake, trying to present the problem in a nutshell. After three tries, the awkwardness of texting him at all overwhelmed her. *There's no point in texting him,* she thought. *I'll just get some big I-told-you-so.*

The elevator door opened, and she pressed the sleep switch on top of the phone in exasperation. She walked to her apartment and went straight to the bathroom. She pulled a make-up remover wipe from the package and began the tedious process of scrubbing the thick broadcast make-up from her face. The face in the mirror gradually came clean.

Karli pitched the last wipe into the garbage can and turned to stare at her reflection, which was framed by the furnished apartment's reflection. Nothing she saw looked familiar or homey. The furniture came from some central hotel supply house, as did the carpet, the draperies, the fixtures, the floors—all of it was as coldly impersonal as a budget hotel, with all the variety of the do-it-yourself styrofoam waffles at the included breakfast.

Karli finished washing, decided against going to the gym, and went to the kitchen to look for supper.

Opening the fridge, she found sparkling water, half a bottle of wine, a half-eaten plastic clamshell of pre-cut fruit, and little foil packets of the condiments that had come with take-out meals. She realized she'd worked late—sometimes very late—every night for the last week, which meant she'd distractedly eaten whatever food the station had ordered in.

She pulled out the wine bottle, filled one of the glasses that had lived in the apartment longer than she had, and took a sip. As she wandered distractedly out of the kitchen, she dragged her fingertips across the table and was surprised to find them dusty.

Is this really what I've been working for? she wondered. *I make really good money now, and literally millions of people know who I am.* She looked out her apartment's huge picture window over the Chicago river. Dozens of other tall buildings held hundreds of flashing windows over the river, and she could see into some of them. Some gave glimpses into shiny, impersonal gyms filled with glistening new exercise equipment and glistening people tramping away on treadmills. Others allowed Karli to peek at tired-looking workers pecking away at computers or talking on telephones. A very few opened into some kind of domestic scene—a dining room table standing ready, a living room with a flat, blank television in front of an empty sofa. She couldn't see any actual people in the apartments.

Nowhere did Karli see any kind of connections. The great compression of people into towering proximity did nothing to foster relationships among them. Each was isolated and alone.

Her iPhone buzzed. She reached for it and saw a text from her father: *Congrats again. You've made a fantastic move.*

At least we're all alone together, Karli thought.

Chapter Thirty-Two

Mid-America Emmy Awards Ceremony
Hilton Hotel and Convention Center
Branson, Missouri
Saturday evening, June 28

Sophia Refai melted at the knees to take her seat, lushly elegant in a sexy, blingy evening gown. She was obviously made up for an evening out rather than for broadcast, her hair up and formal and her makeup darker and more seductive than would ever be appropriate for a newscast.

Jake Gibson slid her chair in under her, then bent to say something into her ear. She turned to him with a smile and a brief rejoinder, followed by a bright laugh. Jake looked across the table to where Jerry Schultz was adding a comment of his own, one that set the entire table laughing as Jake took his chair next to Sophia, who leaned over to him and placed her beautifully manicured hand flat against his chest and focused the bright energy of her smile on him and then swung it to take in the rest of the table, where most of the Three NewsFirst leadership sat.

Karli Lewis stood awkwardly at one of the ballroom's side entrances, her fingers fidgeting with the soft cord atop her clutch. She shook the charm bracelet on her wrist and looked into the chandeliered ballroom from a side-on view of the raised stage and a not very good view of the two-story-high video screens displaying images from the seven or so television cameras pointing all around the room. *Jake in a tuxedo?* she thought to herself. *He looks amazing!*

She locked her eyes on him where he sat on the far side of the room, past the other end of the stage, looking effortlessly comfortable in an obviously not off-the-rack tux. She felt a surge of energy—a mixture of desire, possessiveness, and a hint of jealousy.

Has Sophia already managed to get her hooks into him? she wondered. *That would be so like her—hooking up with some dude when she knows full well that she's moving on to another market.*

She found her fingers tangled anew in the satin cord. *Oh, shit,* she thought. *I guess that's what I did—or what it looked like anyway.*

Karli had flown in from Chicago that morning, with just a small bag and no reservation. By a stroke of luck, the Hilton had a last-minute cancellation and was able to fit her in during one of the busiest conventions of the year. The mid-America Emmys drew countless broadcasters from the region, many of whom arrived with the attitude that it was perhaps their only chance of the year to drink alcohol and flirt with members of the opposite sex. She herself had been propositioned—in varying degrees of frankness—by at least a dozen tipsy sales managers or news directors who had wandered out of the cavernous ballroom searching for bathrooms or more drinks or someone to talk to.

Karli had not arranged to secure actual credentials to attend the awards banquet, though she had put substantial work into looking the glamorous part. Her own long, black Valentino silk dress created the perfect background for her dark blue eyes to sparkle out of their unusually dusky makeup. She had known for some time that the station would be receiving an Emmy award for the work she and Jake had done, and she figured nobody would care about credentials once the award was announced.

And the ceremony was proceeding, with supposedly important but otherwise largely unknown-to-others presenters alternating at two podiums positioned at roughly a third of the way in from either side of the stage. They introduced clips from entries in various categories, and the giant screens played those clips and cutaway shots of audience members, often those who had been nominated.

Karli watched as an announcer stepped up to the nearer podium and, shaking her head, said, "This year a single entry has found its way into three separate categories—something that is so unusual, the entire mid-America board had to vote in favor of permitting it. So, with apologies for taking things slightly out of order, and without the suspense of announcing competing entries, I'm privileged to present this year's winner in each of the following categories: Specialty Assignment Report; Photographer - News; and Writer - News."

As she finished that sentence, the titles of the categories

dissolved to one of Jake's shots of Iowa National Guardsmen filling water containers for Des Moines residents, with Karli's voice describing the things people needed water most urgently for. "The winner in each of these categories is from the Three NewsFirst newsroom in Des Moines, Iowa. For their coverage of the flooding in Des Moines, the winners are reporter Karli Lewis and photographer Jake Gibson!" Karli's heart took off running. She had known they were going to win, but she hadn't known they would win in *three categories*.

Cheers and applause rose from the room. Jake and Jerry rose from their seats, walked to the far side of the stage, and climbed the steps. Once on the stage, Jerry gestured for the photographer to precede him to the podium. As they crossed behind the first podium, the applause died down and the audio from the winning story again featured Karli's voice, setting up a sound bite from a central Des Moines resident who was worried about how the city could stay healthy without water. Then the audio went quiet as Jake leaned toward the microphone.

"Terrible events put people under the kind of stress that requires them to do the best or the worst things they're capable of," he said solemnly. "The shutdown of the water system in Des Moines was unusual and terrible. The people of Des Moines showed their greatness and their resilience throughout that crunch." He paused and glanced up at the exceptional, still-rolling footage he had captured for the story. "The pressure of the catastrophe and the inspiration of a great collaborator required me to record some of the best pictures and audio of my career." The audience, which had been treated to the drive-in-movie-sized version of that footage as he spoke, burst into spontaneous and unusual applause. "Of course I'd like to thank my news director, Jerry Schultz," here he swung his arm back toward Jerry, who raised his hand to an absence of applause, "and Karli Lewis, on whose behalf I am accepting this award tonight. She cannot be here, as she has taken a position..."

Karli laid her hand on Jake's shoulder, and his voice trailed off as he turned and saw her standing next to him. The surprise on his face was so apparent that the audience bubbled with laughter. While Jake had been talking, she had simply climbed up the stairs right in front of her and had walked to where he stood at the near side of the stage.

Under cover of the audience's laughter, she whispered to Jake, "You look amazing in that tuxedo," quirked a single eyebrow at him and then looked pointedly at the microphone. Jake snapped his mouth shut into his reddening face and stepped quickly away from the podium, which gave the laughter a bit more energy.

Just as the audience sounds began to taper, Karli lowered the microphone and spoke into it. "Jake is right, I have indeed taken a new position." Here she looked back to acknowledge Jake, who stood, completely flummoxed, by a broadly smiling Jerry. "But I am thrilled to be here tonight to thank you all for this amazing honor." She looked at the announcer, who had stood by mutely, during the speeches. The announcer stepped forward and handed Karli the little gold statue of a lightning-winged woman holding an orb aloft. Raising the statue, Karli turned back to the microphone and said, "Thank you, on behalf of Jake Gibson and the entire Three NewsFirst team."

Karli turned toward Jake and held her arm out expectantly. Collecting himself, Jake extended his elbow to escort her off stage. Karli raised her face toward him, and he leaned in to listen over the renewed applause. "You said you wanted me to find my own way. Well, I think I'm starting to." She saw the wonder in his face and a smile leapt from her heart and onto her own face. "But first we have to get off this stage without falling down the stairs," she said. "So look where you're going."

Jake laughed for pure joy and paid careful attention to taking one step at a time.

On the way back to the Three NewsFirst table, Jake signaled to one of the staff for an extra chair. While they waited, he helped Karli into the new chair next to Jerry, and resumed his former seat next to Sophia.

"What a surprise to see you here!" Sophia said in ingratiating tones. "That was quite an entrance you made there!"

"I wasn't able to confirm arrangements in time to be here at the table with you," Karli replied. "The Chicago bosses expect about 27 hours of work per day, so getting away was a pretty big deal."

Jerry's face was suddenly covered with a huge, smirking grin. "You're not telling me you're afraid of a little hard work, are you? Because that would be awkward."

"Not at all," Karli said, turning her smile's high beams on. "You know I love the work. Especially when I have a great collaborator like Jake." Saying this, she looked at Jake out of the corner of her eye as he scooted his newfound chair into the space between Jerry and Station Manager Larry Norwich. "Wouldn't you say that a good collaborator is important, Mr. Gibson?" She picked the little statue back up and waved it at him, teasing.

"Of course I would. We made those stories together. Heck, I already miss working with you."

Unable to bear being on the outside of the conversation, Sophia angled for Jake's attention. "Oh, but haven't we been doing some really inspirational stories since Karli left? That one on the homeless people was really special.

I'm hoping that will win us an Emmy next year."

The introverted Norwich cut in ahead of Jake, squeaking out one of his rare sentences. "Won't you be leaving us for Indianapolis next week?"

"Sure," Sophia replied, surprised at the uncharacteristic contribution. "But Karli here came all the way from Chicago for tonight's ceremony. If Jake and I are going to win the Emmy next year, I'm sure I'll be able to come back, too."

Jerry jumped in, apparently sensing Norwich's reluctance to continue in a conversation. "If you win an Emmy, Sophia, rest assured you'll be welcome to come sit with us here at the awards ceremony." He gave her his best sincere-boss face, but Karli was sure he had calculated the odds of Sophia's reporting efforts winning an Emmy to be mostly nonexistent.

"So," Jake said to Karli, "how's life in the big city?"

"It has been an amazing experience, Jake. Even with the insane hours and stuff, I'm still glad I took the job."

"The honeymoon isn't over yet, I take it?"

"Well, I wouldn't go that far," Karli replied. "Let's just say I've learned a lot from working there." She paused, then raised a hand in sudden recollection. "And you should've seen my dad when he came to the newsroom and then saw me anchor a Saturday night newscast with one of my stories in the second segment—all on the television, and *all over Chicagoland!*" She lowered her voice with that last phrase in an apparent imitation of her father. "Mom says the entire bar at the Hotel Intercontinental learned that he was my father that night. Embarrassing, yes, but it was really nice to see him pleased with something about my career."

"What about tonight's award?" Jerry asked. "Every parent of an Emmy winner should cheer until they're hoarse!"

"He's not nearly as excited about the award as he was to be in Chicago and see me on a major-market newscast," Karli replied, a little hesitantly. "He's kind of a quantity-over-quality guy when it comes to journalism."

"That's not the kind of journalist you are, though," Jerry prompted.

"I'm much more proud of this award than I am about the story I did about Mayor Emanuel's plan to create 100 miles of separated bike lanes in Chicago," Karli said. "Not that the Mayor's plan isn't important—even visionary.

"The Mayor is right that encouraging healthy, green transportation is important. But anyone could've reported that story. It didn't require much in the way of background work, it was boringly budgetary and technical, and there wasn't time to delve into the whole argument about the tensions between cyclists and motorists. You know—*bikes always break the law* versus *every car-bike encounter has a guaranteed loser, and it isn't the car.*"

Karli saw Jake's face go suddenly pale. She immediately understood the reason and spoke to him in her most calming tones. "Darrin Anderson's story is the one that mattered, Jake," she said. "Losing that boy got the entire community up in arms. A reactionary city engineer got fired and major changes came fast. There was an entire town's support for creating safe routes for kids and adults on bicycles.

That's different from an impersonal, bureaucratic policy-wonk's daydream. Nobody probably even remembers the story I did in Chicago. *Everyone* in the Des Moines metro remembers the story you and I did. And they remember Darrin, too."

Norwich appeared to sense some of the tension at the table. In a misguided effort to calm things, he resorted to the executive's go-to device: jargon. "Inspirational. That's what that story was," he squeaked in his best Station Manager tones. "It had all the things that Bielfeldt said about inspiration. Memorable. And, um, emotional. Plus the rest."

Although everyone at the table saw the absurdity of the remark, Sophia had been mid-sip on her cocktail just as it was spoken.

Between suppressing her laughter and trying to swallow her drink, she nearly choked. After sputtering into her napkin for a bit, she coughed, cleared her throat, and looked up with watering eyes. "Sorry. That went down the wrong pipe."

The moment of panic had passed, though. Even Jake's face lit up with laughter as he patted Sophia's back and handed her a glass of water. She thanked him and darted a glance at Karli as she again placed a proprietary hand on his arm.

Karli turned so quickly to Jerry that it wasn't clear if she'd caught the needling look. "What new stuff do you have in store for the newsroom, Jerry?"

"We've been struggling to find a replacement for Sophia," he began, giving Karli a look that said he had seen Sophia's tactless gesture. "And we're trying to develop some more large-scale projects. Stuff along the lines of the renewable energy series you and Jake were brainstorming before you left."

"Do you have the reporting staff you need to do that kind of work? I mean, you know I totally agree that exploring big stories takes time, both in the field work and on the air. But you need people who are willing to invest their own time as well as the station's into stories with that kind of scope, right?"

"You convinced us to commit to some documentary-scale work before you left," Jerry replied. "To be honest, finding someone to shoulder that load has been a struggle, too."

"You can't give up that commitment just because Karli's gone," Jake said with genuine worry in his voice. "That work isn't just important for us to do, it's important for the viewers. Those are the kinds of stories that can truly inform the electorate and generate some intelligent debate and opinions. It's not just the sound-bite-*du-jour* stuff that so often stands in for actual reporting on issues. Jerry, you just can't give up on this idea."

Jerry held up placating hands. "Don't worry Jake, we're still committed to the concept. Resources are tight, but we've had help from the entire station," here he gave Norwich an appreciative nod, "and everyone's behind the idea."

Karli's eyes twinkled at this exchange. She smiled up at Jerry and batted her eyelashes while asking, "How are you going to be able to find someone to fill Sophia's huge shoes?" she asked, then glanced down at her own petite feet by way of indicating that

Sophia's shoes were huge because of her feet, not because of her professional ability. "And how are you going to be able to find a reporter willing to do the hard work to support huge half-hour and full-hour reports?"

Jerry just threw his head back and laughed. Norwich even peeped a high-pitched giggle. Jake and Sophia looked around the table in confusion. Jake caught on first, glaring at Karli in mock fury. "How could you sit on news like that?" he demanded.

Sophia caught on just as he spoke. "You? You think you're going to replace *me* at the anchor desk?"

"The feedback from the weekend shows I anchored in Chicago"—she emphasized *in Chicago*—"was quite good."

Sophia's mouth opened and then snapped suddenly shut as she fumed in silence.

"When did this all happen?" Jake asked, his mock fury taking a slightly darker turn towards real anger.

"We didn't reach an agreement until yesterday afternoon," Jerry said, again in placating tones. Then, indicating toward Karli with a tip of his head and a smirk, "She drives a really hard bargain."

"Look, I have to draw the line somewhere, and it just so happens that milking goats is a pretty obvious stopping point."

"Sure, and so are parades and charity runs and all the rest."

"You told me you wanted to hire an actual reporter to both cover the news and anchor the weekend shows," Karli shot back with a grin. "All those public appearances make doing the actual job pretty impossible."

"So, you're really coming home?" Jake asked, obviously worried that Jerry and Karli were playing an elaborate joke.

"Yes, Jake," Karli said, making earnest eye contact. "I am coming home. Because I think I figured out something about what home means, and why I need to come home."

"Really?" he swallowed, his tone this time asking about all the things she'd said and hinted at.

"Yes, Jake," she answered. "Really and truly."

Jake rose from his seat, placed his napkin by the dinner plate, and walked around the table to where Karli sat. "In that case, Ms. Karli Lewis, I request the honor of this dance," he said, holding his hand out to her.

"Jake, there's no music." Karli looked around the room in quick confusion. "There's an awards ceremony going on over there."

"Well, then we will have to find a dance floor," he said, again holding his hand out to her.

She rose to take his hand, and he turned to the table and said simply, "Good night." Karli made sure she had her purse, then nodded to the table generally, looked up at Jake and walked with him toward the main exit. As they passed through the room, several people leaned out from their tables to whisper congratulations. Karli thanked each, but had to walk quickly to keep up with Jake's determined stride.

As they passed through the entrance, Jake leaned to her ear and whispered the question that had been nagging at him since he figured out she was returning to Three NewsFirst: "Are you coming back to me, or just to your *collaborator*?"

Karli could hear the restrained tension in his voice. She took a deep breath, bracing herself for the moment she had anticipated and dreaded for weeks. "I'm coming back to you, too, Jake." She stopped, searching his eyes for a gentle response to the heart she had just laid bare to him.

Karli caught a breath preparatory to speaking, then restrained herself from explaining all the other, professional reasons for returning that were racing through her mind: the Chicago news market placed inhuman demands on reporters, Jerry had given her everything she had asked for, her father's reaction to her Chicago job had made her examine it and her motives for going there much more carefully than she had before going.

She had indeed been trying to address her issues with her father's ambitions for her by landing a job so incontestably huge that even he would see it in a positive light. But it hadn't turned out to be what she wanted. She had realized almost immediately that none of the newsroom staff felt connected to the community—it was nearly impossible to even define the community. The city was so huge that understanding it required learning dozens of formal and informal neighborhoods, not to mention the several counties filled with their countless suburbs.

And quite simply, she missed him with all of her heart. Chicago could never be home with Jake six hours to the west, among his beloved corn fields.

"I know a place where we can have that dance," he said.

***

Karli took in a big breath of surprise when Jake opened the door and gestured her in. "This is amazing!" she cried. "How did you get the station to pay for an entire suite here?" She walked from room to room in the enormous space, which included a complete living room, separate dining room and completely stocked bar in addition to the huge bedroom.

Jake followed her and immediately began moving furniture away from the floor-to-ceiling windows overlooking the Ozark mountains. "The station didn't exactly pay for this," he said. "As a matter of fact, Norwich was so chintzy about this trip that he wanted Jerry and me to bunk together in one of the smallest rooms." As he finished sliding the table away from the huge empty space he had created, he asked Karli what she would have to drink and poured them each a glass of wine from the bar.

"I guess I forgot about your. . .um, resources," Karli said, taking an eager sip of wine. They had walked together over to the windows to take in the astonishing—even at night—view from the 12th floor.

"Sometimes," Jake said, sliding open the glass door to the balcony and inviting Karli to join him, "it's nice to remember that I have *resources.*" He inhaled deeply of the quickly cooling and lovely smelling evening air, and turned to Karli with a smile. "Especially when I don't want to spend two nights listening to Jerry's snoring."

Karli smiled in reply, then leaned her hip against the balcony's railing and looked out over the Ozarks. *This is such a beautiful view. And I'm taking such a giant leap, going back to Des Moines. It feels like it's as big as if I jumped off this balcony. Yet I wouldn't if it didn't feel right to come back.*

She looked over as Jake leaned against the railing next to her, feeling satisfaction with the direction her career was headed. His profile was reassuringly strong and confident, and Karli felt a sense of security looking at him. The feeling was confusing, though, an uncomfortable mish-mash of the professional and the romantic. Karli paused to consider her feelings for Jake, then shook her head and looked back out at the horizon. "This is a glorious view, isn't it?" she asked.

Jake looked at her with surprising intensity. "You have no idea how glorious." He drained his wine glass, held his hand out to Karli, and led her back into the suite. "I think it's time for that dance," he said, taking Karli's glass and fiddling momentarily with a bluetooth speaker. After it began playing a Strauss waltz, he extended his hand to Karli and moved toward the large space he had cleared. "My college ballroom dance class skills aren't much," he said. "But I think I can manage a waltz. How about you?"

Karli curtsied to him in elegant fashion, then batted her eyelashes at him and produced a heavy Southern accent. "Well, I do declare, Mr. Gibson. How could you expect that a woman raised in proper Charleston society would *not* know how to waltz?"

Jake grinned and moved to her, and they circled their arms and stepped right into the beat. Karli felt the sure confidence of his movements through her left hand and arm, where they lay over his right shoulder and arm, and through her right hand's connection to his left. The easy tugs, nudges, and lifts of his direction propelled them together over the improvised dance floor. The sweetness of his wine-scented breath mixed with the familiar spiciness of his cologne to form an intoxicating atmosphere around them. The suite was dimly lit by a few small bulbs, spaced far enough apart to give a sensation of flickering shadows as they turned through the dance.

She knew the waltz and many of its trickier movements reflexively, thanks to many social dance lessons in her teen years.

Yet Jake was unlike any partner she'd ever had: his strength made turns nearly effortless, and his signals made every movement safely predictable.

Karli felt their breathing synchronize as the music took control, and she was transported. *A gallant and handsomely dressed gentleman waltzing me in my finest evening gown, a luxurious setting surrounding me and the stars just outside to shine over us— this is the kind of night I've always dreamed of. And Jake is the very figure of the gallant gentleman.* She looked into his dreamy, chocolate-brown eyes and saw a question—and an answer.

Suddenly the long weeks they had spent apart came crashing down around Karli. The lonely late nights. The cold bed. The never-ending toil. All of those thoughts filled the music's time, but they were distracting enough that Karli was taken by surprise when the music ended.

Jake swept her up in a sudden hug, moved his mouth to her ear and whispered urgently, "You're coming home. And you're my home, just as I am yours." Karli leaned back to respond and found her mouth covered in a kiss that began tenderly and lingered, then changed, suddenly and without warning, into an impassioned, hungry embrace.

As the kiss deepened, Jake's throat rumbled something that was very nearly a growl, and Karli smelled the exotic spice of his cologne as she caught a sudden breath of surprise. She savored the wet softness of his lips and moved her hands up his sternly starched shirtfront to find the beginning of a stubbly five-o'clock shadow on his throat and jaw. She had missed him.

The sudden intense passion of the kiss after the romantic swirl of the dance and her reverie swept her up, where her entire world and every thought, her self-awareness, slipped away and all that remained was *her-and-him* and a keen awareness of how perfectly her body fit within his arms.

Jake pulled back from the kiss and left Karli with a vaguely fuzzy feeling of unwelcome separation.

"This is fast, I know," he said seriously. "Let's move into a new place together. I mean, not the old carriage house. I like it and everything, but it's my space, you know, without accounting for other tastes. So you probably don't much like it or you'd want something not so masculine or something, and I don't want to—"

Karli's half-lidded eyes found Jake's. "Shut up," she mumbled, as she reached behind his neck and pulled him back down to continue the interrupted kiss. She felt his momentary hesitation change to eager enthusiasm, heard his breath deepen, felt the strong pressure of his arms embracing her, and she melted a little more than she had already. She wanted him, and his desire for her was apparent. She moaned into their kiss, feeling the vibrations through her throat and onto his lips and tongue. His growling response sent tingles throughout her body.

No sooner had she felt the quivering begin in her legs than she felt Jake reach down and sweep them up with one strong arm while supporting her back with the other. The kiss stopped only for a moment and resumed in all its intensity and passion as he carried her confidently to the suite's bedroom, then stood her up next to the king-size bed.

Once there, he undid her dress in the back, slipped it from her shoulders and let it fall to the ground, leaving Karli feeling oddly self-conscious in nothing but her heels and her lacy, bought-specially-for-the-gown black bra and thong. Jake had certainly seen her in the altogether many times, she knew, but never when he was fully dressed out in a tuxedo. The formal clothes after the formal dance and the formal event made the scant lacy underthings feel even more revealing than full nudity.

She consciously called to mind the thought that the only place she had ever felt relaxed and sexy and completely herself was in Jake's arms—and the related thought that she had nearly lost the chance to be herself by signing up for the energy- and personality-sink that her Chicago job had turned out to be.

Jake again kissed her, this time tenderly, moving his hands gently along the curves of her hips, waist, and up to her shoulders. He paused as his hands reached her shoulders, and he stood back, holding her at arm's length, his eyes moving hungrily over Karli's face and body. "You rock the hell out of that lace, you know," he whispered. "You look like you need me to attend to you on bended knee, right now."

"Not until you shave, Mr. Raspy," Karli whispered back, though the compliment made her blush with pleasure. As she felt her cheeks heat up, she also felt that her nipples were already pressing hard against the thin lace of her bra, and she realized she was soaking wet. "Your face feels like you haven't shaved in two whole days! Am I going to have to put up with this kind of slovenliness when I come back to Des Moines?"

"I've been kissing you on the lips for about 15 minutes now," he said, again in a throaty whisper, "and you haven't seemed to mind. So I think I can manage to kiss you *on the lips* without causing too much distress," he said, directing a hungry glance at the lace that barely covered her. His hands were still on her shoulders, and they firmly turned and tipped her onto the bed. She sat down as gracefully as she could manage with her gown still fallen around her feet.

It took Jake no time at all to push her back onto the bed and move over her to begin another kiss, this time even more passionate and hungry. Karli felt overwhelmed at the sheer physical size of him, plus the spreading blackness of his tuxedo jacket that swept over her and framed the stark white of his shirt. The bed's first creaks sent shivers through her. The kiss intensified, and she bit his lower lip hard enough to make him grunt and pull away.

Her career—Chicago—as wonderful as it was, had not accounted for Jake. Everything she had ever wanted professionally and personally was all wrapped up in that jet-black tux. Even if it meant returning to Des Moines. She had been in danger of losing herself in her major-market job. Now she could realize her professional ambitions—plus the unknown of a real, enduring relationship with Jake.

When Jake pulled away from their kiss—and her bite—he didn't just pull a few inches away from her face. He kept moving back until he was kneeling at the side of the bed, between her legs. She felt his fingers gently move the lace to the side and heard his appreciative hum at seeing her smoothness. The sudden warmth of his tongue pressed just at her opening but did not enter. Instead, it slid gently and smoothly up and between her lips, probing slightly to find her most sensitive spot.

He picked up her legs and raised them over his shoulders as he explored her pleasure. She felt an involuntary quiver shake through her legs, and she repressed the urge to repress the quiver. Instead, she took a deep breath and gave herself permission to go along with the sensations. And to go along with Jake's ministrations.

He progressed to gently sucking while rhythmically sliding his tongue around and up and down deeply between her inner lips. Karli found the pace of her breath and felt it flow through her, in perfect rhythm with the electric tingling that crackled from her clitoris. Just as she felt herself clenching with urgent need, she felt Jake's fingers slip into her, gently probing her depths and pressing up against her upper wall—the back of the button he was so masterfully tonguing.

She clenched the bedspread in each of her hands and then felt the swooping build-up begin to work its way through her. "Oh, yessss," she hissed, feeling her hips begin to involuntarily rock in surrender to the irresistible wave of consummation that had snuck up on her and that would overwhelm her any second. She lost herself in her feelings, knowing that Jake had brought her to this place where every sensory nerve fired with intense pleasure.

"Oh, God," she whispered, feeling her breath intensify as she continued to clench over and over around Jake's fingers. The throbbing kept on for much longer than usual, until it finally ebbed away, leaving behind it a tingling series of diminishing aftershocks. Karli released the blanket from her tight grip and opened her eyes to a feeling of sudden dryness in her mouth that contrasted with the remarkably dripping wetness below.

Jake kept at her, even though she had obviously finished. His tongue, which had delivered such intense pleasure, quickly became too much to bear. She pressed against the top of his head and twisted her hips to move away from the persistence of his mouth.

"Mr. Raspy, huh?" he chuckled quietly. "I don't think you suffered too much there, did you?"

"Oh my God, Jake," Karli whispered breathlessly. "That was amazing. I just kept coming and coming."

"I felt every throb," he muttered through a devilish grin. "And I didn't want it to end."

"I'm really thirsty," she said, turning her head this way and that, looking for a drink.

"Your wine is right over there," Jake said, rising and indicating to the bar just outside the bedroom. "Or would you like something else?"

"Water, please," Karli said. "And the wine."

He returned and handed her two glasses. Karli sat up on the bed, took the water and drank deeply, set the glass on the floor next to the bed, then sipped the wine. Jake, having managed to carry three glasses altogether, took a drink from his own wine glass. He stood next to where Karli sat on the bed, reaching his hand out to lace fingers with her.

Karli took his hand and looked up and down his tall figure, still fully dressed in his tuxedo, and noted the distinct bulge below the cummerbund.

She took another, deeper sip of wine while her eyes fixed more or less involuntarily on the bulge. *That*, she thought to herself, *is something worth coming back for.*

She savored the wine sliding down her throat, set the glass down next to the water, stood up, and put her hands on Jake's shoulders. "Your turn, now, Mr. Raspy," she whispered in her most seductive tones. She tried to twist him so she could throw him onto the bed, but he just grinned and stood still, controlling his weight and her leverage.

Karli sighed in frustration and looked up at him. "Okay, so I won't call you Mr. Raspy any more," she muttered. "Just cooperate."

Jake chuckled deep in his throat and permitted himself to be twisted and dumped till he was laying on his back across the king-sized bed. "Um, I'm a little over-dressed, aren't I?" he asked in somewhat startled tones.

"Not at all. You're hot in that tux," Karli replied, tugging down his zipper and reaching in to liberate Jake's visibly growing erection. She kept her hand around it as she slid her body up over Jake's chest to kiss his lips, and she felt the racing thuds of his heart through the stiffly starched shirt. Just as their kiss began to deepen and promise to become an extended exploration, Karli broke it teasingly off and moved herself down his body again.

She placed herself between his legs so she could pin them down and keep him from squirming. *I may be coming back to you,* she thought, *but that doesn't mean you're going to be in control.* Then she moved her mouth slowly over his tip, circling it with her tongue and sucking gently.

As she glided farther down his huge erection, she savored the odd contrast between the velvety softness of his skin and the stiffness that filled her mouth. Jake moaned and pushed his hips up against the pressure of Karli's controlling arms. "Damn, that is amazing," he mumbled through audibly clenched teeth.

Hearing his pleasure, Karli gradually sucked harder and moved over him faster, bringing all of him inside her again and again. She then paused near the tip and sucked hard, sliding her tongue across and over the sensitive spot just below the heart-shaped cleft in the top. She felt Jake's fingers run through her hair—not by way of controlling her movements, but rather to connect with her and communicate the intensity of his pleasure.

Karli's own arousal increased as she felt him pulsating against her tongue, and she went with her sensations, letting them overwhelm her. The heat of him, the moans of pleasure and the desperation to orgasm all both transported her and kept her completely in the moment. The thought of how desperately she wanted him inside her in other places and how gorgeously handsome he was both in his tux and out of it renewed the tingling of desire throughout her own body.

The more turned on he got, the more Karli's own body and movements responded, bobbing faster and needing to feel him explode inside her. She felt the moment approach as Jake suddenly tensed and held the breath that had been so heavy. He released it with a deep groan, "Oh, Karli. You're mine."

Then another caught breath escaped with a growl and she felt him fill her with his ecstasy. She took complete control of that moment, making sure she didn't hold enough of his length to be uncomfortable receiving and swallowing, yet keeping up a subtle bliss-preserving movement as he rode the waves of his orgasm.

After he began to twitch from her continued attentions, Karli felt the complete helplessness of his collapse. She moved up the bed to lay on his chest, smiling. His eyes fluttered half-open and met hers. She saw a grin crease his face, in what looked like a mixture of dismay and appreciation.

"You have completely wrecked me," he sighed. "I'll never be any good for any other woman. So you're going to be stuck with me."

She had looked forward to, anticipated, craved this reunion. Yet Karli felt a momentary twinge of resistance, one formed by an entire career's worth of refusing to let her personal life have any priority. She took a deep breath, and let herself feel Jake's closeness, both physical and emotional.

The afterglow of her body and heart's complete surrender flowed back through her with her breath, washing away the practiced refusal to commit. She released her feelings from the strict confinement of long repression, felt the warm embrace of Jake's arms encircling her, laid her head on his shoulder, took a deep inhalation of his familiar spicy scent, and realized that she couldn't imagine ever being with anyone else, either.

"Jake," Karli asked in a sudden and surprisingly serious tone. "When did you start loving me? I mean, once we got going, I can get that it was nice enough to keep going along, but what got you interested in the first place?"

Jake's smile beamed at Karli through the darkness. He plumped up a pillow for Karli's head, then they positioned themselves next to one another on the bed, legs entwined and face to face. "I don't recall some special moment when Cupid's arrow pierced my heart and I suddenly adored you and couldn't think of anything else. Honestly, we were kind of tangled together with work and affection and everything before I even understood that I was falling for you."

"But I wasn't exactly nice to you when we started working together. And you were definitely not nice to me. Are you attracted to mean girls or what?"

Jake chuckled into his pillow and ran his fingers through Karli's short hair. "No. Mean girls do nothing for me. But intelligent women, strong women—they get my motor running. And you are more than just intelligent and strong. You are empathetic. You connect with people. That's evident in your work, and that attracted me. And you are singularly passionate—"

Jake was interrupted when Karli slugged his shoulder. "So you fell for me because we shag well together? That's why you love me? Really? Because if that's it, you're as shallow as every other guy on the planet."

Jake laughed again. "I was talking about your passion for your work and for the stories you tell, silly. That passion and intensity makes you amazingly attractive."

Then he paused and his voice deepened. "But I'd be lying if I didn't say that you are sexy like no woman I've ever been with." He breathed deeply, then bent forward to whisper in her ear. "I very nearly passed out just now. And you make me faint and dizzy so often.

You have a sexual intensity that's just... it's... it's utterly different and more amazing than I ever thought making love could be. And I think that it has to be because it's... because it's you. You're so passionate and I feel so connected with you. I damn near have an orgasm every time you do just because it's so intense to be with you and see how beautiful and amazing you are."

Karli leaned back from his whispering. put her hand to his cheek and whispered in return, "It's just the same for me, you know. Your creativity is amazing, and your stuff was so good it pushed me to do my best work ever."

"And I've never felt such intense pleasure in bed before. It's as big as the difference between high-school kissing and actually having sex. It's mind-blowing. No other guy could ever reach that standard."

Then she heaved a sigh, rolled onto her back and asked the

ceiling, "How are we going to tell my father? And not just that I'm not marrying into Charleston society, but that we're not going to be moving there?"

"Probably not in a text," Jake laughed.

Epilogue

"Here's to happy reunions!" Bailey smiled and raised her glass toward Karli.

"To reunions!" Mary Rose cheered, downing a shot of something.

"I'm thrilled to be back with you guys," Karli responded after sipping her Amaretto Stone Sour.

"That's BS," Mary Rose blurted. "You're thrilled to be back with the sexy Jake-man. You're mildly pleased to be back with us." She quirked an eyebrow at Karli, daring her to contradict.

"Of course she's thrilled to be with us," Bailey cut in. "Who else can she count on to have her back during all the wedding planning?"

"Wedding planning?" Karli fairly shrieked. "He hasn't even proposed yet!"

"Oh, not *yet*?" Mary Rose smirked. "So it's just a matter of what—weeks? And then we'll have to shoulder the burden of putting together a completely epic bachelorette party." Her gaze drifted to the distance as she began to envision what exactly that party would look like.

"Oh, Mary Rose," Bailey said. "Cupcakes with penis candles and everything?"

"No penis anythings!" Karli said. "When my college friends had those parties, they'd get all boozed up and penis-obsessed and then do stuff they don't want to remember." She shivered at the memories. "And the guys they hire for those parties—I wish I could laser those helicopter moves they do completely out of my memory!"

"Helicopters with piercings!" Mary Rose cheered, draining her beer and gesturing for another round. "C'mon, you two! That stuff is so hilarious. And you need to get your blood flowing a little for the glorious wedding night when you lose your virginity to your new husband." She paused momentarily, then looked at Karli with feigned concern. "You *are* a virgin, aren't you?"

"It can be fun to have men completely focused on you having a good time," Bailey mused. "We just need to figure out a way to make it not collegiate-trashy."

"Guys," Karli sighed. "I'm not even engaged. Jake and I haven't talked about anything more than living together."

"How are you going to stay a virgin if you're living in the same house all alone with your future husband?" Mary Rose asked.

"We could have a nice house-warming party," Karli offered. "Just like an actual party with men and women eating and drinking and talking and stuff."

"Oh my freaking lordy!" Mary Rose cried when she saw Bailey nodding. "You two are so dull! What's the good in having Karli come back if we're going to have crappy parties and no pierced helicopters?"

Bailey tilted her head very slightly to the side, considering. "You know," she said, "we could do a really sexy triple-date thing. You know, dress killer and hit a fancy restaurant and catch live music and stuff."

"Do we all get naked together at the end?" Mary Rose asked, her eyes opening wide.

Karli and Bailey together said, "No!"

"And who is my date, anyway?" Mary Rose went on. "And who is your date, Bailey?"

Now it was Karli's turn to raise an eyebrow. "Shouldn't you bring Mr. Dark and Handsome himself, Scott Winstead, the wildly sexy weekend anchor you've been secretly pining after at least since my very first day at Three NewsFirst?"

"Karli, you've done what I thought was impossible," Bailey said, looking carefully at Mary Rose's face. "You've made our girl actually blush!"

"Jake is amazing in a tux," Karli said. "And I'll bet Mary Rose would knock Scott right on his ass in a real dress and jewelry and make-up."

Karli and Mary Rose turned together to face Bailey. "Who is your date?" they asked together.

"Oh," Bailey shrugged. "A sort of long-distance on-again off-again boyfriend is going to be coming to Des Moines this month. You'll have to meet him."

Thank you for reading **Love. Local. Latebreaking.** If you enjoyed it, we would be deeply grateful if you would take a moment to leave a review at your favorite retailer.

Love. Local. Latebreaking. is to be available in e-book format and audiobook format through Amazon, Audible, Apple, and other online retailers.

The Three NewsFirst team will be back soon in **Traffick Report**. You can find updates at my website: hlaurencelareau.com. Thanks!

About the Author

H. Laurence Lareau met his wife 30 years ago in a midwestern television newsroom. He lives with her and varying numbers of their four (some more or less adult) children in downstate Illinois. In addition to his day job and writing, he has spent the last several decades trying to become good at martial arts and singing.

Made in the USA
Lexington, KY
28 October 2017